AN INDEPENDENT LADY

Tarrington's face was like thunder. He reached down and pulled her swiftly to her feet in a single strong tug. "I don't recall, Katherine, giving you permission to ride Sally's mare alone. You could have broken your neck, my girl. Promise me you will never again do something so foolish."

"I am not one of your simpering London misses who can't so much as stroll in the garden without a man to dance attendance on her," she retorted. "You forget, my lord, that I am without position and without fortune. My life is at my own disposal—or was, until you saw fit to overthrow my plans."

Still he gripped her wrists, drawing her closer. "Can you really be such a fool?" he asked softly. "Do you persist in believing that because you have no fortune you must earn your bread as a governess?"

Shivering in the morning breeze, she stared into a pair of hazel eyes, slowly shading to green in the rising light and speaking a language she did not quite understand. She was painfully aware of his lips, firm and masculine and very close to hers, and from being cold she suddenly went to feeling very warm indeed. . . .

FIERY ROMANCE

CALIFORNIA CARESS (2771, $3.75)
by Rebecca Sinclair

Hope Bennett was determined to save her brother's life. And if that meant paying notorious gunslinger Drake Frazier to take his place in a fight, she'd barter her last gold nugget. But Hope soon discovered she'd have to give the handsome rattlesnake more than riches if she wanted his help. His improper demands infuriated her; even as she luxuriated in the tantalizing heat of his embrace, she refused to yield to her desires.

ARIZONA CAPTIVE (2718, $3.75)
by Laree Bryant

Logan Powers had always taken his role as a lady-killer very seriously and no woman was going to change that. Not even the breathtakingly beautiful Callie Nolan with her luxuriant black hair and startling blue eyes. Logan might have considered a lusty romp with her but it was apparent she was a lady, through and through. Hard as he tried, Logan couldn't resist wanting to take her warm slender body in his arms and hold her close to his heart forever.

DECEPTION'S EMBRACE (2720, $3.75)
by Jeanne Hansen

Terrified heiress Katrina Montgomery fled Memphis with what little she could carry and headed west, hiding in a freight car. By the time she reached Kansas City, she was feeling almost safe . . . until the handsomest man she'd ever seen entered the car and swept her into his embrace. She didn't know who he was or why he refused to let her go, but when she gazed into his eyes, she somehow knew she could trust him with her life . . . and her heart.

Available wherever paperbacks are sold, or order direct from the Publisher. Send cover price plus 50¢ per copy for mailing and handling to Zebra Books, Dept. 3325, 475 Park Avenue South, New York, N.Y. 10016. Residents of New York, New Jersey and Pennsylvania must include sales tax. DO NOT SEND CASH.

Crimson Deception

BY THERESE ALDERTON

ZEBRA BOOKS
KENSINGTON PUBLISHING CORP.

ZEBRA BOOKS

are published by

Kensington Publishing Corp.
475 Park Avenue South
New York, NY 10016

Second printing: February, 1991

Printed in the United States of America

To Al, for his patience, advice, encouragement, and love.
To my mother, who is also my friend, and who taught me to love books.

Chapter One

Mrs. Delia Amory reclined on a worn sofa in a dreary sitting room, her eyes tightly shut. She told herself that it was only the ugly wallpaper—improbable roses in an unfortunate shade of green—that induced her to shut out all vision. But true rest eluded her. Try as she might, she could not pretend to ignore the fact that, in the very same room, her daughter and two servants were bustling about amidst a pile of portmanteaux and bandboxes. The sight of these energetic preparations for departure was insupportable, and the lady erupted in a sigh that bore a strong resemblance to a groan.

There was no remark from her daughter, who was directing a manservant to remove the largest portmanteau. Mrs. Amory decided against venturing another sigh, and instead began to grope among the cushions that supported her, but her search proved fruitless.

"Oh, dear, however did I come to be so muddleheaded? I am sure I feel a spasm coming on, and I foolishly told Jenny to pack away my vinaigrette. Katherine, dearest, could you—"

"Here, Mama, take mine," Miss Katherine Amory offered briskly, before the dreaded spasm could take hold. A quick search in her reticule produced the necessary restorative, and then she resumed struggling with the strapping on a worn leather trunk.

"There, it is done at last!" She stood and straightened her shoulders, observing the results of her labor with satisfaction. "I vow I have never enjoyed any task so much as I have enjoyed making ready to leave Whitfield."

Mrs. Amory only adjusted a faded brown curl under her becoming lace cap and observed her daughter's vigorous efforts with dismay.

Katherine was a fine-boned young woman of middling height, with a great deal of lustrous chestnut brown hair threatening at every moment to escape the constraint of innumerable pins. Mrs. Amory could not help noting with pride her daughter's peach-bloom complexion, and the small, even white teeth that peeked out charmingly from between plump rosy lips whenever she smiled.

Yes, she was a delight to the eye and a devoted daughter, but her energy was such that her weary mother often had to close her eyes and beg her to be still, or take herself to another room. No one with Mrs. Amory's delicate system could bear such vitality in close proximity for very long, and how she had contrived to endure it for all of her daughter's nineteen years was a mystery to her.

Now her niece Priscilla, at eighteen, though not as clever as her cousin, was quiet and restful, and though it made her feel deplorably guilty, she much preferred Priscilla's tender ministrations when she was ill than those of her own daughter. Katherine was all too likely to suggest a brisk walk in the fresh air, or a hearty meal instead of calves' foot jelly and a digestive biscuit.

But then, she reflected, watching the sunlight penetrate the threadbare curtains and envelop her daughter's head in a red-gold halo, Katherine followed her own advice to such very good effect. She had never suffered a day's illness, even as a child, and just now she was going about things with her usual brisk competence.

"I confess I do not understand you, my love. Whitfield is the only permanent home we have known," murmured Mrs.

Amory from beneath her handkerchief.

Katherine smiled and stopped to pat her mother's hand, but went on determinedly organizing parcels. "It can't be our home any longer, Mama, and it was high time we formed a plan to secure ourselves an independence. We cannot go on living from one relation to another, you know. Besides, with Uncle Edwin's death, I believe we have run out of relations! And, Mama, you may keep the vinaigrette for the journey. You know I only carry it for your benefit, and I have not the slightest expectation of ever suffering from the vapors or a spasm, except perhaps if something were to prevent us from leaving," she said, secure in the knowledge that nothing of the sort was likely to happen.

"How I wish . . ." Mrs. Amory took another reviving sniff at the vinaigrette. "Unfortunately, it seems we *must* leave, though you know my feelings on the subject." Observing a change in her daughter's expression, she paused, wary of resuming an old disagreement. "I'm sure the earl will want to sell this dear, gloomy old place now that it is his, and we certainly cannot remain under those circumstances," she went on, with the air of one who had not yet abandoned all hope. She sighed and leaned against the faded satin cushions once more. "It was different, of course, when your Uncle Edwin was alive, and was kind enough to give us a home. . . ."

"As long as we catered to his every whim and saved him the expense of hiring more servants," Katherine said bluntly, after the last servant, struggling under the weight of the trunk, had left the room. At her mother's protesting noises, she added, "You must admit that he took shameful advantage of us, of me especially, though, of course, you and Priscilla did your share of the work."

She knelt at her mother's side and took one of Mrs. Amory's soft white hands in her own slender, strong ones.

"These clever hands of yours toiled long and hard to keep us all decently clothed, from Uncle Edwin's shirts even to the scullery maid's apron." She kissed her mother's finely lined

9

forehead. "Now rest, Mama, for we have a long journey to Bath. Once we arrive at Colonel Dawson's you will have naught to do but order the meals and direct the servants. Priscilla and I will see to the children, and you will be almost a lady of leisure."

Katherine stood again and stretched like a graceful cat, with an almost triumphant air. "And at last we shall be free! Oh, to be making my own way, to be no one's dependent!"

Her mother looked at her wonderingly. "Is that what you call it, my dear? How very strange that you should contemplate our fate with such happiness."

Katherine laughed and skipped about the room, causing Mrs. Amory to resort once more to the vinaigrette. "Oh, Mama, how dramatic you make it sound. *Our Fate!* I don't see anything so dreadful about my plan."

She shook out the skirts of her much-mended blue kerseymere travelling dress. "It is almost time to go and meet the coach. Only think, in a few days' time we shall be settled in Bath, and you may even be taking the waters. I'm sure Colonel Dawson won't begrudge you the time for it. Perhaps we shall even attend a concert or the assembly rooms one day," she said wistfully, for hers had been a life devoid of frivolity.

Mrs. Amory smiled affectionately, feeling much better now that Katherine was standing still again. Really, the child was a dear, but sometimes she made her poor mama quite dizzy! "You're a good girl, and I'm grateful to you for thinking of writing to your papa's old friend, but I cannot feel . . ." She avoided her daughter's direct and earnest gaze. "That is, I feel most uncomfortable presuming on the colonel's generosity this way. After all, he is no relation, and he probably has no need for a housekeeper."

"Mama, pray consider! The poor colonel is widowed, with nine children, all but two still in the schoolroom, and you believe it is only out of generosity that he offers us positions in his household?"

"No doubt it is foolish of me, but I cannot countenance

10

living on the charity of a stranger," pronounced her mother from beneath the damp handkerchief which now covered her entire face.

Katherine could not suppress a sigh of frustration, knowing how futile it would be to try the matter further. She confined herself to mentioning the kindness of the colonel's letter, of which her mother had shown her the closing remarks.

"You must admit, Mama, that he showed remarkable concern for your sensibilities in his reply to our letter. Why, we only asked him to recommend us to a good family, never dreaming he would hire us for his own household."

Mrs. Amory winced. "Katherine, please, I have asked you not to refer to this plan of yours in such . . . such mercenary terms. The word *hire*, for instance—"

"There is nothing in the world wrong with it, Mama," her daughter remonstrated. "It is perfectly respectable for us to work for a salary, and you know that there is very little choice in the matter. And haven't I promised you that the moment we save enough, I shall set you and Priscilla up in your own establishment?"

Mrs. Amory fell silent, and sat wringing her handkerchief.

"You know that the colonel said we need only come to Bath, where he was eager to have us take charge of him and the children, and he would see to it that we should want for nothing." Katherine quoted the letter, and considered that the retired military man had expressed himself very delicately.

Not for the first time, Mrs. Amory wondered if she had been wise in concealing the precise nature of the colonel's kindness from her daughter, and did not venture a reply.

According to Mama, Katherine thought with irritation, it was quite acceptable to live for four years as an unpaid drudge to a curmudgeonly old relation, but quite horrifying to accept a paid position as housekeeper to a man who had been her late husband's best friend.

Now that the sickly and irritable Sir Edwin had finally succumbed, leaving Whitfield, a scrubby and bedraggled remnant

11

of the once-vast family estate, to a distant cousin, the Earl of Tarrington, the Amory ladies and Mrs. Amory's niece Priscilla were free to leave the scene of their domestic captivity. Free, Katherine thought, to make their way in the world, an absolute necessity due to the sorry state of their finances. But even Katherine in her bold optimism secretly admitted that doing so was not the approved fashion for ladies of their station.

On the usual manner in which females obtained a sort of independence, Katherine had wasted hardly a thought. There would be few suitors for the hand of a dowerless girl with no important connections to put her forward. Her cousin Priscilla possessed a fragile kind of prettiness, a sweet and dreamy nature, and nothing more. No, they were two young ladies who must depend on no one but themselves, though Katherine's plan appealed as little to Priscilla as it did to her aunt.

With the salaries that Colonel Dawson would pay them (though they had not, of course, discussed anything so vulgar as the exact sum by letter) and Mrs. Amory's small widow's pension, together with a surprise bequest to Katherine from Sir Edwin of a hundred pounds, the three ladies would at least be able to command the comforts, if not the elegancies, of life.

The door squeaked open. "Here you are, Kate, I've been looking everywhere for you!" A breathless Priscilla burst into the sitting room, her auburn hair escaping from its knot in wisps which she brushed hurriedly away from her short-sighted pale blue eyes.

"You must come down and see it! It is the grandest chaise and four, just now turning down the Long Drive . . . at least, Hatchell tells me so," she paused for breath. "Do you think it could be the earl?"

"Well, it ought to be," said Katherine calmly, rearranging a few small parcels before she joined her cousin at the door. "Uncle Edwin has been buried for two months, and the solicitor said that his lordship was informed weeks ago. I wonder he didn't arrive the very day of the burial to turn us out."

"Now Katherine, you know that is no way to speak of his lordship," scolded Mrs. Amory gently as she began to rise from the sofa. "He is now head of the family."

"Which is precisely why, Mama, he may throw us all out if he chooses."

To avoid further reproofs, she followed her eager cousin out into the hall, hiding her own curiosity behind a composed demeanor. She had known, of course, that eventually the new owner or his representative would take possession of Whitfield, and she had hoped to be gone by then. No letter had arrived informing them of it, and at times she had wondered if the earl even knew, or cared, about their existence.

Treading carefully over the worn places on the stair, and averting her eyes from the offense of the peeling plaster at the landing, she made her way down to the entrance hall, once an elegant and imposing semicircular chamber, with painted ceiling and marble floor, but now looking as shabby as the rest of the house.

Before the girls could go out to look for the approaching chaise, the plump, brassy-haired housekeeper, dressed for travelling, sailed in from the passage that led to the servants' quarters, followed by an elderly butler. They were arguing vociferously, with the faithful Hatchell getting the worst of it.

"Look now, Mister Hetchell," boomed Mrs. Burkin, "what's a body my hage want to do in a tumbledown old barn of a house, now that the old maister is gone? Why, that earl what's inherited it'll probably sell it straight away, and then where would I be? No sir, as I told you, I'll just be going to my sister in London what's got me a place with the Quality. Now, you go and tell that pudding-faced boy you call a footman to bring out my trunk, and get out of a body's way!"

The distracted butler had caught sight of Katherine. "Please, Miss Amory," he appealed, his bushy grey brows working, "Tell Mrs. Burkin that she must stay at least until his lordship arrives, which will be any moment now, and—yes, look there, my good woman." He took the housekeeper's bombazine-clad arm and pointed her in the direction of the open double doors. "It will be any moment now. You can see the carriage for yourself."

Katherine had been about to assure Mrs. Burkin that she would not dream of asking her to remain in the wretched place a moment longer, but all attention was now focused on the approaching vehicle. They all crowded outside to get a better look.

It came down the weedy, half-gravelled drive at a spanking pace, a postilion riding the leader, a smart coachman on the box for good measure, and two grooms clinging somewhat precariously to the rear. It was drawn by four powerful looking greys, and their hooves raised puffs of dust that obscured the carriage's underbody and wheels, making it look as though it glided on a cloud to a stop in front of the house.

When the dust had settled, the impression registered by the group under the portico, which now included all of the servants as well as Mrs. Amory, was one of unrestrained awe.

"Only look how fine it is, Kate," whispered Priscilla, squinting at the vision of a large, glossy black equipage with yellow wheels and a gold crest on the panel.

Looking more closely, Katherine could see that although it was perfectly maintained, the vehicle was by no means new. She had seen but few fashionable carriages since coming to live at Whitfield, yet she was sure it was of a style that was no longer of the first stare. Then, too, the livery of the servants was not very grand, and the gilding on the body was downright dull. Was the Fifth Earl of Tarrington a miserly cheese-parer like Uncle Edwin, or merely not so prosperous as they had believed him to be?

These speculations were driven from her head by the emergence from the chaise of two fashionably dressed ladies, who stood blinking in the morning sunlight. Both were slender and rather tall, but one was obviously some years the elder. Before Katherine even had time to wonder who they might be, her attention was drawn back to the vehicle, from which a long-

14

nosed individual, whose dress and bearing proclaimed him to be a valet of the most superior sort, had stepped down and moved haughtily to one side.

The hopes of the group assembled before the door were momentarily dampened by this setback, for they had been expecting to see a real earl, but they were shortly to be gratified.

Just as Katherine had started forward to greet the ladies, for no one had seemed to think of going down the shallow stone steps to welcome them, she heard a murmur from the massed spectators behind her and stopped just in time to see one gold-tasselled and perfectly polished Hessian emerge from the open door of the chaise, followed by another. In a moment, his lordship, the Earl of Tarrington, had leaped down and stood before them.

He was clad in a coat of dark blue superfine, tightly molded to a not unimpressive figure, but not so tightly, Katherine observed, that he would be unable to put it on without the assistance of a servant stouter than his reed-thin valet. The crisp white neckcloth, neatly and precisely arranged, would have drawn approval even from Mr. Brummell himself, and black pantaloons flattered his well-shaped legs.

Altogether, his lordship's appearance was most satisfying to his audience and did credit to the talents of that fastidious retainer who had preceded him out of the carriage. His gaze swept the group assembled before him, and his expression of surprise rapidly gave way to a scowl. Finally he gave an arm to each of the ladies, who stood by looking curiously about them, and they approached the steps. Once there, he surveyed the eager faces with barely suppressed distaste.

"Forgive me if I appear ungrateful, but I was not aware that a welcoming party had been arranged. If one of you would have the goodness to inform me . . . perhaps I have mistaken the directions. This *is* Whitfield, just east of the village of Barton, county of Hampshire, is it not? And if I am correct in so assuming, then may I trouble you for an explanation as to your

15

identity and the reason for your presence here?" He focused his scowl on the three ladies, who stood, surrounded by curious servants.

His tone was laden with sarcasm, and his glance supercilious, but his voice was deep and velvety. Katherine felt a thrilling prickle at the back of her neck at the sound of it, though his words and manner roused her ire immediately. But she forced herself to remain silent. What did his arrogance matter, after all, when she would be leaving within the hour?

Mrs. Amory had just recalled herself to her duties, for she had been lamentably guilty of staring quite as hard as the servants. Though his ungracious speech brought her up short, her training prevailed, and with little nudges to her daughter and niece to follow, she descended the steps, all aflutter.

"Oh dear, did not Sir Edwin tell you? I was sure he had! Katherine, did he not tell his lordship about us when he wrote those letters you posted for him, before he—oh, but why do I rattle on? It is quite rude of me to know who *you* are when *you* do not know—I *am* sorry, my lord. I am Mrs. Amory, and this is my daughter Katherine and my niece Priscilla. My husband was Walter Amory, you know, Sir Edwin's younger brother."

"Indeed ma'am? Then we are cousins, of a sort." The Earl of Tarrington did not appear to be gratified by this discovery. He left his two companions, and climbed the few shallow steps with fluid grace, until he stood, all but glaring down at poor Mrs. Amory.

"I confess I am totally at a loss to know why I was never informed of your existence, madam. My great uncle neglected to tell me that his brother had left any family. However that may be, I am relieved that you at least know who I am. How do you do?"

He included them all in a brief, polite bow, and Katherine felt his eyes linger on her. She returned his glance without embarrassment, for she had had plenty of experience in dealing with outraged, blustering males. But he was already looking away. His gaze travelled up to the dilapidated roof and over the

16

unkempt grounds. He appeared to have lost interest in the inhabitants, and concentrated his attention on the appearance of the house itself.

"Well, it is no worse than I expected. I daresay it will put me to great expense and trouble to set it to rights, but it could have been worse, considering that the house has lacked a fit master for so long."

"We have done the best that we could, my lord!" Katherine heard herself blurt out, and immediately clapped a hand over her mouth. He turned and regarded her with a forbidding stare.

"Have you then, Miss, er, Amory? May I remind you that no one has accused you of any neglect." He glanced piercingly at her for a moment, and then turned to assist his two companions up the steps. Katherine felt that though he had heard her speak and had replied to her, for him, she did not really exist.

He had levelled no accusations, but his attitude had been so disparaging that she could not have resisted the impulse to defend the condition of the house. Nevertheless, she suffered agonies. His iciness left her momentarily tongue-tied.

The younger of the two ladies giggled behind her hand as she approached, but when she met Katherine's eyes she smiled sympathetically.

Katherine felt her face begin to burn, not just with embarrassment, but with annoyance. Of course she should not have said it, but then no one except Sir Edwin himself had behaved quite so arrogantly as this man. Though she had grown to hate Whitfield, she would not suffer a high-in-the-instep newcomer to comment on their care of the place.

The introductions were now swirling around her, and she was made known to the Countess of Tarrington, the earl's mother, and to his sister Lady Colesville. She acknowledged them politely but feeling oddly distracted, she found herself studying the earl more closely. He was not at all the aged and stately nobleman she had been expecting.

His was a face, she decided, that was in danger of being

almost too handsome. He was spared this fate by the intervention of a straight ridge of sandy brows that met above his nose, a pronounced chin, and the fine, faintly discernible lines about his eyes and mouth. Whether these betokened sorrow or dissipation, she could not tell, but she was momentarily struck speechless. She had not expected someone so young and so— she forced herself to admit—compellingly attractive, despite his abrupt and unconciliating manners, and what seemed the perennially disapproving expression of his excellent features.

If one could ignore the disagreeable import of his words, his voice alone would be enough to make one think him the ultimate answer to an unattached female's prayers. The sound made Katherine want to close her eyes and rest her head against the rich, deep flow of it. This, and his air of supreme confidence, fascinated her in spite of herself.

In her years as an officer's daughter, Katherine had known a great many young men very slightly, and two or three old men very well, but she had never known a man who gave such a strong impression of being at the height of his masculine vigor. The Earl of Tarrington seemed to embody the very definition of this category.

His thick reddish-blond hair, revealed when he removed his curly-brimmed beaver, showed not a trace of silver, but his hazel eyes looked as though they had seen much more of life than even the eyes of the soldiers she had known. He was tall, with powerful shoulders and a wide chest under the well-cut coat, but he moved with a grace and economy that brought to mind a sleek thoroughbred.

She found herself staring, too, at his hands, large but surprisingly delicate, with long slender fingers. Suddenly aware that he was watching her as she inspected him, she averted her eyes, angry with herself for feeling so unnecessarily flustered.

"Such an unnerving scrutiny! I trust that I meet with your full approval, Miss Amory? Or may I say, Cousin Katherine?" he drawled, drawing back her gaze again.

"No, sir, you may not. Miss Amory will do, since though we

18

seem to be related, our acquaintance is not sufficient for such familiarity," she retorted, rising to the challenge, her brown eyes snapping.

He stared at her for a moment, then, as amazement spread over his face, replied "No more than I deserved, I'm sure," and gave an ironic bow, his eyes never leaving hers.

Katherine suffered a reproving look from her mother over this. She hoped that by the time they left for Bath the earl did not think her a total hoyden, completely lacking in manners, though of course, she told herself, it mattered not a bit what he thought.

While Mrs. Amory profusely apologized for the oddity of Sir Edwin's behavior in not informing the earl that his inheritance was occupied by the relics of Captain Amory, Tarrington continued to observe them all with those heavy-lidded hazel eyes.

Katherine had the impression that he was judging them, while intending to reveal no more about himself than his physical appearance told them. But it was obvious that he had little tolerance for dissension from his own opinions. She was sure that he cared nothing for what they might think of him.

On the other hand, only the most agreeable condescension was exhibited by the two ladies in his party. Their friendliness, especially that of Lady Colesville, who seemed not much older than Katherine and Priscilla and whose dancing eyes and enchanting dimples promised an infectious sense of fun, could not help but make the ladies feel more at ease with their noble relations.

Although Mrs. Amory had taught the girls not to stand too much in awe of wealth and titles, it was difficult, Katherine felt, gazing on delicate muslins and fashionable bonnets, not to feel like a poor country mouse and a sad dowd in comparison.

"Only think," Lady Colesville was saying, "to have been cousins and never to have met for all these years!"

Her smile was arresting, and with her sandy curls and those same hazel eyes she was remarkably like her brother.

Her mother, the Dowager Countess, shook the hand of each of them with great cordiality and complained bitterly about the trick that had been played upon them. "I never thought very highly of my husband's uncle, but this is the worst I have heard of him. How could he conceal your very existence from us? Well, never mind, now that we have met you we must spend some time together."

Her son did not echo this sentiment. All he would say was that it was indeed a very odd omission on Sir Edwin's part.

Katherine was not very surprised at her eccentric uncle's reticence, because in her years of tending to him she had discovered that he had a wicked and perverse sense of humor, and had no doubt thought it a great joke to keep silent about the Amorys when writing to his heir.

"It was certainly very disobliging of him, to be sure," Mrs. Amory replied, "but then Sir Edwin was very often ill, and he had such odd humors, did he not, girls?" Without waiting for a reply, she went on. "Though, of course, we were exceedingly grateful to him for having us here to live. When my poor Walter was killed, we had not enough left to pay our landlady. Ah"—she sighed—"but that is in the past, and we have gotten along tolerably well. But how remiss of me!"

Mrs. Amory belatedly assumed the role of hostess and finally invited the earl to walk into the house that was now his property, all the while apologizing for the state of things inside.

"You see, we had no idea when you planned to come," she said, leading the way upstairs to the formerly elegant, but now musty and little-used drawing room, "and we are expected in Bath in a few days' time, and with the packing—"

The earl had been remarkably quiet, but as they entered the drawing room, he stopped and stared at his hostess. "What is this? Do you mean to leave here?"

His brows drew even closer together, and his expression was more disagreeable than ever. All at once Katherine felt that, despite her immediate impulse to repress his arrogance, his lordship was not a man whose real displeasure she would like to incur. Now he towered over Mrs. Amory, his uncompromising glance demanding an explanation.

Poor Mrs. Amory was puzzled as to why his lordship, having first been annoyed at their presence, would be equally annoyed at discovering that he was shortly to be relieved of it. She blinked rapidly and searched for the words that would placate him. "Well, my lord, Whitfield is now yours, and of course we should not presume to remain if . . ." She trailed off uncertainly, and looked to her daughter for assistance.

But before Katherine could speak, Tarrington's brow cleared, and he immediately begged her pardon. "I did not wish to imply, ma'am . . . of course I realize that you could not know what manner of man I might be. But though your presence here took me by surprise, I assumed you would still consider this your home as long as it remains in the family. Please do not rush to put yourselves out of my way. There is not the slightest need for you to do so, as my plans for this house do not include my residing in it."

Mrs. Amory gave her daughter a speaking glance, for the earl's reply, in her opinion, had been just what it ought to be, but Katherine leaped in before her mother could commit them to anything, her heartbeat jolted into a sudden staccato rhythm at this challenge to her carefully laid plans.

"You are very generous, my lord, and naturally we are grateful," she said as graciously as she could manage, "but Colonel Joshua Dawson, a great friend of my late papa, has offered us a home with his family in Bath, and as we think it would be beneficial to my mother's health, and we are already prepared to leave—"

"But how kind of the colonel," interjected Lady Tarrington, before her son could break in, as he showed every sign of doing. "Though of course we should be sorry to cut our new acquaintance short. I usually spend a few weeks in Bath every year myself, and shall certainly call upon you there."

"Yes," said the earl, his look quizzical, "we shall be happy to visit you and meet this benevolent military gentleman. He

21

must have been a great friend indeed for he and his wife to offer you ladies a home."

Katherine noted the determined set of his jaw and surmised that his lordship suspected there was more to the story and would not rest until he knew it all. Mrs. Amory only blushed.

Shy Priscilla, quiet until now, was emboldened to oblige him. "Oh, yes, he is a very kind man, that is I believe so. I met him once long ago, but that is not why we are going to him. You see, Katherine had a plan—"

In vain did her cousin direct an admonitory glance toward her. At a distance of five feet, Priscilla's short-sighted eyes could not distinguish smile from frown. "The colonel has nine children," she continued innocently, "and he is a widower, so Aunt Delia is to act as his housekeeper, while Katherine and I are governesses to the children."

The earl's expression was unreadable, but by the sudden tightness of the muscles around his mouth he was obviously attempting to control a strong reaction. He paced beside the sofa on which his mother sat, his changeable eyes turning a disapproving green in the shaft of sunlight from the front window. Ignoring Mrs. Amory's agitated twitterings, he stopped, pivoted on his heel, and looked straight at Katherine. She faced him unflinchingly. Finally, he could restrain himself no longer.

"Housekeeper? Governess?" His disgust made Katherine feel as though they had just revealed plans to go on the stage and dance for their living.

Tarrington's long stride carried him across the room to Mrs. Amory before Katherine could intervene. "Surely, ma'am, with all due respect for my cousin Katherine's ingenuity—"he did not look at her, but Katherine felt her face grow warm— "surely this is not what you want for your future? Not when you still have the offer of a home here at Whitfield?"

Lady Tarrington, seeing Katherine's black look, went to her son and placed a restraining hand on his arm. It was plain that she was no less shocked than he, but was too poised to allow it

22

to show.

"I am sure, Vane, that Mrs. Amory and the young ladies are too highly principled to presume on your generosity, particularly as they have been completely unknown to you until now. Naturally, they must have made their own plans as a contingency. There is no need to upbraid them for it."

At the touch of his mother's hand, his lordship's forbidding expression softened, but he turned again to Mrs. Amory, awaiting her explanation.

That lady's own plans and inclinations were so much in agreement with the earl's that she had little to say but to thank him for his offer and announce that they would be very happy to stay.

"Nonsense, Mama!" Katherine at last burst into speech, her irritation at the earl's high-handed condemnation of her plan goading her into rudeness. "You know very well that we have always been capable of maintaining ourselves respectably, and that our positions in Colonel Dawson's household will be almost as members of the family."

"Indeed, quite like family," murmured her mother, uncertain and feeling the tug of two strong wills.

Katherine turned to Lord Tarrington, her wide brown eyes full of outraged pride. "Naturally your lordship is concerned that we might be entering a life beneath the dignity of those so closely connected to the Earl of Tarrington, but I assure you that we do not consider it at all beneath us."

She ignored the warning implicit in his firmly compressed lips and plunged on. "Please rest assured that we shall do nothing to bring a word of censure upon yourself or your family."

He was silent for a long moment, and regarded her with unconcealed irritation. Katherine imagined that everyone else in the room was unable to resume breathing until he had spoken. The earl, she thought with annoyance, had been too long accustomed to having his own way.

"I fear, cousin Katherine," he said deliberately, observing

23

her heightened color and heaving breast with cool interest, "that despite your words, you hold my consequence to be of little value. The very nature of your plans is an insult to all connected with your family, and I will not stand idly by and see the name of Amory, and of necessity, Tarrington, cheapened by such an imprudent action. However, that is not my only objection."

He came closer, until he stood towering over her. His voice was still deceptively soft, but the look in his eyes told Katherine that he would brook no argument on the matter. "Has it occurred to you that you might not find such a life to your liking? You and your cousin are untrained and unsuited by birth and connection to the labors of the nursery and schoolroom. What do you know of waiting on demanding children, and of the patience and self-effacement a governess must exhibit? You were not destined for such a life." His eyes lingered for a fraction of a second on her lips.

Katherine struggled to ignore a childish desire to stamp her foot. How could she expect him to understand? But he was so certain of the rightness of his views that she could not hold her tongue. "If you had troubled to learn more of the estate you were to inherit, my lord, perhaps you could have ferreted out the secret means by which it has remained standing for the past four years," she said witheringly, heedless of his temper obviously mounting with her every word. "You would also have found that we are all well acquainted with the true meaning of patience. My uncle was a difficult man, and most of my time was spent attending to him and distracting him. My mother has worn down her health laboring over the sewing of the household, and my cousin and I have worked side by side with the few servants my uncle saw fit to employ, in order that Whitfield should not fall completely to ruin."

She ignored the gasps that neither Lady Tarrington nor her daughter could completely suppress. "And you presume to ask, my lord, what we know of patience and self-effacement? We have kept your inheritance in tolerable condition by our

24

labors. Pray take possession of it and leave us go where our efforts will be appreciated."

"That will do, Katherine!" Mrs. Amory could be surprisingly sharp when shaken out of her indolent manner. "Apologize to his lordship at once!"

"Entirely unnecessary, I assure you, madam," the earl's tone was icy, and Katherine could feel his barely controlled anger like a blast of March wind contained by a window-pane.

"Had I known that I owe the preservation of my inheritance entirely to your efforts, I would not have spoken as I did. I sympathize completely, Miss Amory, with your desire to leave the scene of such unpleasantness." He nodded coldly to Katherine. "I shall make no further objection to your plans."

"Oh, but please do not leave so soon!" Lady Colesville stepped between her brother and the defiant Katherine and looked at both of them appealingly. "Why, we have only just arrived, and if you leave now there will be no chance to become properly acquainted." She dimpled and put one slim white hand on her brother's sleeve, the other on Katherine's. "Will you not ask them to stay, Vane, at least for a few days, that we might enjoy a visit together? You know that mama and I planned to stay a fortnight at least with you at the Hall." She stopped to smile at Katherine, and unwillingly, Katherine felt her anger cool under Lady Colesville's charm.

"Grouse Hall is my brother's shooting lodge, barely ten miles from here. If you ladies do not object, we shall stay here instead, until you leave for Bath." She turned back to the earl, whose face was no longer so stern. "And you know, Vane, that Richard, poor dear, cannot escape from London for another month, so he won't miss me!"

Satisfied that his iciness had thawed, she begged prettily of Katherine, "Please stay, do, if only for a little while. And then perhaps you won't— Perhaps we can make plans to meet in Bath."

Katherine had a fair idea of what her ladyship had meant to say, and had an objection ready, but her mother, Priscilla, and both the Tarrington ladies were watching her expectantly. The earl was looking out of the window, but his shoulders were not set so stubbornly as they had been.

Since her father's death, her mother and cousin had come to rely on Katherine as if she were the head of the family, and the burden was sometimes too heavy even for a mind so full of plans and energy as hers; but someone had to take on the role, and neither Priscilla nor Mrs. Amory had the strength for it. Grudgingly, she agreed to stay, and was rewarded by smiles all around.

The servants were notified of the postponement of their departure, a footman sent to intercept the Countess' carriage, containing their bags and Lady Colesville's maid, on its way to Grouse Hall, and Hatchell once more began to importune Mrs. Burkin to remain. Katherine, watching the happy bustle, reflected that it could do them no harm to stay for a week or two to enjoy their cousins' company. Colonel Dawson had himself assured them that they could come whenever it suited them. But no sooner had she reached this conclusion than she heard her mother again pulling the rug from under her.

"I must own," Mrs. Amory was saying, "that I would prefer not to go to Bath."

"Mama, I really think—"

"I would be so much obliged if you could assist us in finding a position with someone within the family. I should prefer it to— That is, I am afraid our resources do not run to even a modest establishment, and Katherine has vowed that she will never again live in rented rooms in a town the way we did when my late husband was away with the army."

The earl, who seemed to have entirely regained his composure after his sparring match with Katherine, allowed a polite smile to cross his face. "Certainly, ma'am, if you wish it, or if you do not"—he forestalled Katherine's unspoken protest with a surprisingly understanding look—"then I promise you I will do my best to see you settled *respectably*, although I cannot help you if you allow my cousin Katherine to have her way and decide to keep your engagement in Bath. I certainly don't think it the proper situation for the family of the man who, had his choice of occupation not estranged him from his father, might even now have been inheriting Whitfield in my stead."

Katherine had not forgotten this aspect of the case, but her dislike of living at Whitfield had prevented her from feeling any resentment on that account. It was true that her grandfather, Sir Philip Amory, had destined his younger son for the church, and had cut him off completely when, a year after his early marriage, Walter Amory had refused the living set aside for him and had used his meager maternal inheritance to purchase a commission in the army. Had he remained in Sir Philip's good graces, Katherine's father might well be alive and now inheriting Whitfield from his older brother. Sent home with a leg wound during the Peninsular campaign, he had come back to make peace with his stern parent, but Sir Philip had remained unforgiving, even on his deathbed.

The frustrated and disappointed Captain Amory had itched for action, and as soon as Napoleon's return to France had given him the opportunity, he had returned to duty, despite his limp. His regiment having in the interium been sent to America, he'd served in Belgium, where he had had his fill and more of action, until a ball in the chest ended his life.

His wife had already grieved for his departure, and after news of his death at Waterloo her health broke down for a time. Katherine had then taken over the running of their tiny household until Sir Edwin had sent for them to come and live with him at Whitfield.

Katherine was as little affected by her father's death as any daughter could be. He was almost a stranger to her. On his visits with them, he had made no pretense of not being disappointed in her sex, but had treated her with gruff kindness when he did not altogether ignore her. Other than to remind her that if she hoped to get a husband she must learn not to sound so much like a bluestocking, he had interfered not a bit with her mother's plans for her upbringing and education.

When the orphaned Priscilla Townsend had come to make her home with them, Mrs. Amory had begun to teach both girls with the aid of her own books and the limited education she had received at the hands of her governess. She had been a general's daughter, brought up to do better than marry an officer forced to live only on his pay, but she had made not a murmur when all her husband's expectations failed, from the moment he'd announced that he had bought his commission. By then her own family was gone, and there was no general to look after his son-in-law's advancement.

When her own resources of learning were exhausted, she bartered her exquisite skill with the needle to procure for the girls the necessary accomplishments of a young lady.

In this way, a poor artist received three fine linen shirts in return for lessons in drawing and watercolor. A struggling musician was able to replace his one threadbare suit of clothes with a new one by teaching the girls to produce music on the wobbly old pianoforte which was the pride of the Amory's shabby set of rooms in a busy market town. Of the French language they learned enough to speak creditably from their landlady, a proud but hard-working emigrée, who in return solicited their help in her kitchen when one of her gentleman residents entertained and required a more elaborate meal than usual.

In fact, the girls were nearly as well educated as those who could claim a string of governesses, music and art masters. It seemed, though, with the exception of one person whom Katherine deemed totally unacceptable, that their accomplishments would never perform their intended function of attracting suitable offers of marriage.

Katherine withdrew from the string of reminiscences the earl's words had evoked, and forced her attention back to the present. Part of her did not at all mind remaining to further her acquaintance with the Tarringtons, and part of her still regretted the delay in their departure for Bath, but seeing the relief on her mother's face, and the pleasure on Priscilla's, she

28

felt that she could not press the issue to any advantage.

"Katherine, my dear," Lady Tarrington claimed her attention. "Why do you not have the servants unload our trunks and boxes? And then, if you do not think me unpardonably rude for suggesting it when I know everything is necessarily at sixes and sevens, could we not order something to eat? Though we had breakfast at our inn, we have been driving since early morning and I am sure we are all quite famished."

Katherine smiled wryly. "Certainly, my lady, but the only servants are the butler, our cook and housekeeper who is leaving today, one groom, a chambermaid, a scullery girl, and one footman. Perhaps his lordship's groom might help our men bring in the boxes?"

The earl nodded and at once gave the order to Hatchell, who was already beginning to stand straighter as a gesture of his approval of the new master. Since the earl's arrival, he had been hovering outside the drawing room in hopes of overhearing that he would not, as Mrs. Burkin had darkly warned him, be tossed out into the road and replaced by a grand London butler.

"There is no need to worry about the meal, even if Mrs. Burkin has left," said Mrs. Amory cheerfully, much revived by all the talk of staying at Whitfield. "Katherine and Priscilla can cook quite as well as anyone, and they shall have something ready in a trice."

The earl, his mother and sister, all fastened horrified gazes on her. "But we cannot allow our cousins to—" The Dowager Countess nearly choked on her words. "Not, my dear," she said with renewed tact to Katherine, "that it is any discredit to you or Miss Townsend that you are able to cook. Indeed, many times have I wished for some skill in the kitchen, when Antoine has taken a pet and threatened to take service with Lady Breye, who is forever trying to steal him from me, but I simply had not realized the state to which the household had been reduced. A house of this size with only six servants! What could Sir Edwin have been thinking of?"

"Of his pockets, very likely," the earl remarked, and he sounded none too pleased. He began to look more carefully about him and observed the worn rugs, faded draperies and crumbling ceilings with disfavor. "I see that though you ladies have done your best, a great deal remains to make this place a fit habitation."

Katherine had been ready to protest, and was slightly mollified by his qualifying remarks, but though she had given in rather easily when a brief stay was proposed, she found herself alarmed by his next proposal.

"What do you say," the earl began, pointedly addressing only Mrs. Amory, "to your remaining here while I set some repairs and refurbishments in train? By then, I hope you will be ready to consider it your home, and if you insist, I will accept a rent from you." He glowered at Katherine, anticipating her reaction, and somehow this steadied her enough so that she calmly defied his expectation.

"An excellent suggestion, my lord," she said smoothly, surprising herself with her own control. "However, as we have already engaged to present ourselves in Bath, we shall be able to stay only until you have completed the repairs and found a suitable tenant."

He looked at her with dawning respect, and Katherine thought his face betrayed an odd disappointment that he had failed to make her angry. She wondered why he appeared to enjoy seeing her in temper. Possibly it was just for the pleasure of having someone openly disagree with him. His mother and sister, she had noted, were careful never to directly oppose him and used only the softest of appeals.

His eyes glinted a deeper green as he finally replied, with perfect calm. "I had no thought of finding a permanent tenant for Whitfield, and it certainly cannot be sold in this condition, and as I have a perfectly comfortable house not far away, I have no plans to live here myself."

He came a few steps closer to her, wincing as he did so at the creaking of the loose boards hidden by the ancient threadbare carpet. "Yet it cannot be left to crumble into dust. I used to visit here when I was younger, you know, and your papa played cricket with me on the lawns when he came down from Oxford for vacation."

She was disconcerted by the sudden change that came over him as he smiled at the memory, a genuine smile of pleasure this time. Out of the light, his eyes deepened again, and the shadows softened the lines etched at the sides of his mouth. Katherine had to struggle to recall that if she did not oppose him now, it was likely she would never leave Whitfield. After four years of servitude there, even the prospect of life in such a quiet place as Bath was enough to do battle for.

"Then I would advise you, my lord, to find a tenant anyway. It will recompense you somewhat for your expenses, and I would guess that you are not in a position to enjoy the luxury of putting money into Whitfield only for the sake of family pride or sentiment."

He countered her gaze steadily, and replied with just a touch of irritation, "I am disappointed, cousin Katherine. I expected you to be too intelligent to pass judgment on a situation of which you know nothing. Namely, my affairs."

Though she had been deliberately provoking, she was not prepared for such a sharp dismissal. With the briefest of bows, he left her side to join the others. Katherine's face burned as if it had been slapped.

But by the time they sat down to luncheon, Tarrington was once again at his most charming, his smile and manner calculated to please.

Even Mrs. Burkin, a woman not easily impressed, had at last been convinced to stay and prepare a final meal. "Not that it won't do me any harm to be able to say I once cooked for an earl," she confided to the chambermaid, who, though her social inferior, had sometimes been her confidante. "And he's a handsome one at that. It would be a fine thing," she informed the maid, who had just passed on his lordship's compliments on the mutton pasty, "if he should marry one of the young ladies."

However, in the dining room, though the atmosphere was all congeniality, such a thought had entered the head of no one. Katherine made no attempt to engage her noble relative in conversation, and he, for the most part, addressed his attentions to Mrs. Amory, who blossomed under them like a young girl in her first season. Priscilla was allotted her share of his conversation, but she was still too shy and in awe of him to do more than smile and nod agreement. They are both, Katherine thought disgustedly, tearing a soft roll, completely under his power.

Yet he was vulnerable, she decided. Her remark about his finances had touched him on the raw, or he would never have given her such a set-down.

Though his appearance was fashionable, there was evidence, on closer inspection, that he was not so well off as might be expected. Why else, then, would his mother and sister be attired à la mode down to the last detail, while the Earl of Tarrington sported not a scrap of jewelry, not even a fob or a watch or a gold pin on his neckcloth? Why should his shirt, though of excellent tailoring and freshly laundered, show telltale signs of fraying on the cuffs, an occurrence with which Katherine was lamentably familiar?

And his coat, she decided, was showing signs of wear. She wondered if he would spend part of Uncle Edwin's fortune on a new wardrobe. She stared until his image blurred, and imagined him attired in elegant black evening clothes, tight-fitting breeches, and a coat just barely containing his massive shoulders. The picture unaccountably made her heart beat faster.

Unaware of having attracted his attention by her close observation, Katherine started, almost dropping a slice of ham from her fork, as the earl's voice penetrated her deep study.

"I fear you are bored, Cousin Katherine. I have been very

rude in excluding you from our conversation, so you have taken refuge in attempting to stare me out of countenance."

"Oh, no," she said hastily, feeling that vexing heat creep down her neck to her bodice. "I am afraid it was I who was rude. I was . . . meditating on our situation."

"Let us hope that your meditations are pleasant ones." Before she could reply, he had raised his glass. "Let us drink to the future of Whitfield."

"Vane, you are always so solemn," complained his sister, picking up her glass. "Besides, we are only drinking ratafia, and mama and Mrs. Amory have tea. You can't make a toast with a teacup!"

The earl's expression so plainly reflected his disgust with the literal-mindedness of females, and so forcibly reminded Katherine of the visits of her father's restless, impatient brother officers, that she relaxed and allowed herself to smile.

She need not worry about the earl's outmaneuvering her. He was only a man, after all.

Chapter Two

With the advantage of congenial company, and the prospect of its refurbishment, Whitfield began to seem less like a prison to Katherine and more like the gracious home it had once been. That the handsome figure of the earl contributed to its new attraction, she would not admit even to herself, but it was certainly a pleasant change to sit down to dinner with a gentleman who enjoyed eating something more than gruel and whose conversation was not confined to the state of his health, the laziness of servants, or the worthlessness of female dependents.

By the time twenty-four hours had passed, all five of the ladies were firm friends, and with the diversion of feminine conversation and the help of the new servants engaged by the earl, Mrs. Amory and the two girls soon found that life at Whitfield could be very comfortable indeed. In a few days even Katherine had ceased to think of Bath as an immediate prospect.

A very grateful letter to Colonel Dawson, and a very civil reply, assuring them that he could manage without them until things were arranged satisfactorily, set the last of her doubts to rest. Mrs. Amory's face gave quiet but unmistakable evidence of her relief at this reprieve, but her reaction to a few lines privately addressed to her on a separate page told her daughter that this comfort was not unadulterated. After clucking disapprovingly at the colonel's going to the expense of including another sheet, she began to read. Katherine heard a sharp intake of breath, and saw that her mother had turned very pale.

"Is it bad news, Mama? You look so distressed." Katherine was accustomed to her mother's sometimes overly refined sensibilities, but she was unprepared for this.

Mrs. Amory seemed not to have heard her. A soft, "Oh, dear!" escaped her and she hurriedly folded the page and tucked it away into her sleeve.

"Mama . . ."

Mrs. Amory started out of her daze and, avoiding Katherine's searching glance, replied, "No . . . no, it is nothing at all. The colonel has said everything kind and proper. . . ."

Further questioning only provoked the announcement of a headache, and Katherine left her afflicted parent to the solace of a darkened room and eau de cologne applied to the temples. She knew from experience that no amount of persuasion could induce her mother to reveal the source of her distress before the proper time, so she very soon put that possibility out of her head. Perhaps it was only a bit of gossip about some old army acquaintance, after all.

Scarcely had the ladies been allowed time to become used to their guests and to the earl's plans for the house, when his lordship stated his intention to set off for London to order new rugs and draperies and to engage whatever workmen the neighborhood could not provide.

"But could you not send to Waring at Northfolde, and instruct him to see to it?" asked his mother as they all sat down to tea on a damp afternoon a few days after their arrival.

"Mother, Waring could no doubt see to it very well, but Whitfield is beyond his responsibilities. He has quite enough to manage at Northfolde. Besides, you know that I have some unfinished business to attend to in town. I told you that I should not be able to stay with you in the country without

36

leaving for a few days now and again."

He flashed a very disarming smile at Katherine as she poured his tea, and she was almost startled into spilling it. His irritation with her had lasted no longer than the hour of his arrival, but she had remained wary of him nevertheless.

Lady Colesville began to tease him for details of his business. "You are so mysterious about it! Whatever can you have to do in town at this time of year? The season is over, and almost everyone is already in the country or at the sea-side. Nothing whatever of importance can happen now." She yawned and stared out of the window at the grey day.

"I may be a trifle too arrogant, as you are so fond of telling me, Sally," the earl replied, "but you are the most impudent chit in the kingdom, and I defy you to explain to me how my business can be any concern of yours."

"Oh, is it a petticoat affair? Have you a dashing high-flyer under your protection, and is she pining for you?" she asked impishly.

Tarrington's displeasure was obvious, and his knuckles whitened as he gripped the delicate handle of his teacup. Katherine watched, wide-eyed, afraid he would break it. Could his sister have struck too close to home?

Before he could retort, the Dowager Countess, like any mother with two squabbling children, stepped into the fray.

"Sarah! One does not speak of such things to a gentleman," she said as sternly as if she were lecturing a schoolroom miss, "even one who happens to be your own brother, and wherever did you learn such vulgar language?"

Lady Colesville's cheeks were pink, but she was plainly unrepentant. "Oh, pish, Mama, I am a married woman now, and even when I was in my first season I was already up to snuff, though of course I pretended not." Her dimples were beginning to reappear. "I was only funning, and I daresay Vane is not half so shocked as you are."

The earl had recovered. The terrible frown was gone from his face, and he tweaked gently at the curl dangling over his

37

sister's forehead. "If it were as you believe, Sally," he said calmly, "I would have to be the greatest fool imaginable to discuss it with my sister. Now, you naughty puss, behave yourself while I am gone. I don't wish to find that you have worried Mama into a decline, or scandalized our cousins, or I'll advise that politically ambitious husband of yours to keep you secluded in the country until you learn some conduct."

"Nonsense! My behavior is always impeccable. I shall make an excellent political hostess." She sniffed as though offended, but her eyes were twinkling. "Will I not, cousin Katherine?"

Katherine replied that she did not doubt it.

She could tell that Tarrington would have responded, and that in a moment she would have found herself a participant in their good-natured banter, but for Mrs. Amory's interrupting with her regrets on the earl's leaving them so soon. She did not know whether to be relieved or disappointed.

By virtue of his concern for her future, Lord Tarrington had made a conquest of Mrs. Amory. She had alternately coquetted him and mothered him in a most diverting way that embarrassed Katherine while it brought a chuckle from Lady Tarrington.

To Priscilla, too, he had made himself agreeable, though she was still very shy of him. But though she was silently admiring in his presence, in his absence she never failed to sing his praises.

It was only Katherine who claimed to be unimpressed by the earl, though after their initial conflict had cooled, she had to force herself to keep up the pretence. There was no denying that he was one of the most attractive gentleman she had ever met, even if his attitudes, she felt, could do with a great deal of improvement.

In spite of her determination not to allow him to dictate to her as he was obviously quite accustomed to doing, she was finding it difficult not to fall under the spell of his smile. Since whenever she was not in direct conflict with him he behaved quite pleasantly to her, Katherine had to take herself sternly to task lest she become as tongue-tied as her cousin.

The night after meeting him, while she tried vainly to fall asleep, something that had never before eluded her, she turned over in her mind the sharp encounter and the odd impressions of the day, and in the end decided to maintain a cordial reserve towards the new master of Whitfield, unless he provoked her into doing otherwise.

Though his assumption of authority irritated her, something about him made her feel strangely vulnerable, as though all her feelings were much too close to the surface, and could be touched off by a single word, a look, or careless touch from Tarrington. It is only, she told herself impatiently as she pummelled a pillow into a more obliging shape, that no one has ever made me quite so angry before.

Now, watching him plant a filial kiss on Lady Tarrington's cheek, she decided that he was altogether too charming for anyone's good. When he was not preoccupied with his own importance, that is, and the thought made her smile in spite of herself, just as he approached to bid her goodbye.

Lord Tarrington almost stepped back in surprise. Katherine Amory had actually favored him with a smile! He had almost despaired of seeing one, so severe and disapproving of him had she appeared ever since his arrival. But no, he thought a moment later, watching her flush as he took her hand. She is only glad that I am going. He had made a bad start. No doubt the girl meant well, but her unspeakable plan . . . had she no sense of her position, her birth, of her potential? He found himself staring for a little too long at her clear smooth skin, stained now with pink, and her large, glowing brown eyes. To waste it all, he mused, as a governess . . . but then he recalled the necessity of his departure and spoke.

"My dear Miss Amory, I hope you are not regretting your decision to stay here for the present? For my part, I am happy it gave me the opportunity to further our acquaintance," he said amiably, though her dislike was palpable, and he well knew that he had hardly spent enough time in her company to have come to know her at all.

Katherine tried to will the color to leave her cheeks, but it seemed to appear at even his most innocuous word or glance, and stubbornly remained. His stare, just then, she thought, was far from an innocent one. No man had ever looked at her quite that way, as if assessing her charms. She wondered for a moment what he thought, but that way lay foolishness.

"Thank you, my lord." She was determined that her voice, at least, would not betray the internal struggle provoked by that flickering green-brown gaze, and was pleased at how calm she sounded. "And *I* am glad that Whitfield has passed on to someone who is eager to see it restored to its former state. I'm afraid Uncle Edwin was sadly neglectful of his duties."

At last that appraising look was gone from his face, to be replaced by a frown of puzzlement. "Would you favor me with your company, Miss Amory, as far as my chaise?"

It was the last thing she had expected to hear, and she could feel the others eyeing them curiously, but she nodded her acquiescence. With another brief farewell to everyone, he took her arm and led her out of the sitting room.

"You found Uncle Edwin to be keeping a tight hold of the purse strings, did you?" he inquired blandly as they made their way to the stairs.

Katherine tried to force herself to ignore the fact that her arm lay securely tucked in his. "Why yes, even when it was a question of repair or maintaining the grounds. If Mrs. Burkin were still here, she would tell you that the table wasn't kept as it was in the old days, either," she said with an attempt at lightness. "I was careful to apply to him in only the direst of circumstances, such as when the kitchen chimney began to crumble, but though I used all the tact at my command, it was nearly impossible to get him to open his purse."

"Quite remarkable to think of the old gentleman being proof against even *your* tact, Miss Amory," he replied.

She could barely refrain from glaring at him. During the past

40

few days, the subject of the former master had barely come up, so eager did everyone seem to exorcise his gloomy specter. Obviously, it was long past the time when the heir to Whitfield should have been enlightened as to his predecessor's true character. Katherine did not exactly begrudge him the Amory fortune, though, to be sure, it would have solved all of her difficulties; but he would not escape without at least hearing a catalogue of Sir Edwin's sins.

"I daresay you are not at all concerned with what we have borne in return for a home here, but you must know that Uncle Edwin continually heaped abuse upon us and took every opportunity to gloat over his fortune, and how little of it he managed to spend. When he was in his most wicked moods, he would actually accuse us of trying to ruin him, and would vow that we should have not a penny when he died! Not, of course, that we ever expected anything more. If he had treated us decently, it would have been enough."

Tarrington listened with particular attention, but his manner reflected no sympathy for her sufferings. "You are too harsh, Katherine. You forget that he was a man who had a great deal of pain to bear."

Katherine grimaced. "But I remember that he inflicted a great deal of pain on the three women who saw to his comfort and managed his affairs for him."

Tarrington grasped her elbow firmly as they took the last few steps to the hall. "Come now, cousin. In another moment I shall begin to think you ungrateful."

Katherine shot him a contemptuous glance. Her determination to remain aloof from conflict had disappeared. "Of course you believe that I should be grateful, as a poor defenseless female to have even *this* leaking roof over my head," she retorted, gesturing with contempt at the flaking ceiling. "But what woman of spirit would not chafe at being cast in the role of dependent and continually reminded to be thankful for her good fortune?"

"Come, come now. Surely you exaggerate. And besides, where else would you have gone, with no one to look after you?"

Katherine bristled and withdrew her arm from his grasp. "With a little planning, sir, we would have found a way to go on, I'm sure, without anyone's assistance. My mother does not enjoy a strong constitution, and my cousin is by far too timid, but *I* am not exactly helpless, my lord! Indeed, even mama says I have a great deal of ingenuity." She lifted her chin and returned his amused gaze with one of defiance.

"Ingenuity is all very well, my dear," said the earl dryly, "but where it is combined with ingenuousness, then we run into considerable danger."

"Your concern is quite touching, my lord, but rest assured that I am well able to stay out of danger. I am hardly an innocent!" At his swift raising of brows she hastily amended this statement. "What I mean is, that though I am young and . . . and inexperienced, I am"—she searched for the words to extricate herself from this tangle, and recalled a felicitous phrase of his sister's—"completely up to snuff!"

For a moment she thought that he was going to laugh.

"Are you indeed?" drawled Tarrington. "I find your estimation of your own, shall we say, *worldliness* rather edifying considering that you were so naïve as to be taken in even by that old humbug, our late lamented Uncle Edwin."

Katherine impatiently waved away the footman who had sprung to swing open the doors. "Whatever can you mean by *that* remark, my lord?" she demanded.

"Simply that you have been soundly hoaxed, Miss Amory, and it only serves to prove to me that you are scarcely fit to be out of leading strings!"

"How dare you!"

"But I do dare, my dear Miss Amory. I was going to break the news to you more gently, but I see that as a—what was it?—a *woman of spirit*, you would have merely resented being cushioned from such a blow." His mouth twitched at the corners. "Tell me, how is it that with all your famous ingenuity, you did not contrive to discover in your years of residence here that there is no Amory fortune!" His smile was maddeningly placid.

"No . . . no fortune? You must be mistaken."

"I assure you I am not. There has not been a fortune for many years. Sir Edwin was enjoying a rather pathetic joke at your expense, my dear."

Katherine digested this news in silence for a moment. "Well, I must say, I'm disappointed in dear old Uncle Edwin. It would have been infinitely shabbier had he built up our expectations and allowed us to believe we were heiresses."

The earl looked at his cousin in amazement. She did say the most remarkable things.

"Just so," he murmured. "Poor man must have been slipping in his dotage."

"But you, my lord . . . it does appear that you have lost rather more by this than I. I, after all, have only lost my pride. You on the other hand . . . oh that explains it!" she exclaimed, turning innocent eyes on him. "No wonder you are always rude and odious beyond all bearing!"

"My dear Katherine—"

"No need to apologize," Katherine said sweetly, "To a man like yourself, who is no doubt up to every rig, the prospect of inheriting a shambles of a house, when you expected to come into a fortune, must have been a dreadful blow, I'm sure. I quite sympathize, and give you leave to behave as badly as you please."

"You do me too much honor," the earl replied, his eyes gleaming appreciatively. "I am quite overcome."

The earl's chaise, with his prime greys harnessed to it, awaited him at the bottom of the steps. Katherine was certain that he had had his fill of verbal jousting, but he took her arm once more and prevented her from bidding him goodbye as she had planned.

In the greenish light of the overcast morning his eyes were

deeper in color, and there were shadows beneath them. She was tempted to ask him outright if he had really been disappointed by his inheritance.

But a little reflection convinced her that she had taunted him enough. Had she not already provoked one setdown by presuming to know too much about his lordship's affairs? If he was really impoverished, then this inheritance was surely a burden. However, if she mentioned it he was sure to say that it was none of her affair. And she was not altogether certain that he would not be right. If only he weren't so infuriatingly secretive! Surely he would not be the first man of position to have fallen upon hard times?

The greys were fresh and eager to be off, and Thomas, his lordship's groom, was struggling to hold them. "If you please, m'lord!" he called.

"All right then, I'm coming."

Tarrington paused, and seemed to be considering something. "I do hope that this news has not been too shattering for you, cousin. I had not meant . . ."

Katherine glanced up at him, quickly enough to see that his expression had softened. But by the time he continued speaking his chin had regained its usual arrogant set.

". . . I had not meant to be quite so abrupt. However, it must be a great comfort to you to that Sir Edwin so far recalled his duty as to leave you a hundred pounds."

Katherine shrugged. "I daresay it is more of a comfort to Mama than to me. I would much have preferred to have been treated with dignity while he lived. But my mother hated to think so ill of a relation, and it brought him up in her esteem that he had not forgotten his duty as head of the family to make some provision for his only niece."

"Yet you remain unimpressed by such a small amount."

"That is unjust, my lord," Katherine snapped. "Though it is certainly not enough to allow me independence or comfort, I cannot but be grateful that my uncle remembered me at the last."

44

The earl bowed. Katherine wondered if that was as much of an apology as his pride would allow him.

"Perhaps, cousin, it would be unwise to inform your mother of Sir Edwin's duplicity in the matter of the fortune. I should not like to think of the spasm that might ensue."

Katherine glanced up sharply, but the earl's look was all innocence.

"On the other hand," he continued, "it might be best if you did inform Mrs. Amory. It will complete the destruction of Sir Edwin's memory, and perhaps then your mama will be more willing to accompany you to Bath if she comes to regard Whitfield as the scene of a cruel deception."

Katherine allowed herself to succumb to a tiny smile. To her complete surprise, Tarrington was smiling too. She bemusedly allowed him to take her hand.

"Really, Katherine, can I not persuade you to give up your plan? Even you must realize that it is quite unsuitable."

There was a sudden sinking in her middle and Katherine wrenched her hand away. It was obvious that his sudden turnabout was meant to confuse her and make it easier to mold her to his will.

"Indeed, my lord? And I suppose that you have a better suggestion as to how we should contrive to support ourselves?" she inquired coolly.

"Of course, Miss Amory! Why not stay here and keep house for me? I would be the ideal employer, you know. Why, I doubt that you would see me more than a fortnight out of the year." His voice was light and teasing now, which only contributed to her annoyance.

With a great effort she managed not to rip up at him immediately, but to force a frigid smile instead.

"Though the prospect of your absence throughout most of the year is, I admit, quite an inducement, my lord, I really think Bath would suit me better. And I must warn you, I would require an exorbitant salary. In view of your failed expectations here"—she gestured at the ruin around them—"I seri-

45

ously doubt that you could afford me!"

The earl fixed steely eyes on Katherine and bowed abruptly. "Good day to you, Miss Amory."

In a moment he was climbing briskly into his chaise. A footman had slammed the door, the groom had let go of the horses, and the carriage was rolling down the drive. Katherine felt that she had won the skirmish, but that the real battle was yet to be fought.

The day suddenly seemed greyer and damper than ever, and no sooner had the chaise disappeared from sight than the rain, which had begun very slyly as a clinging mist with fits and spurts of drops every now and again, finally came down with a vengeance, and she hurried up the steps into shelter to give the news to her mother and cousin.

Priscilla took it philosophically. "Even if there were a fortune, Sir Edwin made it clear enough that he would leave none of it to you. We should still be in the same circumstances." She blinked up at Katherine and smiled. "And the earl has been so kind, that we are not really badly off at all."

It was too true, Katherine reflected. She began to despair of ever being able to move her mother and cousin to Bath. Mrs. Amory admitted to being shocked by Sir Edwin's deception, but her feelings were relieved very speedily by a series of oh, mys punctuated by "What your dear father would have said."

The earl had been too optimistic by far in his supposition that knowledge of her brother-in-law's perfidy might encourage her to leave. She was quite comfortable as she was and whenever Katherine mentioned Bath she became apprehensive of an attack or found something requiring her attention in another room.

Though she now had more leisure than she had ever known, and more pleasant company, as two or three days passed, tranquil but strangely flat since Tarrington had gone, Katherine began to dread the arrival of a certain caller whose visits had occurred with distressing regularity for the past twelve

46

months, and who could be expected to present himself, with his distasteful proposals, at any time.

But she clung to the slender hope that Mr. Oldbury had heard of the arrival of the Earl of Tarrington and would shrink from interrupting a family party. She put the thought aside and enjoyed her freedom for another few days, and then a letter from the earl arrived, along with the workmen, to break up their domestic amusements for a while.

Tarrington wrote that he would return sometime within the next fortnight, and that he might bring a guest, but that otherwise their plans could commence unaltered. Accordingly, the ladies arranged to move for the duration into a formerly unoccupied wing of the house, which had long been closed off for reasons of economy. Aside from dust and mustiness, it was not in any worse condition than the center section which would undergo repairs first.

They had resigned themselves to the inconvenience, and for the Tarrington ladies the experience was more in the nature of a novelty than a hardship, but only hours after the men had begun their labors, Lady Tarrington and her daughter decided regretfully to take leave of their cousins, as the dust and dirt that the work occasioned caused the Dowager Countess to sneeze mightily. A few coughs from Lady Colesville reminded her mother that as a child her lungs had been delicate, so they planned a swift remove to Grouse Hall.

On a close, humid morning the ladies gathered to bid each other goodbye, with the promise of many visits to console them for their separation.

"I shall ride over to see you one morning soon," promised Sally Colesville.

"And when my son returns we will all dine at the Hall and spend an evening together," added Lady Tarrington. "Delia, my dear, if he and his guest should prove troublesome, you are not to hesitate to send them straight to the Hall. You are inconvenienced enough already, what with all the sawing and banging." She punctuated this opinion with a sneeze and a

47

flourish of a lacy handkerchief.

"Oh, my lady, I should not dream . . . that is, to order his lordship out of his own house." Mrs. Amory looked scandalized, but the earl's sister only laughed.

"Mama is right, Aunt Delia, and Vane is sometimes a great deal too demanding, so you must not hesitate to order him about when he needs it."

Katherine giggled at the dismay on her mother's face, and wondered at the casual teasing that came so easily to Tarrington and his sister. Though she knew her pert replies had provoked him, she could not imagine, even had she known the earl twenty years, ever feeling comfortable enough to actually poke fun at him. But then, she was only a poor dependent cousin, and could never aspire to such intimacy. She bade the ladies goodbye, and Whitfield became tedious and confining once again.

The weather worsened that afternoon, and after two days of drenching rain and intermittent thunder, the sun came out warmer than ever, and the servants exclaimed that they had not seen so warm a start to June in many years.

Katherine and Priscilla varied their day with some short walks, returning with their boots covered in mud, in between assisting Mrs. Amory, who, with less to do and more time to rest, had found her health much improved. Yet finally such a cloudless sky, and the heavy green scent of the new summer growth, together with the drying of the roads, tempted the girls to be away.

One afternoon, with the excuse of a list of trivial items to be obtained from the village shops, they left Mrs. Amory resting with the curtains drawn against the sun and climbed into Sir Edwin's aged gig, the only occupant of a once-full coach house. They were attended, at Mrs. Amory's insistence, by an equally venerable groom riding alongside on a long-suffering roan hack.

An hour or two of careful shopping and much wishing over hats and ribbons and bolts of muslin, followed by a hearty tea at the Black Horse, quenched their restlessness somewhat, and after they had made one false start for home, with their cob casting a shoe, they were eager to be on their way.

By the time the horse had been attended to, with the groom, Peters, standing alongside muttering through his grey bristles while the smith did his work, it was very late, and a faint purple dusk was already shading the hills in the distance, while a moist wind had picked up and begun to sway the boughs of the trees that thickly lined the road, producing an eerie moaning.

The mournful baying of a dog somewhere was all that was needed to set Priscilla shivering, despite the lingering warmth of the setting sun, and her fertile imagination supplied the rest of the details.

"Are we almost there?" she asked fretfully, squinting into the space between the horse's ears for a glimpse of Whitfield, which was usually visible on its rising ground for quite a distance away.

"Not yet, but soon." Katherine tried to project a calmness she did not really feel. Though normally she was not at all fanciful, the awful stillness between those sighing gusts of wind, and the shadows, as clouds moved in to cover the remains of the sun, had their effect on her own nerves. She knew better than to say so, as it would only increase her cousin's anxiety.

Peters, leather palmed and toothless, and less silent than usual due to an afternoon spent in the alehouse waiting for them, glanced at the gloomy lanes hung with branches on either side of the road, and shook his hoary head.

"This were the exact spot where they say Mister Bracken's dairyman were nearly kilt by one o' them footpads—last spring it wor. This stretch, afore ye come to the fields, be the worst," he said darkly. "O' course there were no moon that night," he conceded, but in the next breath he had sealed their fate. "Nor yet tonight neither, aye." He nodded significantly.

Katherine told him firmly that she would thank him to keep his stories to himself, and assured her trembling cousin that the isolated stretch of road would afford slim pickings for any highwayman worth his salt. Privately she recalled, not without a twinge of fear, that though not many travellers used this route, several wealthy merchants with business in the larger towns beyond the village of Barton were known to pass this way now and then. Still, it would have to be a desperate character who would prowl such a deserted country road.

She scolded herself for communicating her fear to the horse, for the cob was becoming restless, and required her fullest attention. As they reached the narrowest stretch of road, he snorted at a squirrel, and the harsh cawing of a bird made him start as if a pistol had gone off behind him. It was while Katherine was engaged in controlling his tossing head that a furious rustling came from just ahead, and as they rounded a sharp bend, the horse was frightened anew. A ragged figure, a spotted kerchief tied round half his face, charged out of the woods on a powerful horse and, brandishing a pistol, cut off their escape.

Priscilla screamed, Peters cursed, and Katherine fought to keep the cob from rearing in the shafts. The groom was unarmed, and too frail to put up a fight. The highwayman's eyes above his kerchief were wild and dangerous and his pistol-hand jerked nervously. Katherine only hoped that their scanty purses would satisfy him. She had only one piece of jewelry, a gold locket that had belonged to her grandmother, and she was glad she had worn it beneath her bodice.

The shrieking Priscilla was harshly adjured to "stubble it" if she did not care for a "douse on the chops." That all but silenced her except for a low moan of fear, but she was too terrified to move when the thief demanded their money. Katherine flung her reticule to the ground beside his horse, and urged her cousin to do the same. Though she did not scream, indeed, she did not think she could produce a sound from her throat at that moment, she was trembling almost as violently as Priscilla.

Keeping the pistol unsteadily trained on them, the highwayman was preparing to dismount and collect his booty when both he and his victims were jerked out of their rapport of terror by the sound of hoofbeats, accompanied by what was unmistakably drunken singing in an uneven baritone.

Katherine's hopes, momentarily raised, were dashed again when the tune was interrupted by a distinct hiccup. It was not likely that any man in such a condition would be of much use. More likely, he was an accomplice of the thief.

But the figure that emerged from the trees was like nothing her imagination could have prepared her for. Mounted on a flashy chestnut, waving what appeared to be duelling pistols of an antique but deadly aspect, was a young gentleman of fashion, attired in garb that even to Katherine's untrained eye spoke instantly of London and the highest ton.

He wore exquisitely fitted buckskin inexpressibles, a toilinette waistcoat of a delicate shade of cream, beneath a dark blue, tailored riding coat, with an artfully arranged cravat and stiff shirt points climbing towards his ears. He rode as unsteadily as he sang, his feet, shod in top-boots that gleamed even in the filtered light of the sinking sun, and he clutched spasmodically at the sides of his horse, so that animal and rider proceeded in a peculiar jerky dance to the scene of the crime.

His appearance startled the already uneasy highwayman, whose weapon wavered. Katherine was terrified that he would instantly shoot the new arrival, but she could not have been more surprised at what happened instead. No sooner had this fashion plate focused his bleary eyes on the scene, than he waved his unwieldy weapons, huge pistols covered in silver filigree, and swayed lightly in the saddle.

"What the de—" He noticed the ladies and stopped. "You there, what's 'a meanin' of this?" The significance of the scene began to penetrate his fog, and with a glare almost comic in its ferocity, he urged his horse towards the thief.

"Holloa! There's a fine gallows'-bird!" He discharged one of his pistols, without troubling to aim, and the ball whizzed past the nervous highwayman's ear. Crying, "Come on then, men,

51

let's at him!" to some unseen companions, he gave a final kick to his poor confused mount, which reared in a convincing display of rage, and charged the criminal.

Katherine swiftly pulled her cousin to the floor of the gig, lest they find themselves the target of his next wayward missile, but her caution proved unnecessary, for he galloped straight past the gig without firing until he was nearly upon the highwayman.

To Katherine's astonishment, that jittery bandit must have assumed that this wild fellow would soon be joined by a host of others. Thinking better of his attempt and leaving the ladies' reticules where they had tossed them, he turned and fled into the woods on an unseen path, managing to dodge the second ball sent hurtling in his direction.

When their rescuer was satisfied that he had routed the villain, he returned to the victims who were dusting off their gowns with shaking hands after stepping down from the gig. Peters, once again as placid as his old horse, dismounted and offered the gentleman a gnarled hand.

"Beggin' your worship's pardon, but I ain't never seen such a spectacle! A fellow mor'n half-sprung scarin' off the likes of one of them rascals, and with bad shootin', too!"

The young man somewhat bemusedly accepted this doubtful praise, but then Katherine and Priscilla, the former giving the old servant a speaking glance while the latter stared raptly into her rescuer's face, added their thanks to the old man's words in a rather more complimentary way.

"May we ask to whom we owe our deliverance?" Katherine inquired. "Please accept our deepest thanks for your courage." She was perfectly serious, despite the unconventional nature of the rescue. Now that the immediate danger was over, she saw the humor of it. But though the gentleman was undoubtedly intoxicated, he had such a kindly face that she could not bear to mention it.

"Why certainly, ma'am," he replied, reaching down and shaking first her hand, then Priscilla's, a little too vigorously.

52

"Rodney Thatchbreed, Lord Knolland, at your service," he said, sweeping off his hat, which had miraculously remained firmly set on his unruly blond curls throughout the adventure. Unfortunately, he attempted to make them a deep bow while still in the saddle, and in doing so nearly unseated himself. At last he dismounted unsteadily, with Peters' help, to bow properly before them.

"Beg pardon," he murmured, his eyes barely focusing on the intent, admiring face of Priscilla. "Daresay it was the claret. Had more than was good for me. Can't hold my drink like the other fellows. Very fine stuff it was, though!"

"Oh, sir," cried Priscilla, "how can we begin to show our gratitude for your bravery?"

Lord Knolland swayed dangerously, and it was only the timely assistance of Peters which prevented him from falling in an inglorious heap at the rescued maidens' feet.

"No need, miss . . . thing is," muttered their hero, his balance precariously restored, "feeling dashed queasy; done up, you know."

"Won't you let us help you, my lord?" Priscilla begged shyly. "You are ill and shouldn't travel any farther tonight. Come home with us, or if you would rather not"—a moment's reflection served to remind her how odd her aunt would think it if she brought home an intoxicated young lord for dinner—"then let us send a servant with you on your way."

Lord Knolland, whose slightly protuberant pale blue eyes could just be seen in the fading light, grinned down at her unsteadily. "Yes, I am a bit too disguised to be jauntering about alone, ain't I? No miss, you're right to think it. Your kind offer gratefully accepted." He put his hand to his brow and a puzzled look crept over his face. "Where was I off to, anyway? Visit . . . the pistols . . . can't seem to— Oh, well, I daresay it'll come to me." He shrugged off the forgetfulness, an unwise move, which brought another wave of dizziness. He clutched at Peters' supporting arm, and gingerly remounted his horse.

"If your man'll ride by me, I'm bound to remember sooner or later. Can't have been going far; I've got hardly any clothes with me!" It was true that he carried nothing but two bulging saddlebags, and the pistols. "Meanwhile, I'm going to stow these poppers safely away." The groom handed him the one which he had dropped after chasing away the highwayman. The other was still in his left hand.

Katherine watched with apprehension as he handled the weapons, but he reassured her. "No need to be alarmed, they're both empty now." He shuddered at the realization. "I *did* shoot 'em, didn't I?"

But neither of the girls could keep from wincing as he flourished them, preparatory to bestowing them either in his coat pockets or in his waistband, a decision he appeared to have difficulty making. All of them had been far too absorbed to pay any attention to the sound of hooves and the creaking of wheels that announced the approach of a vehicle.

In a curricle drawn by matched bays, of which Katherine heard Lord Knolland mutter, "Never seen such commoners; fellow must be a flat to've parted with his blunt for those slugs," sat a stocky young man with a ruddy face, who, seeing his lordship with pistols drawn and the two ladies standing before him in the road, jumped to a not unreasonable conclusion. He pulled up behind them, shouting "Hold hard, villain!" And drew his horse-pistol on the astounded Lord Knolland.

"Get down. Dismount, I say! Scurvy rascal, thief! Coward, preying on unprotected females! I should deal with you myself if I was not sure that you will swing at Tyburn for this!"

"If you please, sir . . ." Peters was stung into an attempt to explain.

"Silence, old fool!"

His lordship ceased goggling at his accuser and began to protest on his own behalf. "Really, my good fellow, got it all wrong, not a thief at all. Coming it a bit too strong."

For answer, the newcomer, who Katherine had already recognized as their neighbor and her irritatingly tenacious

54

suitor Mr. George Oldbury, discharged his weapon. Lord Knolland's high-bred chestnut, already in a nervous state due to the unsteadiness of his rider, took offense at this insult and reared, throwing the unfortunate peer to the ground this time, where he lay insensible.

Priscilla screamed and ran to him, while Katherine tried to make it clear to Mr. Oldbury that he had grossly misinterpreted the situation.

"Really, sir, you are quite mistaken! This man is not guilty of anything. In fact—"

Oldbury, however, in delight at his brave and gallant behavior, was in no mind to listen to the cold voice of reason.

"Back away, Miss Townsend, he may still be dangerous. I shall deal with him," he said, stooping to confiscate the silver-mounted pistols, then looking them over appreciatively before handing them to his groom and muttering, *"Evidence."*

"Or rather, the magistrate shall, when I get this scoundrel back to Barton. No, Miss Amory," he addressed Katherine, not having heard a word of her explanation. "Don't plead for mercy on his behalf. Why, the fellow's naught but a worthless stain on the face of our country, and shall be dealt with just as he ought."

This reaction was not promising; nevertheless Katherine continued to press for his understanding, in the hope that once the initial excitement had passed, reason would return. But she was well enough acquainted with George Oldbury to know this for the slenderest of hopes.

"Indeed, Mr. Oldbury, I tell you it is not at all the way it appeared! This gentleman is no highwayman."

Mr. Oldbury remained unimpressed. " 'Gentleman,' you call him? Rather say villain and have done!" His broad face, handsome in a florid way, was filled with triumph and righteousness, and his chest, over the beginnings of a paunch, was bursting with pride. "I know you tender ladies have a weakness for these rogues, these so-called gentlemen of the road. You are easily impressed with their boldness, and their liking for finery"—he pointed accusingly at Lord Knolland's elaborate neckcloth—"but you are misguided, though your sentiments do credit to your kind hearts and delicate sensibilities."

Katherine knew from experience that once he began on such a harangue he would never allow the demands of common sense or even common courtesy to interrupt it, so she ignored him and looked over at her cousin.

Priscilla sat in the dust of the road, heedless of her gown, with Lord Knolland's head in her lap. Having long shared with Katherine the duty of ministering to Mrs. Amory in all her spells, she never went anywhere without her supply of lavender water and hartshorn, or a vinaigrette, and it was the last of these that she was employing in an effort to revive their rescuer.

"Kate," she sobbed, "oh, Kate, I believe Mr. Oldbury has killed him!"

There was a muffled groan from the depths of her blue muslin skirt. Lord Knolland pushed the vinaigrette away from his nose, and attempted to sit up. "Killed? Never say so! Take more than a rotten smell to kill me." He swayed, and Priscilla waved the vinaigrette again. Her hero waved it away, caught sight of the angry Mr. Oldbury, and hurriedly closed his eyes again. "Feel as though I might be better off dead, though," he raised a hand to his temple, groaning.

"That is a wish that can easily be gratified," pronounced Mr. Oldbury, who strutted over to his captive and stood over him, glaring.

If it had not been for the forlorn look on his lordship's face and the tears on Priscilla's, Katherine would have been in whoops. The lightning thought crossed her mind that his lordship the Earl of Tarrington would have enjoyed such a scene immensely, and then she was sorry it had, for she had almost succeeded that day in putting him out of her mind.

Calling his groom over to assist him, Mr. Oldbury began to drag Lord Knolland away, and heaving him upright on shaky legs, towed him towards the curricle.

"No, you must not!" Priscilla leaped up and ran after them, and Katherine, who had never seen her cousin so affected before, followed and added her own entreaties, but Oldbury would not be moved from carrying out what he had declared to be his duty to king and country.

His lordship, in no condition to put up much resistance, sat limply in the curricle, looking pale and queasy, and shot a hopeless glance at the ladies. He did endeavor to clear himself once more.

"Good fellow!" he approved, "Patriotic duty and all that, but you've got the wrong man, that's it. Meant no harm, I assure you. Came along, let go with a round, drove the curst fellow off. Would never harm a lady; not at all the thing, you know."

To these applications, as to all others, Mr. Oldbury turned a deaf ear, and only advising his prisoner to save his speeches for the magistrate, ascertained that the ladies were unharmed, adjured the amazed Peters to take better care of them in future, and drove back towards the village.

The ladies stared, horrified, after him, Priscilla crying quietly, Katherine deep in thought.

"There is no help for it," she decided, "we must go back to the village and clear him before the magistrate. They'll probably keep him under lock and key at the Black Horse for tonight." There was no gaol in the tiny village of Barton.

"Please don't cry so, Priscilla, it isn't seemly. Why, you are barely acquainted with that gentleman. Besides, when we explain to the magistrate exactly what occurred, I am sure he will listen to us like the sensible women we are." She gritted her teeth at the thought of the odious Mr. Oldbury's refusal to believe her explanation. It was no different than his usual conduct towards those of the female sex, and it was one of the things she despised about him.

No exertion on her part would ever convince him that she had a rational, well-informed mind and was capable of using it. He was always ready to insist, especially when she continued to

57

refuse his monthly applications for her hand, that she did not know her own mind. He was sure there could be no doubt of his desirability as a suitor to a young lady who, he was fond of telling her, had nothing but the transient attractions of youthful beauty to recommend her as a wife, a beauty which seemed to impress him little.

She had seethed under these and other similar remarks, but had never yet allowed herself to respond in kind, or to let him feel her wrath, not caring to bandy words with such a blatant fool.

Mr. Oldbury, unfortunately, was always kindly received by her mother, and by virtue of being the son of Sir Edwin's late boon companion, he was the only neighbor who had visited Whitfield in the days of her uncle's rule. No one else was ever admitted to the house, and they had long ago stopped calling, as Sir Edwin had quarrelled with or insulted all of their neighbors.

Not a day had passed but that her uncle had urged Katherine to accept Mr. Oldbury's offer. "Take him," he had advised, chuckling dryly, in between choking coughs. "Haven't got a penny, and never will. You ain't exactly hatchet-faced," he would say, screwing up his rheumy eyes at her, "and you've got a figure on you, but you're as good as a beggar, you are," and he would laugh hoarsely, losing his wind, until his valet would solemnly pound him on the back.

Katherine knew all this quite as well as her uncle could, but she was not so desperate to form her own establishment as to be lost to all sense and propriety. To marry a ridiculous prig like Oldbury, who had never even pretended any affection for her, would be nothing less than a crime.

She knew from the servants' gossip that he had already been rejected by several young ladies in the neighborhood, and that his fortune was all in his art collection, the only thing for which he had obtained some local notoriety. His birth was considered no more than respectable, and much of his land had been sold off by his father. With these deficiencies, in addition to his personal ones, Katherine was not the only one to consider him ineligible.

The oddest thing was that her suitor had never really evinced more than a cursory interest in her, until the day a little over a year ago when he had visited Sir Edwin and emerged from the sick-chamber with a peculiar light in his watery grey eyes, and a determined set to his rounded chin.

Since then he had made it his business to address Miss Amory promptly in the first week of every month, returning undeterred after each refusal as if it had never occurred. He would always begin by assuring her with a calm certainty that made her wild with irritation that her hand had already been bestowed upon him by her nearest male relation, and that it wanted but for her consent, a negligible formality in his eyes, to make it official.

Despite her firm, but apparently not violent enough refusals, he had continued to present himself at Whitfield even after Sir Edwin's death, and with a new urgency in his manner, which baffled Katherine even as it annoyed her. She had despaired of ever making him give up, until she had conceived the Bath scheme. But now that she was staying at Whitfield it was sure to begin all over again.

Forcing her attention back to the situation at hand, Katherine waited for Peters to mount his weary hack and to take the reins of Lord Knolland's much more impressive mount, and then continued on the road for home, wending her way carefully along the dark road, shivering as she remembered the unholy gleam in the highwayman's eyes.

"But wait, where are we going?" Priscilla's voice was shrill with agitation. "Are we not going back to the village to clear his lordship from Mr. Oldbury's charges?"

Katherine turned to her in astonishment. Was this the same cousin who had been so painfully shy and timid all these years? "Surely you cannot think I meant to go tonight, Pris? Why, there is hardly a sliver of light left, and that highwayman might still be lurking about."

Priscilla shivered and looked about her warily, but she persevered. "Then poor Lord Knolland will have to spend the night as a prisoner, and they will be so unpleasant to him! And he is hurt; suppose he took a serious injury when he fell from his horse?"

Katherine smiled. "Silly, he was only very drunk, and it was more of a slide than a fall, I think. I daresay he will be fine but for a severe headache tomorrow. Besides, Mr. Oldbury does not believe us and will insist that his lordship be kept anyway."

These excellent reasons made no impression on her cousin. "But we must try, Kate, indeed we *must!*"

"Have you forgotten that my mother will be wild with anxiety for us? It is two hours since she must first have looked for our return. I fear her nerves won't be equal to the strain."

Priscilla looked conscious at this, but soon had an answer for every objection. "We will send Peters back to Aunt Delia with a message after we bring Lord Knolland's horse to the inn, so that she will know we are safe. Then she can send someone back to the Black Horse to escort us home after we have discharged our debt to that poor brave gentleman." Her voice trembled, but there was more decision in it than Katherine had ever heard.

After a little consideration, she could find no fault with this, though she did not relish the dark drive. But it seemed that Peters knew horses better than he knew the sky and its vagaries, for contrary to his prediction, there was going to be a moon that night. In fact, she could see the pale, fat lopsided crescent at the edge of the sky. She turned back towards the village, amidst cries of thanks from her cousin.

Katherine was above all, surprised at Priscilla's unexpected inventiveness, and thought about it with much amusement on the way back to Barton, where she directed a grumbling Peters to return with all dispatch to Whitfield and inform Mrs. Amory that they were safe, and to ask for another servant to come and escort them home.

Giving the reins into the hands of an ostler in the inn-yard, she had a few qualms about the wisdom of two unescorted young females appearing there in the evening, but as they were well known to the landlord, he swiftly conducted them, after his first look of surprise, past the noisy taproom and the curious glances of its inhabitants, into a small private parlor.

Before they could reach this sanctuary, and just as she was congratulating herself on not encountering anyone who might have recognized them, Katherine's eye was caught by the sight of a gentleman who could have been the twin of the earl of Tarrington ascending the narrow wooden stairs in company with a burly, coarse-looking fellow in a frieze coat. She stared in horror as his broad back disappeared up the stairs.

It was bad enough that she had allowed her cousin to convince her to turn back, when tomorrow would have done just as well, but to have the earl find them there at the inn after dusk, chasing after a strange gentleman, would be disastrous. She could imagine his reaction, and wondered if he would order them home immediately, without waiting for an explanation. At the very least, it would certainly confirm his belief that they were unable to fend for themselves.

Then it occurred to Katherine that though the propriety of her own presence at the Black Horse was questionable, his arrival there required an explanation as well. They had had no word of his return, and it was certainly odd that he would choose to go to the inn rather than return to Whitfield. And who, she wondered, could his oddly dressed companion be? As yet she could not discuss it with Priscilla, who was busy explaining their errand to kindly old Hewes, the inn's proprietor.

He chuckled and said, "Indeed, miss, young Mr. Oldbury has the poor gentleman in the next room, and is in-terrogatin' him something dreadful, though anyone could see the young gent's of the Quality and ought to be treated more respectful. Not to mention he looks to be too unsteady on his pins to harm a kitten, let alone hold up your gig."

He hastened to assure Priscilla, who had not ceased praising

Lord Knolland's courage, that he had done all he could for the young man. "There's no saying but that he was a trifle bosky, and beginning to feel the worse for it by the time Mr. Oldbury got him here. I gave him a cup o' my special remedy, and loosed up that infernal contraption around his neck." Hewes snorted his disgust at the frivolous turn in gentlemen's fashions. "He'll do, that is, if young Oldbury'll let him be."

Priscilla's gratitude for these kind attentions to her hero were cut short only by her concern that Mr. Oldbury should immediately be made to understand his lordship's innocence.

Hewes promised to bring both gentlemen to wait at once on the ladies, brought them two branches of candles, and after they had declined his offer of refreshment, he bustled away.

"It is the oddest thing, Pris," said Katherine, "but I saw a gentleman who looked very much like Lord Tarrington—just a moment ago, going up the stairs with a rough-looking fellow."

She flung down her reticule, and nibbled her lower lip. "If it should be him . . . Oh, it is so vexing! I only hope that we can leave here without him seeing us. I am sure he would not at all approve and I am much too tired to quarrel."

Priscilla looked up in surprise. "I did not think you cared that much for our cousin's approval, Kate."

"Of course I don't! It is nothing to concern him. But he is of an interfering disposition, and I should not enjoy being read a lecture about something that does not even concern him. Does it not seem strange to you, Pris, that he should have come here and not to Whitfield, or at least have sent a message—"

"Are you quite sure it was he?"

Katherine paced the parlor, stared out of the small-paned windows, and saw nothing of interest in the lantern-light of the yard. "There could not be two such men with those looks in this part of the country," she insisted.

Priscilla came out of her anxious daze long enough to say, "Perhaps he is only taking his dinner here in order not to inconvenience your mama. It is rather late for him to appear, especially when we are not expecting him."

"Hmmph! I doubt if such a man would care how much he might inconvenience anyone."

His determination to convince her to change her plans still angered her, but at the same time she had been continually struggling with thoughts of how, depending on his company, his haughtiness could turn to teasing and then to exasperation, of which of these emotions she was most likely to precipitate in him, and of what behavior she ought best to assume towards him when he returned.

The most infuriating part of it was that she seriously doubted if a single thought of *her* had even crossed his mind since the moment his chaise had pulled away. He seemed to be assuming far too important a position in her ruminations, and somehow she must put a stop to it.

And now there was the sudden possibility of meeting him here, under these difficult and admittedly indelicate circumstances. It made her wretchedly anxious, and she could only hope that they were well away before he came downstairs again. She was sure that if Lord Tarrington ever found out, he would violently disapprove of their actions, and, due to her own scruples, she did not feel fully prepared to defend herself should he object. Disabusing Mr. Oldbury of his mistaken assumption would require quite enough effort as it was, and her patience was close to being exhausted.

Aloud, she continued to ponder possible explanations for his presence at the inn, and the identity of his ungentlemanly companion.

"Perhaps it has something to do with his business . . . no, not likely. He was with such a curious fellow, who wore an old frieze coat, and a dreadful spotted neckcloth. And they both had this . . . this *furtive* look about them. I can hardly credit it's being Tarrington."

Priscilla favored her with a nearsighted, very uninterested stare. "Then it could not be him," she said absently, and seated herself on a small, straight chair by the window, only to leap up again at the entrance of a pale, shaken Lord Knolland, who was followed by Mr. Oldbury, not at all pleased to see them.

"Miss Amory, Miss Townsend! What can you mean by this? Surely you can trust me to do all that is necessary to see that this evildoer is brought to justice?"

He gestured contemptuously at his prisoner, who, weak-kneed, had sunk into a chair. Priscilla promptly seated herself at his side and began searching in her reticule for a restorative.

Katherine squared her shoulders and prepared to do battle. It was obvious that her cousin's concern was only for Lord Knolland. It was up to her to convince Oldbury of his mistake. "No, sir," she retorted, "I cannot trust you to do something as simple as giving me your attention when I speak to you. You have made yourself and all of us ridiculous by this . . . this farce!"

She had never spoken so vehemently to him before, even when he had persisted in offering for her. "This gentleman, Lord Knolland, whom you have dragged away as a common criminal, is the person who rescued us from a real highway-man, with less flourish and foolishness than you have displayed in dealing with an imaginary one."

Of course, this was not strictly true, but Katherine thought she preferred Lord Knolland's methods to Oldbury's.

"I demand that you set him free immediately," she declared.

She had flung this speech at him so forcefully that Oldbury had begun backing away from her until he was almost at the door, appearing so puffed up with wounded pride that Katherine wondered he did not burst. But after a long spate of sputtering and half-hearted objections, his outrage dissolved as her words sank in. He cleared his throat and made a cold and correct apology to his lordship, who received it with a good humor it did not deserve.

"Oh, certainly," he said faintly, "mistakes happen. My fault, you know, pointing the pistols at the ladies that way . . . empty, though, so no harm done. Wouldn't mind so much if it weren't for this infernal headache." He rubbed his temples, and Priscilla, lavender water at hand, proceeded to bathe them with her handkerchief, while he gazed up at her with a grateful and entirely foolish expression.

"Well, Rodney my friend, it is you, is it not? In what manner of scrape do I find you this time?" inquired a cool, amused voice from the doorway.

No one had heard the door open, but Mr. Oldbury suddenly found it necessary to jump away as a large masculine figure filled the frame behind him. This put him in the unfortunate position of appearing to lurk behind the door, and Katherine almost laughed at his pained expression, except that she was too chagrined to do so.

The Earl of Tarrington stood surveying the scene, one eyebrow raised quizzically, a polite smile on his face, as if he had just walked into a play which already bored him excessively.

"T-Tarrington!" uttered Lord Knolland in astonishment. *"Now* it all comes back!"

The other occupants of the parlor looked no less surprised, and despite his affectation of ennui, Katherine could tell that the earl was excessively diverted by their reaction. She wondered how he came to call such a likeable fribble as Lord Knolland his friend.

That poor gentleman, his neckcloth undone, his blond curls tousled, looked as though his eyes were about to start out of his head, while Priscilla, her bonnet askew, interrupted in her ministrations, still held a dripping handkerchief over her hero's forehead. She stared at the earl as though he were a ghostly apparition.

Katherine had been trying hard to convince herself that the man she had seen could not be Tarrington, and was very nearly as amazed as the others, but she still stood in the attitude in which she had confronted Mr. Oldbury, so the first glimpse the earl had of her was of a proud and angry bearing, with her cheeks flushed, her eyes sparkling, and wisps of hair escaping their tight confinement to frame her face in becoming tendrils.

For a moment he simply stared at her, but then allowed his gaze to travel around the room, returning to his left in time to hear an irate cough and the squeak of the door as Mr. Oldbury pushed it shut again and emerged from his temporary obscurity.

"And who the devil are you, sir?" he blustered, to the horror of everyone present. "This is a private parlor, and I will thank you to leave it immediately. You have no business here."

Tarrington's eyes met Katherine's briefly. His glance was a combination of equal parts of astonishment and accusation, but she only glowered at him. If only he had remained upstairs! She was doubly vexed at the thought that he had probably heard her raised voice from the corridor, and it was thus her own fault that he was a witness to this foolish scene. Before the earl could respond to Oldbury's rude command, Lord Knolland spoke.

"I tell you, it's all very odd, Tarrington—you'd scarcely believe it! I was on the road for that new place of yours, and happened to fall in with these ladies, who were being attacked by the most ruthless-looking villain you'd ever care to meet," he offered, rising shakily to extend his hand to the earl.

Tarrington clasped it, and let his glance travel briefly over his lordship's disheveled figure, lingering for a moment on the ruin of his neckcloth, at which he shook his head and clucked softly. "I see," he said calmly, disregarding the outraged sputterings of Mr. Oldbury, who most decidedly did not like being ignored. "But how did you come by your present disgraceful condition, I wonder?" he mused.

He glanced at Katherine once more, frowning. "And to what do we owe the presence of the ladies? This is no place for you and your cousin, Miss Amory. Surely I do not have to remind you how improper your presence here could seem at this hour."

Katherine was about to retort, but Priscilla, made bold by her outrage over poor Lord Knolland's mistreatment, forestalled her.

"It was all because of Mr. Oldbury," she cried, pointing an accusing finger at that gentleman, who looked indignant but was prevented from defending himself as she poured out the story.

"Lord Knolland had just saved us from a dreadful highwayman, and was putting away his pistols, when Mr. Oldbury drove up—"

"His *pistols?*" interjected the earl on a rising note.

"—and accused him of trying to rob us!" Priscilla interposed her body protectively between his lordship and the bristling Mr. Oldbury, while the earl watched with evident appreciation. "He wanted to bring Lord Knolland up before the magistrate, but we came back to free him."

"Indeed," was all that the earl said, but his eyes were eloquent and it was all Katherine could do to hold back a giggle. The absolute absurdity of the situation had gripped her.

After the earl had gently commiserated with Priscilla on her ordeal, he turned to Mr. Oldbury at last.

"*You,* sir, I take it, are the person who mistook my friend Knolland for a . . . a highwayman?"

He said it rather mildly and with just a hint of incredulity, but there was a light in his eyes that told Mr. Oldbury he was dealing with a very different specimen of man than his erstwhile captive. Nevertheless, discretion made up little of Oldbury's character, so he gathered the shreds of his pride about him and prepared to defend himself quite offensively.

"Once again, sir, I ask, who are you and what concern is it of yours?"

Priscilla gasped at his audacity, and Lord Knolland even flinched in sympathy for his former tormentor, but Tarrington, with no visible discomposure, replied with cool courtesy to Mr. Oldbury's graceless demand.

"I beg your pardon, sir. The reception of this extraordinary news quite drove from my mind the fact that you and I are unacquainted. Permit me to make myself known to you. I have the honor of being Earl of Tarrington and the pleasure of being an old friend of my Lord Knolland, and cousin to Miss Amory."

His lordship and the ladies exchanged satisfied smiles at this revelation, while Mr. Oldbury gulped and blanched. Katherine thought it high time, too; for his face had been growing so red

67

that it was almost purple, but she knew that he was not sensible enough to give in graciously. His next attack, however, came from an unexpected direction.

"Then my lord, as her cousin, perhaps you could induce Miss Amory to behave more circumspectly in future. This running about after gentlemen when dusk has fallen could prove injurious to her reputation, a reputation that, may I say, I hold as dear as my own, as it is some time since I was first convinced that in the near future she will do me the honor of becoming my wife."

Katherine stifled a cry of indignation. She was not about to make a spectacle of herself by arguing with her suitor in front of the earl.

"Indeed?" his lordship inquired, producing the quizzing glass from his waistcoat pocket and leveling it at Mr. Oldbury as if he were gazing on an insect of the most remarkable insignificance. Katherine was amazed, for a man less likely to affect a quizzing glass she could not imagine, and Lord Knolland's look of pleased anticipation informed her that she was about to witness a remarkable performance.

"Well then, Mr., er, Oldbury, is it? Since Miss Amory seems to be unfamiliar with any of these felicitous plans for her future, I suggest that you make yourself better acquainted with her wishes before you publish the banns. Your assurance seems rather premature."

He dropped the quizzing glass and walked over to his friend, saying casually over his shoulder, as if it were of the least possible concern, "As for that other matter, I am sure you have found my good friend Knolland here to be remarkably charitable and forgiving. Although your offense is calculated to induce even the most saintly gentleman to demand satisfaction."

"S-satisfaction?" Oldbury, Katherine noted with glee, was now as white as he had formerly been red. For all his bluster he was a coward. Her contempt for him tripled.

The earl stood, glancing briefly out of the window, with his hand on the shoulder of the seated Lord Knolland, who made a sorry attempt to look angry at last, contorting his face into what was meant to be a menacing frown, but succeeding only in making Katherine and Priscilla choke on repressed giggles.

Tarrington turned and fixed Mr. Oldbury with a solemn look. "If that should be the case," he said, taking in with a sweep of the quizzing glass Oldbury's pale flabby hands and rotund stomach, "I should have no hesitation in acting as his second. Although for your sake, sir, I hope that he does not retract his hasty forgiveness of this grave insult."

Lord Knolland started, and would have spoken, had not his friend's hand been pressing him firmly into his chair.

"There now, my good fellow, be easy," the earl told him. "Try to control that temper of yours."

"But I—"

"Your *temper*, Rodney . . ." the earl warned.

At the reminder, Knolland suddenly resumed his affectation of fierceness, this time attempting to lower his brows menacingly, but it only looked as though his headache had suddenly become worse.

By this time Mr. Oldbury had begun to resemble a cushion with all the stuffing removed, Katherine observed with mingled satisfaction and dismay. How dare Tarrington reduce the greatest annoyance of her life to jelly with a few well chosen words and a silly quizzing glass! His presumption annoyed her, but at the same time she could not help enjoying it.

The earl had not yet done with Mr. Oldbury.

"In our circle, you see," he expounded, "Lord Knolland is known to be a keen marksman—I daresay I have lost count of the number of wagers I have won on his ability to hit a wafer at a hundred paces—and among his fellows at Jackson's Saloon, where the Gentleman condescends to spar with him, he is known as 'Lord Bruiser'."

By now Katherine and Priscilla were at their last resources, and steadily avoided looking one another in the eye, while Lord

Knolland himself was agog at his friend's fabrications. Nothing loath, Tarrington continued. "And with the sword, of course . . ." But he needed to say no more.

Mr. Oldbury, despite what he thought of as his courage in rescuing the ladies from a supposed highwayman, did not at all relish the thought of pistols at dawn with a noted Corinthian, and with no female audience to play-act for. He was already bowing and backing out of the room.

"My sincerest apologies . . . a most dreadful misunderstanding . . . only doing what I perceived as my duty, you see . . . thank you for your patience and consideration, my lord. . . ." His words tumbled over one another, and Lord Knolland was moved to comment on his friend's extravagant testimony to his prowess, but was fortunately prevented from doing so by the timely application of Miss Townsend's foot to one of his shining top-boots.

In another moment Oldbury, with a last confused glance at Katherine, was gone.

"Come now, Miss Townsend, just look what you've done to the finish on that! My man will be in a regular lather when he sees it!" said Lord Knolland, anxiously inspecting the damage that lady had inflicted on his footgear.

She apologized demurely, but the earl defended her. "Rodney, don't be such a cod's head," he said, clapping his friend heartily across the back and further unsettling him. "If Miss Townsend hadn't kicked you, you would have been certain to confess to that fellow that the only time you'd ever been near a sword was when they buckled that unwieldy family heirloom onto you for your Presentation, that the pistols you were so valiant with today are the ones I asked you to pick up at Manton's for me, and that only the lowliest of Jackson's assistants have ever consented to instruct you in the rudiments of the Fancy on the rare occasions you have patronized the establishment."

Lord Knolland sheepishly admitted that his friend's assumption was correct. "Sorry, Tarrington, didn't think for a moment. But *such* a rum tale!" He shook his head gingerly. "Could have ruined it, couldn't I, with this flapping tongue of mine?" He flashed a self-deprecating smile at Priscilla, who seemed not at all put out to discover that her savior was less than a paragon of manly accomplishment, and then wrinkled his nose at the earl.

"Not like you at all, Vane, to tell such bouncers. 'Lord Bruiser,' indeed!" He laughed good-naturedly at his own expense. "Fellow Oldbury must be a regular muttonhead to be taken in by such a hum."

"Muttonhead . . . exactly," murmured Katherine, thinking how suitable was this designation for her stubborn suitor.

"Not to mention, my lord," reminded Priscilla, "that he was silly enough to mistake you for a highwayman, when you are obviously far too"—she looked down and her long golden lashes veiled her cheeks—"far too much the gentleman."

"Why yes, I suppose. . . ." His lordship was torn between the necessity to agree politely with a young lady and his natural disinclination to praise himself. In the end he returned to Oldbury. "Deuced unpleasant fellow!" forgetting for a moment that there were females present. "Had all I could do to stop myself from planting him a facer," he declared. "But you put him in his place, Vane, right enough. I always did say there's nothing like one of your set-downs. Much obliged to you."

"Your gratitude unmans me," replied the earl placidly. "And now we must see about getting you ladies home. I assume, Miss Amory, that you are aware of how fortunate you are that I happened on the scene." A brief smile crossed his face. "Did you really think that you could convince that ridiculous fellow of poor Rodney's innocence?"

"I had already done so, my lord, before you entered the room," she informed him, turning indignant brown eyes on him. "I have been acquainted with Mr. Oldbury for quite some time now, and I know just how he is to be dealt with."

Tarrington's brows rose. "Ah! Then perhaps I owe you an

apology. I was under the impression . . ." His lips twitched. "But perhaps you have actually been welcoming the fellow's attentions. Have I chased away your only suitor? In view of your ambitious plans, I assumed—"

Katherine had never felt more like boxing anyone's ears in her life.

"No, I do *not* welcome his attentions! In fact, I find him despicable, and I would not consider—"

"Well then, I accept your gracious thanks for extricating you from your problems this evening. It was, of course, a harebrained scheme, and highly improper into the bargain," he added.

Katherine's eyes blazed with fury. Be calm, she reminded herself. Do not give him the satisfaction of knowing he has made a hit. A deep breath somewhat restored her serenity.

"In fact, my lord, it was a perfectly rational scheme, with nothing whatsoever improper about it," she said, blithely ignoring her own previous misgivings. "We are quite private here, and if you had not happened along, I am sure we would have been on our way home at this moment." Inspiration struck. "And pray what is *your* explanation for being at the Black Horse this evening, my lord? We received no word of your return, and I assure you that we are quite as surprised to meet with you as you have been to find us here. However, I did see you withdraw upstairs with your companion, and have been cudgeling my brains ever since to discover who he might be." She smiled, and awaited his explanation.

"My presence here, dear cousin, is nothing to concern you," he said abruptly. His eyes were a murky hazel in the sputtering candlelight. "And I haven't the least idea to whom you are referring. I came alone. Come now, we must see about getting you ladies safely home."

"Why how kind of you to offer to escort us home, my lord . . . as you are so providentially on the spot." She looked at him challengingly.

A grim smile touched his lips. "I regret that it is not possible," he replied smoothly. "I have some business to complete here, and I shall be returning to Whitfield quite late."

Katherine shot him a penetrating look from under her lashes. Did he really think her such a gudgeon as to take him at his word? Obviously, whatever his business was there must be something irregular about it if he would lie outright. She was more and more certain that it had been he on the stairs earlier.

The earl occupied himself with polishing his quizzing glass and did not look at her. For a moment Katherine wished that Lady Colesville were with them, for she would most certainly ask that interesting question, "What business?"—especially in view of his denying being with the man in the frieze coat. But Katherine could not bring herself to do it.

Besides, he had already refused to enlighten his own sister, it was hardly likely that he would be more forthcoming now. She wondered if it really concerned something as simple and as disappointing as a female of easy virtue, but somehow that did not seem likely. Of course, it was none of her concern, but there was something so unusual, even sinister, about all his secrecy that she could not put it out of her mind for very long.

Temporarily accepting defeat, she explained the arrangement they had made for their return journey. When Priscilla, her experience having, curiously enough, made her brave, earnestly assured the earl that he would not at all discommode them no matter how late he returned to Whitfield, it was on the tip of Katherine's tongue to add that it was, after all, his house.

In a few minutes a knock on the door informed them that their servant had arrived, and Lord Knolland, who stated he was feeling much more the thing, was detailed to accompany them home.

"Please convey my apologies to Mrs. Amory," said the earl to Katherine. "I shall see you in the morning, Cousin, and we shall confer on the improvements. I hope that once the work is done, you will find Whitfield much more comfortable."

"And give up my plans?"

Tarrington shrugged. "It is too late in the day for you to be picking quarrels with me, Katherine. I suggest that you return to your mother and think over your impetuosity this evening. A lady who prides herself on her independence ought to know better than to put herself in such a compromising position."

Katherine felt her face burn, but she haughtily lifted her chin and stepped past him out of the parlor.

The earl saw them safely into the gig, instructed the young footman who had come from Whitfield to beware of highwaymen, with a wink at Lord Knolland, and waved them away.

Before she drove out of the yard Katherine obeyed an impulse and turned to look behind her. Tarrington was just about to re-enter the inn, and in the flare of torchlight, she saw a stocky figure join him at the door. Two heads, one noble and groomed, the other shaggy and hatless, were bent in conversation. They were alone, and again, Katherine thought there was a furtive air about them. She saw the two men glance about and then disappear inside. After that there was nothing else to look at but the road ahead.

Chapter Three

"When I think of the near escape you had, my love, I confess I am quite prostrated!" cried Mrs. Amory, submitting to her niece's attentions and allowing herself to be tucked into a warm blanket.

Katherine, who sat at her mother's bedside, was inclined to make light of the matter, but was not permitted to do so.

"Oh, my dears, only think if his lordship had not come to your rescue! All of the terrors I was imagining when you were so late returning were as nothing compared with the truth!" Her face paled with the horror of it, and Katherine fixed her cousin with a stern glance. Priscilla had the grace to look ashamed.

"But indeed, Kate," she whispered to her, "I could not have gone home again without assuring myself that Lord Knolland would be freed."

In her heart, Katherine forgave her cousin for causing her mother such distress, for Priscilla's sudden determination to rescue the rescuer had amazed and delighted her. In Katherine's opinion, it was long past the time when Priscilla should have been done with her adolescent shyness and become aware of her own attractions. Before this, in the presence of any gentleman, she had always shrunk into the background and become as inconspicuous as a pattern on the wallpaper.

But Mrs. Amory was not done. "I shall be eternally grateful to his lordship for risking his life to save my dear girls. So courageous!" Katherine was unwilling to disillusion her, and only exchanged a little smile with her cousin as she remembered the scene of their salvation.

"As soon as I feel well enough, I shall thank him in person. No, perhaps I should go immediately. It would not do to be remiss in such an attention," she said with as much determination as anyone could muster while reclining against three fluffy pillows and wearing a ruffled lawn nightcap trimmed with ribbons.

She was easily dissuaded from doing so, luckily for Lord Knolland's reputation as a hero, Katherine thought. She doubted that he would make much of an impression on her mother in his present state of dishevelment and while still suffering from the aftereffects of his overindulgence in some very fine claret.

"There is not the least need to tease yourself over it, Mama," Katherine assured her, thinking it time that she brought the discussion to an end. "I daresay the ruffian would have gone off with our reticules and left us quite unharmed. Lord Knolland will be happy to make your acquaintance in the morning. Since he is Tarrington's guest, I daresay he will be with us long enough for you to thank him a dozen times over if you wish. I am only sorry that you should have had so much anxiety on our account."

She saw that Priscilla was looking sheepish again. Neither of them had mentioned that it was mainly at her urging that they had turned back to the village, and Katherine did not think her mother would believe it.

They had arrived home to find Mrs. Amory already retired to her bed, thrown into a spasm by the message Katherine had sent with Peters, who had not been able to restrain himself from painting an exaggeratedly vivid picture of the dangers that had attended their journey.

The two girls had hurried upstairs to Mrs. Amory's chamber, and that lady's relief at their safety had been so great that at length they were able to persuade her to partake of a cup of broth and a piece of cold fowl, while they enjoyed a somewhat heartier repast at her bedside. Lord Knolland was left to the care of the servants until the earl's late arrival, when both gentleman dined bachelor fashion upon a cold collation downstairs.

Lord Knolland, looking somewhat more like his usual bright-eyed self after a good meal washed down by nothing more potent than coffee, shuddered as the port was offered to him, waving it away. The earl, though not unsympathetic, laughed and strongly advised his companion to forego the habit of becoming drunk so early in the day, or, indeed, of drinking beyond his capacity at all.

His friend looked mournful. "Don't know how it came about. Knew I'd arrive before you, didn't want to put out the ladies, being a stranger and all—you'd told me they were staying on here—so I stopped at a posting house in Basingstoke. A long ride puts a devilish thirst into a fellow! Before I knew it, I was so well to live I'd forgotten what I was doing in these parts at all." He shook his head. "Should have brought Finster. He'd have looked after me, seen that I'd eaten first. I've no more brains than m'aunt's pug. Silly animal will eat every bonbon she feeds him till he's lost them all over her carpet."

The earl shuddered at this vivid description, and his friend returned once more to the absent Finster. "Dashed inconvenient for the fellow's father to have chosen just this time to cock up his toes."

The earl nodded solemnly, but with a twinkle in his eyes. "Most inconsiderate. Finster senior should have been more circumspect in choosing the hour of his demise."

"Not at all! Didn't mean . . ." Comprehension dawned on

Lord Knolland's face. "Oh, you're ragging me again, as you always do. I can't help it if I am a bit paper-skulled sometimes."

"I assure you, my friend," the earl said, sipping at his port, "I would not like you half so well if you were not."

His lordship glowed under this approval, but grew uncomfortable as Tarrington began to praise his accomplishment.

"You certainly are the intrepid one today, Rodney. It seems not to have turned out badly at all. Quite the hero! Especially in the eyes of Miss Townsend, if I may be so bold. Her defence of you was very affecting."

"Not at all," mumbled Lord Knolland, "duty of a gentleman. Couldn't allow that villain to threaten the ladies, you know, so I shot at him." He frowned into his coffee. "Ought not to have missed, though."

The earl laughed, and replaced his glass on the weathered oak table. "My dear fellow, you have not shot a pistol above a dozen times in your life, and you've never held these particular weapons before today. I would say that you have done exceptionally well, and am only amazed that you contrived to avoid hitting your own foot."

Lord Knolland grinned, not at all offended. "I say, Tarrington, those were very fine pistols, though. French?"

"Spanish," replied the earl. "Part of my father's collection, or I should say, what's left of it." He sighed, and reached for the bottle again. "It looks as though these will go, too. I may have a buyer. I had brought them in to Manton's to be looked over."

He stopped with his glass in midair. "I suppose I shouldn't ask this, but why were you riding with the pistols loaded?"

His lordship's smooth, boyish face became pink. "Oh, er . . . it was a wager with Charlie Rushwood. He claimed I couldn't carry them loaded for even an hour without shooting myself in the foot." He immediately brightened. "Looks like I won, then. It don't count that I discharged them," he added hopefully.

When the earl had managed to contain his amusement, and both gentlemen had settled once more into a companionable silence, Lord Knolland ventured a question.

"Is it all . . . gone, then?" he asked timidly. "Have you had to part with everything?"

The earl, drinking, did not answer for a moment. "No, not yet thank heavens. I've still got many of the paintings—the finer ones, or so that dealer told me. I'm too ignorant to tell the difference."

His lips tightened momentarily. In the past that ignorance had nearly exacted a heavy price. "But almost all of the other things are sold, slowly, discreetly, but . . . gone." He put his glass down so hard that the crystal rang. "The devil of it is that it's entirely my fault. I can only thank Providence that I've come about in time to handle *this* disaster." He gestured around at the soiled and faded walls of Whitfield.

Lord Knolland hated to see that look of despondency take possession of his friend's features. His immediate impulse was to distract the earl before the gloom could settle on his brow.

He laughed and slapped at the yellowed damask tablecloth. "Didn't know I was such a top-of-the-trees Corinthian. A regular out and outer, you made me sound back there. And me barely knowing the business end of a gun!"

Tarrington smiled at the recollection, his grim mood momentarily lightened.

"I'd had a good mind to consider the whole episode dashed good sport," his lordship continued, "at least until that cork-brained fellow came along and took me for a highwayman. Wants to marry your cousin, too. My advice is, don't let him. Fellow must have windmills in his head! Not that Miss Amory ain't a fine sort of female." He suddenly recollected himself. "I meant about me being a highwayman. I tried to explain how it was, the ladies, too, but would he listen? Never met with such a—"

"Quite right, my dear fellow," the earl cut in hastily, for the amusement of the story was wearing off quickly with repetition. He was more interested in Knolland's opinion of his cousin Katherine. In his bungling way, he had hit upon exactly the right description.

To men of their circle, surrounded by beautiful women of every size and form, she was at first glance just another young, vital and attractive female, but on closer inspection, she was very "fine" indeed.

Her features were not strong enough to be called handsome, nor delicate enough to be called merely pretty, but her high forehead, small straight nose, and soft full lips were classically simple and pure.

Her brown hair was shiny and thick but then the fashion was for brunettes these days, so she could be said to have an unfair advantage. Tarrington recalled how it had from the first appeared to him to be a living thing, struggling to unbind itself and fall in its full glory about her shoulders. He wondered idly, before stopping himself in amazement, just how it would feel to entwine his fingers in those soft gleaming curls. Instead he concentrated on how she had looked at the inn, proudly facing up to the ridiculous Oldbury, head up, eyes ablaze, and those intriguing waves and wisps escaping to frame her lovely face.

It reassured him that hers was nothing like another face he had known, heart-shaped, gay, and lively, crowned by guinea-gold hair and lit by laughing green eyes. He quickly returned to the inner contemplation of his very different cousin Katherine.

Her eyes, he thought, dominated the face, being large, deep-set, and full of intelligence and determination. Her figure, though tending towards slimness, gave a promise of lushness to come.

Her home-fashioned gown of pale ecru muslin became her not at all. Such ivory skin and rich brown eyes called for more vibrant color, he thought, and then painful memories of the last time he had attempted to guide a woman's taste in dress began to intrude, so he shrugged away the thoughts of how he would like to see Katherine clothed to more advantage, allowing only a last recollection of how straight she had stood and how well she carried herself. His last experience with the fairer sex had assured him that he was not fit to think of a lady in that way ever again. But it was only reluctantly that he surrendered the pleasing image of Katherine.

Lord Knolland was unaware of his friend's reverie, and was prattling on. "Thing is, what the devil are you doing out here? Told me you'd inherited the old Amory estate, but I can't fathom what you'd want with such a tumbledown old pile. And why are the ladies here?"

"It's very simple, Rodney. The ladies lived here with my great-uncle Edwin, and they are practically penniless. They had some wild scheme in mind to go to Bath and keep house for a retired officer."

"You're bamming me!" Lord Knolland choked, some of his coffee having painfully found its way into a passage which was not intended to convey anything other than air.

"I assure you I am not." The earl smiled. "Miss Amory, at least, was quite set on it; I found them on the doorstep ready to leave the very day I arrived. But we made an arrangement that they would stay and look after the place while the repairs are made, and after that . . ." He shrugged. "I said that of course they must do as they wished, but I have high hopes of convincing them to stay at a nominal rent. Her mother would be very willing, but my cousin Katherine is a proud one, and can't bring herself to accept my charity."

"I should say!" ejaculated Lord Knolland, strongly moved. "And charity it would be, to let 'em have this great barn of a place for a penny a quarter. Why, you could very likely get a thousand a year for it. You know, Vane, you ain't exactly as rich as . . . as . . . well, whatever the fellow's name was, and if you won't think of it, then your friends must."

The earl's eyes crinkled in amusement. "What's this, now, Rodney? A moment ago you called the place an old pile and demanded to know what I did here, and now you are ready to have me turn my own flesh and blood out into the world, so I can rob some family of a thousand a year to live in a drafty old barn?"

Lord Knolland, whose affection for his friend prompted him to jealousy guard that gentleman's interests with a vigor otherwise foreign to his nature, defended his assertion. "Well, I don't say that you ought to turn the ladies out, but it don't seem right that you won't get the chance to recoup. I should think its costing some to get this place back together." He looked around with disfavor. "I hope, at least, that he left you something more than this."

Tarrington shook his head. "Not even a ha'penny. No debts, thank God, but there was no more than two hundred pounds in the funds, and he liquidated it, spent half, though on what the Lord knows, and left the rest of it to my cousin Katherine. It's only fair," he said, forestalling his friend's protest. "If her father hadn't quarreled with the family, it would all be hers. There's no one else. She has little enough."

"But how will you manage? Bound to cost a fortune to make the place fit."

"Never fear, I'm not as badly off as you think." He gazed with amusement at the slightly frayed cuffs of his shirt. "With a little personal economy, I have managed to set my affairs to the rightabout, but I shall have to order some new clothes sooner or later. It wouldn't do to have an earl look as though he were about to go to the poorhouse. I'm sure Miss Amory thinks I am another Uncle Edwin. She has very sharp eyes."

Mulling over this, the earl decided that sharp was a poor description for those luminous brown orbs. They were disconcertingly searching, to be sure, and he must take care to avoid their sweet entrapment in the future, for her sake as well as his. He doubted that she had any serious thought of attracting his interest, but he must guard himself nonetheless. If he were careful, he could guide her as a brother would, but keep them both out of danger of anything more.

"Dash it all, Vane, you know I'd lay out any sum for you, you'd have only to name it, but my uncles have got it all so tied

82

up it's all I can do to present a respectable face to the world."
Lord Knolland pulled impatiently at his ruined neckcloth,
which in Finster's absence he could scarcely contrive to tie.
"I'm nearly rolled up at the end of the quarter as it is, and I can
only touch the interest until I marry. Even then I won't be
what you'd call a Nabob!"

"I wouldn't dream of allowing you to assist me. Perhaps I
shall sell my hunters," Tarrington mused. "That ought to
bring enough for a new roof. . . ."

"Sell your hunters! Have you gone mad?"

"Why keep them eating their heads off at Northfolde, when
they will bring in more than enough to keep me on course, even
if it turns out I have to rebuild this house from the cellars to
the attics?" inquired Tarrington. "I can always buy more when
I'm flush again."

"Damn it, Vane," said Lord Knolland agitatedly, "Won't do
at all for people to think you're in the suds—as they would, I'll
wager my best waistcoat, in the space of a day if you was to put
a single one of your hunters on the block. You can put about
some sort of tale about selling the collection, should anyone
hear of it, but not your horses. You don't want the entire ton
whispering behind their hands, do you?"

The earl's expression darkened. "No," he said shortly. "I
believe I have already afforded the ton quite enough meat for
their scandal-broth already."

"Tell you what," offered his friend, blithely ignoring the
change of mood, "you ought to look for an heiress. Had any
number of females dangling after you this year and more. No
doubt their papas would be glad to give them to the earl of
Tarrington."

"Please, my good fellow, do me the honor of thinking before
you propose such a course of action," said Tarrington in precise accents that Rodney knew from experience indicated his
iciest disapproval. "If the ton has already been buzzing about
my activities, what do you think will be said when I begin
hanging out for a rich wife? Especially after—"

"Deuce take it, Tarrington, it's about time you thought of marrying again. It has been three years and more since—"

"You forget, my friend, that I do not care to speak of it," the earl said quietly.

Either his affection or his natural heedlessness prodded Lord Knolland to continue. "Vane, I'm your friend, as you say, and it ain't easy when you're liable to become as sulky as a bear when I only tell you for your own good that—"

"Not now, Rodney!"

For a moment Tarrington looked as though he would like to draw a dagger on his persistent companion, but it passed, and he put his head into his hands again.

"I'm sorry, I know I seem unreasonable to you, indeed to everyone. Even so, three years, nay, a hundred, would not be sufficient to make me forget."

"No doubt," agreed his companion, "especially when you spent one of the three buried in the country with no one but your groom and your dogs for company."

"Don't forget," the earl said, forcing a grim smile, "my cellarful of companions, who spent many a night entertaining me, until I was so completely castaway that I fell asleep in my chair in front of the library fire."

He shuddered, recalling the utter blackness of his despair, an emotion from which he was not yet entirely free. But his sufferings had given him a new purpose and resolve.

"Do you know how humiliating it is to be found by one's servants in that condition, when all of them have known you since you were in leading strings, and worse, to receive never a word of reproach, but to see their eyes full of pity?" His hand was trembling a little as he picked up his glass.

Encouraged by his frankness, his friend dared a question. "What about those wild rides over the hills? Damme if they didn't say it was a miracle you never broke your neck."

"It sufficed to keep me from thinking," Tarrington replied. "The wonder of it is, that none of it eased my pain. I ranted, I cursed God, I drank and rode like one possessed, but I couldn't get her face out of my mind. Cassandra . . ." The name was a dead, hopeless whisper.

"Here now," Lord Knolland interposed, dismayed, "my fault for bringing it up. You're right. Three years is too soon to expect a fellow to forget."

"Yes," Tarrington said softly. "A woman like her . . . after the accident I couldn't bear to hear her name mentioned. I couldn't face your mother."

"I remember." Rodney moved uneasily in his chair. "But Vane, none of it was your fault. In fact, you ordered her not to try it. If only she had heeded you for once . . ."

With sudden fury, the earl stood up, sending his chair teetering back, just short of crashing onto the floor.

"That is exactly my point! I was always hovering over her, always warning, scolding, instructing—more like a damned governess, not like a lover! No wonder she began to doubt my affection for her. No wonder I drove her to defy me, drove her to her death."

"Coming it too strong, Vane! The girl was heedless, never had a care for anything, and spoiled into the bargain. I can vouch for that. Stands to reason she would lead you a merry chase. Not your fault."

"Rodney, I hope the day will come when I begin to value you as I should." Tarrington sat down again, heavily, but managed a grave smile.

"Fustian!" Lord Knolland squirmed at this tribute. "Everyone knows I ain't a clever fellow like you, but a friend is a friend, and I won't let you blame yourself for that curricle accident when likely my sister meant to have her own way no matter what you said or didn't say." His pale blue eyes were watery with unshed tears. "As pretty a filly as ever stepped, Cassandra was, but when she'd taken the notion to race your curricle with that wicked team of blacks poled up, there was no one, not even you, who could stop her."

The two men sat in silence for a while, the quiet broken only by the chiming of a hall clock, distant and muffled, and the clink of the stopper as the earl replaced it in the crystal decanter.

"I've no one to blame but myself," Tarrington finally said. "And I have my good friends to thank that I didn't let it destroy me in the end. I'd have let my affairs go completely to the devil, if it weren't for you and Charlie, and my mother. My losses towards the end of the war, while I was dead to the world back at Northfolde, were almost enough to ruin me. I'm a fortunate man, but I won't trust my luck any further. I shall not marry again, Rodney."

"Don't say that, old fellow. You haven't gotten over it yet, is all. Someday—"

"No."

Lord Knolland stared vacantly into the flickering flame of the candles that had lighted their repast, temporarily accepting defeat. The effort to distract his friend had nearly exhausted him, and today there was something else that had arisen to plague his indifferently ordered existence.

He had planned to risk a little friendly mockery in order to obtain the earl's advice, but one look at the shadows under Tarrington's eyes and he knew that he could not. His friend had already had his fill of problems. Besides, this was one even Tarrington could not solve. He made one more attempt to put the memory of Miss Townsend's delicate, pointed face from his mind.

At length they parted to seek their beds, and after bidding the earl good night, Lord Knolland startled the servant who lighted him to his chamber by suddenly muttering, "Settle it on my own, that's what. But damme if I know how."

The first down to breakfast the next morning were Katherine, always an early riser, and, to her surprise, Lord Tarrington. He bowed to his cousin and drew out a chair for her, wishing her good morning, but scrutinizing her in the most discomfiting way. She tried not to fidget in her seat as the servant placed the coffee-pot before her, but when he had gone, she looked up and demanded to know at what he was staring.

"I beg your pardon, but it occurred to me that last night your hair looked very different, so much looser, less restrained." His appraisal was cool and incurious. He might have been commenting on a change in the weather.

"Why, I suppose," she said, strangely relieved that his stare did not mean disapproval, "that it was falling out of the pins after such a long day with no opportunity to rearrange it. It very often does."

"It was rather becoming," he said casually, addressing a plate of ham with the utmost unconcern. "Pity you can't loosen it all the time."

Who would have guessed, Katherine thought, that the Earl of Tarrington would trouble himself with so trivial a matter? Though she had little vanity, she could not help but wonder if she should not take up the suggestion.

She had long ago ceased to really have a care about her appearance, though even when she was too young to be noticed by gentlemen she remembered her papa occasionally glaring at some bold young buck who might have ogled her on their way to church on a Sunday.

By the time she was of an age to be interesting to the opposite sex, she was already sequestered at Whitfield and had suffered only the solitary attentions of Oldbury. Therefore she had never had the heady experience of being admired, and she wished that it had not begun with someone as elevated and as infuriatingly self-confident as the earl.

Yet there was still that restraint in his manner, which made her doubt if admiration played any part in his noticing her hair at all. Very likely, she thought, buttering a slice of toast, it was just part of his domineering way to oversee every aspect of the lives of his dependents. While this explanation satisfied her sense of indignation at being still under his protection, it was not very satisfying to her in any other way.

87

He smiled at her over the coffee-pot, as if he were able to divine her thoughts, and she hastily turned her attention to her food.

They were soon joined, to Katherine's relief, by the others, except for Mrs. Amory who sent down word that she would remain in bed that morning. After an uneventful meal, during which Priscilla and Lord Knolland took turns darting shy glances at each other across the table, the gentlemen set off for a riding tour of the estate, and Katherine and Priscilla returned to Mrs. Amory, to read and stitch by her bedside. The morning was not far advanced when a housemaid sent by Hatchell came upstairs to announce the arrival of Lady Colesville.

Mrs. Amory at once began to look more lively. "A visitor! I am feeling much more the thing, and it has been too long since we have seen either of our cousins. I confess I believed that they had forgotten us. Jenny, tell Hatchell I shall receive her ladyship in the blue saloon, and then come back and help me to dress. Girls, do go down and say I shall not be a quarter of an hour."

Priscilla and Katherine willingly obeyed, eager to see their lively cousin again.

"We have missed you all dreadfully," Lady Colesville assured them when they reached the blue saloon, "but Mama has had a horrid cold all week, and she was so afraid that I had caught it too that she forbade me to leave. All's well now, though, and I have come to bear you company, and Mama is coming along in the carriage. We mean to bring you back with us for dinner tonight."

She was attired in a modish riding habit, and a tall hat with a blond lace veil had screened her gleaming hazel eyes before she lifted it away. "I rode over on my new chestnut mare. I have been meaning to try her paces this age. Vane chose her for me, you know—he has such an eye for horses."

Katherine was not at all surprised to hear it. She had observed, even from her limited experience, that it was a rare gentleman who did not claim to have a good eye for a horse, but in the earl's case she thought it was very probably true. There was an indefinable something in his glance that revealed a searching intelligence, a deep knowledge and understanding of many things that she could not even name. Something else in his face, voice, and manner hinted that much of his understanding had been dearly won.

I am becoming nearly as fanciful as Priscilla, she thought, chiding herself, and then her mother came in, just as Lady Tarrington's carriage drew up outside. Both their ladyships were delighted to hear of the earl's unexpected arrival, and expressed pleasure at the prospect of meeting Lord Knolland again.

The Dowager Countess urged Mrs. Amory to go for a drive about the countryside with her, to accompany her on a few visits she had planned. Katherine and Priscilla exchanged a glance, and Katherine was just about to speak, but her mother had already begun.

"Oh, it is very kind of you," said Mrs. Amory uncertainly. "I am feeling much better, and an airing would suit me very well, but . . . that is, we have never . . . I mean to say I really could not . . ." She trailed off in embarrassment.

"What Mama means to say," Katherine explained, "is that we have never visited anyone in the neighborhood, and since Uncle Edwin long ago quarreled with all of his neighbors, they were none of them ever welcome at Whitfield."

"What!" Lady Colesville was astonished, her mother no less so. "To be cut off from every form of society, to have no intercourse with your neighbors at all, this is a punishment, indeed!"

Lady Tarrington now redoubled her efforts to budge Mrs. Amory from the house. "We can and must make it up to you. To live without society is intolerable, and you will allow that now that Sir Edwin is gone, there is no reason for you to continue the absurd policy of not making or receiving calls. I know several very congenial families in the neighborhood, and it will be my pleasure to make them known to you and the girls."

She took Mrs. Amory aside, and whispered conspiratorially, "It is especially important, is it not, my dear Delia, when one has young ladies to provide for, that they enjoy as wide a circle of acquaintance as possible?"

"Oh, yes, that is, I should like it of all things if they were to meet some fine young men." She stopped. "But my lady, you know it to be impossible, as I do, that I should have any hope of seeing them creditably married, though of course it has been the dearest wish of my heart these three years and more. Although they are well-looking, pretty-behaved girls, there is not a penny between them, except what Sir Edwin left to Katherine, and that is not likely to be of much use to her. And no matter what I say, she refuses to accept poor Mr. Oldbury's offer, though he has persisted in his suit for an entire year!"

If the Dowager Countess thought the gentleman's perseverance very odd, she did not say so, but only clucked sympathetically.

Mrs. Amory was concluding. "I fear, ma'am, they are neither of them accustomed to going about in company, and Priscilla can be dreadfully shy, while Katherine, I blush to admit, has a distressing tendency to be quite pert. Aside from their dear sweet selves, what have they to offer to the kind of people with whom you are no doubt acquainted?"

"Do not be concerned about that," advised her ladyship. "They are charming girls of respectable birth, and not every unattached gentleman of our acquaintance is hanging out for a rich wife or unwilling to settle for anything less than an Incomparable," she said with a gleam in her eye.

"Even disregarding every expectation of that kind," she went on, "would it not be very pleasant to have a circle of friends here? Although you cannot, of course, do much in the way of entertaining, the excuse of mourning Sir Edwin and the repairs to the house will serve for now, and before you leave the neighborhood you will have formed some very useful acquaintances."

Lady Colesville, meanwhile, had been trying to persuade Priscilla and Katherine to ride with her. Upon being informed that, not only had they never ridden in their lives, but that aside from the cob, a cart horse, and one aged hack, Sir Edwin had kept no animals in the vast, tumbledown stables, she declared that she had never been so shocked in her life.

"But of course you must learn," she insisted, her eyes showing green flecks in the sunny room. "Do not be afraid," she said, for she noticed Priscilla shrinking back and paling at the mention of it. "I will teach you, and our groom Thomas will help. It is the greatest fun imaginable, and a very healthful exercise," she added.

They looked at her doubtfully. Katherine, after one glimpse of Priscilla's white face, was thanking Lady Colesville and politely declining her kind offer when they were interrupted by the return of the earl and his friend, and all discussion of the matter was suspended while Tarrington kissed the hands of his mother and sister, and Lord Knolland uttered a few muddled but sincere compliments.

"Is this the savior of my dear girls? How may I thank you, my lord?" Mrs. Amory rushed to Lord Knolland and squeezed his hand fervently.

His lordship reddened and assured her that it was nothing at all. "Anyone would have done the same, ma'am," he said, his eyes on Priscilla, who smiled shyly.

It was not long before the earl had satisfied his sister that he had carried out the various commissions with which she had burdened him before he had left for town, and, after her sly inquiry, that his own business was proceeding apace.

Both the Tarrington ladies were horrified at the harrowing adventure of the night before, but when they heard of poor Rodney's apprehension as a common criminal, both mother and daughter, in identical fashion, pressed their lips tightly closed while their eyes danced with laughter. Then they commiserated with his lordship most politely.

Through all of this the earl stood to one side, leaning carelessly against the mantel, his arms folded across his chest, and Katherine was sure that he was studying her. She was determined to resist looking back to confirm the suspicion, but she was released from this self-discipline by Lady Colesville's attempts to pry from her brother the details of his mysterious mission to town.

Katherine paid close attention to the exchange, but the earl continued to deny that he had done anything more interesting than to hire a new plasterer and to choose striped silk for the drawing room and a green figured carpet for the hall.

Over a light luncheon, Lady Colesville abandoned this line and once again brought up the proposal of teaching her cousins to ride.

"You, Sally!" the earl gasped, hurriedly swallowing a sip of wine. "Why, it was all we could do to get you to stay on your first pony, and to this day Thomas has to remind you to watch your hands."

"Well, he has been with us forever, and you know that old servants permit themselves to take liberties," she replied, unruffled. "Besides, you must own that my seat, at least, is very good."

His lordship admitted that this was true, but still he insisted that she was not fit even to teach a child to bestride a hobby-horse.

"No, my dear sister, I am afraid it will not do. However," he turned to Katherine and Priscilla, "I shall be happy to give you the benefit of my experience, before I leave you in the capable hands of my sister's groom, who taught us to ride, at my late papa's insistence, almost as soon as we could walk."

"So very young as that," murmured Priscilla.

"Thank you, my lord," Katherine said quickly, "but we wouldn't dream of taking up your time with it. We have lived till now without the ability to ride horseback, and I doubt not that we will be able to pass the rest of our lives without lamenting the lack of that skill."

She was gratified at his offer, but she preferred not to spend too much time in his company, lest he attempt yet again to embroil her in a discussion of her proper place in life. Of course, she had also to consider Priscilla's fear of horses, and the disheartening reflection that no such thing as a riding costume had ever graced either of their wardrobes.

Priscilla voiced her own disinclination for the scheme. "Thank you, my lord, but I don't think I ever could get so near to a horse as to ride one," she said, her blue eyes round with terror.

"Mustn't talk that way, Miss Townsend," Lord Knolland intervened, suddenly realizing how much to advantage he would appear while assisting his friend to instruct the ladies in the rudiments of the one gentlemanly accomplishment he had mastered. "It's never too late to learn something new," he said, proud at having produced this nugget of wisdom all impromptu.

"Besides, it's all the crack, you know! Look dashed fine in a riding habit." He turned his placid gaze on the object of his admiration, and Priscilla blushed. "Hats à la Hussar, and all . . ."

As he was patently racking his brains to come up with some more solid inducement to take up the sport, he was as surprised as anyone when Priscilla suddenly said, "Oh, yes, let us learn, Katherine, I should like it of all things!"

"But my dear," said Katherine ingenuously, "you are terrified of horses. Ever since we first arrived here, when Uncle Edwin's stallion kicked at you that day . . ."

"That was a long time ago, my love," interrupted Mrs. Amory hastily, for invalid though she was, she still maintained a discerning eye when it came to the young people in her charge. "Surely Priscilla is over that fright by now, and I think it would do both of you a great deal of good. You have been too much indoors. Riding would put the roses back in your cheeks."

Too late had Katherine seen the reason for her cousin's sudden interest in becoming a horsewoman, but she remedied her error by objecting no further to the scheme, though she vowed to learn quickly so as not to be under Tarrington's eye for very long.

Lady Colesville clapped her hands like a child. "Good! Then it's settled. I am sure you will both come to love it as I do," she said, as Katherine and Priscilla looked at her doubtfully. "Now, if you have never ridden I am sure you do not have the clothes for it, but I can remedy that. There are some of my old riding habits at the Hall that can be made over to fit you. We shall try them tonight after dinner, and the lessons can begin as soon as they are ready."

Only the afternoon's activities remained to be decided, and it was not long before the two older ladies set off for a series of calls, while the younger ones decided that they would join the gentlemen for a meandering walk through the neglected park. Katherine and Priscilla hurried upstairs to change into outdoor shoes, and the garden was appointed their meeting place.

Katherine had laced up some old but serviceable half-boots and had just emerged from her room when a flustered house-maid informed her that Mr. George Oldbury had called and requested speech with her. She bit her lip in vexation for she could not endure the thought of his embarrassing her before the earl again, and with more annoyance than ever before, reflected that it was just about the time when he customarily renewed his offer of marriage.

Feeling ill equipped to deal properly with his harassment, for the first time she told the maid to deny her to the caller and to say she was just gone out.

But the evasion was unsuccessful, for as she entered the main hall and hurried to the door leading to the gardens, the stocky figure of Mr. Oldbury strolled purposefully towards her.

"Ah, Katherine, my dear, I knew you would not think that little, er, contretemps yesterday would make me forget my mission. And of course I knew that you had not gone out;

indeed, where have you to go? I knew it must be a mistake, or else just one of your odd humors." Despite his barely concealed displeasure, he was making an effort to be genial. However, his approach produced in Katherine precisely the opposite response from that he desired.

"I am afraid it is you who have made a mistake, Mr. Oldbury. I have not yet left the house, but I must surely have done so in the next moment. I am engaged to walk in the park with my cousins and Lord Knolland, and since they have been awaiting me this quarter of an hour, I am afraid I must go." She turned away, knowing it was horridly rude to leave him so, with no one else at home to receive him, but suddenly not caring a bit.

He caught her by the arm, and she was surprised at the sudden strength of his grip, surprised and not a little frightened. Idiot, she scolded herself, there's no reason to be frightened of this great bag of wind. He smiled knowingly at her, and her fear left her as she became inspired with the urge to slap his face.

"Ah," he said as if to a naughty child, "I see you do know what day this is! Your modesty is admirable, my dear, but it is very wrong of you to keep your faithful suitor in suspense for so long. Come, now, let us have our accustomed interview. Your cousins cannot want you."

He paused, surveying her appearance. Recalling the earl's comments, she had taken the time to rearrange her hair, allowing freer rein to her natural waves and letting wisps and curls play over her forehead. Her mirror had told her that Lord Tarrington's opinion of the effect had been correct, but Mr. Oldbury did not agree.

"I see you have altered the style of your hair. I beg leave to think it was for my sake, but really, my dear Katherine, I much prefer your usual modest way of wearing it. Such fripperies are quite wasted on you."

As sensible conversation would be wasted on *you*, she would have liked to reply to this impertinence, but she confined herself to saying, "Indeed, sir, you are mistaken in believing that I

had the idea of pleasing anyone but myself in this matter."
Though she knew that this was not strictly true. She had the
oddest wish to hear the earl approve of her appearance.

She had not spoken coldly enough to discourage Mr. Oldbury, for he only shook a finger playfully at her, and she was
amazed at the anger which was beginning to seethe within her.
She had always found his proposals distasteful, but never
before had they stirred her to such outrage. If only there were
not so many of the servants finding an excuse to pass through
the hall, she would have given him a taste of her temper then
and there, but it would not do to make a scene.

Knowing that the only way to be rid of him was to allow him
to say his piece one last time, and it *would* be the last, she
assured herself, she led him silently into the nearest room. It
was the morning room, presently shuttered and unused, and
she thought with satisfaction that the dust, gloom, and
shadowy furniture draped in holland covers combined to
produce an atmosphere that would quench the passion, real or
imagined, of the most eager suitor.

Emboldened, she decided not to let him begin his usual
speech after all and instead attacked at once, leaving the door
open. Although he had never attempted to physically demon-
strate the supposed warmth of his feelings, his rough grip on
her shoulder made her more uneasy than usual about being
alone with him.

"Mr. Oldbury, if you are honest with yourself you will admit
that I have given you absolutely no encouragement to believe
that I would ever accept your offer. I continued to receive you
for the sake of my mother, who has ever been a friend to you,
and in the past because my uncle would not allow me to do
otherwise. However, it seems that I have not been forceful
enough in my refusals."

To her dismay, he calmly shut the door and approached her.
He reached for her hand, but she denied it to him, and he only
smiled, sighed, and shook his head, with its thinning brown
hair, over this further evidence of her shyness and modesty.

"Allow me, my dear, to say that I know there can be no personal objection to the marriage, for we get on very well, do we not?"

Perceiving that it was long past the time when she should have been severe with him, she made up her mind to put an end at last to his pretensions.

"No, sir, we do not get on as well as you believe, for it is obvious that we do not understand one another in the least!" She noted with glee that he winced a little as she raised her voice, but she was completely ready to bring the house down around them with her screams if necessary. She had never felt quite so free before, and she found it invigorating.

"Oh, but I understand you very well," he replied, outwardly calm, but with an edge to his voice that informed her she was beginning to make progress. "You are afraid that your mother needs you and would not wish you to leave her. Have no fear on that score, for of course I was prudent enough not to address you without her consent, and you already know I had Sir Edwin's."

Katherine knew that her mother looked too kindly upon Mr. Oldbury, who courted her assiduously. His own mother, who had died during his boyhood, had been a silly and doting parent, and his father, a spendthrift and noted rake who had for years been the disgrace of the neighborhood and the boon companion of Sir Edwin in all his youthful debaucheries, had paid his prosy son little attention.

"Still, sir," said Katherine, walking a few paces so that a ghostly, draped sofa stood between her and her suitor, "with her consent or without it, you are still lacking *my* consent to your offer, and once again, and I hope finally, the answer is no. We should not suit. I take no pleasure in imagining a life at your side. I am angered and insulted by your continued insistence, and if you do not cease to press me, I shall instruct the servants to deny the house to you. Have I made my feelings clear?"

She had never before been quite so blunt, though very

nearly so, and she could hardly entertain a doubt of failure this time. He would have to be the greatest fool in existence to persist after such an insult as that!

That he loved her she could not credit, and since she had no fortune and he had never bothered to profess being struck by her beauty, she could only be amazed at his persistence. It gave her absolutely no pain to be rude to him. In fact, she was quite beginning to enjoy it.

When Oldbury started and cleared his throat nervously at her unaccustomed vehemence, Katherine perceived a hint of desperation in his countenance. She briskly bid him good day and went to the door, but he blocked her path with his bulky body.

"You are young, Katherine, and inclined to be fanciful and romantic, like all young ladies," he said in a voice deepening dramatically. "You have not yet come to realize that it is unnecessary for there to be any affection between partners at the inception of a marriage. That may come with time."

"In this case, Mr. Oldbury, I most seriously doubt it!" She could not keep from laughing full in his face, as she had never had a fanciful thought in her life, and well he knew it.

Everyone, including Katherine herself, knew her to be a sensible, steady young woman, never one to indulge in the kind of romantic fantasy so dear to the heart of her cousin Priscilla.

Oldbury's face betrayed a strange apprehension, and it was plain that he was determined not to let her go. Till now she had been reluctant to really abuse such a pitiful specimen, but now there was no choice. He was an immovable object in the doorway.

"Get out of my way, sir! You are a fool, and if you do not cease to plague me with these idiocies I shall have the servants remove you."

He cringed at her voice, raised this time far above her usual ladylike tones, and she took heart. "You obviously have no great impression of my beauty, and you have not the slightest notion of my character if you think me so modest. I am much

98

too proud, Mr. Oldbury, to continue to suffer your odious attentions."

His face was now livid, and as he drew nearer in a way she could not fail to interpret as menacing, Katherine had a brief return of fear. She began to regret having moved away from the protective barrier of the sofa and scurried back behind it, but not before Oldbury could follow and place damp, heavy hands on her shoulders.

"Such passion!" His eyes were glassy, and his lips hung loosely open. "Now I see why my courtship has not pleased you. Can it be that you hunger for my embrace? Are my words not enough? My dear Miss Amory, your loveliness tempts me to prove to you, in a way that renders words superfluous, my intense desire to unite our lives, our destinies, our *fortunes.*" He jerked her body up against his, his moist mouth smearing her cheek with an inexpert kiss.

"Oh!" She tried to wrench her shoulders out of his grasp, but he managed to place one arm tightly around her waist, and to graze her lips wetly. Summoning up all of her strength, she wriggled partially free of his embrace, turning away to claw at the back of the sofa, but she only managed to catch hold of the covering and pull it partly off as he tried to drag her away. She clung fiercely to the Holland cover as if to a life-line in a tempestuous sea.

Oldbury was surprisingly quick, and this maneuver left her in a worse position than before. She kicked with impotent fury as Oldbury, puffing with exertion, now held her from behind and frantically pressed his lips to her neck. In a moment she was pinned down by his beefy stomach, bent double over the sofa, with the Holland cover coming off in her hand and a cloud of dust rising to choke her.

She could barely utter a word, let alone scream, and the ludicrous nature of her predicament made her reluctant to attract anyone's attention to it. Her feet flailed wildly, and a grunt from Oldbury told her she had succeeded in kicking his shin, but otherwise her writhings and squirmings were futile.

"Ohhh . . . *ahhh* . . . I shall teach you to love me, Kate!" was all the response elicited from the clumsy, panting form that imprisoned her.

The only thought that gave her any comfort was that the sofa was ancient and massive, and hardly likely to tip over beneath their struggles. The heavy carving along the top of it dug into her middle, pressing the breath out of her, but she struggled to speak.

"Stop this at once . . ." She coughed and choked as dust entered her throat and the tickling it evoked rendered her even more incapable of speech. "Release me this instant, sir." She gasped. Then dust rose into her nose and she sneezed.

Mr. Oldbury, though winded and beginning to choke himself, was undaunted. "Oh, my sweet Katherine . . . say you will be my . . . ah . . . ah . . . chew!" Not even his sneeze discouraged him. "I shall not free you until you say the word that will join us for eternity!"

"*Oh, you ridiculous, nonsensical* . . ." A sound from the door silenced her. Katherine could not be sure, but it seemed as though there were voices in the corridor, and she was mortified to think that the servants might be aware of the scuffle. There was the unmistakable sound of a knock, but Oldbury seemed oblivious, and made no attempt to extricate them from their immodest pose. Her struggles became frantic. She kicked madly, but Oldbury had moved his vulnerable shins and her feet met only the empty air.

"Have you run mad, sir?" she cried. "Release me this *instant!*" She alternately panted and choked from the strain of moving the bulk that secured her in this highly uncomfortable and indecorous position, but she only succeeded in upsetting Mr. Oldbury's balance so that he fell even more heavily over her. To her horror, she toppled headfirst over the sofa back to land with her face in the dust-covered cushion, Oldbury still firmly attached, his arm now pinned beneath her.

This time the cloud of dust rose higher and thicker, and just as Katherine became aware of the terrifying sound of the door being opened, their exertions reached a crescendo. Oldbury grunted as he tried to extricate his arm, Katherine cried out in spite of herself, the dust overcame both of them, and they thundered with simultaneous sneezes.

"Might I be of some assistance?" A sharp and unmistakable voice from the doorway jerked Oldbury to attention, and Katherine's heart sank to the pit of her stomach.

The earl of Tarrington, having firmly closed the door behind him, stood just inside the room surveying the straining bodies that were making such unconventional use of the shrouded sofa.

Intense relief and gratitude, quickly suppressed, were Katherine's first emotions at the sight of his tall and angry figure, but her mortification was so extreme and her breath so short from her struggles that when Oldbury's surprise enabled her to move her head, she could only flash a look of pure hatred at her rescuer.

His timing was infelicitous, to say the least. She only hoped her stockinged legs were not as visible as she believed them to be, but from beneath the hair that had fallen over her eyes she could see Tarrington examining them with interest as he approached.

"Thank you, sir, but I think not," she managed to wheeze from the dusty cushions. "I don't believe that anything you can do would be of any material value at this moment."

Tarrington stood much too close to them now, and if she twisted her head she could see his sardonic smile. "Yes, I see that I am *de trop*. No doubt I should only be in your way."

Oldbury remained motionless and speechless until Katherine administered a sharp jab to his stomach with her elbow. With a final grunt he heaved himself off her and rolled unceremoniously from the sofa to his knees. Then he picked himself up and immediately began to dust off his trousers and coat as if he had merely suffered a tumble from his horse. "Ahem!" was all he managed to say, assiduously avoiding Tarrington's eyes.

"I am sure there is a reasonable explanation for this extra-

101

ordinary behavior, sir," the earl began, his drawn brows and clenched fists belying the calmness of his voice, "and I should be most interested to hear it, so I suggest you begin at once."

Oldbury opened and closed his mouth, stared stupidly at Lord Tarrington, and did not make a sound.

Katherine, relieved of her suitor's not inconsiderable weight, began to scramble, no more gracefully than Oldbury, out of her humiliating position and back to her feet. It required much effort to avoid tumbling heels over head, but she was determined to regain her feet at once instead of first falling forward and exposing more of her legs to Tarrington's scrutiny.

By the time she had managed to do so, she was quite as angry with herself for being discovered in such a situation as she was with Oldbury for having maneuvered her into it. A quick glance showed that a battle between mirth and outrage was being waged on the earl of Tarrington's countenance.

"If you have aught to say about this, my lord, I suggest you speak to *me*," she said when she could regain her breath.

Outrage seemed to have won. "Well then, my dear cousin, perhaps you will enlighten me. I can only suppose that either Mr. Oldbury has been offering you a grave insult, or that you and he were searching for a lost sixpence under the cushions."

Once again the quizzing glass was out, and Oldbury was subjected to that relentless inspection calculated to reduce him to the state of a blancmange. At last he recovered enough to see the chance that was being offered him.

"My lord, pray do not jump to conclusions! Of course I meant no disrespect, but by my honor, I will gladly bestow the protection of my name on Miss Amory, lest any word of this . . . er, accident, become general knowledge. I rely on you, my lord, as her protector, to convince her of the necessity of it." He watched the earl's face expectantly.

But the earl was awaiting Katherine's explanation.

She bit back her denial and tried to still the trembling in her hands as she rearranged her rumpled gown more decorously.

Tarrington's gaze unnerved her as she shook back her loosened hair from her face, wondering how best to proceed. It would not do to have him think that he had rescued her yet again from a situation she was not prepared to cope with, when she had assured him of her ability to conduct her own affairs without the help of a man.

"Nothing at all has occurred to induce me to resort to such a drastic measure, my lord. In fact, it was all quite innocent," she informed him, her eyes flashing defiance. "Mr. Oldbury called just as I was about to join you in the garden, and we came in here to"—she cast a hasty glance around the room and the painting over the mantel caught her eye—"to discuss this painting." She pointed. "Mr. Oldbury is something of an art expert, you know, and I had meant to ask him his opinion of it."

Oldbury stared at her flabbergasted, his eyes bulging.

Tarrington gave a casual glance at the painting. "I see."

His expression did not soften. In fact, Katherine had the impression that he had become a simmering pot ready to boil.

A second look informed her of how unfortunate it was that she had lighted on this particular painting as an excuse for being alone with Mr. Oldbury. It was a scene, supposedly from mythology, with some extremely plump naked ladies, improbable animals, and fat cherubs frolicking under the trees by a stream. It was nothing, in short, that would have adorned any room presently in use by the ladies, and certainly a most improper subject for discussion between an unmarried young lady and a gentleman caller.

Mr. Oldbury was flattered enough at this mention of his expertise to expand on this explanation. "Hrrmph, exactly as Miss Amory said, my lord. To be certain of the, er, authenticity of the work, I ventured to ask if I might take it down and examine it more closely, and in consequence of my attempt"— he gestured towards a worn footstool that stood nearby—"I stood upon that, lost my balance, and—"

Katherine took up the tale. "And he fell, pushing me, quite

by accident onto the sofa. So you see, my lord, it was really very trifling—"

"And perhaps a sudden blast of wind came down the chimney and blew Mr. Oldbury clear across the room to the sofa," mused the earl, his eyes as implacable as his voice was casual. "Yes, I see exactly how it must have happened." He glared at Oldbury from beneath his brows. "How foolish of me to have questioned your intentions, sir, when you have already announced your plans to marry Miss Amory. Am I then to wish you happy?"

"No!" Katherine cried. "I—I mean, n-nothing has changed in that regard, my lord." Katherine's glance bored into Oldbury, daring him to refute her assertion. But the poor man had had quite enough for one day, and did not take up the challenge.

"Well!" he said briskly, searching for his hat. "I must take my leave of you, and"—he found the dusty brown beaver peeking out from under a shrouded chair—"as I said, Miss Amory"—he nodded towards the painting—"it is most definitely a Balsini, fifteenth century, most probably acquired by Sir Edwin many years ago on his tour." He sighed and shook his head. "But for the continual warfare, I, too, might have made the Grand Tour and returned with treasures beyond compare, and now, though we are at peace, my circumstances do not permit it. It is one of the regrets of my life."

He seemed to forget his uncomfortable predicament for a moment, and his eyes misted over as he gazed on the painting. "Ah, Balsini. Such a master at portraying all the characters of myth and legend. . . ."

Tarrington was watching him thoughtfully, and Katherine wondered whether she might yet escape this whole affair without having to listen to a scold. The earl approached the mantel and examined the work.

"Balsini, yes, but *fourteenth* century, and he was not best known for his mythological subjects, but for his portraits of the family of his patron, the Duke of Navona. This is a rare work, cousin," he informed Katherine. "If I were you I would see it is taken down and stored while the workmen are here. The dust might damage it."

Katherine stared at him, open-mouthed, while Oldbury looked chagrined. She knew very well that he prided himself on his knowledge of art, his only real accomplishment, and for a moment she almost pitied him, faced with the earl's careless assurance. It was quite unbearable, she thought, that the man should consider himself an authority on everything.

"As you say, my lord, a most valuable work," said Oldbury hurriedly, and bowed to Katherine. "I must bid you good day. I found our . . . discussion most stimulating, and I pray that we will continue it at another time, my dear Miss Amory," he added, with a significant nod, and fled from the room.

"Come, Katherine, admit that once more you have proved yourself no more capable of looking after yourself than a babe in a cradle. If I had not arrived—"

"—I would have been spared a deal of embarrassment, my lord. Do you think that I cannot hold my own against such a fool? Just because I have not had your advantages and the benefit of a little town polish does not mean that I am a social cripple! I have long since learned the delicate art of rejecting an ineligible suitor. The situation was perfectly under control," she said, meeting his haughty and amused gaze with anger that could no longer be suppressed. In truth, she was at least a little grateful for his interruption, if only it had not been so late! It was just like him, she fumed, to come to the rescue only when the situation was most compromising. It was almost worse than not being rescued at all.

"Of course, if that is how you customarily discourage your unwanted suitors, Katherine . . ." His eyes travelled to the sofa, the cover rumpled after their assault upon it. "I own it seems a rather ineffective form of discouragement, but who am I to argue the case? A young lady who would consider going into household service, who declares herself independent and in no need of protection from the stronger sex, will no doubt have discarded many of the rules and mores of her class. Perhaps on the next occasion I shall leave you to fend for yourself, my dear, and you will see just how difficult it is to be an unprotected female in a world where circumstances conspire to lead you into danger."

"There will be no other occasions, my lord, and I pray you will not interfere again in matters that do not concern you," she cried. "I declare you put me all out of patience, and you are quite beginning to sound almost as pompous and prosy as Mr. Oldbury himself!"

His expression changed abruptly. "Am I really, Katherine?" His eyes searched her face, and she looked away, not having meant to be so rude. "You are unjust. Now, if that fellow should insult you, I expect you to inform me so that I may deal with him. That is my final word." He led the way to the door, and held it open for her.

She strode past him silently, with head held high.

Having had the last word, he seemed satisfied, and ignored her coldness. "Come, my sister is fretting to be off, and threatens to leave without you." He took her hand and placed it firmly on his arm. For a moment she tensed, but then she let it stay there.

It would be very easy, she thought, recalling how safe she had first felt at the sight of him, to tell him the whole story and then let him deal with Mr. Oldbury for her.

Interfering Tarrington might be, and most certainly engaged in some mysterious activity whose purpose she could only guess, but something told her that his rigid code of behavior would make him not only arrogant but most definitely a man on whom his friends could rely.

Still shaky from her unaccustomed bout of anger, she admitted to herself that the support of a strong arm was welcome. If only it was not *his* arm! His nearness had a strange and uncomfortable effect, and no sooner did the weakness depart than an inner disturbance took its place. Her body seemed alternately too hot and too cold, and her stomach quaked.

Her mind sought the cause of it, but soon she began to scold herself for being fanciful. It was no wonder that she felt a bit light-headed after the ridiculous ordeal she had endured.

They did not speak until they reached the garden, and she moved over to her other cousins as soon as she decently could, feeling clear-headed again immediately.

When questioned by the impatient Lady Colesville, Katherine only apologized for keeping her waiting and explained that she had come downstairs too late to be denied to an unexpected caller.

If her curiosity was piqued by this and by Katherine's strangely rumpled appearance, Lady Colesville did not show it, but only gave her brother a searching glance and sighed, finding nothing informative in his bland expression.

The walk passed off pleasantly, and as they followed a path of sunlight that filtered through the leaves overhead, Katherine felt herself being lulled into a seductive comfort. The agitation of the previous hour burned away under the warm June sun, and even the earl seemed to mellow and forget himself enough to chuckle with them over Lord Knolland's acrobatic attempts to avoid obstacles, help Priscilla over them, and keep his boots from being scratched all at the same time.

Lady Colesville from time to time distracted her brother with suggestions for redesigning the overgrown park, as she was much impressed with the current craze for making all appear as natural as possible, though it took as much labor and artifice as the rigid formal landscaping of the past.

Now and again she pointed out a view that might be improved, or begged him to build a scenic ruin or rustic cottage to add interest to the prospect.

"Our neighbors at Chipham have had Mr. Repton in to do theirs, and it is the loveliest sight imaginable. Perhaps he could build just such a wilderness, and then an ornamental lake with a bridge, as he did for the Sedgeworths."

"I have no intention, Sally," said the earl calmly, in the face of his sister's protests, "of calling in Repton or anyone else to work this ground. I shall certainly do all that is necessary to restore it to order. I'm sure that we can persuade our cousins to make their home here even without the temptation of a false ruin or a rustic bower to divert them." His self-satisfied look challenged Katherine, but Lady Colesville still claimed his attention, insisting that the Amorys deserved better than such a paltry effort.

She contented herself with extracting a promise that he would send his own head gardener from Northfolde to oversee the work, smiled knowingly at Katherine, and troubled him no more.

Katherine did not wish to resume quarrelling with the earl when they were all enjoying the beautiful day, but she did not see any help for it if he *would* insist on provoking her in this way. He knew very well that she had not relented one bit in her determination to leave for Bath eventually.

"I would appreciate it very much, my lord, if you did not base the extent of your repairs to Whitfield on the assumption that we will be making our home here. I should not," she said in a superficially sweet voice edged with steel, "wish you to be put to such a great expense when, as you no doubt have forgotten, we will be on our way to Bath very soon. I could not forgive myself if a strain were to be put on your finances merely because you sought to make this place more comfortable for us."

"And I, Miss Amory, would be unable to forgive *myself* if I allowed you to carry out your plan without offering you a reasonable alternative." He tossed this remark over his shoulder, but his voice revealed that he did not mean it casually.

"We have already declined your kind offer, my lord," she insisted, following close behind him with Lady Colesville.

"And I do not accept your refusal."

The earl had stopped walking abruptly, and Katherine and his sister almost walked straight into him before they realized it. Lady Colesville laughed and steadied herself on her brother's arm, but storms were gathering in Katherine's eyes, and she stepped fastidiously away from him.

"And I do not recognize your right to dictate the manner in which I should conduct my life, my lord."

They faced each other, gazes locked in mortal combat, while a fascinated Lady Colesville looked from one to the other of them.

Priscilla and Lord Knolland brought up the rear, and seemed to be far too deep in an inane conversation regarding a field of bluebells that had once moved Miss Townsend deeply to notice anything amiss.

"You have had your own way for much too long, miss," he began. "It is high time that—"

"*I* have had my own way? Why, you can see no farther than your own nose."

"And it is extremely selfish of you to think of nothing but your own ambitions, while totally disregarding the wishes of your mother and cousin."

"How can you say so? Why, all my care in this matter is for their benefit. It is because I wish to save them from—"

He laughed mirthlessly. "Save them from what dire fate? That of living a comfortable life on the family estate, provided for and protected, with only the lightest of responsibilities and free from want? How cruel of me to insist on it for them!" He eyed her flushed and angry face contemptuously.

"You are insufferable! You know that there is much more to it than that!"

The earl turned to Priscilla.

"Miss Townsend, please be so good as to give me your frank opinion of your cousin's plan to lead all of you into servitude in Bath. Tell us whether you would not, in actuality, prefer to remain here instead, and live like a lady."

Priscilla's lower lip trembled, and she glanced at Katherine

109

uncertainly. Katherine clenched her fists into balls of frustration. It was certainly unfair and unsporting of him to pick on the weakest link in the chain! Priscilla would never dare disagree with such an august presence as the Earl of Tarrington. She waited in stony silence for her cousin's reply.

"I . . . I expect that I might . . . might find Bath very pleasant, my lord," she ventured.

Katherine let out the breath she had been holding.

"But . . . I own I would prefer not to be Colonel Dawson's governess. And in spite of"—she averted her eyes from Katherine's—"in spite of everything we suffered before, I *do* like it here. Especially now." A smile worked its way onto her lips, and her glance slid unconsciously towards Lord Knolland who stood at her side listening to it all in complete bewilderment.

The earl turned fiercely on Katherine. "Do you not see what you have done? You have bullied her into going along with you, and probably your mother as well."

"How dare you insult me so!" Katherine felt the tears well up. "I was only trying to make us independent."

He tossed her a scathing look. "I pray you, Miss Amory, do everyone a favor, and stop deceiving yourself. Such an independence may be what *you* desire, but to those you profess to care for, it obviously takes another form. Such selfishness as yours is vastly unbecoming."

He turned on his heel and continued, slapping angrily at the overhanging branches that blocked his way.

A hush had settled over the others and nothing was heard except the birds, the sound of Tarrington's boots pounding ahead, and the crackle of dead branches. Priscilla was almost in tears at what her innocent admission had cost her cousin, but Katherine shrugged off her repenting words and comforting hand.

Lord Knolland, who had not the slightest idea of what to make of any of it, stood gulping and red-faced with embarrassment, unsure of whether to follow his friend or to remain to comfort Priscilla. The earl's sister, meanwhile, behaved as if nothing out of the ordinary had occurred.

"Don't dwell on anything Vane says when he is in a temper," she advised cheerfully, taking Katherine's arm and following in her brother's wake. "Ten to one he will come and beg your pardon in a few hours." But she watched Katherine anxiously.

Katherine stumbled along in misery, not replying, and her companions ignored her and chatted uneasily among themselves.

Lady Colesville dropped her arm, then wandered ahead; but when she called to Katherine to come examine a coppice of young beech, near an outcropping of rock, which she was sure would be the ideal spot for an elegant stone bench, Katherine did not reply, but trudged forward alone, angry tears almost blinding her, not caring what direction she took. What right had that infuriating man to insult her, to dictate what her life should be?

It was bad enough that her mother and Priscilla had agreed, that they were so ungrateful to her for all her planning and care, but she could not hate them for it.

Instead, she was beginning to hate Lord Tarrington for his interference and his arrogant assumption that simply because she was young, female, and had lived retired all her life, she was unfit to help provide for her family. As for her selfishness, that accusation had stung, perhaps because she had considered it and she could not deny that there might be a grain of truth to it. "Hateful man!" she muttered, kicking a stone out of her way.

A voice called to her, and she could not help but recognize it as Tarrington's, though it sounded more concerned than angry. Nevertheless, she could not bear to face him again so she began to run, but she soon had lost the narrow path and had caught her foot in a tangle of dead branches and vines.

In a moment she was on the ground, having instinctively broken her fall with her hands, which were now scratched, bruised, and bleeding. Tarrington was beside her in an instant, though she had been unaware of his firm step directly behind her.

"Can you sit up?" He assisted her to do so, while Priscilla caught up to them, panting, and then cried out at the sight of Katherine on the ground. In an instant she had her vinaigrette ready to wave under her cousin's nose.

"Yes, my lord, I . . . oh, do leave off with that, Pris, I am fine . . . it is only my hands. . . ."

"Let me look at them," the earl commanded, and she obeyed unthinkingly, putting them into his. His touch was warm and dry, and his expression was unemotional as he gently prodded the joints of her hands and fingers. Their argument might never have taken place. "All seems to be in order here," he said.

Katherine realized that she was staring into his eyes, so close now to hers, and made herself look away. Their expression was very different from what it had been only moments ago at the height of their dispute. It was almost . . . gentle.

Her face grew warm, and she suffered more discomfort from the train of thought this provoked than from her injuries. "Really, my lord, it's not necessary . . . it was only a little fall," she said, and pulled her hands away.

"How do your legs feel? Do you think you can stand?" he asked, ignoring her protest.

"Of course," she said brusquely, trying to hide her confusion as he placed his hands on her waist to help her up. She had never been this close to a man before. She only hoped that he could not feel the banging of her heart against her ribs. It seemed to her as though the bodice of her pale rose muslin afternoon frock must rise and fall with it so that he could not help but notice.

She was on her feet, but he would not let go of her till she had obeyed his order to take a few experimental steps. When she experienced no pain or difficulty, he finally let her go.

Katherine thanked him somewhat breathlessly, and he

coolly shrugged off her thanks. He would have done the same thing, she thought, if it had been his sister who had fallen, and she felt very foolish indeed for even suspecting otherwise. His manner towards her had changed so quickly that she had not known what to think.

"My goodness, Katherine, I'm so sorry I ran off like that," Lady Colesville apologized when she had been called back to the scene. "I had no idea that you were not following me. I didn't see you heading off the path."

"It is of no consequence, Sally," Katherine assured her. "It is just that I was wool-gathering and did not expect the path to branch off that way."

The earl took her arm once more, and Katherine did not bother to protest. "Paths have a way of doing that at the most unexpected times," he said. "It is difficult to anticipate, and often we fail to notice the choices at all."

"A very common failing, I believe, sir," was all she could say, but she could not help sneaking a glance at his face. His mask of hauteur had descended once more, and she wondered if she had imagined the concern he had shown for her. But no, she could clearly recall the sensation of his fingers moving over her wrists, careful not to cause her pain. Why, she wondered, was he ashamed to show this other side of himself? Just the same she was almost glad that this new mood of his seemed to have passed. It made her even more uncomfortable than when he was angry with her.

Upon their return the walkers were greeted by Mrs. Amory and Lady Tarrington, and when they sat down to their tea, Katherine flashed a grateful smile at the Dowager Countess, for Mrs. Amory, after her day's outing, appeared more energetic and animated than her daughter had seen her in a long time.

"What do you think, my love?" Her gentle brown eyes had a new sparkle, and her skin was for once suffused with a healthy color. "Everyone was so kind and pleased to make my acquaintance, and they were positively apologetic for neglecting us while Sir Edwin was alive. And Mrs. Littleton, who lives at the manor house on the other side of the village, has invited us to a ball she gives for her eldest daughter in a fortnight."

"Aunt Delia!" Priscilla's voice squeaked with excited disbelief. "Why, we've never been to any evening parties, except for one card party Madame Dichot had at our lodgings, and I did not like that at all." She wrinkled her small, upturned nose at the memory.

But in the midst of the general rejoicing, her eyes met Katherine's and both of their faces fell.

"Why, whatever is the matter?" inquired Lady Colesville, noticing the cousins' changed expressions.

Priscilla reddened in chagrin, but Katherine managed to smile as she explained the problem. "This morning, dear Sally, you were kind enough to offer to teach us to ride. I wonder if we could impose on you for some instruction of a different sort?"

The earl, perceiving the difficulty at once, smiled and told Katherine she need not be ashamed. "It was very shocking of Uncle Edwin to have kept you from the enjoyment of your neighbors' society. I am sure, if you had mixed with them at all, you would long since have learned to dance."

Mrs. Amory looked stricken. All her careful bartering for lessons for the girls had not been able to get her any agreement with a dancing master, and it had always distressed her, though until now the girls had never had occasion to use such an accomplishment.

"You mean you have never—" Lady Colesville recollected herself and her cousins' feelings. She resumed more calmly, "Well, of course, you were never given the opportunity to dance! It is the simplest thing in the world to remedy, I assure you. I am sure that Vane and Lord Knolland will oblige us when you have learned the steps and are ready to practice with partners."

Both gentlemen assured the ladies of their willingness to assist. Lord Knolland's eagerness surprised no one, since he had played the gallant to Priscilla during the whole of their walk in the park and even now could not help staring at her whenever his attention was not required elsewhere. The earl's acquiescence, however, and the reassuring smile he turned on Katherine, troubled his mother very much. Katherine's returning it bothered her even more.

Though he was as discreet as any gentleman could be, Lady Tarrington could not help but have discovered that since he had come of age, her son had taken several women of easy virtue under his protection, until his brief, tragic marriage to Cassandra.

She had noted of late his taking up of his old habits, and had no doubt that his frequent visits to town were at least partly to assuage the loneliness of whichever barque of frailty was currently allotting him her favors.

The dowager countess, though she had long prayed for him to find more suitable and permanent companionship among females of his own kind, had never before this known him to drop his pose of hauteur for any lady other than herself or his sister.

Hoping that the circumstance of Katherine's being a relation was the origin of his more than polite attentions to her, she observed the girl closely and was alarmed at what she found. Though Katherine's voice and expression betrayed nothing suspicious, there was a certain softness in her eyes whenever the earl addressed her in that particularly gentle tone that was meant, one assumed, to be brotherly. Lady Tarrington could not but fear for the safety of the girl's heart.

There was a glow about Katherine now that had been absent before the onset of Vane's attentions, she noted. It was all the more disturbing because Lady Tarrington doubted her son's ability, since his tragedy, to give affection as well as to inspire it. She told herself that she would have a talk—but with whom? If she approached her son on the subject, he would no doubt retreat behind that icy wall that came down between them so often now since Cassandra's death.

115

If she approached Katherine, she was even less sure of her reception. The girl was friendly enough, but there was a reserve about her that frustrated all attempts to acquire a more intimate knowledge of her character.

The Dowager Countess accepted another cup of tea from Priscilla, then sat back to watch the play of emotions, reflecting that it would be a shocking crime if her son were to make that poor child Katherine Amory fall in love with him.

Chapter Four

"That's it, Miss Townsend! Don't be frightened, it seems a gentle enough nag. Keep your hands a bit lower, don't hold him so tightly . . . just so . . . splendid!"

A grim-faced Priscilla bounced gamely in her saddle on the placid old riding horse, trying not to let her fear overcome her. Katherine watched her, amazed at her cousin's determination, and hard put not to laugh as Lord Knolland continuously shouted his encouragement.

She herself was having by far the easier time, mounted on Lady Colesville's sweet-tempered mare, which had been loaned to promote the success of the scheme. Katherine gave a pat to the mare's neck, stuffed her reins into one hand in order to tuck away a rebellious curl that had stolen out from under the borrowed green velvet riding hat, and gazed over the treetops, in complete enjoyment of the experience.

"I know that the clouds are uncommonly enchanting today, Cousin Katherine, but please don't forget your horse. She's intelligent, but she needs your guidance. There, you have let your wrists down—shocking!" A teasing voice roused her out of her contemplation of the sky, and she hurriedly drew her attention back to the management of her reins, shooting a sideways glance at Tarrington, who rode beside her, laughing.

His presence was distracting, but he made a competent

teacher, his instructions precise and calm, his approval devoid of flattery. He meted out praise with care, and only when she had done something extremely well. Still, such attention was almost more than she could comfortably endure. It was difficult to defend oneself against someone who could be icily arrogant at one moment, but brotherly and kind the next.

Perhaps that was why she had begun to chafe again at her confinement at Whitfield, though her current existence was far removed from what it had been during her uncle's lifetime. Somehow the riding helped, giving her a sense of mastery over herself and the horse. It encouraged her to hope that soon she would have more than just the horse's reins firmly in her hands, that she would be directing her own fate as she had always meant to. But it was not without a pang that she thought of leaving this comfortable life, and earning her own way. As for her mother and cousin, they simply avoided discussing it.

They rode quietly along a wooded path, the clop of hooves muffled on the soft damp ground, for the first time away from the stableyard where for a few days they had practiced the rudiments and become acquainted with their mounts. Katherine's eye was caught by a bright splash of yellow, a cluster of daisies that seemed to have just sprouted under her glance, much like the possibilities that she suddenly saw all about her, many more than her retiring and restricted life had ever contained.

Her thoughts strayed again to her problem. She was sure that there was something very important in store for her, and she was not at all certain that it awaited her at Colonel Dawson's in Bath. But her plan was the only thing between her and disappointment, so cling to it she must.

These morning rides, in the gentle summer air, the hoofbeats accompanied by birdsong and laughing voices, were the only occasions that Katherine could not escape the earl, and he unwittingly cooperated by spending much time closeted away with Sir Edwin's solicitor, or one of the tenants, or riding off somewhere without a word and returning in a contemplative mood.

When he was in her company, he behaved to her in much the same familiar, fraternal way he related to Lady Colesville, though never overstepping the bounds of propriety and the tenuous family connection. At rare moments when she thought no one observed her, she allowed herself to bask in his attention, but she did not feel altogether comfortable with even the casual interest he showed in her.

His first suggestion about her appearance, concerning the style of her hair, had been followed by a few others, equally subtle, offered in a matter-of-fact manner that made Katherine feel as if whether she took them up or not was a matter of the most complete indifference to him. She was at a loss to know what these suggestions signified.

But she had taken them up. During an idle discussion of fashions and gossip, Tarrington had made his sister giggle and had astonished his friend Lord Knolland as he gave his opinions with all the confidence and decision of a Brummell.

"Of course," he had said, affecting a drawl and a haughty pose, "I feel that the true brunette does not do justice to her coloring with these pastels that are now all the rage. A fine, deep jewel-tone is much the most becoming for a lady such as Miss Amory." They had laughed, but Sally pressed him to admit that he was serious.

How could anyone take offense at an opinion expressed in such a way? Katherine had thoughtfully tried on one or two older gowns that she had put away as being too unfashionable even for someone closeted in the country, and had reluctantly come to the conclusion that he was right.

In her newer gowns, few as they were, made after the current fashion in pale wispy muslins, her hair, skin and eyes seemed to fade away to obscurity. Now she wore only the brighter colors, like garnet and sapphire, and had even been prevailed upon, after the discussion, to accept an evening dress of bold emerald silk from Lady Colesville, which, she said, made her look sallow, but would suit her cousin exactly.

She had held the fabric up to her face, and could not deny

that it complemented her creamy skin and brought out the highlights in her deep brown hair, which, with a little help from a housemaid who had ambitions to be a dresser, she now always wore in loose curls over her ears and forehead, with the rest softly pulled back.

The first sparks of resentment at Tarrington's casual suggestions were dampened by Katherine's innate sense of justice. Standing before her mirror, she had to agree that he was right.

When on her twentieth birthday, a few days before, Sally had presented her with a simple, but elegant pair of pearl earrings, and had promised to pierce her earlobes for her, she had at first shied away from the idea, reluctant to be seen, as she thought of it, decked with jewels. It would be foolish for a future governess to become accustomed to such fripperies.

But the earl had made her realize in his usual quiet way, that the dangle and gleam of the earrings emphasized the curve of her jaw and cheekbones, and added sophistication to her appearance.

A length of fine sapphire silk that had been his mother's gift was already being made up, under Mrs. Amory's skilled hands and with Lady Colesville's advice, into a fashionable ball dress.

The earl's gift, which had surprised and delighted her, was a book of Venetian sketches. She wondered how he had found out about her interest in drawing, and her love of landscapes, and decided that her mother was the culprit. Mrs. Amory was inordinately proud of her daughter's accomplishments. Before she knew it, Katherine had found herself showing the earl her sketchbook and even her first tentative watercolors, and secretly treasuring his careful criticism.

It was almost too difficult to accept all this unobtrusive but flattering attention from a man she had not quite ceased to think of as her enemy. When he was not annoying her with his assumption of authority or urging her to reconsider her plans, Katherine found it a great strain to keep her anger fresh, or remind herself of the oddity of his activities. These, however, she had not ceased altogether to ponder.

Whenever possible she had tried to catch a glimpse of his callers, but none of them had been any more mysterious than the local sporting vicar, who came to angle for an invitation to shoot at the Hall in the autumn. The man he had met with at the inn had never appeared at Whitfield. Or had she been wrong?

Her self-possessed cousin seemed much too proud to lie. Evasion she could easily suspect him of; outright deceit, never. Just then she was startled out of her musings as the earl himself caught up to her again, and passed her, with an admonition to pay more attention to where she was going. He had fallen back to help counsel Priscilla at an awkward moment when neither her timid signals nor Lord Knolland's vigorous encouragements could induce her lazy mount to progress to a trot.

Lord Tarrington rode two horse lengths ahead as the path narrowed, and Katherine stared at the back of his trim, broad-shouldered figure, so straight in the saddle. She had watched him ride; he seemed to move neither hand nor leg, yet the horse obeyed him instantly. She sighed, tried to arch her stiff back and shifted the knee hooked over pommel of her side-saddle, knowing she would never gain such control.

Tarrington slowed his horse and waited for her to catch up to him. The stallion's nostrils flared, and he swung his head towards the mare, but the earl held him in check. His eyes travelled disapprovingly over Katherine.

"Am I to despair of ever finding you an accomplished equestrienne after all, Katherine? Here I leave you to your own devices for a moment, and the next thing I see is that your seat has degenerated into a shocking slouch."

She stopped the mare uncertainly, and the animal, sensing that she did not really mean it, chose to sidle and snort rather than stand properly, the skin on her withers rippling, her ears set back.

"I don't know what you mean, sir. I have not moved an inch from where you placed me." Too late did she guiltily recall her readjustments of her leg. She blushed and tried to regain con-

121

trol, but the mare did not cooperate. Sally had warned her that the horse needed a good gallop to "shake the fidgets" out of her, and so far the earl had permitted her nothing more than a sedate trot.

To her horror the chestnut mare tossed and dipped her head and the reins slid from Katherine's unwary fingers. She could have kicked herself for being so foolish. By this time she certainly should have known better. But it was too late. The horse was sauntering off the path, quite of her own accord, and Katherine could feel the coiled power in the animal's haunches as they slowly picked up speed.

The pressure of her heel was ineffective in slowing her mount, and without the reins Katherine was helpless to change her direction. She twisted round, holding tightly to the cantle with one hand and the pommel with the other, and saw Tarrington, his face a mask of wrath, following between the trees on his bay stallion. She faced forward again, in time to duck under a low branch.

Katherine fumed at her own inadequacy. A wretched horse would never dare use Tarrington so! But very likely his mere arrogance gave the creatures the impression that he was to be the master. They passed under a still lower branch, at a brisk trot now, and Katherine's bonnet was knocked back, and her forehead scratched. Her bottom was beginning to be quite sore as well. How could she ever have thought that she was enjoying this? But she disdained to cry for help.

Tarrington had gained on them, wending his way between the trees. Katherine could hear the cries of the others far back along the path, and she spared a thought to hope that Lord Knolland was keeping Priscilla well away from the scene, lest her fears return in earnest. Finally the earl approached on his nervous stallion, one arm outstretched to help her correct the situation, but the mare, close to being in season, sensed the other horse's increasing interest and whinnied shrilly, coyly presenting her flank to the oncoming stallion.

In spite of her predicament, clinging gamely to the pommel,

Katherine observed with some satisfaction that the earl was having no easy time himself. He had reined in the stallion so tightly that she wondered he was not afraid of ruining the horse's mouth, as he had preached that she must never do. She ' d suffered his sharpest corrections whenever he thought her ᴜndling of the reins too rough.

The stallion was all but under control now, but his eyes rolled, and in spite of all Tarrington could do he continued to make for the mare, dancing sideways whenever his rider prevented him from making a forward movement.

As for Katherine's mount, she had apparently decided that it was early days yet for romance. Had the area not been so thick with trees and undergrowth, Katherine had no doubt that the mare would have taken off with her at a wild gallop. As it was she continued to weave her way around the more obvious obstacles, stumbling several times, and Katherine felt her heart fall into the pit of her stomach each time the animal's head dipped. At last, however, either tired or confused, the horse slowed her pace.

Katherine saw her opportunity and leaned forward, poised precariously, in an attempt to snatch the reins from where they hung. She could only thank Providence that they had not by this time tripped up the horse. She strained, but could not reach them. Mercifully, a clump of juicy grass suddenly appeared very enticing to the tired horse, and she finally stopped. She put her head down and began placidly munching at it, all innocence, as if the events of the last few minutes had never happened. Katherine had quite a mind to teach her a lesson, but she did not dare move.

The mare was a good sixteen hands, perhaps too much horse for a lady Katherine's size, though perfectly suited to the much taller Lady Colesville. Katherine looked down from her perch, wondering how she was to get down without hurting herself. She wanted nothing so much in the world at that moment but to feel her feet on solid ground. She was about to unhook her knee and try sliding while the mare was occupied. The ground seemed awfully far away.

A voice called her name sharply. Tarrington was almost upon her, but he stopped a few yards away and came no closer. "Very well, Miss Amory." His voice was a little breathless and very disdainful, though he seemed unable to hide a hint of worry. "Since this is your doing, and I should only make matters worse by coming much closer, let us see if you can dismount without assistance."

His tone brought Katherine's irritation to the bursting point, and she abandoned her attempts to get down. She sat as though quite comfortable, and looked at him expectantly.

"You surprise me, my lord! You are the last man on earth I should suppose to be lacking in solicitude for the gentler sex. Should not the gentleman always assist the lady to dismount? I should not wish to flaunt a displeasing independence. I know well how it vexes you."

She was well aware that she was in a difficult position and entirely dependent upon his good will to extricate her from it, but she could not resist this jibe. Besides, the mare stood very quietly now, entirely preoccupied with her unexpected snack, and most of Katherine's fear had dissolved.

The lines deepened at the sides of Tarrington's mouth. "If I could trust Charger to behave with an attractive female of his species so near, I would dismount this instant and take you over my knee. You deserve nothing more than a good spanking, my girl, though I'm sure that after your extensive trot it would be somewhat redundant."

"You wouldn't dare," Katherine hissed.

"Shall you risk it?" he asked, looking as though he itched to try it. "Now, before I lose what little patience you have not already stolen from me, be so good as to unhook your leg and slide slowly down. Hold on to the saddle as long as you can. She'll stay, now that she's had her little jest with you."

Katherine decided there was nothing for it but to comply. She regained her reins and obeyed his further orders to slowly walk the mare back to the path.

She could not resist tossing him a resentful look as she passed him, but he only answered with an approving nod. Once she had begun to capitulate, he showed no further interest in her predicament.

Katherine took her tone from his and during the remainder of the ride diverted herself with thoughts of how enjoyable it would be to strangle him with her reins. This rugged exercise of her emotions left her quite dizzy, and she wished herself anywhere else but at Whitfield. The rest of her free time that day was spent in stewing over her failure to triumph over him, and in heartening herself with the reflection that he had not yet managed to force her to give up Bath.

In fact, Tarrington had not mentioned again the subject of the Amorys' future, neither insisting that they continue to remain at Whitfield, nor bringing up their departure for Bath. Mrs. Amory and Priscilla, in fact, seemed to have forgotten poor Colonel Dawson entirely.

Katherine's days had taken on a comfortable pattern, the mornings devoted to attending her mother, seeing to the running of the household with its new servants, reading and sketching whenever she had a moment to herself, and visiting or being visited by her cousins at the Hall nearly every other day.

To these quiet domestic pursuits was added the novelty of dancing lessons. Sally Colesville was an exacting taskmistress, determined that Katherine and Priscilla should do her great credit on the dance floor as well as on horseback. Lady Tarrington graciously assisted by providing the music, as eager as her daughter for the girls to shine at the ball.

Priscilla picked up the figures of the country dances quickly, and soon progressed to being partnered by Lord Knolland, who, when the earl was not in need of his company, always stole away to the drawing room to observe their practice.

Katherine had felt stiff and awkward from the very first, though she enjoyed the music and had a natural sense of rhythm. It was simply that she found herself reluctant to take part in any activity that would draw the attention of the room. She scolded herself for being silly, but still she moved without grace, head down, eyes on her feet.

"Not so carefully, if you please, Cousin Kate," ordered Sally, "Step lightly, as though you were a puff of cloud, or a frolicking brook bubbling over the pebbles!" She giggled at her own nonsense, and Katherine took a breath and tried to smile.

"Hold your head high," Sally continued, "and try to look as though you were enjoying it. Everyone will be staring; the neighborhood has been abuzz with curiosity ever since mother introduced Aunt Delia to them. They will be falling over each other to see the hidden ladies of Whitfield."

At this, Katherine went rigid with anxiety. How could she, simple, unadorned Miss Amory, ever bear up to the scrutiny of a gossip-hungry neighborhood? Her dancing worsened, if possible, from that moment. Though she knew the steps, her body executed them as if each movement were torture. But soon Sally lost patience.

"Good enough, Katherine. And now it is time to call Vane in to practice with you."

"That's the very thing, Kate!" cried Priscilla, with her hand still in Lord Knolland's, though Lady Tarrington's fingers no longer moved on the keys of the pianoforte. "It is so much easier than prancing about by yourself. Besides, even if you know the steps, you must learn how to move with your partner."

"Absolutely correct, my dear Miss Townsend," Lord Knolland added his approval to the suggestion. "Much more enjoyable, may I say." He looked down at her with an idiotically infatuated expression, until he recalled that he still held her hand and let go of it reluctantly.

"And if anyone can make you relax, Katherine, it would be Vane," Sally added innocently. "He is an impeccable dancer. It is such a pity that he rarely dances nowadays. Perhaps he will oblige us both and engage you for your first dance at the ball. Then everyone will be sure to watch, and you'll have no need

126

to worry about being partnered for the rest of the evening." Her merry face beamed with satisfaction.

Katherine thought this unlikely to promote her enjoyment in any way but tried to seem grateful when the earl appeared all too quickly at his sister's summons.

Tarrington was very quiet, and Katherine had the impression that his mind was far from the cares of Whitfield's rejuvenation and the anticipation of a country ball, but he took her hand with alacrity and did not offer a word of criticism as they began their dance under the sharp observation of Lady Tarrington and the approval of Lady Colesville.

Katherine was wretchedly embarrassed, and her hands felt quite damp while her mouth was too dry for speech.

"I—I beg your pardon, my lord," she managed to croak, as she trod on his foot for the second time.

"It is of no concern," he replied. His gaze was fixed somewhere over her shoulder, and Katherine had the impression that he had forgotten her existence. Either that, or her clumsiness had displeased him.

The next time the dance brought them together, she tried again, unwilling to let him think it was her own idea. "I do not think my skill is sufficient for me to inflict myself on a partner, but your sister—"

"Once Sally sets her mind on a thing, it is practically impossible to impede her," he said.

They parted again, but the next time they caught hands, he glanced down at her with a brief smile, and an odd relief flooded through Katherine. "I pity my poor brother Colesville," he said, "Fortunately, he has politics to distract him whenever his home becomes to hot for him."

Katherine, too, began to pity the unknown Lord Colesville, for Sally, not satisfied that her brother was dancing, continually called out observations and suggestions for his benefit, until he froze her with a glance that would have had even the most imposing *grandes dames* of the ton shrinking under their turbans.

His sister only laughed, and advised Katherine, "If you think that *I* have been severe with you, cousin, only wait until Vane begins to advise you on your steps. I only hope he will not frighten you into immobility." She made a rather disrespectful face at his lordship, who loftily ignored her and continued to dance without comment until the music stopped.

Curiously enough, Katherine was not really faring any worse with Tarrington as her partner. After a while she had ceased to step on him, and truly, the dance involved so little contact that it was not much different from dancing alone or with Sally.

When Lady Tarrington assured them that she was not too tired to give them another piece, Katherine began it with more confidence than before. Except for the afternoon sunlight streaming through the tall windows of the drawing room, Katherine could have imagined herself in a ballroom.

It was now freshly painted, its wide-boarded floor newly polished, the worn rug, not yet replaced, rolled back, and the massive old chandeliers restored, the missing crystals replaced and reflecting rainbows onto two large mirrors at either end of the room.

For an instant, in Katherine's mind, the tinkling of the pianoforte became the inspiring strains of a full orchestra, the furniture pushed back against the walls was transformed into chairs full of elegantly dressed, murmuring neighbors, their eyes fixed in fascination on the handsome couple as they progressed down the set, lighter than air. Her old cerise afternoon dress became a filmy bejewelled ball gown, and the earl appeared to her in all his evening array, the most elegant man in the room, her partner.

This fantasy reassured her, though it also made her want to laugh at her own absurdity, and she very soon forgot to think of her feet.

The next time Sally spoke it was to congratulate her on her rapid improvement. The earl added his own praise, which jolted her into awkwardness for a moment, but he immediately directed her back into the figure, then made a few quiet suggestions that made everything seem easier.

She was amazed at his gentleness with her. It almost seemed that he was a different man from the one who had upset all her plans, met with a ragged stranger at the village inn, and traipsed off to town for some mysterious purpose.

They ended their dance to the sound of applause from the others. The earl accepted their homage with a dignified bow, and Katherine managed a playful curtsey. Strangely enough, Tarrington's presence had given her a confidence she did not have, and she began to believe that Sally was right. If he claimed her first dance she would do very well the rest of the evening. The ball no longer seemed so fearsome a debut.

"You do my sister credit, cousin Katherine," the earl was saying. He had not called her "Miss Amory" for a long time, though she still called him nothing but "my lord."

"The young men of the neighborhood will find you a graceful partner."

She stumbled over her thanks for the unexpected praise. "I—that is, it is kind of you to say so, my lord."

He smiled. "Not kind, true. In fact, I wish you would save one of your dances for me. A waltz, perhaps? Or has my scatterbrained sister neglected to teach it to you?"

"Of course I have taught them the steps, Vane," protested Lady Colesville. She bustled forward indignantly. "But I don't think they do very much waltzing at these country balls. Still, I was going to ask if you and Lord Knolland would—"

"With pleasure." He already had his hand on Katherine's waist, and the warmth of his touch spread quickly, her heart thudding in anxiety or excitement, she was not sure which. She stared fixedly at the crisp creases in his neckcloth and struggled to appear as unruffled as he.

"Mama, would you oblige us?" he asked.

"Of course, though I confess I haven't played in so long I wonder any of you can keep the beat for all my stumbling." She smiled at her son, but beneath her complacent exterior, she was worried. She had managed to say exactly three words to him on the subject of his cousin Katherine before being shut out by that chilly curtain the earl invariably drew down when others trespassed on an area he did not care to discuss.

Even his own mother, she fumed as she began the waltz, was not exempt. And now there were definitely stars in the girl's eyes, she thought, watching as Katherine placed one hand in the earl's, and her other tentatively on his shoulder.

Katherine felt flushed and overheated before she had even circled the room once in Tarrington's arms. Though he held her very correctly, almost stiffly away from him, she had never in her life been held this way by a man, her hand in his firm, but gentle, clasp, his shoulder reassuringly solid beneath her fingers. The music helped, giving her something on which to focus her attention besides the unnerving proximity of Tarrington's elegant masculine form.

She looked past his ear, trying to concentrate on the steps Sally had taught her. They seemed suddenly unfamiliar, with her partner's steady gentle pressure directing them. She was surprised for a moment by an unexpected turn, but the earl said nothing when she did not execute it correctly. The next time, his body communicated such unmistakable signals that she could do nothing but twirl competently in his arms. Her heart was beating riotously as she faced him again, and she only met his eyes briefly. They were a warm green in the sunny room, but their expression was unreadable. His mouth had relaxed into a half-smile, and she wondered if he were secretly laughing at her.

As the music ended Katherine slipped quickly out of the earl's grasp. He thanked her for the dance, still smiling that half-smile, and turned to his sister. "There you are, Sally. Your students are ready to make their debut, and you'll have nothing to blush for, I'm sure, in their performance."

"Of course not!" cried his sister. "Our cousins will be the belles of the neighborhood, and they are going to enjoy it all immensely. I only fear that once their neighbors discover

130

them, they will be in such demand that we shall never see them. They will be far too busy." Her dimples appeared and her eyes danced.

Katherine and Priscilla laughingly protested that they could never treat their cousins so shabbily, and in any case, Katherine was still looking forward to her belated introduction to society with more anxiety than pleasure.

But she was happy about it for Priscilla's sake, not only because Priscilla was a year younger and far more impatient for dancing and balls and such, but because Lord Knolland's very particular attentions did not seem to be leading anywhere.

Doubtless, Priscilla had her dreams, but she was too innocent to know that such a marked preference for her society should quickly develop into something more substantial. Her mother, she was sure, knew perfectly well that in any other circles her niece would be considered to have had her hopes raised with little expectation of fulfillment, but very likely she was too happy at the life they were leading to demand an accounting from Lord Knolland.

That left only two people, and Katherine knew she could never ask Tarrington to interrogate his friend on the subject. It will have to be me, she thought. But she dreaded approaching Lord Knolland. For all his apparent toying with her cousin's affections, she knew she would never find it in her to be stern enough.

"Going to be very jolly, looking forward to it m'self," the object of her meditations contributed to the conversation. "Beg leave to hope that you'll save me the first dance, Miss Townsend." He fixed eager eyes on her, while she became suddenly shy, though she had been whirling about in his arms with the utmost confidence only a moment before. She whispered her assent and looked at the floor.

Hoping that her own confusion was not as plain to everyone, Katherine became uneasy when she heard Lady Colesville begging her mother for another tune, but before she could begin, Hatchell appeared at the door and attracted her attention with

131

a discreet but effective cough.

"My lord, there is a . . . a person, who desires speech with you." His face spoke eloquently of his opinion of the caller.

The half-smile vanished from the earl's face, and to Katherine it seemed as though his eyes snapped to attention. "And the, er, person's name, Hatchell?"

"He gave no name, my lord," said the butler, "but he requested that I give you this." He produced a dirty white dog-eared card held very gingerly between thumb and forefinger.

Katherine was all attention during this exchange, reminded of the earl's odd companion that evening at the Black Horse, and she was gratified to see his expression change abruptly as he took the card. It was as though a shutter had been drawn, leaving his face blank to all onlookers.

"Please excuse me," he said to the company in general. "There is some business to which I must attend." With a brief bow in the direction of the ladies, he was gone.

Katherine had to suppress an overwhelming urge to follow him. Only by telling herself that it was none of her concern should her cousin be in the habit of meeting with disreputable-looking men, or of haring off to town out of season, or of seeming to be less rich than he ought to be, could she force herself to remain in the drawing room.

She seated herself at the pianoforte, recently vacated by Lady Tarrington, and thought about all she had observed, letting her fingers seek out a tune that she knew well, leaving her mind free to ponder the enigma that was the Earl of Tarrington.

Lady Colesville, though sometimes teasing her brother about his mysterious jaunts and his lack of care for his dress, seemed unaware of anything really wrong. But Lady Tarrington, Katherine had observed, sometimes fixed her son with a look of mingled pity and anxiety, and just as obviously was at least partly in his confidence.

Lord Knolland was almost too plain in his eagerness to pretend that all was as it should be, she mused, striking a chord, but she had the notion that no one was completely a party to his secret, whatever it might be.

Then the earl was back in the room, his expression bland, but his eyes and the set of his jaw had a grimness about them that belied his casual manner as he approached his mother.

"I am afraid, Mama, that my visitor"—he wrinkled his nose as if the person had offended his fastidiousness as well as Hatchell's—"has brought me word of something I must attend to in town. I apologize for leaving my cousins again so soon after prevailing upon them to stay." There was just the hint of a smile on his lips as he glanced at Katherine.

She could hardly keep from showing her interest in his sudden departure, but she let Lady Colesville remonstrate with him while she listened.

"Not again, Vane, not so close to the ball!" Sally pleaded, grasping his hand.

He brought her hand momentarily to his lips. "I promise, dear sister, that I shall return in time to show off your pupils at Mrs. Littleton's event."

Katherine only murmured her regrets with the others, but he surprised her by approaching and taking her hand. She met his quizzical gaze uncertainly.

"And you, cousin Katherine, will you not scold me for being such a poor host?"

"I should never presume, my lord," she said innocently, "to question how you conduct your affairs, of which I, of course, know nothing."

He threw back his head and laughed, and for a moment the blank mask dissolved. "You never fail to surprise me, my dear."

The others in the room, especially, she noted, Lady Tarrington, were watching them curiously. Katherine studied the carpet with increasing interest as she felt Tarrington's eye on her. She had no idea how to reply, or what he meant by the comment.

Lord Knolland was clearing his throat, bobbing up and down

133

to attract his friend's attention. "Ah . . . thing is . . . go with you if you like. Whatever it is, two can take care of it quicker than one, that is, if I could be of any help . . . get home sooner, you know." He raised round hopeful eyes to Tarrington.

"Thank you, my good fellow, but it is nothing that you need be concerned about. I can attend to it alone, and besides, within an hour of stepping out of the chaise, you know very well that you would end up at White's entering some ludicrous wager that would only oblige me to wait for you to collect or pay, and we should be twice as late getting back."

Lord Knolland did not hesitate to admit that this was true. "Can't seem to resist it." He shook his head, mystified. "Fellow has only to offer a bet on anything—anything at all— and I'm off. You're right, better go alone. Besides"—he brightened noticeably—"got to have a man here to protect the females. These country fellows get up to all sorts of tricks."

His face fell when he was reminded pertly by Sally Colesville that for propriety's sake he would have to remove to the Black Horse until his host had returned. "Else you should scandalize us all, my lord. You do not have the excuse of being family, and the ladies cannot entertain you alone."

Lord Knolland reluctantly agreed, and went off, with a sorrowful glance at Priscilla, to see to his belongings being shifted to the inn. Katherine was sorry to see her cousin looking equally besotted. It looked very much as though it would be necessary to speak with Priscilla as well. How could she tell her that in the way of the world, no amount of infatuation was likely to make up for her lack of fortune and position? She did not want her cousin to be hurt. Or is it I who am in danger of being hurt, Katherine's honesty prompted her to wonder, as she watched Tarrington's broad back disappear into the corridor.

Lately it seemed as though her every thought contained some reference to the earl, she noted irritably. Perhaps his brief absence would teach her to put her mind on other things. She turned again to the instrument, and began to play

134

something long, dull, and difficult as a punishment. But still her mind wandered.

Katherine knew little of love. The closest she had come to experiencing it was a brief girlish attachment to a pale young artist, whose soulful eyes and long slender fingers had captivated her fancy during the month in which he gave her lessons.

Though they had been suitably chaperoned by her mother, and not a word had been spoken out of place, she had lived for his every syllable of praise, his tiniest smile. But even as she'd gloried in his company, her nights were undisturbed by dreams of him, and she concocted not even one thin fantasy in which he would come for her on a moonlit night to bear her away to the Border.

When the lessons were over, and he had returned to his garret, never to visit again, his image had disappeared all too quickly from her mind. Left with her brushes and pens, her palette and her inks, she had turned her attention to her work, and during the hours when she and Priscilla had escaped to the meadows and fields outside the town, she'd concentrated to such an extent on capturing exactly the shape of a gnarled old tree, or just the right shade of blue for the sky, that in the end she had scarcely recalled her sole experience with infatuation. Her only hope now was that this foolish fascination she seemed to have developed would disappear as completely, and as soon.

That it would be hopeless and unsuitable to indulge in a romantic daydream about the Earl of Tarrington was not the only reason she tried to clear her mind. His abrupt departures and all the other little puzzles about him were almost as worrying. These thoughts stirred her, and she broke off her playing, with no protest from anyone, as all the ladies were gathered around the latest issue of *Ackermann's* and were deep into the fashion plates.

No one made a murmur as she quietly quit the drawing room, making her way outside just in time to see Tarrington's groom leading his big, high-strung black stallion up to the house. Another horse, a shaggy, rawboned beast of indeterminate color, already stood placidly by.

Conscious that her curiosity was not really warranted, Katherine walked down the steps and a little way into the shrubbery between house and stables. It was still overgrown and tangled, and she was effectively hidden, though she could see out.

In another moment the earl, dressed in buckskin breeches, polished, but well-worn, top-boots, and a blue riding coat emerged from house and directed the groom in the arrangement of two small saddlebags. Katherine thought it strange that he should ride all the way to town carrying so little, but perhaps he would not be away very long. The ball was only three days away, and her heart gave a traitorous leap at the thought.

The earl mounted his horse, and as he did a small, dilapidated figure arrived from the path leading to the kitchen door. He was no more than a boy, rather dirty, dressed in worn, stained, toast-colored breeches and scuffed boots a shade too large. A huge brown beaver hat that had seen better times flopped over his tangled ginger curls, and bright black eyes peered out from beneath it as he mounted the disreputable-looking animal that awaited him. Next to the glossy, high-bred stallion, it looked to be no more than a farm horse.

Katherine was just close enough to hear some of their conversation, carried on a fortunate breeze.

"Did they give you something to eat in the kitchen?"

"Yessir, m'lud." The boy bobbed his head, his eyes fixed admiringly on the stallion.

"Good. Do you think you can take me to this Mr., ah, Smith, before nightfall?"

Once again the head bobbed, the hat-brim flapping.

Before nightfall! He could not, as he had told them, be going to London, not this late in the day. Katherine stepped a little way out of the sheltering bushes, hoping her bright dress would not draw attention to her presence among the greenery.

"M'master told me to tell you old Smith be the one yer

136

lookin' for. 'E knows the fellow you mean, does old Smith, an' can put you in the way o' some fine things."

Even from a distance she could see the expression of satisfaction that appeared on the earl's face, and she wondered exactly what "things" he needed this Mr. Smith's assistance to find.

"And just how is your master so sure of it?" Tarrington asked the boy.

The child looked knowing and altogether too sharp, Katherine thought, for one of such tender years. "Smith 'as a sister who 'as a flash ken down Bow Street way—right cheeky, I calls it." He flashed a gap-toothed grin. "They all runs their rigs there right in the laps o' the runners."

"A flash house, eh?" the earl mused aloud. "Smith must have many useful and interesting acquaintances. Our man is probably the least of them."

Katherine wondered what a flash house was, though from the boy's reference to the audacity of its proximity to Bow Street, she concluded that its inmates must be flaunting some illegality literally in the face of the law.

As she was puzzling over this, the breeze shifted and she strained to hear more, but the rest of the exchange was lost. Tarrington had turned his horse and begun to walk him towards the drive when suddenly a startled hare ran through the tangled growth near Katherine, and she jumped, just managing to restrain a cry of surprise.

She knew she hadn't made a sound, but the earl turned sharply in the saddle and for a long, anxious moment it seemed that his eaglelike gaze searched for her in the shrubbery. She shrank back, hardly daring to breathe, while reminding herself how ridiculous she would seem if she were found crouching among the bushes spying on the Earl of Tarrington. Just as she was about to emerge, quickly inventing a plausible excuse for being there, he turned away and set off down the drive, followed by his odd little companion.

Chapter Five

The Earl of Tarrington warily eyed the glass his host offered to him. It was not very clean, much like the hand that proffered it, but he accepted it with a small nod of thanks.

"Fine brandy, sir, I assure you," the little man at his side twittered nervously. "The final cask from the last run before the revenue men—ah, but I do let my tongue run away with me. . . ." He gulped at the brandy in his own glass, his hard grey eyes fixed on the earl's calm visage.

"The source of your spirits does not concern me, sir," Tarrington told him, sipping first cautiously, then appreciatively at the brandy. "It is of other sources that I come to speak with you."

"Of course, Mr. Vane, I . . . I should be most happy . . . but a moment, if you will . . ."

Mr. Smith had achieved no visible relaxation from the consumption of his fine brandy. He scrambled about in his pockets for a full minute before bringing to light a rather battered silver-coated snuffbox. His stained fingers and the grains clinging to his soiled neckcloth already proclaimed his habits.

The earl declined an offer of the mixture and observed his host's snuff-taking ritual with increasing impatience. After the little man had clumsily opened the box, pinched what looked to Tarrington like an enormous amount of the brown snuff between his fingers and raised it to his nose, he still had to wait for "Mr. Smith" to complete a series of quick tiny sneezes, culminating in one gigantic one for which he brought out a yellowed handkerchief before he could obtain the information he had come for.

It had been a long and difficult trail, Tarrington reflected, sampling the brandy once more, but it was at last at an end, here in this modest cottage on the outskirts of an undistinguished Hampshire village. The fellow Smith, his contacts had assured him, was the last link in the chain leading to the man he had been seeking for the better part of a year. It only remained to inform certain people, and, most difficult, to ensnare the man himself.

Smith had secreted the snuffbox about his person once more, probably, the earl reflected, only to forget its whereabouts in a moment, and now he fastened his rodentlike gaze on Tarrington. He appeared doubtful that such a plainly dressed fellow could provide adequate recompense for his trouble. But Smith's sharp eyes had not failed to notice the prime horseflesh Mr. Vane had arrived on, and he was not without hope of earning a few guineas for very little work.

"My friends in London tell me that you know where one can find treasures of art for a comparative pittance. Of course I have no curiosity as to where these pieces originate," the earl added casually, placing his glass on a water-scarred mahogany stand. "As our mutual friend Mr. Lyons told you, I am sometimes in the way of disposing of one or two items to people of wealth, and I should be interested in, ah, . . . replenishing my stock at the lowest possible cost."

He had been careful, before leaving Whitfield, to don his plainest coat, and to tie his neckcloth simply, lest he awaken suspicions that he was not what he seemed, "Mr. Vane," a well-connected businessman of somewhat dubious probity. Smith must not be alarmed by too ready a display of power or position, and of course, he must protect his identity.

"Ah! Well, sir"—Smith had concluded the preliminaries—

140

"I have in mind a fellow who can put you in the way of some very nice things indeed. A gentleman, too, if you can believe it." He snickered and rubbed his yellow fingertips together. "Fallen on hard times, no doubt, and come up with an ingenious way to restore his fortune without parting with any of his precious possessions. Of course, it is not he who does the actual work involved, but . . . that is not our concern." He trotted over to an old, dusty desk, and rummaged in a drawer stuffed to bursting with papers.

"Ah, yes, here it is," he said, extracting a wrinkled sheet. "This is where you can find him. I don't say he's easily approachable, now. To my knowledge he hasn't ever arranged such a job for anyone but himself, but he has been generous to certain friends of mine . . . put them in the way of some business."

Tarrington followed Smith behind the desk, and conquering his disgust of the little man, bent with him to read the name and address scrawled on the greasy paper. His shock at what he saw there did not in any way prevent him from feeling just a bit of triumph, now that success was within his grasp.

However, it was still a dangerous situation, the fellow being so close to Whitfield, and to his family. It would be difficult work, and he knew that though his sister and Rodney were unaware of his activities, his mother and his quick-witted cousin Katherine had noticed something peculiar.

To his mother, he had explained it away as some tiresome business dealings to do with preserving the remains of his fortune. To Katherine, he attempted to show a bland exterior, though he was not too confident of the success of this ploy. It was becoming more difficult to stick to his original intentions where she was concerned.

He wondered if she knew anything at all about his past, and decided she did not. His mother and sister, he knew, had always honored his request not to speak of his tragic marriage, and he doubted that even Knolland would venture on the subject without his permission. Tarrington had a sudden intense

141

desire to confide in Katherine, a desire which he instantly suppressed. No matter what she claimed, she was far too innocent of the unpleasant realities of life, though she would perhaps understand, but his good sense told him it would be far better for both of them if she were not involved.

In the back of his mind there was a faint hope that one day soon he would not have to restrain those feelings she roused in him, feelings he had almost thought were dead. Rodney was right. He had been premature in deciding that another marriage was out of the question. But it was not for the present. For now he must keep Katherine out of this infernal mess he had gotten himself into.

When it was all over, he mused, unknowingly clenching the hand that had taken the paper from Smith, then he could do what he had been longing to do ever since he had first met that accusing wide-eyed gaze. But not now. No, he could not do justice to his wooing with this weighty and uncertain business on his mind.

He only hoped she could be persuaded to continue to postpone the Bath scheme. He had a sense that though she was outwardly compliant with everyone's wishes, she was only awaiting the right moment to carry out her own. For the moment he could only look forward to her company at this little country ball.

In general such evenings heartily bored him, though he had always carried out his social obligations with precise courtesy, and he could not believe how his heart quickened at the thought of leading Katherine onto the floor for the waltz. He could still recall the feel of her waist, pliant yet firm under his hand, and the shy touch of her fingers on his shoulder. He was determined that at the very least, he would waltz with her and enjoy it to the fullest. If the temptation to do more overcame him . . . he would deal with it somehow.

Suddenly aware that he had quite forgotten his purpose in his contemplations of Katherine's charms, he turned back to Mr. Smith, who was eyeing him curiously.

"Yes," he said hurriedly, "this is exactly what I want to know. Of course, as our friend promised, you shall be recompensed for your assistance...."

In a very short time Tarrington was mounted again and riding away in the dusk towards a hostelry in which he knew that yet another curious fellow awaited him, while the little man with the snuff-stained fingers was happily counting over the contents of a small leather purse filled with coins.

Though the earl's finances were by no means settled, he did not begrudge a penny of the payment. Satisfaction, he reflected as he dismounted in the inn yard and threw his reins to an ostler, was something worth more than gold.

The day of the ball dawned grey and dismal, but though a morning shower threatened to last into afternoon, by the time Lady Tarrington and her daughter arrived at Whitfield for an early dinner, bringing their French maid and their ball ensembles, the rain had stopped and the sun was drying the ground again. The air was warm, the breezes were soft, and indoors and out, Whitfield was experiencing an unaccustomed excitement that was infectious.

Sally was continually appearing at either Katherine's door or Priscilla's, her filmy petticoat covered by a dressing gown and her own hair half-done, to the despair of her maid.

"No, Priscilla. You must let Minette arrange your hair, I insist!" Checking on Katherine's progress, she gave her unqualified approval of the new sapphire silk gown.

Mrs. Amory had studied the fashion plates to excellent effect. The shimmering blue stuff was made up into a low-necked, high-waisted gown, trimmed with tiny crystal beads around the bodice and sleeves, while crystal-studded silver net drifted down to be caught up in festoons just inches from the floating hem. Her hair was supported by a silver Grecian ornament lent by Sally, which, all the ladies said, made her look uncommonly elegant.

143

The tiny puffed sleeves seemed to cradle her creamy shoulders, and the low-cut bodice emphasized the slender grace of her neck and the rounded fullness of her bosom. In truth, she felt quite exposed, but even Mrs. Amory allowed that it was perfectly proper.

Her only ornament, the gold locket, was deemed unsuitable, and her mother surprised her by producing a small sapphire pendant that was one of her few remaining jewels.

As the necklace was clasped around her neck, she stared into the mirror at this new Katherine. The simple healthy glow that had always been her chief asset was accented by a new polish and sophistication, thanks to the upswept hair and the jewels. She raised her chin and decided that she would not be put out of countenance by the stares of the neighborhood. Though soon she might be only a governess, now she was an Amory of Whitfield, and that was enough.

So far there was almost nothing that did not give her satisfaction. Her cousin Priscilla was looking charming in a new pale yellow satin enhanced with bunches of satin rosebuds and seed pearls. Mrs. Amory, too, quite did them all proud in her elegant lavender half-mourning, for she told them, though she could not pretend to have liked Sir Edwin, she knew the respect that was due to family.

"For they will think it so odd, my dear, that we do not observe mourning for at least a year, considering—"

"Considering that he despised *them* and practiced a gross deception upon *us*," Katherine finished for her. Mrs. Amory only shook her head and clung to the proprieties.

In short, there was nothing wanting, except that the Earl of Tarrington, contrary to his promise, had not yet made an appearance. Very soon the ladies were getting carefully into the carriage and still there was no sign of him.

I was wrong to put any dependence on his being there, thought Katherine. Yet she felt betrayed by her own imagination. Last night she had dreamed of twirling in his arms to the admiration of all her neighbors, and now, despite her pleasure

144

in her new gown, she was suddenly afraid. This might be her only chance to enjoy a little success before the stark realities of life overtook her. It would be dreadful if she were to fail.

She was not the only one, of course, to be disappointed by the earl's continued absence, but his mother took it calmly and his sister went so far as to assure them that he would probably join them at Mrs. Littleton's later in the evening.

"I know my brother," she stated firmly, as she demonstrated the proper use of the fan to Priscilla. "If he makes a promise, nothing will prevent him from keeping it."

Their arrival at the ball was greeted with unabashed curiosity on the part of their neighbors, all of them intent on getting the first glimpse of old Sir Edwin's niece and her cousin. To the girls' delight and the dismay of Lord Knolland, who had rushed to meet them, only to be forestalled by a dozen strangers, Katherine and Priscilla were immediately surrounded by gentlemen seeking introduction from their hostess.

There were several handsome men among the neighborhood bachelors, some too young and some much too old, Priscilla whispered to Katherine, but they met all of them with pleasure, and very soon they were both engaged for several dances. Lord Knolland, for the moment, had to be satisfied with having already secured the first set. So anxious had he been that he had arrived almost early enough to embarrass his hostess, to whom he was a perfect stranger, and had his town companions heard of it he would have been soundly ridiculed.

Katherine's feelings alternated between confusion and gratification, but she could not keep her mind from the earl nor her eyes from the door of the large chamber that served as their ballroom, an exercise that provided no satisfaction.

However, she was soon obliged to turn her attention elsewhere, as her first partner claimed her. He was a pleasant, ruddy-faced young man from one of the neighboring houses, and his dancing was not so polished as to intimidate her, so after a moment of fear on that score, Katherine found that she

145

was enjoying it very well.

"How cruel of you ladies, Miss Amory, to keep yourselves hidden from us all!" her partner teased. "Were you only trying to increase our eagerness? Could you only know the expectation you have excited among us!" He cocked his head and smiled in a way that could only be described as flirtatious. "However, I shall not scold you, since my expectations have been exceeded by the reality."

His eyes were full of appreciation, and though the sensation was foreign to her, Katherine found it very thrilling to be admired.

"If you don't take care, sir, I shall soon be dreadfully spoiled by flattery," she replied, amazed at how easily banter came to her. "It is too rich a diet for one unaccustomed to it." It was not very difficult, either, to return his warm smile.

"I would then warn my friends to be sparing of it tonight, Miss Amory, but I fear they will not be able to help themselves," he riposted.

She hoped she could keep from blushing too often. It would not do, she thought, to be red as a beet the entire evening. How silly did her fears seem now! Whether Tarrington keeps his promise or not, she thought, I am bound to enjoy myself; and she determinedly put him out of her mind.

Her next partner also twitted her on her late debut in the society of the neighborhood. "Were you really all kept locked away by old Amory? Sounds awfully like one of those horrid novels m'sisters always read. Dilapidated old castle, eccentric master, beautiful young females . . ." He remembered himself in time to add, "No intention to offend, Miss Amory. It's just that we hadn't much of an opinion of your uncle—especially since he withheld from us two of the most charming girls in the county."

The evening was passing swiftly in a whirl of dancing, mild flirtation, and at intervals the approving smiles of her mother and Lady Tarrington. Sally, though her mother sternly took her to task, enjoyed the full advantage of her status as a married woman and danced and flirted as heartily as everyone else. When pressed she admitted that it was because she missed her husband dreadfully, but she swore the girls to secrecy lest she become a figure of fun. "For it is terribly unfashionable to be so attached to one's husband, you know," she declared before she was swept away again on another gentleman's arm.

Priscilla, Katherine noted, attracted her share of attention as well. Her short-sighted stare gave her a dreamy look that enhanced her already delicate appearance, and she danced as lightly as a fairy, floating from one partner to another.

Lord Knolland's increasing discomfort with this state of things almost made Katherine laugh aloud. So far he had managed only one dance with her cousin, and no more. For the most part, he had surrendered the field and stood against the wall glaring.

In a moment between dances, when Katherine sat briefly with her mother, he approached her and stood silent for a moment, watching Priscilla sip punch brought to her by her latest partner, while three other hopeful swains attended her. He murmured darkly, hopeful of a sympathetic ear, "These country fellows are a rum lot. Not that Miss Townsend ain't looking particularly charming tonight, and deserves the attention, but . . . you'd think a fellow who's known her a fortnight would at least get the first crack!"

"Why don't you ask her to dance again, my lord? I think you have given up too easily," Katherine said, taking pity on him. She was secure in the belief that now her cousin had tasted a bit of flirtation and success, she would get over her infatuation with his lordship. She even, for a heady moment, believed it true of her own situation.

The disappointed suitor repudiated her suggestion. "No wish to be making a cake of myself, Miss Amory, among these bumpkins. Ain't at all the thing. Won't do to shoulder my way through that crowd." He turned an anxious gaze on her. "Suppose she turns me down?"

He looked so forlorn that Katherine suppressed a smile and

147

was moved to say, "I don't think she'll do any such thing. In fact, I think she would be happy to waltz with you. I know I would be so much more comfortable waltzing in public for the first time with a gentleman with whom I was well acquainted. It is rather an uncomfortable dance to perform with a stranger."

"It is, isn't it?" he said hopefully. Taking courage, secure in the knowledge that his evening attire was of the first stare, now that the absent Finster had finished attending to the obsequies of his late parent and had joined his master at the Black Horse, he smoothed an infinitesimal crease in his neckcloth, straightened his shoulders under his exquisitely cut black evening coat, and sailed off to take his rightful place among Miss Townsend's admirers.

Katherine smiled, watching him go, but the episode did not amuse her for long. Despite her early success, and amidst all the new sights and sensations of her first ball, a twinge of disappointment still hovered in the back of her mind. Whatever else might be unfathomable about him, her cousin Tarrington had seemed to be a man of his word. Obviously his peculiar journey with the ragged boy had been a greater attraction than the prospect of standing up with her at a country ball.

Her disillusionment was complete when she overheard the dowager countess say to Mrs. Amory, with an odd hint of relief in her voice, "Oh, Vane will certainly not arrive in time to enjoy any of the evening, my dear Delia, for all his promises. It is just like a man to be so caught up in all his affairs as to hold such an engagement to be of little importance. In fact, I have already made his excuses to Mrs. Littleton. . . ."

With this, Katherine felt entirely free to accept the hand of one of her hostess' tow-headed sons for the upcoming waltz. Lord Knolland shot her a grateful look as he led Priscilla out onto the floor, but just as Mr. Littleton took Katherine's hand, a deep voice in her ear and the appearance of a strong, well-manicured hand on young Mr. Littleton's shoulder forestalled them.

"Please accept my most abject apologies for my late arrival,

148

Katherine, but I must also beg leave to claim this dance for myself. I believe I secured it before I left Whitfield."

She turned to see Tarrington, in impeccable evening dress, staring coolly at Mr. Littleton, awaiting his retreat. By his appearance, no one would have guessed that the earl had but three-quarters of an hour ago leaped from his horse, run up to his chamber, and hurriedly washed, while his valet flung his evening clothes at him with all possible speed.

The carriage being in use, the lowly gig was made ready for him, and to it he had harnessed one of his prime greys, apologizing to the proud animal for subjecting it to such an indignity. This unlikely equipage had brought him to the ball just in time to steal Katherine away from the son of the house, a piece of rudeness he ordinarily would not have attempted, save for his stubborn intention, held in the back of his mind during all of his two days of machinations, to dance with her as he had promised.

Katherine felt heat rising from her breast to her forehead as his eyes, sparkling with greenish flecks in the candlelight, took in her appearance with obvious appreciation, catching her off guard.

The sapphire silk clung to her curves, and drifted to her feet in the most flattering way, he thought, while the crystals at the bodice shimmered and swung with her slightest movement, reflecting the glow in the depths of her eyes, fixed on his face in startled fascination.

Tarrington thought her appearance fulfilled her promise and more. Only, as he frowned at the lingering Mr. Littleton, who stood stupidly with Katherine's hand still in his, he reflected that it was inevitable she would attract other gentleman who had long wondered what treasures the forbidden walls of Whitfield had concealed.

But Mr. Littleton's youth and inexperience and the determination of the earl, a nonpareil if the young man had ever seen one, was enough to make him think twice of defying the late-arriving guest.

He gulped, apologized, surrendered the lady's hand, and bowed his way out of it, leaving his astonished partner incensed at the success of the earl's high-handed tactics. This was the first time Katherine had been able to become angry with him in a long time, and her irritation gave her the strength she needed to resist the smile he now turned on her full force, as well as the unabashed admiration in his eyes.

"I hope you are proud of your excessively bad manners, my lord," she began at once, before he could lead her onto the floor. "I, for one, am thoroughly mortified. You know as well as I do that we had no such engagement for this particular dance. You took shameful advantage of poor Mr. Littleton who is, after all, our hostess' son!"

He ignored her protests, and with a firm hand at her waist, drew her into the dance, the music having already begun. Privately he thought her high color became her extraordinarily well, but he said, "You must try not to seem so perturbed at my little deception, dear Katherine. I fear our quarrelling on the dance floor would cause some remark." Then he smiled into her eyes in a way that could not fail to silence her, as she became conscious of his closeness and, when she swung by them, the stares of her mother and Lady Tarrington.

Katherine assumed as placid an expression as possible, and though her heart was thumping and her throat felt constricted, she tried again.

"The business that called you away so suddenly must have been unsuccessful for you to be detained so long. I hope nothing is amiss?"

Though he still smiled, there was evidence in the deepening of those lines about his mouth that her interest in his affairs did not please him. But he replied calmly enough, "On the contrary, it went better than I expected, and that is why I must beg your indulgence for claiming our dance so late. I shall, of course make my apologies to Mrs. Littleton and our respective parents."

Katherine studiously ignored him for the rest of the dance,

intent on concealing her excitement at his presence and hoping he had not seen the flash of joy she had been unable to hide when she found him beside her.

As if it meant anything! Tarrington, she decided, had used this ruse to make everyone focus on his sudden solicitation of her hand, rather than his mysterious absence and late arrival. He did look, though, as if his mission, whatever it was, had been successful.

Tarrington, too, seemed lost in thought for the remainder of the dance, though he missed not a step, and continually challenged her with elegant turns. Katherine thought it impossible that he should be as conscious as she was of the way his fingers spread out over the small of her back, gently holding her at a correct but disturbingly close distance, and how he clasped her hand so carefully, as if he were holding a rare, delicate bird he was anxious not to let escape.

It was a delight to be so close, a delight and a torment, to be at eye-level with the crisp folds of his neckcloth, to inhale his spicy, leathery scent, and to see the flawless upright carriage of his broad shoulders and firm jaw. A heat emanated from him that seemed to penetrate the thin silk to her very flesh. In a strange contradiction, it made her shiver. After that he held her a tiny bit closer, and for a moment she lost control of all rational thought and was only caught up in the sensation of the moment.

Neither of them made casual conversation. There was nothing to say, or perhaps, Katherine thought, there was too much. Too soon, it was over, and when the earl handed her over to her mother, she dared to breathe once more, certain that she had had a narrow escape. She dared a glance at him, but his face was once again a mask. It was impossible, she thought, that he could have felt anything resembling her own experience.

If the earl was disappointed that the remainder of her dances were spoken for, he gave no sign of it. Katherine, endeavoring to control a slight trembling as she formed with the others the last set of a country dance, watched him for a moment as he charmed his hostess and a group of local matrons. She did not see him glance at her again and again as she progressed down the set, intent on the figures.

He had danced once with Priscilla, and had conferred briefly with Lord Knolland. That gentleman had sunk once again into gloom, though he had performed a duty dance with Miss Littleton, watching Priscilla all the while. The evening was almost at an end when Katherine returned to her mother's side to find the earl already there with their wraps.

"It looks as though your tutelage was a dazzling success, Sally," he was saying to his sister, "But here are our protégés themselves to tell us if they enjoyed their first ball." He smiled kindly at Priscilla, who was still flushed and radiant from a last lively romp.

"Oh, yes, my lord, I don't believe I have ever enjoyed myself more, though of course I have not much to compare it with," she added honestly.

"And you, cousin Katherine?" The earl turned his quizzical gaze on her. "I hope you at least enjoyed our waltz?"

Sally instantly came to her cousin's defence. "It is shameful of you, Vane, to tease Katherine so! Look, she is blushing." For so she was, much to her fury. "Even if you were a clumsy oaf who trod all over her toes, she would be obliged to say yes, thank you, sir, it was the highlight of the evening."

Such an unwarranted scolding evoked Lord Knolland's support of his friend.

"Here, now," he protested, "Tarrington's a deuced good dancer! Never trod a lady's toes in his life, I'll warrant. Manners a trifle at fault sometimes." He glanced apologetically at the earl. "Cheeky of you to descend on poor Littleton and steal his partner away just as if you'd been here all along, but no one's ever said Tarrington's not as graceful as one of your Frog dancing masters!"

The earl's laugh echoed in their corner of the room, and even Katherine had to chuckle at the comparison.

It was at times like this when the earl showed his lack of concern for pride or consequence, laughing good-naturedly at his foibles or those of his friend, that she felt most drawn to him. But she struggled to bring to mind instead the memory of the earl's secret meeting at the inn, his sudden journey with the ragged boy, and his early victory over her determination to go to Bath. Thus she was prepared to resist the overwhelming temptation that faced her next.

"Can we leave you at the inn on our way back, Lord Knolland?" Lady Tarrington asked.

"Oh, yes, much obliged," he replied, revived at the thought of another half-hour in Priscilla's company.

No sooner were they informed that the carriages were ready, and they had taken leave of their hostess and stepped out into the sweet-scented summer night, than the earl spoke again to Katherine.

"Due to my unforgivable tardiness I was forced to resort to the gig. Won't you take pity on my solitude and bear me company on the way back?"

It was all she could do to suppress a gasp of surprise. His manner was so direct, his voice and expression so engaging, that it was only after a serious internal struggle that she was able, keeping the thought of her own peace of mind ever before her, to reply.

"I confess, my lord, I have a horror of that old gig, especially since our frightening experience in it. I am afraid I grow sadly decadent, but the comfort of your mother's carriage is too great a temptation. Then too, the night air . . . I would rather not ride in an open carriage." She gave this speech to the empty air beside his left ear. She did not dare meet his eyes, or all her good intentions would be swept away.

To her dismay, his features lost their warmth and his eyes grew distant in the flare of the flambeaux set before the drive. Still, she was not prepared for the iciness of his answer.

He gave a stiff bow, and said, "Yes, I see precisely what you mean. How thoughtless of me to entice you away from the comforts of a well-sprung vehicle. And of course," his voice became perceptibly sarcastic, "everyone knows the night air is positively treacherous, even to a healthy young lady like yourself. I shall order a fire in your room tonight, cousin, lest even this small exposure have already done you some irreparable harm."

Everyone, even Lady Tarrington, who, Katherine noticed, seemed to have been holding her breath after the earl's invitation, looked away in confusion. The air that night was positively balmy, and even Mrs. Amory, practiced invalid that she was, could have had no objection to driving four miles in an open carriage.

Only Lord Knolland seemed oblivious to the undercurrents of the exchange. "Now don't go calling me a cod's head, Tarrington, but even I can see there ain't no harm in a warm night like this. Since when do you subscribe to all those notions? Why, you told me that even in December, you sleep with a window open and not wearing so much as a—"

Before any of the ladies could raise an eyebrow, but not before Sally had stifled a giggle, the earl interrupted his friend, with a sigh of resignation.

"Very well then, Rodney, why don't *you* join me in the gig and I can explain how I came by my new opinions."

"But . . . I'm staying at the Black Horse . . . Finster and all m'things are—"

"We shall send for them at the crack of dawn, my friend, and in the interim I shall lend you a razor and a nightshirt." The earl's lips curled at the corners. "I do own several, you know, despite the unfortunate impression I may once have given you."

Loyal to the core, Lord Knolland obeyed, not without casting a wistful glance at Priscilla, and after helping the ladies into the carriage, the men moved off into the night.

If Priscilla was disappointed because she was thereby deprived of Lord Knolland's company on the journey home she gave no sign of it, but her curiosity awakened, she searched

Katherine's face in the light of a sickle moon. She was not the only one who wished for an explanation of her cousin's refusal, bordering on insult, to drive with the earl.

Mrs. Amory, however, was too fatigued and too happy with the obvious success of the young ladies in her charge at their first ball to ponder it for long, and Lady Colesville, breathing in the fragrances of a still summer night, was achingly reminded of how long it had been since she had seen her husband. Lady Tarrington, for her part, was merely relieved that Katherine was showing such good sense, and she told herself she could stop worrying that the child would be hurt.

Katherine herself, much like Sally, sat quietly, outwardly composed, observing the way the moonlight turned the road before them to bronze, now and then looking out of the window, let down to catch the slight playful breeze. It seemed a perfect night for discoveries, for talking quietly, just two in a little gig meandering its way home behind a plodding, nodding horse.

These were dreams, fantasies, she told herself firmly, and though she had developed the regrettable habit of resorting to them so late in life, she had best lose no time in curing herself of it.

Reality told her that she was a poor nobody, a dependent relation, whom no earl, especially one in difficulties, could afford to marry, and that the object of these insubstantial fancies was involved in something secretive, and therefore suspect.

It was these thoughts that she repeated over and over to herself while trying to fall asleep, a task made more difficult by the heat of the fire the confused housemaid had insisted, on his lordship's orders, on laying in her grate. How angry he is, she thought, and yet it was so ridiculous that she wanted to laugh. Too tired to protest, she had let it burn until it went out. But it was a long time before she sank into oblivion. The treacherous night air had already done its harm.

Chapter Six

Whether it really was the night air or perhaps only the excitement of the ball that was to blame, Katherine did not trouble to wonder, but when dawn filtered lazily through the dusty blue curtains at her window, she was already awake, having hardly closed her eyes at all. She sat up in bed, listening to the sounds of the house awakening.

The servants were already stirring, soft-footed, in the halls, and she knew the workmen were getting their breakfast in the big stone kitchen, preparing for another day of tearing down and propping up the neglected old house.

Unable to stand another hour or two of her own fevered reflections on the ball, she got out of bed shivering, for the mornings were still cool, and the vexatious fire that Tarrington had forced on her the night before was long since dead. On an impulse, she dressed in a made-over, amber velvet riding habit Sally had given her.

Katherine had not yet ridden alone, but she was so confident of her abilities that she felt she could very safely go just a little way by herself. There was a hillside only a mile or so away that had been tempting her to capture in her sketchbook, and it would be the very thing, she thought, to clear her head.

She stood before her dressing-table mirror and noted with satisfaction that she did not look nearly as bad as she felt.

Though there were shadows beneath her eyes, and she was pale, something of the glamour of the ball still hung about her. She twisted her hair up loosely and secured it with a ribbon before donning the tall, curly-brimmed riding hat, almost mannish but softened by its lace veil. Then she found the crop the earl had presented to her, and made her way quietly downstairs.

She managed to slip out of the house and out to the stables without attracting the notice of any of the servants, and luck remained with her, for instead of the eagle-eyed Thomas, who she knew would insist on accompanying her, she found only a recently hired, sleepy boy, who saddled the mare for her and did not protest when she stated her intention of riding out alone.

In a few minutes she was walking the mare down the drive, and once out on the road she broke into a trot, proud of her ease in the saddle. She knew she should not be riding unattended, but it was so very early that few people would be abroad, and therefore no one could be shocked to see Miss Amory riding alone through the countryside. Besides, she needed to be alone, to settle her thoughts, and to decide what to do now that she had offended Tarrington.

Despite her suspicions and fears, she had not wanted to make an enemy of him. But the interest he had shown last night—what could have been his intention? It could not be any honorable one, though she found it difficult to believe that he would suggest anything improper. It seemed impossible, as well as unpleasant, that he might have destined for her for an easy flirtation, or even something immeasurably worse. Poor and unprotected as she was, she might be seen as easy prey by any man who had mere dalliance in mind, but surely not by her own cousin, and an earl.

Katherine turned it all over in her mind, and half-concluded that she ought to try to be more conciliating today, still keeping him firmly at a distance nevertheless. She was not altogether satisfied with this decision, but it would serve until Tarrington did or said something to force another reaction from her.

The mare balked at a squirrel, but Katherine brought her attention back just in time to take her firmly in hand again, and soon they had reached the lane that led up the hillside. She had tucked her sketching materials into a saddlebag, but when she reached the top, the long expanse of good ground and the fresh morning air were too enticing, so instead of getting down, she kicked the mare into a canter and rode until she was breathless, with the wind in her ears and her eyes fixed on the feathers of mist as the sun burned them away. The mare seemed to enjoy the run as well, and though she had never ridden so hard alone, Katherine was too exhilarated to be frightened.

Too soon she came again to sloping ground, and to her relief the mare halted obediently at her signal. She took in the delightful view of the other green hills in the distance, the thick trees below, and a stream, a glittering line of silver, meandering away between them. Remembering what Thomas had told her about cooling her horse, she noted the poor beast's heaving sides, and turned around, guiding it back at a more sedate pace to where she had decided to do her sketching.

The spot, in the shelter of a very old oak with a trunk just made for an artist to lean against, looked out over the village, away from Whitfield. She slipped down and tied the reins loosely about the trunk. Then she set her pencil, pens, and ink carefully beside her in a notch between two roots and turned to a fresh sheet, but as so often before, her mind buzzed with problems and instead of capturing the village view as it revealed itself between wisps of fog, she found herself noting down once more the elements of her Plan.

It had begun during her uncle's last bout of illness, when everyone was sure he would soon die. Katherine had looked gloomily into the future and had seen nothing but poverty and boredom, a useless cramped little life in squalid rented rooms. Her mother would supplement their meager income by taking in sewing for as long as her strength would hold out, and she and her cousin would be reduced to doing housemaids' work, as well as the marketing and cooking. What leisure hours came their way would be devoted to re-reading their small collection of books, and, if she had managed to save enough pennies to buy paper and ink, in sketching, though she doubted they would make their home in any locale worth recording her impressions of.

Then there would always be the diversion of devising ways to extend the life of their wardrobes without appearing too threadbare. In short, it would be the constricted life of the shabby-genteel. She had lived it already, and dreaded its return. Not much better was the prospect of finding yet another relation to drudge for. Even Whitfield in its improved state was only a variation on that theme. No, the time had come for drastic action, and if it meant going into paid service, so be it.

The list grew under her pen, and she wrote so fast that she blotted her page and spilled drops of ink over the grass as she dipped her pen. "When the summer is over write again to Colonel Dawson" it began, and "Do not encourage Priscilla to be taken in by Lord Knolland" followed, right before "Make plan to save most of salary to set up house for Mama."

Katherine sat writing for a long time, her lower lip caught between her teeth, her mind filled with ideas and schemes to pull her family out of the cycle of their dull existence by the main force of her will, if necessary. She was oblivious to everything but the soft breeze on her cheek and the sunlight gilding the steeple of the village church.

Thus it was not surprising that she failed to hear the hoof-beats muffled by the thick grass, or the low voice uttering her name, or to notice anything until a shadow fell over her paper. Even then she was not startled, only looked up, annoyed, to see what had blocked her light.

Tarrington towered above her, his arms folded, his face like thunder.

His voice, however, was deceptively soft. "I don't recall ever telling you, Katherine, that you might ride Sally's mare alone.

160

I saw you from down there." He gestured to the path below. "There are rocks and rabbit holes here. You could have broken your neck, my girl."

His eyes were blazing, and he frowned not only with his mouth, but with his entire face, with alarming effect. Katherine's heart began to pound and her mouth went dry, almost as though she were a child who had been detected in some naughtiness. The thought sparked an answering anger in her, but before she could retort, he had reached down and pulled her swiftly to her feet with a single strong tug.

"Promise me that you will never again do something so foolish. Why did you not let the groom come with you?" he demanded. His face was so close that she could see the tips of his golden lashes glinting in the sun, and his eyes never left hers. "You should always be escorted, even if you had been riding all of your life."

She would have expected a flirtation or a smart set-down, after her insult last night, but never this plain and simple scold. She felt like a disobedient child under his chilling glare.

"I am not one of your simpering London misses who can't so much as stroll in the garden without some man to dance attendance on her," she said hotly. "You forget, my lord, that I am only an ordinary girl, with no position and no fortune, whose life is at her own disposal, or was, until *you* arrived to overthrow my plans."

Still holding her wrists, he drew her closer until she was almost against his chest. His eyes held hers, and there was still anger in their brownish-green depths, as well as some other emotion which Katherine was too agitated to distinguish.

"Can you really be such a fool?" he asked softly, "Do you persist in believing that simply because you have no fortune you must earn your bread as a governess?"

He laughed, and she felt his body moving against hers, which did nothing for her efforts at self-control. But with the laughter his mood changed. He scolded no more, and his voice became teasing.

"Silly little cousin Katherine," he said, loosing one of her hands, then tweaking a curl that had escaped from under her hat. "Don't you know what you were meant to be?"

Now Katherine was thoroughly frightened, and it seemed as if her pounding heart had climbed to choke off her very breath. All of her worst speculations were being proven, and along with her fear, she felt an overwhelming sadness, as if at the loss of something precious.

"Oh, yes, my lord," she cried, "I know all too well what I must do, though it is far from your offensive implication. I pray you will never again suggest such a thing. To believe anything but that I must learn to fend for myself, I would indeed have to be the fool you think me!"

Yet, to her own disgust, she could not force herself away from him. He still had one of her hands, and she knew that if she attempted to withdraw it he would let it go, but she could not even try.

She was shivering in the moist morning breeze, and there was an irresistible warmth radiating from him. She looked at him in mute desperation, and his eyes lit with a sudden flash of understanding.

"No, my dear," he whispered, sweeping a gentle hand over her head to push back her hat and smooth the tumbled curls out of her eyes. "I'm sorry. You're no fool. Perhaps it is I who am the fool. Yet I . . ."

Katherine was still trembling, and Tarrington was not unaffected by the sweet wonder in eyes turned up to his, or by the promise of her soft full lips, so tantalizingly close. But he resisted.

It was perhaps one of the hardest things he had ever done, considering how each shiver brought the softness of her body, its lushness covered but barely disguised by the close-fitting velvet habit, brushing against his. His blood had turned to flame from the first moment he had pulled her up against him, but somehow he overcame the desperate urge to crush her to him and sip the sweetness from that unkissed mouth.

162

He had been teacher to her before, and he longed to be her teacher in love as well, but his honor would not allow it. Her feelings towards him after last night, and her vehement rejection of his very delicate advance could scarcely be discounted. Katherine was ripe and ready for his touch, but he could not bear the prospect of having her pull away and denounce him as a seducer and manipulator. If he did not restrain himself now, he told himself, there would never again be another chance to prove to her that she was wrong.

To Katherine it seemed an eternity in which she was lost in a dream, staring into a pair of hazel eyes slowly shading to green in the rising light of morning, speaking a language she did not quite understand. There was a thrilling and unfamiliar tension in the bare inch of space between their two bodies, moving closer with every breath and every trembling moment. She was painfully aware of his lips, firm and masculine and very close to hers, and from being cold she suddenly went to feeling very warm indeed.

But all at once it was over, as if it had never been, and the sense of loss was so sharp that Katherine almost cried out. Abruptly he let go of her hands, and with one step back he destroyed the delicate, shimmering link that had joined them to each other for one moment out of time.

Tarrington was once again His Lordship, slightly disapproving, brotherly, and self-possessed. "Have I frightened you, Kate?" He smiled, a little stiffly, as if he were forcing his features to assume the correct expression. "You were very wrong to ride out alone, but I apologize for, perhaps, being a little too harsh with you. I know you have not been used to considering yourself as a lady in every sense of the word as it is used in polite society, but I suggest that you begin to do so. Now that you have been introduced to people, your prospects are not so bleak as you think them."

He stifled the beginnings of her protest by going on. "I hope you do not forget all of your eager partners last night. Do you see? That is all I meant, my dear." By the time he had finished

163

and put some distance between them, he almost believed it himself.

Katherine struggled to regain her composure. For a long moment she had forgotten why she had been angry with him. It almost seemed as if the entire episode had sprung from her own imagination. There was certainly none of the vile seducer in *that* speech, she thought.

Her mind in confusion, her peace thoroughly cut up, she could not try to sketch with any degree of comfort, especially with Tarrington still looming over her. So she packed everything away and allowed him to help her remount the mare.

His hands seemed to linger for a moment on her waist after she was settled in her saddle, but when she glanced quickly at him his face was empty of that alarming intensity that had filled it when he had first pulled her to her feet. In fact, it was distressingly impassive.

"I don't wish to interrupt your ride, my lord," she said, gathering up her reins. "I can find my way back to Whitfield."

"Alas, I have been quite ineffective, when I thought that I had delivered the most thundering scold," he replied, but his voice was only impatient. "No, I shall certainly escort you back . . . or perhaps . . ."—for the first time, she noticed a hint of uncertainty—"perhaps you would like to ride with me if you are not too fatigued."

Katherine was surprised to find that despite everything, she very much wanted to ride with him. Something told her that he would say no more odd things to her that day, and that the few seconds of delicious confusion, which she was now ready to admit she had probably imagined, would never be repeated.

"I should enjoy that," she replied, and nudged her horse up beside his.

As she had thought, his behavior from that moment on was calculated to put her at ease, except for the moments when he reverted to riding instructor and called out sharp comments regarding her management of the mare, which despite her fine bloodlines and upbringing on the finest fodder, was all too prone to eat grass when she could get away with it.

Tarrington led the way down the hill and onto the road where he finally allowed his pupil to have a good gallop, until he signalled her to slow down at last, and they turned back towards Whitfield at a sedate trot.

He was barely winded himself, but Katherine had ridden almost to the limit of her strength, so at the entrance to the gravelled drive they slowed to a walk.

Katherine's cheeks were pinker than he had ever seen them. Her hair, which she had stuffed quickly under her hat, had escaped again, and the hat itself threatened to topple off her head. Her lips, when they were not parting for her rapid breaths, were rosy and smiling.

Tarrington was unable to restrain himself from reaching out a hand to her, but instead of stroking her cheek, he made himself pat her hand instead. She was so flushed and invigorated that she almost did not notice.

"You are a fine natural horsewoman," he told her. "But as yet your endurance does not match your skill. I think we should practice a bit every day, until you are able to go as far as you like without becoming too tired."

For a second Katherine's heart fluttered at the thought of it, but soon anxiety replaced elation. Still, no matter what the danger to her heart and mind, she could not bear to deprive herself of his company. If not Tarrington, then she would have to ride with a groom, and the prospect did not please her at all.

Very soon, she assured herself, she would regain control over those feelings that had almost overwhelmed her today. She reminded herself that she was above all a practical, sensible young woman, and that there was no room in her life for these distracting fancies. Ride with him she would, and nothing more.

As she assented to the proposal, it occurred to her that perhaps she would also be able to discover more about the earl's strange comings and goings and acquaintances. That alone, she decided, should be daunting enough to keep her from becoming too interested in the other distractions of his companionship.

If he was disappointed at her lukewarm reaction, he did not show it. When they reached the house, he helped her down briskly and, tossing the reins to Thomas, who shook his head reproachfully at Katherine, he accompanied her into the breakfast parlor.

The entire family was present, even Lord Knolland, who looked none the worse for not having had the use of his own razor or the attentions of the excellent Finster. Sally and Lady Tarrington were making ready to return to Grouse Hall, from whence they would set out in a few days for Bath, having accepted an invitation to stay with some friends there.

Sally complained of the dullness of it. "Bath is so stuffy, full of nothing but army pensioners and vulgar encroaching shop-keepers. I'm sure there will be no one at all amusing there at this time of year."

"Do you include your husband in this collection of boring people, my love?" inquired her mother with a smile. "I suppose you forget that he is to join you in a fortnight."

Sally giggled. "Of course not, Mama. I did not mean . . . But I should prefer to have our reunion in the country. Richard is even less fond of Bath than I am. However, I want Katherine and Priscilla and Aunt Delia to meet him. Would you do us the honor of coming to Pensley for a few weeks in the autumn, ma'am?" she asked Mrs. Amory.

"What? . . . Oh, yes, thank you . . . so very kind . . ." Mrs. Amory, who had sat silent and pale all through breakfast, eating little, swayed in her seat.

"Mama, what is it?"

"Aunt Delia!"

Katherine and Priscilla leaped to her assistance, calling for burnt feathers and waving a vinaigrette under her nose. Tarrington disappeared for a minute, then returned with brandy, which he poured and himself held to Mrs. Amory's lips.

She gasped and choked on a sip of it. "It is nothing . . . only perhaps I shouldn't have risen so early after last night," she said faintly, closing her eyes, her face drawn and alarmingly grey about the lips. She seemed to breathe with difficulty, and pressed one hand to her chest.

"We must get you up to bed immediately, Delia," Lady Tarrington said firmly. "Indeed, I told you it was unnecessary for you to come down this morning only to bid us goodbye. We would have come to your room."

When Mrs. Amory was settled in bed, propped on several pillows, Lady Tarrington surreptitiously felt her pulse, and leaving her in the care of Priscilla and one of the housemaids, gestured Katherine out of the room.

"I don't wish to frighten you, my dear, but I think we should call in the apothecary immediately, or even a doctor if one can be found. Her pulse is very rapid and weak, and I don't like her color or her breathing."

Katherine thanked her and rushed to give orders that Mr. Gunn, who oversaw the health of the neighborhood, should be sent for.

The rest of the day was spent in waiting on Mrs. Amory, who seemed to grow weaker and struggled for breath, and after she had been examined by Mr. Gunn, everyone gathered in the sitting room to hear his impressions.

Lady Tarrington and her daughter had refused to leave until they could be assured of Mrs. Amory's recovery. The earl, once he found that his assistance was unnecessary, had remained discreetly but comfortingly in the background, ready to relay messages and orders, or to procure anything necessary for the invalid. Lord Knolland alternated between offering incoherent but gratefully received reassurances to Priscilla, and pacing the drawing room until Lady Tarrington sent him out of the house, for the resultant squeaking of the floorboards drove them all to distraction.

The two gentlemen came in just before Mr. Gunn began to speak, and the earl sat beside Katherine, and squeezed her hand reassuringly. She was too worried to do more than glance at him. Her own problems had been quite driven from her head by this alarming attack of her mother's. Though Mrs. Amory had always been easily fatigued, she had never experienced such severe symptoms, especially after a period of improved health, and it was frightening. She exchanged a worried look with Priscilla, who sat twisting her handkerchief.

"Your mother is out of danger for now, Miss Amory," Mr. Gunn told her, sipping gratefully at a cup of tea, and rummaging in a plate of little cakes. "But her condition warrants a consultation with a good physician. As far as I can make out her ailment is not a fever, but a chronic weakness of the heart. I have given her a draught to relieve the pressure and will send over some pills which I will make up, but if possible, she ought to go to London, or perhaps Bath. Yes," he mused, munching on bread and butter, having demolished two of the cakes with incredible speed. "I should take her to Bath, if I were you, miss. I have seen many cases greatly improved by a water cure. I can recommend a very good physician there."

"But she was feeling so well, and had so much more energy of late," said Priscilla, squinting with tearful eyes at the apothecary. "Why is she suddenly so ill?"

The rotund little man frowned and, making a steeple of the tips of his fingers, stared balefully through it.

"Perhaps it was only a temporary stimulation, caused by a felicitous change in situation." He gave a half-bow to Lady Tarrington. Like everyone else, he had heard of the arrival of the earl and his family at Whitfield. "However, this imbued her with a false confidence, and I am afraid that she overreached her strength."

"She went to Mrs. Littleton's ball with us last night, and got up early this morning, though we warned her to stay in bed," Sally admitted.

"Ah, that, no doubt, would have precipitated it," he concluded sagely. Having finished his tea, he bowed to all of them and left, the earl following him into the hall.

"Bath!" Katherine was saying as Tarrington came back into the room. "I only hope we can manage it. Even with my legacy, though to be sure a hundred pounds is more than I had ever looked to have—will it be enough to hire lodgings, and a servant, and the services of the physician?"

"Why, Miss Amory," Lord Knolland interrupted her, "a hundred pounds is not so very much—why, it would not bring you more than one good riding horse."

"Oh, hush, my lord!" Sally scolded him, and he subsided, red-faced.

Katherine looked accusingly up at the earl. "Mr. Gunn's fee—" she began.

Tarrington frowned. "Do not speak of it, Cousin Katherine. While your mother remains in my house I shall see to such expenses. After all," he said, his face softening, "it is at my request that she is here, instead of being already in Bath."

"That is it," cried Katherine, astonished that it had not occurred to her immediately. "Colonel Dawson! I shall write to him immediately. Perhaps he will take only me and Priscilla, and our wages might be enough to cover Mama's cure. If he will but give her a room, when she is better, she can—"

"No!" Tarrington said sharply, startling everyone.

Katherine glared at him. His assumption of authority was having a salutary effect. At that moment she quite forgot that she had ever considered him anything but overbearing.

"It is not necessary," he said coolly, "for you to take up your positions at Colonel Dawson's. In fact, with your mother ill, it would be most unsuitable."

Katherine was about to inquire coldly if he had any better suggestion when Lady Tarrington spoke.

"Of course it would be unsuitable, especially when we are going to Bath anyway. With a little contriving, it will all be settled. We shall not stay with the Brocktons, Sally," she told

169

her daughter, who grinned at Katherine and Priscilla. "We shall take a house ourselves, and Mrs. Amory and the girls will stay with us. There, it is all settled."

The earl, smiling, went to his mother and kissed her hand. Katherine and Priscilla looked at each other, full of hope for a moment, but Katherine said, "Oh ma'am, I am very grateful of course, but how could I allow you to—"

"Hush, child, no nonsense," said Lady Tarrington. "Of course you will be our guests. We feel partly responsible, after all, for as Vane admitted if it weren't for our selfish desire to have you stay here your mama would have been at Colonel Dawson's close to the waters and the physicians, and no doubt she would never have exerted herself enough for this to happen in the first place. It was my silly idea to take her jaunting about with me that caused it."

"Oh, no, my lady," cried Priscilla. "She was so happy to be among people again, and she was so pleased, she told me, to see Katherine and me dance at the ball last night. I am sure she felt nothing but gratitude to you for introducing her to the neighborhood."

Katherine, realizing that this was the only chance to restore her mother to health, resigned herself to being beholden to her cousins and thanked them quietly. "However," she said uncertainly, "there is still the matter of the treatment . . . if it should take a long time . . . and I could not go to Colonel Dawson and leave Mama and Priscilla alone . . . would my hundred pounds be enough, do you think?"

"I should hope it would!" cried Sally. "After all, Bath waters are not precisely champagne, and the doctors fees—"

"Keep your hundred pounds, Katherine," her brother said at the same time.

Katherine looked from one to the other, and finally the earl hushed his sister, and continued. "Please allow me to assume the expense of your mother's care. You should not be deprived of your only inheritance. I assure you, I would be seriously displeased if you did not permit me to do this."

He did already look very displeased, with his sandy brows drawn together and his mouth quite serious. Suspecting what she did about his circumstances, she could only be overwhelmed by the offer.

She met his eyes, and saw that they were full of concern, and that though he was stern, there was not a hint of the old arrogance about him. For that moment he seemed only to want to be of assistance, and her heart swelled. Why, she wondered irritably, did he have to be such a friend to her when she was desperately trying to find reasons not to like him?

"You are . . . you are too good, my lord." Katherine faltered and had to look away, but it was enough.

Lord Knolland, at first unhappy at the prospect of bidding a premature adieu to the object of his admiration, brightened immediately.

"That's famous," he said in a relieved voice, smiling at Priscilla. "The Bath physicians are first-rate. At least, my grandfather always said so. Kept him alive till ninety. Just the thing for Mrs. Amory. She'll be in plump currant again before you know it," he assured Katherine. "In fact, had a thought of going to Bath myself. Haven't been there in an age." He cast a sidelong glance at Priscilla, who gave him a brief, shy smile.

"Daresay we could find something to amuse us; assembly rooms, concerts, you know, while the ladies wait for the cure to take effect." He looked hopefully at Tarrington, who was regarding him with fond amusement.

Sally was the first to reply, and could not resist teasing him. "You, my lord, in Bath? Why, I've never heard anything so absurd. Whatever would you do with yourself there? Don't tell me you would actually go for a stroll in the pump room every morning?" She dissolved into giggles, and the others had to smile as they pictured it.

Rodney, however, recalling his near failure at the ball the night before, was just clever enough to know that Bath out of season was likely to be the one place where he could be sure of no rivals for Priscilla's affection. "Nothing absurd about it," he defended himself. He screwed up his face and put a hand to his stomach. "Fact is, not feeling so stout myself just lately. Shouldn't be surprised if the waters wouldn't do some good as well."

"Very well, Rodney, come to Bath and be our guest," said Lady Tarrington, suppressing a laugh. "But I warn you, the waters won't be at all to your taste."

"Doesn't matter," Lord Knolland replied, looking at Priscilla. "I'm sure I'll find something that is."

Sally hid her smile behind her hand, and Lady Tarrington looked indulgent, but Katherine found herself distinctly annoyed. Priscilla had no hope of making a good marriage, any more than she herself did, and it was high time everyone stopped trying to encourage her to believe in a dream.

It occurred to her that she must cease postponing the serious talk she had meant to have with Lord Knolland. When the earl announced his intention of escorting his mother and sister back to Grouse Hall, where they planned to write letters to Lady Brockton begging her pardon for failing to keep their engagement in Bath, she detained Lord Knolland.

"If you please, my lord, I should like to have a word with you."

He started guiltily, and withdrew his glance from the retreating figure of Priscilla. "Oh! certainly. At your service, Miss Amory."

He stood, shifting his weight like a nervous horse, until she had crossed the room and reseated herself opposite his chair. Then he sank unsteadily down again, mechanically working a finger beneath his collar.

Katherine had to smile. "Don't be frightened, I'm not going to eat you! It is only . . . well, I could not help but notice that you seem to be paying very particular attentions to my cousin, my lord."

Lord Knolland blinked his round blue eyes. "She's a deuced fine girl, Miss Amory! Sorry, I ought to watch this tongue of mine, but I suppose you get my meaning. Thing is, never met anyone I've admired more than Miss Townsend."

His resemblance to a pleading puppy softened her some-what, but she knew she must carry on for the sake of Priscilla's welfare.

"I shall be honest with you, my lord, if you will do me the favor of being equally honest."

"Of course!"

"I have reason to believe," she said, recalling her cousin's glowing face, "that she would not be averse . . . that is, she seems to welcome your attentions." She lifted a hand to prevent him from breaking into eager speech before she had done. "But I pray you will take something into consideration, for I fear you are already in danger of trifling with her feelings."

Lord Knolland stoutly avowed that he would never dream of doing such a thing.

"Not intentionally, no. I would not accuse you of it," she told him. "But the plain facts are these. Priscilla has even less than I. She was left an orphan, totally dependent on my mother, with no other living relations, and not a penny of her own."

His lordship's face fell, but he said with an attempt at manly pride, "See here, Miss Amory, I ain't one of your fortune hunters. Stands to reason she wouldn't have stayed here living under the thumb of that old humgudgeon—beg pardon, Sir Edwin—if she'd had the blunt to set herself up in style. But I have to admit, it comes hard to learn that she's without a cent. My trustees won't like that, not a bit." He sighed, and ran a hand through his already disheveled locks.

"Your trustees, my lord?" Katherine asked. She had not thought it quite so complicated. "I wish you would tell me about your situation," she invited.

"You see," he said, getting up and beginning to pace, "my uncles hold the purse strings, Miss Amory, until I'm married, and only with their approval. It's all because we've had a couple of loose screws in the family, ran off with the daughters of shopkeepers, adventuresses, opera-dancers—well, you realize it ain't at all the thing for a marquess to do."

173

"Indeed," she agreed, keeping her composure with difficulty.

"Before my papa wound up his accounts—liver, you know—he determined that I wouldn't follow that path. Not that it's a great fortune. No more than comfortable, you understand, but there's the title and that barn of a place in Northamptonshire, and one or two other . . . well the jist of it is . . ." Here the bleakness of his future overcame him, and he halted before her to drop into his chair again, rubbing his temples energetically.

"I'm doomed, Miss Amory, doomed to a life of solitude and poverty," he pronounced. "Those uncles of mine are such high sticklers that practically no one but a duke's daughter would do for them. Doomed, that's what I am."

Katherine fought to maintain a dignified expression and begged him not to despair.

"You are talking foolishness, my lord," she said in an attempt to be bracing, though she pitied him and her cousin both. "I'm sorry to say that Priscilla's connections, though respectable, would probably not appeal to your uncle's sense of position, but there will undoubtedly be another young lady who does, someday."

"Respectable, yes," he said, and raised his head from his hands, regarding her anxiously. "But she ain't connected to any tradesman or anything of that sort? Only tell me that, and there may yet be hope."

"No, of course not, silly," Katherine replied without thinking. Already he seemed like a foolish younger brother in need of her guidance. He took no offense, but only begged her to tell him of Priscilla's family.

"Well, her mother was my mother's younger sister. And *their* father was a general, and their mother was the daughter of a baronet, but that line has died out. Priscilla's father, alas, was only a country clergyman, with little fortune and no family. In fact, he went through Oxford on scholarship and—"

Lord Knolland uttered a groan which stopped her. "No, no.

It won't do, it just won't do. Not a viscount, or an earl or any such thing among 'em?"

She shook her head.

"I'm doomed," he repeated. He sat quietly for a moment, expressing his anguish only in sighs, while Katherine sought for words to comfort both him and Priscilla, with whom she planned to have the next interview.

"An earl," he muttered. Suddenly he looked up. "There is one hope," he said, looking at her with interest.

"What might that be?" Katherine was almost ready to giggle. He was so absurd in his extremity that she couldn't help it.

"Miss Townsend ain't well connected now," he admitted, "but she could be."

"Whatever do you mean?" Katherine wondered if he had finally lost what little sense he seemed to have.

"Well, if *you* was to marry someone my uncles couldn't take exception to, then they couldn't object to Miss Townsend, because she's your cousin!" he said triumphantly.

"Not, my lord, that I should balk at anything when it comes to obliging you," she said gently, fearing for his sanity, "but how do you suppose I am going to induce a duke to offer for me, when I have only a hundred pounds to my name, and am not well connected myself?"

"Oh, it needn't be a duke," Lord Knolland assured her, a grin spreading across his face. "An earl would do quite as well, you know. And luckily, we have one to hand. Tarrington's always been a great favorite with my uncles. In fact, he's the only one of my friends they approve of, even though the scandal took them aback a bit, but all in all—"

"But my lord," Katherine sputtered in indignation, "do you seriously believe *I* could marry the Earl of Tarrington? And what is this about a scandal?"

"Oh, nothing to signify, though very sad, to be sure." He shrugged it off. "But whyever shouldn't you? You like him, don't you . . . and I'm sure he must like you or else why would he still be here?" He gazed up at her innocently.

"Why indeed?" said Katherine coldly. She stood up. "Lord Knolland, I regret that if this is the only way I can help you obtain your trustees' approval to marry my cousin, then I must decline. I beg you will put this fanciful notion of marrying me to Lord Tarrington quite out of your head. I assure you, nothing could be more unlikely."

"Beg pardon, Miss Amory." Lord Knolland leaped to his feet and took her hand to pat it reassuringly. "No doubt I frightened you by mentioning the scandal. Please let me explain."

Slowly she sat down again, and nodded her acquiescence. Though Knolland's idea was, of course, absurd, she admitted to some curiosity about the alleged scandal, and wondered if it had anything to do with Tarrington's present activities.

"It all had to do with his marriage, you see."

"Marriage?" Katherine's eyes flew to his face in momentary shock.

Lord Knolland twitched uncomfortably. "Not exactly sworn to secrecy on it, but . . . promise you won't let on that I told you?"

She promised impatiently. "Go on, please do my lord!"

"You didn't know he had been married? Well, no one likes to remind him. . . . Three years ago he was wed to my sister Cassandra." Knolland's face grew serious. "Led him a merry chase, she did. Too hot for any man to handle, maybe. Anyway"—he sighed—"she died in an accident, a stupid curricle race. Vane tried to forbid her of course, but"—he shook his head—"no one could say her nay when she'd set her heart on something. Aye, and plenty of heart she had, too."

"Oh, I—I'm so sorry, my lord," Katherine whispered. "I only wish I had known." She immediately wondered why she had said that, for how could it have made any difference in her dealings with the earl? Perhaps he was still in love with the memory of his wife, she thought, and then rejected that idea. He didn't look to be wearing the willow for anyone. In fact, he seemed perfectly content as he was. But what was so scandalous about the situation? she wondered, though admittedly racing a curricle did not seem quite the proper behavior for a countess.

Her companion obliged her before she could ask. "And then poor Vane was so crushed—all about in his head. For a year he stayed secluded at Northfolde and would receive no one, and—" He stopped, and suddenly realized that he would not make the proposition of marriage to his friend any more attractive if he mentioned the financial distress occasioned by Vane's overwhelming grief. "Well, eventually we managed to bring him out of it. He's over it now," he assured her.

Katherine looked at him sharply, and he returned her gaze with unflinching innocence, but she suspected that there was far more to it than he was telling. Yet, recalling his behavior since she had known him, perhaps it was only something embarrassing that loyalty to his friend would not permit him to reveal.

Lord Knolland interrupted this train of thought. "So you'll think about it, then?" he begged, brightening once more. "You needn't think I won't do my part," he assured her. "All it needs is for me to drop a hint or two of your tendre for him."

"What tendre?" Katherine rose abruptly, and felt her face crimsoning. "Upon my word, this is going too far! I beg you will do no such thing, my lord. I am very sorry, of course, that your situation prevents you from offering for Priscilla, but this absurd plan of yours is *not* the solution!"

His lordship looked crestfallen. "Of course, Miss Amory, if you feel that way . . . only a suggestion. Damme if it wouldn't work, too," he muttered.

"Why then, my lord, I suppose you would be damned, for nothing could be more unlikely," she said, losing all patience with him. "I wish you would abandon this ridiculous and fantastic notion. And please make an effort not to encourage my poor cousin. It will only make things more painful for both of you."

She stalked out of the drawing room, and his voice trailed

behind her.

"What's fantastic about it? Nothing could be plainer. . . ."

It was not difficult, in the days that followed, for Katherine to avoid Lord Knolland and the earl, because she spent most of her time in attendance on her mother, first in her bedchamber, and then, when she was well enough to get up, by her side in the garden with her embroidery.

It had never before seemed so dull, and soon she resorted to her sketchbook, drawing her cousin seated on the grass playing with a kitten, roses blooming in the background. Then she began a watercolor of the newly planted flower beds, clear of weeds for the first time since they had come to Whitfield.

By now the house had begun to regain some of its former grandeur. Though there was still a long way to go before both wings and the main hall were completely restored, and the gardeners had made only a start on the tangled growth, Whitfield was decidedly improved. With the disappearance of shabbiness had gone the memories of Sir Edwin's irritable, clutch-fisted ways, and the loneliness that had been their daily lot.

Neighbors now came to call on the invalid, assuring her that a sojourn in Bath would be the very thing, and young ladies who had been there told Katherine and Priscilla about the shops and circulating libraries, but warned them of the over-abundance of elderly men and the dearth of young handsome ones.

Altogether they were so well occupied that Katherine hardly missed the two gentlemen, whom they saw only at dinner. Lord Knolland had honored her request and had ceased to pay quite so much attention to Priscilla, though she often saw him looking yearningly in her direction.

Poor Priscilla was at a loss to know what she had done to deserve this desertion, but Katherine had not the heart to tell her that her hero was hampered by her lack of fortune, and she postponed indefinitely the talk she had meant to have with her cousin.

She will soon be distracted enough in Bath, Katherine thought, and it is better that she think him fickle than that she believe him no better than a fortune hunter. She even began to hope that Lord Knolland would not accompany them after all, but, seeming to have no other intention but to torture himself, he made no mention of any other plans.

So far she had not yet had to face Tarrington alone. Katherine only hoped that his well-meaning but foolish friend had not mentioned the marriage scheme to him. Though she had not forgotten about her promise to ride with him in the mornings, she had the excuse of her mother's illness to save her from a tête-à-tête, and she was vastly relieved. Even the thought of it, after Lord Knolland's embarrassing assumption of her "tendre," was enough to cause her face to burn.

On their last day but one at Whitfield, she rose early, hoping to have her breakfast quickly and then do her last-minute packing before the earl came down. Unfortunately, he was the sole occupant of the breakfast parlor when she entered.

"Good morning, Katherine. I haven't seen very much of you lately. Under the circumstances, though, I forgive you for breaking our engagement to ride in the mornings." He regarded her cheerfully enough over his bacon.

"Oh, my lord, I was sure you had forgotten it. I'm sorry if I inconvenienced you." She concentrated stonily on her coffee, after risking a brief glance at him. He was still smiling.

"Not at all. I merely rode alone. But you must promise to ride with me later. I'm sure Priscilla can sit with your mother for an hour."

Katherine prayed, not for the first time, that Lord Knolland had not spoken to him, and considered refusing, but knew it would be churlish, after all the assistance he had given her family. Not that we asked for it, she fumed inwardly.

He finished his breakfast and left to make a last inspection of the repairs, and Katherine did not see him again until later,

179

when he sent a maid to the sitting room to ask her if she was ready to ride. She sent the reply that she would be at the stables in twenty minutes, and excused herself, ignoring the curious glances of her mother and cousin.

Lord Knolland, who had been sitting with them and reading, at Mrs. Amory's request, very haltingly from Shakespeare, looked up, winking and nodding encouragingly. He turned a page in the big volume, and a mischievous grin spread over his face.

"'This bud of love, by summer's ripening breath, May prove a beauteous flower when next we meet,'" he quoted, mightily pleased with himself.

Mrs. Amory looked up, puzzled. "I am sure that is not right, my lord. Are we not still in Act One?"

Katherine spared a moment to glare at him before she went. "'Bud of love,'" indeed! He must be totally witless if he thought that she would entertain his absurd suggestion. She only hoped he had not been as candid about his plan to Tarrington. If the earl ever found out, she was sure she would die of shame.

When she had put on another of Sally's made-over riding habits, this one of slate gray with burgundy braid trimming, and a fetching white lawn ruffle at the neck, she went to the stables to find both the mare saddled and her riding companion ready as well. He was dressed more casually than she had ever seen him, in a tobacco-brown riding jacket, worn buckskins, less than glossy top-boots and, of all things a spotted kerchief tied casually about his throat. He waited, slapping his crop against his muscular thigh.

For a moment she stopped and stared, but he misinterpreted her surprise. "You are wondering how my restless sister can bear to do without her new horse for so long. Rest assured that she has as many horses as she can ride at the Hall, but no time to ride them as I am sure she is busy packing and writing letters to all of her acquaintances. Never fear, she and her mount will be reunited in Bath. I'll have one of my grooms ride the mare while you ladies travel stylishly by chaise."

"Of course," Katherine murmured, but recovering, and thankful that this offhandedness must indicate a complete ignorance of Lord Knolland's plans, she said, "I am not surprised to see your sister's horse still here, for she told me of it herself, but it is just that your . . ." Her eyes were mesmerized by the spotted kerchief. She had never seen a gentleman wear one, though she knew, of course, that some men affected such a studied carelessness in their dress. She had often heard her uncle deplore such mannerisms. "Can't think what's gotten into them all, aping their grooms and coachmen," he would grumble.

He saw her expression and laughed. "Come now, cousin, admit you are impressed. I am told that the ladies find this style quite captivating. No, really, pray don't be insulted that I have not put on my best for you. It is only that most of my clothes are packed away by now, and Skempton, my valet, would hand in his notice if I disturbed his arrangement, though in truth it made him almost ill to see me go out dressed like this."

"You mistake me, my lord, I . . . I rather like it," she said. With his starched neckcloth he seemed to have discarded some of the starch in his nature. He looked younger, she thought, his hair tousled by the stiff breeze that had blown up, his face relaxed, his eyes glowing unmistakably as he took in her appearance. No, he had most decidedly not been speaking to Lord Knolland about her.

"I'm glad you approve." He waved away the groom and tossed her into the saddle himself.

They headed, as if by silent agreement, to the hilltop where they had met that morning—barely a week ago, Katherine was astonished to recall. Her feelings towards the earl had undergone so many changes since then that it was as though they were two different people entirely. Now that she knew of his tragedy, pity was uppermost in her emotions. But from what she had learned of his character she knew it would be a mistake to show it. Simple kindness would suffice.

181

They rode in companionable silence for a while, Katherine preoccupied with these thoughts and with her mother's illness and their forthcoming trip to Bath. It occurred to her that, once her mother had recovered and her own plans could be carried out, she might never see Whitfield again, and despite the unhappy years there, it saddened her. But perhaps, she told herself, it was not Whitfield she was going to miss once she had become governess to the Dawson children.

Tarrington was equally distracted, and Katherine, glancing at him now and then, got the impression that he was almost on the point of saying something, but kept biting back the words before he could utter them.

It began to intrigue her, so in spite of her intention to be kind in light of his loss, she could not resist inquiring, when they reined to a stop at the summit, "You haven't been troubled by any business appointments lately. Is it possible your affairs will allow you to stay in Bath with us?"

In fact, his affairs were not proceeding as planned. After the visit to Mr. Smith, the next step in his search had turned out to be more difficult than he had imagined. The man he must see was proving surprisingly elusive, not so surprisingly, Tarrington reminded himself, considering the treatment he'd received from him before he'd known who he was.

He wondered if it were simple disinclination for his company, or something more. On both occasions when he had visited, his quarry was said to be not at home. He had gone so far as to leave a note, discreet but pointed, regarding his business, to no avail. It's my own fault, he grumbled to himself. I've scared the fellow off. It was frustrating, so close had he thought himself to his goal.

Perhaps, he thought, it would not be too dangerous to take his cousin partially into his confidence. Though it would no doubt be distasteful to her, she might be able to help.

"Unfortunately," he belatedly replied to her question, "the trip to Bath will hold up my business for a little while, as I must transact the greater part of it between here and London, but I do not begrudge the time." He dismounted, and reached up for her, smiling. "I believe I am entitled to some amusement on occasion."

She was startled to hear him talk of his business so casually, after all his evasions, and could not help pressing for more details.

"I hope, my lord, that your accompanying us does not cause you to miss a favorable opportunity. Is it that you are trying to dispose of some property?" she ventured, while she still had the courage. It seemed logical enough, for a man who did not appear to be very prosperous.

To her utter surprise, he only smiled again. "How clever you are to have guessed it, Katherine. Yes, I have been unlucky in my investments, ever since . . . a personal misfortune a few years ago. I was forced to sell my father's collection of paintings and *objets d'art*." He walked his horse a few steps and looked out over the village.

"In fact, I was wondering if you could be of some help. I hear there is someone in the neighborhood who is an avid collector, and I had wondered if I would meet him, but he hasn't presented himself here with the other neighbors."

For a moment Katherine simply stared. Was this the sum of the enigma? Though she had suspected him of suffering an embarrassment, somehow this admission made it all seem quite dull. After all the secrecy . . . though, to be sure, it was not a thing he would want to advertise to all the world. And suddenly he wanted her help. She knew, of course, of whom he was speaking.

"Why, you have met him already," she began, and recalling the circumstances, looked away from him. Though that mortifying scene in the shrouded sitting room seemed to have occurred a hundred years ago, she did not like to remind him of it. "He is Mr. Oldbury, my erstwhile suitor. I—I believe you have already been treated to a show of his expertise," she said slyly, looking at him only through her lowered lashes, to see how he would react.

The earl gave every appearance of one searching for an elusive memory. "Ah, yes . . . the admirer of Balsini. Shockingly clumsy fellow. However, I daresay that footstool wasn't up to his weight. How fortunate for you both that such a commodious sofa was at hand."

A wicked grin spread over his face, and Katherine blushed. She should have known that he would not forget a single detail of her embarrassing incident—nor allow her to.

But he seemed inclined to laugh at it now, for which she was thankful.

"Between us we have probably scared him so badly that I doubt he could be persuaded to come and look at any of your art," she ventured, watching his face anxiously. "Perhaps Mama will assist us. He has always been a favorite with her. If she will write him a note, he might consent to come to you at Northfolde when you return from Bath."

"I should be very grateful if she would. But he need not come so far as Northfolde, and I would like to finish it while I am still in the neighborhood. I have several things right here at Grouse Hall which might interest him. It has been in the family almost as long, in fact, as our seat. My father spent a good deal of time there, and liked to have his things around him."

The horses were fresh, and made it clear to their riders in no uncertain terms that all this standing about on a beautiful summer day when the grassy hilltop called was quite unacceptable. So without more ado they abandoned their conversation and with the earl in the lead, rode a long sloping path that wound down the hill and into a wood, where Katherine found the cool shade most welcome after the sun beating down on her kerseymere-clad back.

The path was stippled with the sunlight breaking through the thick leaves, and the wood smelled deliciously of summer, almost chasing away the memories of the cold winds of March. A brook chattered close by, the sound not quite muffled by the clop of their horses' hooves, and ahead Katherine could see patches of blue sky above and a green meadow below them in the breaks between the trees.

The path widened momentarily, and Katherine, intent on enjoying the day and the ride, passed Tarrington, laughingly ignoring his protests. He called to her to slow down, but she kept on, even though the path soon narrowed and began to be littered with fallen trees and undergrowth. Still, she persisted in running the mare over every patch of clear ground.

With a really good stretch before her, she had settled into a comfortable canter, feeling so confident that the sight of a huge log lying across her way did not unsettle her in the least. She determined to jump her horse, though she had never done such a thing, and urged the animal on, when it would have slowed.

But at the last moment, the mare, knowing better than her rider, balked and refused the jump, swinging her haunches up and to the right, catapulting Katherine out of the saddle, to land, luckily, in a stand of wild shrubs.

The earl was off his horse in a moment, and at her side.

"My God, Katherine!" he cried, and she opened her eyes, only slightly dazed and short of wind, to see his face, white and drawn, above her. His eyes had deepened into a woody brown, and the lines around his mouth were suddenly more pronounced than ever.

She felt his fingers probing her head, and then her neck, working their way feverishly down her body. "Does this pain you?" He pressed and prodded, until finally, frightened by her fall and his touches, she struggled to sit up.

"No . . . please, my lord, I'm fine. Really, you must not—"

"Lie down again, at least until you're not giddy."

"But I'm not giddy now. Please . . ."

At last, convinced that she had broken no bones, he let her sit up, but supported her on his shoulder.

"You silly little fool. What made you think you could jump her?" His voice was harsher than she had ever heard it, and it made her shiver.

"It was only a little log," she had to protest.

The earl got up abruptly, leaving Katherine to support herself as best she could by leaning back on her elbows, and she winced at the soreness of the hip and shoulder on which she had landed. Tarrington went quietly to the mare, making soothing noises until she stood still and allowed him to take her reins. He peered over the log.

"That may have been only a log, you stubborn girl, but there was a huge pit on the other side of it, screened by fallen branches. Sally's poor horse would have broken her forelegs, and you your head, if she had not had the intelligence to prevent you."

Katherine had managed to get to her feet, and stood swaying with dizziness and anger. "I admit that it was poor judgment on my part, my lord, but you needn't go on scolding so! One would think that I was a wayward schoolgirl. There, I promise never to do it again." She choked on a sob, but recovered herself enough to scowl fiercely at him, breathing heavily, the color beginning to return to her face.

He led the mare back to her, and stood very close, returning her angry look, until she finally dropped her eyes in shame, knowing of course that she had been wrong. She shivered as she recalled Lord Knolland's description of Tarrington's late wife. How cruel of her to put him through such a fright, after he had lost his countess through just such headstrong risk-taking!

"I beg your pardon, my lord," she said softly, unable to meet his eyes again. "I did not mean to frighten you. I honestly thought I could do it."

As she spoke he was starting to say, "Katherine, my dear, I—" But she did not look at him, and his hands, raised to her shoulders, then slid down again to his sides.

The earl apologized stiffly. "I was out of line, but you must never try anything so stupid again. Do you feel well enough to ride home? We'll go very slowly."

Katherine quietly assured him that she was able to ride, and he brought the mare to her and helped her onto her saddle again. Tarrington was silent, memories of another headstrong girl freshly painful in his mind, and of the accusations that had flown at him whenever he had tried to tighten the reins. But no, he told himself, Katherine Amory is no Cassandra.

Still, the incident had shaken him, and he brooded as they walked the horses all the way back to Whitfield. By the time they arrived it was very late in the afternoon and the family were gathered in the sitting room before going up to change for dinner. Mrs. Amory blanched when she saw Katherine's dusty habit, disheveled hair and scratched chin.

"I'm all right, Mama." Katherine hastened to her side. It was only a little tumble. I haven't broken anything, and I got up right away."

"My darling child, you do look a frightful sight! But I'm sure you were safe. After all"—she shifted her glance to Tarrington—"his lordship was with you." She turned her sweet smile on him.

He returned it and sat down near her to devote himself to reassuring her that her daughter had suffered no injury. Katherine heard the name Oldbury mentioned, saw her mother smile and nod, heard her ask Priscilla to bring her paper and pen. Altogether the two of them were thick as thieves, Katherine thought, and she wondered if her mother was beginning to harbor as wild an idea as Lord Knolland's.

Well they are all bound to be wretchedly disappointed, she thought grimly. All of them except me, of course, for I know better. After today's episode it was plain that Tarrington regarded her as only slightly less of a nuisance than his sister Sally, and in much the same light.

His veiled suggestions about her future were made, no doubt, only because he could not bear to let the Amorys live their lives without his good advice. The only thing that salved her wounded pride was his new readiness to confide in her. Perhaps when they returned from Bath— But she was brought up short by the realization that there would be no return from Bath. No. Certainly this time no one, not even Tarrington, would prevent her from carrying out her Plan.

When her mother had recovered and she and Priscilla had had enough amusement, they would go to Colonel Dawson, and life would settle into a safe, secure routine. The earl need not be troubled about the fate of his cousin Katherine any longer.

But thinking of it, reviewing each detail mentally as she had done a hundred times since Sir Edwin's death, did not bring with it the pleasure or sense of autonomy that had once raised her spirits so. This time the prospects seemed bleak, rather than cozy, lonely rather than busy and fulfilled. She did not look forward to being once again a dependent, no more in charge of her destiny than when she had been under her uncle's thumb.

That awareness was very sobering, and for a moment she wavered. But no, she was committed to the plan in every respect, and after all, what else was there? Curse Tarrington, she thought, watching him completely charm her mother. Before his arrival, she'd had not the slightest doubt that her decision was correct. Now his presence, his advice, his companionship, had shown her simple dreams for the pale and dull things they were.

Katherine found it impossible to shake this mood, even caught up as she was in the preparations for their departure. The next morning, with Tarrington, they left Whitfield very early, not without a few tears on Mrs. Amory's part and a sigh on Priscilla's, intending to breakfast with the Dowager Countess and Sally at the Hall, from whence they would get into the earl's travelling chaise.

The earl himself would ride alongside their carriage, and Lord Knolland bade them all a lengthy but temporary farewell. On the advice of the stern Finster, he would post home to London to replenish his wardrobe and pay his respects to his uncles, and within a few days join them in Bath.

Of course their carefully laid plans did not proceed quite so smoothly. While they breakfasted, Sally jumped up and left the breakfast parlor several times, consulting with her maid, searching for last-minute things forgotten till then, and ordering one portmanteau unpacked and repacked twice. Her mother scolded her for being a rattlebrain and not having seen to it all during the past sennight, but there was no help for it.

Tarrington, too, seemed restless, occasionally pausing on his way to the sideboard, to gaze out onto the drive, plate in hand. The morning was more advanced than they had foreseen when they finally collected their lap-parcels and were ready to embark.

So Katherine was not the only one to stifle a moan of frustration when one of the earl's servants announced a visitor. With all the bustle and coming and going in the house, the family could not possibly deny being at home so he was shown in, and Lady Tarrington, in her son's momentary absence, went forward to greet Mr. Oldbury politely as he was shown into the breakfast parlor.

"I fear I am intruding," he said after sweeping the ladies a bow, in which Katherine thought he included her only grudgingly. He had not called on them since she had given him that well-deserved tongue lashing, and it seemed that the memory still smarted.

"Not at all," Lady Tarrington was forced to say, though it was obvious that five ladies and their maid, dressed for travelling, surrounded by various small parcels, were not at liberty to entertain visitors. "As you see, we are just about to leave but if there is something of importance I am sure we can spare you a few minutes. I don't believe we are acquainted, sir." She raised an eyebrow questioningly.

Katherine stepped forward and hastily performed the introduction. Lady Tarrington acknowledged it and shot Katherine a quizzical look from under her lashes, as did her daughter. No doubt, Katherine thought, her mother had confided all the details of Mr. Oldbury's courtship to them.

For a moment he looked uneasy, and Katherine wondered what had brought him to the Hall. If it was her mother's note, then he had responded with curious urgency.

"In fact, I come on a very particular business to see his lordship the earl. I shall not detain him any longer than necessary, I assure you." He bowed again and Katherine noticed for the first time that his hair was thinning on top, and stifled an urge to giggle. She hadn't realized what the freedom from his unwelcome attentions really meant to her until now. Once in Bath, she thought triumphantly, she need never see him or think of him again.

In a moment Tarrington had come in, and Oldbury started at the sight of him, then seemed to recover. He went over again his apologies for disturbing them at this busy time, and Katherine was diverted to see that instead of shrugging them off brusquely as she might have expected, the earl received them graciously.

Finally Mr. Oldbury came to the point, expressing his desire to consult with the earl on a business matter. How humiliating it must be, she thought, for her noble cousin to have to court the interest of such as Oldbury in order to dispose of his property. Surely it could have been done much more easily through an intermediary.

But she had to save her questions, for the earl had asked his guest to step into his study, and he'd assured the ladies that he would be ready to leave within a quarter of an hour.

Sally sighed, watching the backs of the two men disappear into the wainscotted study. "Fiddle! I thought we might hear something of it, whatever it might be. I know there must be a good reason why Vane is willing to speak to that fellow. Isn't he the one who has been plaguing you, Katherine, and the one who tried to have poor Rodney arrested?"

"Oh, yes," Priscilla answered for her. "He is the most odious man imaginable, and I don't blame Katherine a jot for not wanting to have anything to do with him, though Uncle Edwin was forever pushing him on us, and Aunt Delia dotes on him." She wrinkled her already turned-up nose. "He is nothing but a puffed-up bag of wind!"

"Why, he is just a harmless, lonely boy," Mrs. Amory declared, "and so knowledgeable about art. To be sure, he is a bit unguarded in his behavior and his manners are not the best, but—"

"Nevertheless, you think I should have accepted him," said Katherine hotly.

At this Mrs. Amory smiled and looked pointedly at the earl's curly-brimmed brown beaver hat, which rested on the side table where he had dropped it. "Perhaps once I did, but no longer. I feel sure that there is something better in store for you, my love."

Katherine squirmed at this, and Lady Tarrington took pity on her and asked her if she would be so good as to fetch from the sitting room across the way a fine evening shawl of spider gauze that she had meant to present to her as a gift to wear in Bath.

"What with Sally's throwing us all into confusion I had quite forgotten it, and it will be just the thing for you on those warm evenings."

Katherine thanked her with real gratitude and affection, and slipped out of the room. But temptation overcame her as she passed the half-open door of the study. Though she had no real reason to doubt the earl's tale of wanting to dispose of his art collection, something about it all did not ring entirely true, especially when she thought back to the first few times he had given her cause for suspicion.

Her curiosity overruled her sense of propriety, and after hurriedly fetching the shawl from the sitting room, she found herself unable to return to the breakfast parlor without determining how the negotiations with Mr. Oldbury were proceeding. Rationalizing that Oldbury was a sly and selfish fellow, and that the earl could hardly know him as well as she did, she pressed herself against the wall next to the doorway, with the opening to her right. By turning her head she could easily see both the earl and his guest, without any fear of them seeing her. The hall was deserted of servants, the other ladies

191

no doubt preoccupied, so she settled herself to observe whatever she could. It was, she told herself, for his lordship's own good.

Just to the left of the hall was Tarrington's study, and he was steadying himself to receive Mr. Oldbury's inquiries casually, afraid of giving away too much. All his sniffing about had finally brought results, and Mrs. Amory's note had brought the prey to his own turf. Now, he thought, outwardly cool, offering his guest a glass of wine, now I bait the trap.

Oldbury, gaining confidence from the earl's polite reception of him, refused an offer of refreshment, and looked around the little room, his eyes devouring the framed prints and paintings. He seemed almost to forget his host's presence until the earl spoke again.

"Well, Mr. Oldbury, I am sorry to be abrupt but we are just about to set off. It won't do for me to keep five impatient females waiting, will it?" He smiled disarmingly. "How can I assist you?"

Oldbury's glance finally settled on Tarrington. "Forgive me, my lord, but you have quite a few very fine things here . . . in fact, it is about some of your art that I have come to see you. Dear Mrs. Amory wrote that if I was interested in adding to my collection, I ought to consult with you. As you see, I have wasted no time. Her ever obedient servant, am I." He bowed in the direction he assumed faced the breakfast parlor where the ladies were ensconced.

Tarrington bit back a laugh and thanked Providence that his cousin Katherine was spared the attentions of this buffoon. Of course, if his suspicions were correct, Oldbury was more than the fool he seemed.

"Of course, you must know that I am considered a collector of some repute in this county." Oldbury cleared his throat importantly.

"Indeed?" Tarrington showed as little interest as possible.

"Yes, my lord. Mrs. Amory seemed to indicate that you might be willing to part with some items from your father's collection, and I did wonder . . ." For a moment he savored the power this knowledge gave him. "I only hope that your lordship has not come upon any misfortune?" His eyes gleamed, and for once he met the earl's gaze.

Tarrington contrived to appear unconcerned, and employed his quizzing glass to good effect. Oldbury dropped his gaze.

"We all have our interests, Mr. Oldbury. Mine lie elsewhere, I'm afraid. A matched pair before a splendid sporting carriage means more to me than a few pretty pictures." He gestured casually around him.

Oldbury reddened. "My lord, I must take issue with such a description. The attraction of an exquisite work of art extends beyond mere prettiness! The joy it brings the possessor, the incomparable pleasure of a home filled with rare and delightful objects, the feast for the eyes . . ." His voice had risen in pitch and his eyes were glassy.

Tarrington almost shuddered. This fellow, he thought, is gone far beyond mere appreciation. Is this what drove him to do what I suspect him of? He is clearly obsessed, but that does not excuse him. His trickery could have ruined what is left of my reputation, and he shall not escape me easily.

He smiled politely at his guest, and pretended to suppress a yawn. Oldbury's mania drained away, leaving only eagerness, which he was at pains to disguise.

"Perhaps I could accommodate you, sir. But the time left to us is short, and I shall not be home at Northfolde before Christmas. However, you are welcome to inquire about anything here that catches your eye, though I regret there is not very much to interest the serious collector." He gestured at some charming but ordinary hunting prints, and then at a lovely Chinese bowl that graced a side table. "Pretty baubles, these, but surely you have seen their like before."

He turned away, and busied himself sorting out a few papers on his desk, instinct telling him that Oldbury must notice the very picture he had chosen as his bait.

It was a small landscape by a little-known Dutch artist, whose work, however, had recently taken the fancy of the Regent himself, and many collectors, Tarrington knew, had found the works of the long-dead artist valuable for that reason alone.

This particular painting was deceptively simple, though skillfully executed, and showed merely a low grassy field, dotted with cows, a sweep of ground behind them, wildflowers swaying in an imaginary breeze, and a picturesque windmill in the distance. But the sky was subtly tinted, here azure, here turquoise, there so pale as to be almost silvery white. Altogether the effect was peaceful, charming and serene, and someone like Oldbury, he knew, would not be able to resist the temptation it represented, especially as its very simplicity suited it perfectly to the purpose he had come to investigate.

"This is rather charming." Oldbury, suddenly realizing that staring raptly was no way to insure himself a good bargain, nodded casually at the painting. "Of course, it is not up to the standard of the rest of my collection—I have a very fine Rembrandt and Canaletto, though till now I have concentrated mainly on the decorative arts, and have not really the space for a true gallery. Hmmm . . ." He moved closer to where the painting hung over a small settee, and examined it with eyes that were becoming glassy with greed. Then he turned abruptly, and named a figure.

The earl had all he could do not to raise his eyebrows at the size of it, but pretended to waver for a moment, forcing himself to frown gravely. Imagine, he thought, what profit could be taken if Oldbury did what he expected him to do with the painting.

"Very well, sir," he said finally. "It is yours. I have no idea what my father originally paid for it. The Regent, with whom he had the honor to claim friendship, recommended the purchase to him, and no doubt the price was a good deal inflated."

He walked over to the painting himself, seemed to hesitate,

194

and out of the corner of his eye saw Oldbury visibly holding his breath. He wants it very badly, Tarrington thought. It was not inconsistent with his reputation as a collector, but was suspicious nevertheless.

It was a delightful work, to be sure, worth a bit more than the amount he had offered. But his offer was exactly the right price at which a distressed nobleman, concerned about speed and discretion, would sell some property that meant little to him. It was perfect bait, and no doubt, by the time he returned from Bath, or even sooner, if his customary informants did not fail him, he would find out what breed of animal he had caught in his trap. There was little doubt of it in his own mind, but proof was required, and proof he would get.

Recalling the ladies waiting for him, he quickly concluded arrangements with Oldbury. The butler was called to take the painting down and wrap it securely, a sum of money changed hands, and Oldbury left, after shaking Tarrington's hand with rather too triumphant an air. There was an entirely satisfied smirk on his round red face, which promised this was not the end of the affair; and though the ladies greeted him with cries of impatience, the earl did not grudge a moment of the delay.

Katherine noted every glance, every change of expression, and every word that passed between the earl and Mr. Oldbury. It all seemed very straightforward on the surface, but she had the distinct impression that on another level something other than the mere sale of a painting was being accomplished. There was nothing solid on which to fasten her suspicions, but she puzzled over it nonetheless, until she saw Tarrington reach for the bell pull. She leaped away from her post just before the butler emerged from the nether regions at this summons, and at the same time as he was carefully wrapping the painting, she was seated once more in the breakfast parlor, admiring Lady Tarrington's generous gift of a very lovely silver gauze shawl and promising Priscilla that she might borrow it.

Chapter Seven

Katherine lay fully clothed across a silk coverlet on a divinely comfortable bed, listening to the muffled sounds on the street three stories below, and stretched her cramped limbs with satisfaction. In Bath at last! But to her dismay, a little reflection showed her that her satisfaction was due more to the end of a tedious journey than to the proximity to the scene of all her carefully laid plans.

She turned her head and groaned, catching sight of the sketchbook page on which she had made one of her many lists, with the words "speak with P. about K." heavily underscored.

Lady Tarrington had insisted that to hurry their journey would be dangerous to Mrs. Amory's health, so Katherine had spent two slow days with her cousin in a creeping chaise. Priscilla had spent the greater part of her time either thinking or talking of Lord Knolland, and that situation had brought Katherine to the decision that she must not put off this conversation any longer.

Accordingly, as soon as they had arrived at Lady Tarrington's rented house in Gay Street, and were being shown to their rooms, she had whispered to Priscilla to come to her room as soon as she unpacked. Her cousin had fixed curious, innocent blue eyes on her, and said, "Certainly Kate, if you wish it, but . . . is anything wrong? Are you unwell? Should I not ask Aunt Delia if—"

"No, no, it is nothing like that," Katherine had been forced to say, while the curious housekeeper looked on. "I only want to ask your advice on . . . on a gown."

This only puzzled Priscilla the more, because though she had often gone to her cousin for advice, the reverse had never been true. She almost asked Katherine right then and there what all the mystery was about, but fortunately they had reached her room, and Katherine had hurriedly followed the housekeeper across to her own.

Now, much sooner than she had expected, there was a soft knock on her door, and she sat up, hiding the telltale page in her sketchbook, and called out to Priscilla to enter. Her cousin looked as though she had found herself in a fairyland. Her fine-boned face was animated and her eyes were sparkling.

"Oh, Kate, I like it here already! Even though it is raining, and we could hardly see anything as we drove in, but only think what fun we shall have! Lord Knolland promised me that there would be dancing and music and cards, and that in fine weather we could drive out to some very picturesque places. Oh, I cannot wait till he arrives." She finally ceased her raptures, while Katherine winced inwardly at having to be the one to prick the bubble of her cousin's happiness.

Priscilla seated herself in a comfortable armchair covered in rose satin, then looked up at Katherine, who had begun to pace back and forth between the bed and the window.

"Now, what is it that you want to talk about, Kate? I knew that you only said that about the gown because of the house-keeper—why her ears were stretched as long as a donkey's! But that is nonsense; you never need my advice on anything. You know ever so much more than I do. Lord Knolland says that you are the smartest female he ever met."

Looking into her cousin's hopeful face, lit with a smile as ever when his lordship's name passed her lips, Katherine felt that she must be a monster to want to put an end to such an innocent affection. But she steeled herself for the task with the reminder that the more involved Priscilla became, the worse she would be hurt in the end.

She sat down, took a breath, and without another moment of hesitation told her cousin the entire story, exactly as Lord Knolland had told her, of the restrictions on his fortune and marriage, leaving out, of course, the suggestion he had made regarding Tarrington.

With each word Priscilla's face drooped a little more, till her chin was sunk in her hands, her elbows on her knees, and a tear ran out of the corner of each lovely blue eye. Then she stood up, brushed away the tears, and, with a muffled "Oh, Kate!", ran from the room. In a moment Katherine heard the door across the hall slam shut.

Mrs. Amory rested on a sofa in the elegantly furnished drawing room, and tried to express her gratitude. "You are all a great deal too kind, and I beg you not to think of me when you make your evening engagements. I shall be quite happy to have Minette sit up with me until I go to sleep, and in the morning you can tell me all about it."

Her niece Priscilla, sitting close by her, patted her hands and assured her that by next winter she would be attending the assemblies, but Katherine only agreed absently. She stood near her cousin Sally at the window, taking in the street scene below. Since their arrival two days ago, in a horrendous storm of rain, exhausted and cramped from the journey, they had been kept inside by a continuance in the bad weather and by some loss of strength on her mother's part.

She had had no chance so far to see anything of the city, not even a glimpse of a view as they approached it, for the afternoon had darkened prematurely in all the rain. But today Lord Knolland had arrived, and he and Tarrington had promised to escort the ladies on a walk about the town.

Katherine and Priscilla, subdued and awkward with each other after their painful interview, were impatient to escape the house and explore Bath, and though Sally assured them that it was nothing so wonderful, even she admitted that the shops were very good and the circulating libraries were an attraction.

On the paved walk below there was a continuous stream of passers-by, dressed fashionably and otherwise, of all ages and conditions. But Sally was continually bemoaning the lack of company.

"There is hardly a soul in Bath I would care to meet," she complained, though the city looked very full, indeed, of quite interesting people, to girls who had spent the last five years secluded in the country. They were eager to be out among them.

What was more, Katherine had determined that to save all of her legacy from Sir Edwin would not advance her scheme of independence by very much, and she had announced to her mother and cousin that they would spend part of it on replenishing their wardrobes, so that they would not look so poverty-stricken in this fashionable city. Besides, it would not do to go to work for a gentleman like Colonel Dawson without some respectable clothes. Their positions would be uncomfortable enough, she thought, without the lower servants looking down on their threadbare appearance.

This reminded her of something she had been meaning to do. "Mama, do you not think it proper for us to call on Colonel Dawson today? It would be rude of us not to let him know we are here, after his kindness, and you would not let me write to him from Whitfield."

Mrs. Amory avoided her daughter's eyes, and spoke hesitantly. "Perhaps you and Priscilla could call on him some morning. It is not so urgent as that. It is really a very trifling matter." She picked up a book which she had just set down and did not look up from it again.

Katherine raised her eyebrows at this lapse of manners on her mother's part. It had been a continual puzzle to her why her mother was so reluctant to have anything to do with

Colonel Dawson, and now that they were in Bath she meant to find it all out. She resolved that she and her cousin would call on him as soon as possible.

"Are you ready, ladies? I did not forget my promise to show you as much of the city as your energy will allow in one morning. I must warn you of the hills!"

Katherine turned to find Tarrington at the door, regarding her with amusement. Lord Knolland hovered behind him, resplendent in doeskin and cream toilinette, his eyes searching for Priscilla, who turned away.

Tarrington joined Katherine and stared down into the street. "I can tell that even the little you can see through the window fascinates you, Katherine," said the earl with a fond expression on his face that set his mother to worrying all over again. "Shall I fetch a guidebook? Your eyes are all questions."

It might be true, she thought, but the questions that, as always in his presence, filled her mind had nothing to do with the city of Bath. "It would be poor spirited of you, my lord, to rely on a book. Surely a gentleman of your experience is equal to such a paltry challenge. I know too little to be able to ask any difficult questions."

By the time Katherine had reached the end of this speech, the teasing tone had gone out of her voice and uncertainty had crept in, for Tarrington's face closed up at her reference to his "experience" and she could have bitten her tongue for her forced attempt at lightness. Perhaps he is aware, she thought, that Knolland has told me of his first marriage and thinks I have made a casual reference to it. Of course, she had not had any such intention.

Out of the corner of her eye she saw Lady Tarrington and her daughter exchange a worried look, but the earl only smiled, less warmly than before, and said, "Then let us go and we shall see if my knowledge can satisfy you."

Tarrington had been oddly distant on the journey, though of course as he rode his horse while she sat in the chaise, there had not been much opportunity for conversation, and during their frequent stops she had been occupied with seeing to her mother's comfort. But that had not stopped her from wondering if their uneasy friendship was once more in decline.

"I am ready, my lord" was all that she said, and she tentatively placed a hand on the arm he offered, after making sure that her mother had everything she wanted about her, and being shooed away by Lady Tarrington.

"Go, child, and enjoy yourself. I shall sit with your mama and we will have a comfortable cose."

Lady Colesville sighed. "Yes, and I must go and call on a dreadful old dowager—Richard's aunt—such a dragon!" She hurried away to change her dress.

Lord Knolland had approached Priscilla to offer her his arm, and she hesitated, but with a sigh took it, while he asked her with exaggerated politeness how she did.

"Not very well, sir," she said faintly. "I fear Bath will not be what I expected."

In short, they looked perfectly miserable, and once more Katherine felt a pang of regret for the necessity of making them face reality. Resolutely she ignored their uncomfortable silence and let Tarrington escort her downstairs.

Katherine looked around with great curiosity, admiring the fine appearance of the terrace houses in a glimpse of the Circus to her right and of the park beyond. Glad to have the sun on her back once more, she resolved to purchase a parasol when they reached Milsom Street.

While they wandered over the sloping streets, Tarrington related to them something of the history of Bath, and Katherine was surprised at his knowledge. Perhaps, she thought, he really *had* studied a guidebook. He told them of Mr. Ralph Allen, whose fortune had been made in reorganizing the country's mails, who had commissioned John Wood to begin constructing some of the buildings and squares which had so beautified the city; and of Mr. Richard Nash, who for over thirty years had overseen and regulated the conduct of the mixed society that was attracted to Bath.

It was he, the earl told them, who had formed the code of behavior that had smoothed the way for visitors of all classes to enjoy the diversions of the city. "There is still a master of ceremonies in Bath," he said, "and had you not already been acquainted with someone, you and Miss Townsend would have relied upon him for introductions at the assemblies."

"Oh, I do not think I should have liked that," cried Priscilla. "It is so difficult to talk to strangers."

Lord Knolland gulped and, looking straight ahead, said bravely, "No, indeed, Miss Townsend, I think it is something you might try to become accustomed to." He directed a pleading look at Katherine, who had turned to observe them as they paused at the first of the shops. "I know *I* shall," he said mournfully.

Katherine frowned at him, while Tarrington looked on curiously, and Priscilla only said, "Oh!" She directed a wide-eyed glance at Lord Knolland, but he was gravely studying the contents of a baker's window, his attention apparently fixed on a currant-studded bun.

Katherine was quiet, wondering how she could convince Lord Knolland to let the matter rest. If he was going to be continually reminding her of his ridiculous idea, then life was going to become horribly uncomfortable. She wondered why he had not simply remained in London and thus made it easier on all of them.

A voice broke in on her thoughts. "You are remiss, Katherine," the earl remarked.

She glanced up and saw a teasing smile. "You are supposed to own yourself properly grateful for not having to be put to the extremity of relying on the master of ceremonies. You must express how fortunate you are in my acquaintance."

"You are a great deal too presumptuous, my lord," she could not resist replying, with a little smile. "I suppose that a master of ceremonies would have it in his power to introduce me to a great many people I should find just as agreeable." She glanced mischievously up at him from under her lashes, unable to resist quizzing him in return.

The earl stopped walking, cocked his head to one side, and pretended to study her in amazement. "My dear Katherine, I do believe you are flirting with me!"

"That's the ticket!" she heard Lord Knolland say just loudly enough for her to hear, and she glared at him repressively. She was overcome with confusion at Tarrington's words, but he was still laughing at her. She didn't know what imp had prompted her to behave this way, after all her careful restraint; and in utter embarrassment, she abruptly looked away from him and began to walk again.

Tarrington caught up with her and regained her arm. "Don't be so alarmed, Katherine, I was only teasing you. Besides, you must learn to flirt. It becomes you, and I'm sure you will find it vastly useful here."

She could not miss the sarcasm in his voice, and wondered if it were intended for her, or for the crowd of valetudinarians that were passing them on the other side of the street. She decided it was the latter, with some relief, because he said in a low voice, close to her ear, "Your friend Colonel Dawson is not the only wealthy widower in Bath, Cousin. And the ones who are not stricken too badly with gout no doubt like to dance with pretty young ladies. Perhaps you need not carry out your plan after all?"

She knew he was only teasing her, but was still hurt and puzzled by these odd high spirits, after the events of their last few times alone together. Sensing it, he immediately sobered and apologized.

"Forgive me, I have let my tongue run away with me. It is just that—"

A thought had occurred to her. "Your . . . business? It is going well?"

"Yes." It was only one word, but in it was a world of satisfaction, and she immediately forgave him for vexing her with his nonsense.

For the rest of their walk he behaved impeccably, patiently waiting outside the shops she and Priscilla could not resist inspecting, or accompanying them into some and venturing to give an opinion on a shade of ribbon or a pair of gloves, even selecting a charming frilled sunshade for Katherine, until a bemused Lord Knolland had to protest when the ladies stopped before a milliner's window.

He laid a hand on his friend's arm and looked up at him imploringly. "Say you're only quizzing us, Vane," he begged. "You ain't serious about going into the milliner's, *too?*"

Tarrington began to grin. "Why should I not, my friend?"

"For one thing, it ain't the thing for a gentleman to do, be seen escorting a petticoat into such a shop—beg pardon, a lady, of course. For another"—but recalling his own needs, he began a late retreat, his usually ingenuous expression becoming almost calculating—"Miss Amory's a charming girl, and she thinks the world of you, but even she wouldn't expect you to—"

"I was not aware, Rodney, that you had been made my cousin Katherine's confidant." Tarrington endeavored to look stern, while enjoying his friend's confusion.

"No, not at all," Rodney hurried to assure him. "She hasn't said a word . . . not that you'd expect her to . . . but she seems to like you well enough. . . ." His words trailed off as he plainly began to regret his attempt to further his plan for Priscilla's social advancement by the marriage of her cousin.

The earl indulged in such hearty laughter that a number of people began to stare, and Katherine and Priscilla were distracted from their study of the fashionable bonnets in the window.

"I'm much obliged to you, my lord," said the earl to his friend, ignoring the ladies' startled looks, "for that piece of information"; then he suggested that they turn around and return to Gay Street. "You have seen most of the principal shops, and that should satisfy you until tomorrow when Sally will introduce you to the joys of the circulating libraries."

Katherine hardly heard him, so busy was she mulling over what she had overheard of his conversation with Lord Knolland, and that night sleep eluded her as she agonized over the earl's reaction to his friend's remark. She would rather not bring up the subject again, but it might be best if she discreetly requested Lord Knolland not to attempt to arouse a partiality for her in the earl.

It was too humiliating to bear contemplation, that Tarrington should believe she had conceived a tendre for him. Despite those few blazing moments on the hilltop, she was certain that she was no more to him than another dependent, an unprotected female, not "up to snuff," as she had told him, but in dire need of his experience and guidance.

And even if Lord Knolland's scheme could be carried out, though, with a sudden catch in her throat, she assured herself it was impossible, she doubted if it would raise her penniless cousin Priscilla any higher in his uncles' esteem.

Despite an uncomfortable night, Katherine rose early enough to attend her mother to the Pump Room, see her comfortably settled and watch her drink her prescribed two glasses. She even swallowed, grimacing, a sip or two herself. She wondered at the resolution of all the invalids who submitted their palates and stomachs to such an indignity twice a day, only to later immerse their bodies in the odorous waters.

Her expression was mirrored in Priscilla's face, and they laughed as they hastily put down their glasses. Leaving Mrs. Amory with Lady Tarrington and Mrs. Brockton, who was to have been her ladyship's hostess but who behaved very civilly to Mrs. Amory, the cause of the disruption of their engagement, they promenaded the room. They were disappointed to see nothing more interesting as yet than other invalids.

"Oh, Katherine, that stuff is so horrid, I wonder it does not make them all sicker! How can they bear it?"

Priscilla shuddered as she watched an elderly gentleman, his gouty foot propped before him, swallow a glass of the water in large, resigned sips.

"Perhaps being weak in body strengthens one's spirit to endure such things," Katherine said absently. Her attention had been attracted by a very extraordinary person who was making a noisy entrance, calling as much notice to himself as he possibly could.

The new arrival was a man of early middle age, with thinning reddish hair dressed in fashionable disorder. He was attired in skin tight yellow pantaloons that showed his bulky figure to poor advantage, while a vividly embroidered white satin waist-coat vied for attention with an impossibly high collar and intricate neckcloth, thrusting up from a bottle-green coat.

"Here now, my good man, take care you don't crush it," he admonished his servant, a frail man of mousy aspect to whom he was carefully surrendering his gleaming beaver hat. He nodded and spoke to several of the occupants of the Pump Room, with total disregard for their proximity to him, his hearty voice correcting the limitations of distance.

"General Bradwood, how do you do? . . . My Lady . . . so glad to hear you are over the bilious complaint . . . Miss Harper, you look burnt to the socket. Did I not warn you against attempting a card party the evening after the musicale? . . . Ah, Stanley, my friend, it does me good to see you in such plump currant. . . ."

The gentleman in the bottle-green coat seemed to know every denizen of the Pump Room, and with his diminutive servant in train, made his way in a cheerful progress to the pump, was served his water, and downed it in one swallow, hardly stopping to breathe before setting off on a circuit of the room, loudly greeting each of his acquaintances while Katherine and Priscilla stared unabashedly, having never encountered such a person at any time in their lives.

"Good heavens." Priscilla grasped her cousin's arm. "Look, Kate, he is stopping to speak to Aunt Delia and Lady Tarrington. Let us go!"

They reached the ladies just in time to meet this fascinating personage.

"Ah, the girls are here," said Lady Tarrington. "Mr. Fellowes, I should like to present you to Miss Amory and Miss Townsend. Girls, this is Mr. Fellowes, an old acquaintance and the most well-known man in Bath. I vow, my dear sir, you are quite in danger of becoming an institution here!"

"Ah, never say so, dear lady!" He was already executing a very neat bow, to the accompaniment of creaking corsets. "I am far too youthful in spirit to permit myself to become anything so stodgy as an institution, even in this, my dear city. And I do not wish the charming young ladies to think of me as such, when I might, one evening, wish to solicit a dance with one of them. Nay, do you wish them to think me so ancient as to be unable to cut a caper like any young buck?" And he blithely demonstrated a little jig step for the amazed eyes of everyone near them.

Katherine and Priscilla giggled and he was delighted, squeezing their hands and planting great smacking kisses on them. He was too odd looking to be attractive, with his small, bright black eyes and little pointed nose and round face, but his impish smile was irresistible and his good humor was infectious. In a very short time, both Priscilla and Katherine felt they had found a valuable friend in Mr. Fellowes.

"Now, madam," he said, addressing Mrs. Amory, "I hope you will permit me to give you some very good advice on pursuing your cure."

With this he sat down at her side and delivered a spirited dissertation on the efficacy of various water cures, the skill of the Bath physicians, and the potency of the water as compared to Cheltenham's. At the end of it, Mrs. Amory was so convinced that, with a little time, the waters of Bath would restore her to health, that she accepted Mr. Fellowes offer to escort all of them to a musicale on Friday.

In fact, when the dandified little man took his leave of them,

Mrs. Amory was beginning to look like her former self, and it was only at Lady Tarrington's urging that she consented to be taken back to Gay Street by chair for a nap.

As the four ladies emerged from the Pump Room, greeted by the cries of the waiting chairmen, Mrs. Amory, who was gazing across the street towards the Abbey, suddenly turned pale again and clutched at Katherine's arm. "Hurry, my dear," she said faintly, "I'm afraid I have exerted myself too much." They quickly ushered her into a chair and she was carried by two stout fellows off to Gay Street.

"How strange, to be sure," murmured Lady Tarrington. "I would swear that she has been feeling better today than in a sennight."

Katherine, too, wondered at the sudden relapse, and she followed the direction of her mother's glance to find herself confronted by Colonel Dawson, who had just crossed over from the Abbey. She had not seen him since her father's death, but he had changed very little. He was still tall, though heavier than before, but his upright carriage had not deserted him, and if his weatherworn face had a few more lines, it was still as kindly as ever.

"Miss Amory . . . little Katherine!" His disbelieving voice boomed out, prodding her to step forward to greet him. He took hold of both her hands, looking over her with fondness. "Why, you are quite the young lady now! And to think you were just a wisp of a girl five years ago. Ah, child"—he sighed—"it has been too long. But what's this? How do you come to be here? Has your mama changed her mind?" he asked eagerly.

Katherine was puzzled by the emphasis he put on this last question, since she clearly recalled that their last letter to him had contained nothing of her mother's reluctance, only the news of Tarrington's arrival.

"Indeed, sir, I must apologize. We have been in Bath only two days, and what with the preparations, and Mama's illness, there was not leisure to—"

"Illness? Is Delia ill?" His voice rose in alarm.

209

"She is recovering," Katherine assured him. "In fact she was just with us in the Pump Room, but we sent her home for some rest. We had meant to call upon you in Henrietta Street as soon as—"

"By God, I had no idea," the colonel muttered. "I knew she was delicate, but—"

"Pray, sir, do not excite yourself so," said Katherine, at a loss to discover the source of all his emotion at the news. "Mama had a rather bad attack a fortnight ago, and Lady Tarrington was kind enough to invite us to be her guests here until she is quite well again. She is taking the cure, you know. Of course, when she is recovered, we should be quite happy to take up our prior arrangement with you."

But the colonel did not seem to hear. "I did not know Delia's health had deteriorated so. It is my fault." His face reddened. "I should never have let her go to live with that Sir Edwin. Your father and I knew him for what he was, my girl, and it is his coldness and stinginess that has brought her so low. If only I could have persuaded her . . ."

Suddenly he noticed the other two ladies listening curiously to this exchange, and remembering his manners, ended his litany of regrets and allowed Katherine to present him to Lady Tarrington. He then greeted Priscilla, whom he pronounced a fine pretty girl, and made her blush.

"I am expected inside," he nodded at the Pump Room, "by some of my cronies, but I shall call to see how your mother does." Katherine gave him their address.

"One of these evenings you must do me the honor of dining with my family," he said and, bowing to them, strode away.

"He seems a very kind man," her ladyship remarked, staring after him, "so concerned when he heard that your mother was ill! And to think he was prepared to take in all three of you. . . ." She gave Katherine a sidewise glance.

For a moment Katherine was baffled, but after reflecting on her mother's sudden haste to leave, which seemed to have been occasioned by the sight of the colonel approaching, she thought she might be beginning to understand.

Why would the colonel have blamed himself for her mother's illness? And why would he invite them to dine with his family when they were to have entered his house in the capacity of servants, not guests? But the thought was dismissed almost as soon as it had formed.

Surely if the colonel had that kind of interest in her mother, he would scarcely have been ready to hire her as his housekeeper! Besides, she thought, Mama would certainly have mentioned it.

But if the colonel did call in Gay Street, it must have been while Katherine and Priscilla were out, and in the following days they were out a good deal of the time. Mr. Fellowes, while escorting them to the musicale, without Mrs. Amory who had pleaded fatigue, had begun to introduce them to all of his acquaintances, and that acquaintance was large indeed.

This led to invitations to the numerous private parties that formed the higher social life of the city, and although many of the gentlemen were too old to be of interest to Katherine and her cousin, there was a sprinkling of younger, unattached gentlemen who began to vie flatteringly for their favor.

Tarrington and their other former companions were, of course, not abandoned. In fact the earl and Lord Knolland accompanied them to several evening parties. But for poor Lord Knolland it was not much better than a repeat of the Littletons' ball, between his unsteady determination to heed Katherine's request to end his courtship of Priscilla and the attention she attracted from the gentlemen she met. His only chance to monopolize her came during the day, when he assiduously escorted her to her favorite circulating library, or when he took a family dinner with them in Gay Street.

Tarrington, however, seemed satisfied at the way events were unfolding. Katherine noticed that he rarely made a push to dance with her, once she had made the acquaintance of some gentlemen, and when she ventured to mention a desire to ride, he only offered to hire another horse for her, as Sally had taken over the use of the mare again. He did not offer to accompany her, and only reminded her not to go out alone.

He seemed preoccupied as of old, as though for the first week he had been expecting something to happen and that he was impatient when it did not. He spent much of his time out of the house, only occasionally dining with them, though they sometimes met him later in the evening, and he only once attended them to the Pump Room. When his sister chided him for his neglect, he shrugged it off lightly.

"No, Sally, do not think to make me guilty of abandoning you. Colesville is coming soon to carry you off, is he not? You ladies certainly have enough to fill your days, and our cousins have a flock of admirers that would do credit to the belles of the season."

Tarrington stood in the hall, clad in well-fitting riding clothes that Katherine could swear were new, and rapped his crop impatiently against his thigh, as was his habit. He glanced at Katherine, as if feeling her stare, for she had not been able to help it, and his smile was as easy and casual as the one he gave to his sister. In a moment he was gone.

From then on Katherine indulged herself in the diversions of Bath society, and tried to enjoy the admiration of the gentlemen she met and danced and dined with. None of them were too assiduous in their attentions, though, and a frank conversation with Mr. Fellowes, who had appointed himself their unofficial social sponsor, much to Lady Tarrington's amusement and to her son's annoyance, explained this phenomenon to Katherine.

"I know I need not remind you, my dear Miss Amory," he said one day while they were momentarily alone in Lady Tarrington's sitting room, "not to refine too much upon Lord Jamison's flattery. He is really very poor himself, as these things go, and is entirely dependent upon the generosity of an aunt. *Not* the man for you! In other circumstances, perhaps"—he stopped and thoughtfully chose a meringue, nibbling at it like a mouse—"but, alas, he has never been known to offer for anyone without at least a moderate fortune."

Katherine assured him, as she had done many times, that she was not looking for a husband. But his casual reference to her lack of fortune startled her. "Does *everyone* know that my cousin and I are penniless?" she asked bluntly.

Mr. Fellowes was taken aback, and nearly choked on his tea. "My dear Miss Amory! Please, do let us stick to euphemism. You know, I believe your mama is right, you seem to have a distressing tendency towards the absolute unadorned truth. It does mar your otherwise perfectly charming nature somewhat. Ah, you protest . . . but a little trimming never did harm to a plain gown, my dear."

"But an excess of it, sir, will obscure the figure of the wearer."

"And do you not agree that some figures are better obscured?" Mr. Fellowes, hesitating between an iced cake and a thin slice of buttered bread, leaned over in a way that made his corsets complain exceptionally loudly, and Katherine laughed at the look on his face.

"Hmmph!" He straightened up, his cheeks a bit pink. "In any event, I should prefer to say that you and Miss Townsend are well-bred young ladies of little fortune. That has already become, as these things do by some mysterious means which have yet to be discovered, general knowledge among every unmarried man in Bath. But there are always those gentlemen," he assured her, gazing at her earnestly with his bright little eyes, "neither young nor old, neither rich nor poor, but lonely, and willing to sacrifice fortune for beauty, charm, and intelligence. In short, my dear Miss Amory, I believe that you do not have to look very far to find such a one." He reached over to take her hand, but before she could even begin to wonder whether or not she should be alarmed at these words, they were interrupted.

"I had thought I might find you here, Katherine." A stern voice from the door made Katherine start, and Mr. Fellowes dropped some crumbs on the carpet as he jumped in his chair.

"My scatterbrained sister has no doubt left you to entertain callers alone, for a 'tiny bit' as she would put it, but you know you should have called one of the maids to sit with you when she did not return." Tarrington's face was as full of displeasure as his voice, but even though the faces of both the occupants of the room stared back at him with innocent surprise, his mouth drew into a hard line as he turned to the visitor.

Poor Mr. Fellowes was clucking over a tea stain on his pale buff pantaloons.

"But you, sir, with your many years of experience and the position you maintain here in Bath, you should know better than to allow a young lady to entertain you alone." Tarrington strode over and stood towering over the dandy's chair.

"My lord!" Mr. Fellowes stood up, scattering another shower of crumbs to the floor. "I assure you, there is no need—"

"I am afraid there is just such a need," the earl replied smoothly, though plainly enjoying the man's discomfiture. "For in the absence of a father or brother, I must stand in the place of a protector of my cousin's welfare and reputation."

"You are being absurd, my lord!" Katherine finally burst out. She barely noticed Mr. Fellowes slide past them to reach the door, murmuring under his breath, "Foolish young pup . . . last time I attempt to do *you* a good turn."

Embroiled in their dispute, they did not hear him. "It certainly is absurd that you are constantly to be found in that old dandy's company," Tarrington lashed out.

"Mr. Fellowes has been very kind," Katherine retorted with dignity. "He has introduced us to everyone and made sure that we know how to get along. Besides, he is old enough to be my father! How could you . . ." She then recalled that the earl had told her, jokingly, about older men who were willing to dance and flirt with pretty young ladies, and color swept over her face when she remembered what Mr. Fellowes had begun to say before the earl's entrance.

It is too ridiculous, she thought. Mr. Fellowes, she was sure, could not have been talking about himself. If it wasn't so improbable, I might think that his lordship is . . . jealous!

This absurd thought made her smile, and Tarrington demanded to know what she found so amusing.

"Nothing at all," she replied, quickly schooling her features into indifference. "I am sorry if you think I behaved badly by entertaining Mr. Fellowes, who, after all is your mother's friend. I assure you that there was nothing at all improper in it." She could not imagine the friendly, plump old fellow making improper advances to a girl less than half his age, but her conscience gave her a twinge just the same. "Have you not realized by now that I am well able to fend for myself?"

He looked at her, his anger fading with every moment that passed, then drew his hand across his eyes and sighed. "I'm sorry, Katherine. I don't know why I let myself become so— It is just that what I said about standing as your protector is true, and I feel that my responsibility . . ."

The tiny glow that the suspicion of the earl's jealousy had produced died like a snuffed candle flame. Of course, he was only worried about her reputation. She forced herself to make light of it, swallowing a lump in her throat.

"How like a medieval knight you sound, my lord! I doubt that poor Mr. Fellowes could compare to a dragon or any such thing. I shall take care, my lord, never again to so distress you." And she left him staring after her, her trembling legs carrying her as quickly as they could out of the room.

The next week saw such a great improvement in Mrs. Amory, that she took to attending some of their evening engagements with them, though to be sure Katherine and Priscilla noticed some oddity in her behavior. They discovered, through a chance word dropped by the butler, that she had made it a habit to instruct the servants to deny her to callers when she was alone in the house, which, as she might be sleeping, was not so unusual, Katherine had told her cousin.

But they also noticed that she kept a very sharp eye out for any notes brought to the house or left on the hall table, and sometimes was seen to snatch one up and scurry away with it in a most peculiar manner.

Katherine could make nothing of it, but one morning she found her mother looking as though she had just been crying, though smiles alternated with her frowns. Every so often she shook her head, and said, "Oh, my . . . oh, dear."

"My dearest mama, whatever has disturbed you?"

"Oh!" Mrs. Amory gave a start and swallowed something from a medicine glass. Then she confided, "I have had a visitor, Katherine. It was . . . Colonel Dawson."

To this unsurprising news Katherine replied, "Well, then, I told you that he knows we are here, and he was very concerned when he heard of your illness. Did he come to invite us to dinner?"

"Yes . . . that is, no . . . I . . ." Mrs. Amory searched about her for her vinaigrette. She inhaled deeply, then collapsed back against the sofa. "Don't mind me, child, I'm just being foolish. It was a very touching reunion . . . your dear father . . . We dine at the colonel's on Thursday, before the Brocktons' rout. Now run along, you and Priscilla, and try on those gowns we are making up for you. I want to be sure of the flounces."

Katherine would have preferred to discuss it further, but she was glad that the colonel had not been offended at their failure to inform him of their change of plan. She was confident that as soon as her mother was well enough they would become part of his household. She tried to cheer herself with the thought that they would never have to be beholden to the Earl of Tarrington, or anyone else, for the rest of their lives, but it was poor consolation. She had to admit that life as she lived it now was infinitely more satisfying than the dutiful future she had mapped out for herself.

That afternoon, the young ladies were about to set out on a last shopping expedition to purchase some hair ornaments to wear with their new gowns to the Brocktons' rout. Sally insisted on flowers, Priscilla argued for a satin toque she had seen in a milliner's, and Katherine laughingly suggested feathers.

"No, no! You are much too young, Priscilla, to appear in a toque, and you, Katherine, are altogether too bad to be teasing us about feathers. Never for a summer rout party in Bath!" Sally scolded them good-naturedly, and pulled in her pink lower lip, thinking. "I have it exactly! Do you still have Mama's *Ackermann's?* There was a plate with the sweetest flowered headdress that would just suit both of you. With a little contriving, I am sure we could make one up just like it."

Priscilla volunteered that she thought Lady Tarrington had taken it back to her room, and reached to ring for a servant, but Katherine forestalled her.

"I'll look for it," she offered, feeling very restless and not averse to climbing the stairs.

Leaving the other two young ladies to argue over wreaths, sprays, and garlands, she jumped up and took the stairs at a less than sedate pace, arriving somewhat breathless at the door of Lady Tarrington's bedchamber. She did not trouble to knock, knowing her ladyship was out with her friend Lady Brockton, and would not at all mind if she just went in for a moment to take the magazine.

But on the threshold she was brought up short. "Oh, excuse me, my lord!"

She had made the most dreadful blunder. This was not Lady Tarrington's chamber, but her son's, and at the moment he was very much in use of it.

He stood before his dresser wearing only tight, dove grey pantaloons, the view of his broad, muscle-ridged back and firm, curved buttocks unimpeded by shirt or coat.

After her first astonishment receded, Katherine was reminded of the drawing of a beautiful but scandalous Italian statue she had once been shown by her art master, when her mother wasn't watching. Tarrington's pure, unadorned masculinity was so very well defined, his essence so revealed in this candid pose, that she felt her legs go weak.

She knew she should leave immediately, but for a moment she was transfixed by the splendor of him, and then she noticed that he hadn't moved except to fasten his nether garment, and was watching her with appreciation and amusement. His total lack of embarrassment stopped her from running out at once. Obviously he expected her to do just that, and she decided to deny him the pleasure. He would see that she was not a simple country miss who would be flustered by the slightest thing out of the ordinary!

"I—I beg your pardon, my lord," she said as calmly as she could under the circumstances, forcing herself not to look away. "I had not realized that this was *your* room. I was looking for Lady Tarrington's."

There, she thought, quite pleased with her affectation of indifference, especially when her heart pounded harder with his every fluid movement. He was reaching unhurriedly for his shirt, and now that she had begun looking she could not keep her eyes from travelling the length of his arm to his bare shoulder, tracing the lines of muscle under smooth flesh that was like living marble.

Finally her eyes met his, and it was too late to look away. She stood watching breathless and trembling as he slowly and deliberately pulled on the shirt, holding her gaze locked all the while. He shrugged his powerful shoulders into it languorously, and Katherine stood like a statue herself, the door half-open behind her, her nerves screamingly aware of him and of the danger of someone passing by the room, but unable to move. Her face grew warm, despite her determination not to blush.

By now the weakness had moved through her legs and up into her body, and she thought she might actually collapse if she tried to turn and go. Her tongue cleaved to the roof of her mouth. She swallowed and tried to speak, but not a sound emerged from her lips. Finally she managed to back away exactly one step. But by then he had advanced on her, his shirt front left carelessly open, exposing the light curly hair on his chest. She hardly knew where to look. Her eyes seemed to stray over his body without her conscious control.

"Apology accepted, Katherine." His voice was deep and intimate, and he made no attempt to force her out, or to continue dressing. "I hope my state of deshabille has not alarmed you. I doubt that you are accustomed to seeing a gentleman without his shirt."

He moved closer, and she took an involuntary step back. There was a teasing note in his voice now, and he obviously expected her to squirm and blush. She had come this far, and she was determined to see it through. Slowly the strength began to return to her limbs.

"Why . . . why, not at all, my lord!" Katherine tossed her head. "When I was just a girl my father's friends quite made our lodgings their own. I expect I have seen at least three or four men looking quite . . . er . . . rumpled."

To her dismay, she found that she had backed up too far and had closed the door altogether. What an uproar there would be if she were seen leaving the earl's room! Oh, why did he not have his valet with him? It was his own fault!

Tarrington smiled a slow, easy smile and advanced on her, hands on his hips, until he was less than a foot away. Katherine retreated until she felt the hard door against her back, and stared at him helplessly. Her courage was rapidly draining away under the onslaught of his scent, the fragrance of fresh starched linen and clean, warm male skin. It filled her nostrils and made her head float as if she had just sniffed an exotic Eastern perfume.

"How interesting. And what a sad comment on the social and domestic habits of our army officers. I shouldn't think your mother would approve of letting young men run about bare-chested before her impressionable daughter. See how unusually bold it has made you!" He reached out and chucked her playfully under the chin.

Katherine made a sound that was a mingled whimper of fear and shame. "Please . . ."

The earl let out a long breath, so close that it cooled the burning flesh on Katherine's bare neck. He studied his unfastened cuffs and frowned. "In fact it seems quite out of the realm of possibility, considering your mother's upright character and Christian upbringing." He grinned at her wickedly, took her unresisting arm, and pulled her away from the door.

"Trust me not to allow a word to escape of your sudden lapse, my dear Katherine," he said, and opening the door, performed an elegant bow.

"How dare you! Oh, you . . . you twist everything I say . . . you know I didn't mean . . ." She had been so intent on convincing him of her ability to look after herself that she had fallen neatly into his trap. It is so frightfully difficult to appear to be mature and up to every rig when one has, in reality, been kept wrapped in cotton wool for so long, she thought, scrambling for a suitable reply to his lordship's infernal impudence. But there was nothing she could say. Careless of witnesses, she flung herself out of the room and slammed the door behind her, to the echoes of his laughter.

"My goodness, Kate, whatever has kept you? We have been waiting an age!"

"I'm sorry. Here it is." She handed the publication, which she had finally found in Lady Tarrington's room a little further down the hall, to Priscilla. Her legs still felt weak, but she had stopped to splash some water on her face, and her mirror had told her that the telltale blush was gone.

"Why, Katherine, you don't look well. You should have let us call one of the maids," Lady Colesville said, taking her hand. "Your skin is so cold, and your face so pale! I think you had better stay here, else you will be too ill to attend the rout."

Katherine insisted that it was nothing at all. The last thing she wanted was to be left alone in the house with Tarrington. Who knew what idiocy she might betray herself into this time?

220

It was all too easy to do when she was faced with that infuriating, irresistible smile. Her feelings were becoming all to clear to her, and they meant nothing but trouble. She could only pray that her mother would recover quickly or that Lady Tarrington would tire of Bath. Colonel Dawson's beckoned like a safe port in a tempestuous sea. Katherine was afraid that if she had to remain much longer under the same roof as the earl, a shipwreck would be inevitable.

The night of Lady Brockton's rout arrived at last, and the young ladies were well prepared. By dint of careful shopping and Mrs. Amory's skill, Katherine and Priscilla had two new evening gowns each and had bought some relatively inexpensive ready-made morning dresses. They had also purchased hats, shoes, gloves, fans, and stockings, enough, as Priscilla had said in amazement, to last them for years.

They were both confident of being in their best looks that night, and Katherine did not feel they suffered very much even when compared with Lady Colesville in her London-made gown.

Lord Knolland, who had made a gallant effort to obey Katherine's wishes in the matter of Priscilla, still suffered under this neglect of his tender feelings. He had attempted to discuss their dilemma with the object of his admiration, but Priscilla had confided to Katherine that it was too distressing to bear thinking of, and instead she treated him with distant kindness, and gave a successful impersonation of a young lady quite satisfied with the attentions of the less decrepit specimens of Bath manhood.

Only Katherine knew the real state of her feelings, and many a night she heard muffled sobs as she passed her cousin's door, but obedient to Priscilla's wishes, she refused to discuss the subject with Lord Knolland, however much he pleaded with her.

However, his lordship was determined to procure for himself the solace of securing the first set with his beloved, and before they left for dinner at Colonel Dawson's Priscilla was finally prevailed upon to give him her promise.

"But only once, my lord," she said with a false little giggle that somehow fell flat, "else my other gentlemen friends would scold me for unfairness."

So his lordship snatched at her hand and kissed it, and, with only one sighing glance, left them early in the afternoon to take dinner with an acquaintance of one of his uncles.

The earl was likewise engaged elsewhere for dinner, a fact Katherine noted with suspicion, for on passing the kitchen stairs that morning she had caught a glimpse of that same oddly dressed boy who had come for him at Whitfield. As Tarrington did not volunteer the identity of his dinner companions, she supposed that this was no mere coincidence. She had avoided him since their last memorable encounter, though she was not so sure that she had yet lost the desire to box his ears. She told herself she was not at all afraid of him, but she made sure they were never alone, nonetheless.

All thoughts of the earl and of his activities were driven from her mind by the extraordinary warmth of their reception at Colonel Dawson's house in Henrietta Street.

They sat down *en famille*, with only his eldest son and daughter coming downstairs, the others still being of schoolroom age. The colonel greeted the Ladies Tarrington and Colesville cordially, and expressed his gratitude for their care of his "dear Delia." The ladies exchanged glances of the utmost surprise, except for Mrs. Amory who only blushed delightfully, and Katherine began to have the oddest sensation that she had been set down on a stage to play a part in a completely unfamiliar play, without having seen her lines.

Colonel Dawson proceeded to fret and fuss over her and Priscilla, taking pains to see that they were neither too warm nor too cool, that they liked their seats, and that they were served as much as they wanted of the dishes that appealed to them from the tremendous selection spread on his long dining table. Though Katherine felt awkward on this account, she did murmur to her mother, "It is so kind of him, Mama, not to remind us in any way of what our *real* position will be here," only to receive a sheepish glance which was hurriedly averted.

But the biggest shock was the sight of how the colonel treated her mother. A duchess could not have been plied with more flattering attention or elevated to higher notice among the company. From the moment she walked into the drawing room, Colonel Dawson was gallantly at her side, raising her hand to his lips, procuring a footstool and firescreen; for though it was warm he imagined it too damp for an invalid, and so had a fire blazing in the drawing room hearth. In short, his attentions were like nothing so much as those of a man in love, and Katherine was not ready to face this momentous truth. But it was becoming obvious that there would soon be no turning from it.

"Ah, Miss Amory, to think that by her own determination, which I admire as much as I deplore it, your mama has condemned herself to this ill health. Had she only allowed me to be of assistance, as I gave my pledge to Walter to do, as he lay breathing his last . . ."

The colonel stopped, and gazed upon Mrs. Amory, overcome. Blushing and shy in a way that Katherine had never seen her, she scarcely looked at him. Finally she spoke.

"My dear Colonel Dawson, I could not—you should not have—" She stopped in confusion, and Katherine recalled that at the time of her father's death the colonel's wife had still been living. "You had your own responsibilities then, and it would not have been seemly."

This was all that Mrs. Amory could be persuaded to say, though he pressed her again and again to admit that she should have accepted his offer of help, an offer that Katherine had not known of until now.

She thought it more than just curious that he mentioned not a word of their previous arrangement, and did not seem at all put out that they had not discussed their duties with him. Several times she attempted to open the subject, but to her utter amazement, her mother always interrupted and diverted the conversation onto some other topic.

After the fourth time, Katherine desisted, but her head was beginning to whirl with the implications of it, and when, after dinner, the colonel forbore to sit in solitary splendor with his port, and joined the ladies in the drawing room, devoting the entire time to close conversation with her mother, Katherine felt that she must have dreamed the entire arrangement, and that her plan was now fallen into ashes.

By the time they all set off for the rout, the ashes were long cold, and Katherine's hopes wavered on the edge of a vast pit of uncertainty.

But she had no leisure to meditate on what tomorrow might bring, or where her new future might lie. Before Katherine could steel herself to tell Priscilla of her discovery, they were at the Lady Brockton's and the music had begun.

Mr. Fellowes had already bespoken her hand, and as she took her place opposite him, her eyes were drawn to the door. Lord Tarrington was just arriving, alone, and dressed flawlessly enough to please even his tyrannical valet. In black breeches and tail coat, his shapely, muscular legs bearing him confidently into the room, his sandy curls gleaming in the candlelight, he was easily the handsomest man in the room, and she could not look away.

His eyes met hers momentarily, like a beam of clear hazel light from the doorway. She nodded briefly, her lips in a taut smile, as she saw his gaze move disapprovingly to her partner. Mr. Fellowes was in rare form that night, his robust figure struggling to contain itself in the extravagantly tailored but encasing suit of evening clothes, his cravat tied with fussy perfection, and an assortment of fobs and seals decorating the front of his white brocade waistcoat.

His keen little eyes followed her glance, and with a pleasant nod to Tarrington, he led Katherine proudly down the set, performing his part with a light step, despite his stoutness. Katherine felt the curious eyes on her, and was relieved to see that there were some friendly, familiar faces among the crush. She noticed Tarrington making the acquaintance of Colonel Dawson, and turned away. It would not do, she thought, were she to spend each dance staring at him, and she fully expected to have almost every one of her dances spoken for. She only hoped he would not appoint himself her "protector" here as well.

The set ended, and Mr. Fellowes, with a compliment on his lips, took her back to where the rest of their party, who were not dancing, had been seated. But Tarrington was gone, as well as Colonel Dawson, and though Katherine could see her mother's new Norwich silk shawl draped over a chair, and Lady Tarrington's black ostrich fan lying on another, they were none of them there.

"Oh, dear, it seems as though your friends have deserted you, Miss Amory," Mr. Fellowes said, darting little glances about the long room, and up to the gallery. They waited a little while, talking desultorily of the company, but none of Katherine's party appeared.

"I'm afraid this may be difficult, my dear Miss Amory," said Mr. Fellowes at last. "Quite awkward indeed. You see, I have promised the next dance to—"

But Katherine had already seen the blowsy female, with hair of a very suspicious shade of titian, nodding and smiling at Mr. Fellowes from across the room, and she knew she would have to depend on either Lord Knolland, who had not yet brought Priscilla back, or the earl himself to give her company until another partner appeared.

"Oh, how vexing! Wherever can Mama have gone?" She looked about once more and saw no sign of her mother or the colonel. If it were not for fear of how it might look, she would have felt perfectly comfortable sitting quite alone, but it would be much remarked and frowned upon, and she had by now enough of an acquaintance with the habits of the less gentlemanly class of Bath visitors to know that it would leave her prey to some unwanted advances. With a relative dearth of company, even private society in Bath could be quite inexclusive.

But Mr. Fellowes, at her side, was looking nervously across at his new partner, rising up and down on his toes and bobbing his chin as if he were a puppet on strings, so that finally inspiration struck her and she said, "Don't worry, sir, I believe I see his lordship coming this way. I am sure he will take me to my mother or Lady Tarrington, and you may join your partner and stop worrying about me." She smiled reassuringly, and he trotted across the room just in time to take his partner into the set.

Despite her intentions, her solitude began to feel conspicuous, and she searched the room desperately for someone she knew. She could locate none of her party, and had almost resolved to search them out in the card rooms when she actually saw Tarrington, as if her lie had brought him to her, walking in her general direction. Already her solitary state was beginning to attract attention, but she had little choice in the matter. Reluctantly, yet with more relief than she had expected to feel, she succeeded in attracting his attention.

"What? Has that absurd old fellow gone and left you unattended? Has he no sense of propriety?" These were Tarrington's first words as he reached her side, and his frown deepened the lines in his face forbiddingly.

"Surely you cannot pretend to be a slave to it yourself," Katherine reproved him. "I have known you to ignore it on at least *one* occasion." It required an effort to smile knowingly, but she wanted him to be aware that she could consider their last meeting as coolly as he, though the memory of his bare body was burned into her mind.

"As I recall, Miss Amory, on the occasion to which you undoubtedly refer, the error was all yours. However," he said, before she could deliver the blistering retort she had prepared, "this wins no points for Mr. Fellowes. He knows very well that he should not leave you alone." Tonight he was all arrogance

226

and assurance again. The playfulness was gone.

"It was not Mr. Fellowes' fault! I assured him that you would escort me to my mother, and it would be rude of him to keep his next partner waiting."

"Very well." The earl's expression softened a little, and he did not take his eyes from her until he had absorbed every detail of her appearance. To Katherine's surprise, her face did not feel even slightly warm, and with a confidence born of her recent practice, she kept her head high and played coolly with her fan until he had done.

"I hardly know you these days, Katherine," he said softly.

"And I hardly know, my lord, whether or not to take that as a compliment!"

His eyes glowed with appreciation. "Have a care, country cousin. Before you know it you will be renouncing your noble plan for more worldly ends."

"I hope not, my lord," she retorted, "but even a governess must know how to go about in the world. And if you had dined with us, you would have seen something that would make you think Colonel Dawson's establishment a veritable paradise for governesses."

In a moment she was sorry she had gone so far, though the temptation to unburden herself was great, for he remarked wryly, "Why, it doesn't seem to please you, Cousin. Could it be that you prefer to wear a hair-shirt, and play the martyr to the hilt? What more could you want than paradise?"

"Martyr!" Katherine said in disgust. "How little you understand me, my lord, though I thought I had made myself perfectly clear. It is just that the colonel . . . I mean my mother seems . . . oh, let us forget I mentioned it. It is nothing of consequence."

"Katherine, if it worries you then it is of consequence." His voice was suddenly warm and concerned, and the cynical look had gone from his face.

For a moment she was sorely tempted, but with a sigh, she snapped shut her fan, and placed her hand on his arm. "No, it is nothing that need concern you. Let us go and find my mother, if you please."

"Certainly." His tone was stiff now, as if her refusal to discuss it with him had hurt him, but Katherine told herself that her nerves were becoming ridiculously sensitive, and they proceeded in silence out into the antechamber.

"The last glimpse I had of Mrs. Amory," said Tarrington, "she was strolling out on the gallant colonel's arm. By the way, I quite liked him, the famous savior of the Amory family." He glanced sideways at her, and she found it difficult to maintain a blank expression.

"Oh, he has been hovering around her all evening, and if I were Mama I believe it would drive me to distraction," Katherine said, before she could prevent herself.

"Really? Well, your mama did not look at all distracted. In fact, she looked as though she were rather enjoying herself."

She bit back a reply, as they stood looking about the large chamber and hall. She had no desire as yet to put her fears into words, for then she would have to cope with the total overthrow of all her plans and face the future as the dependent of yet another man, kind, this one, and nothing like Uncle Edwin, but with habits of command, and children of his own who would of course be dearer to his heart.

"And where is Lady Tarrington? I have not seen her since I went to dance," she said instead.

Tarrington laughed. "Oh, one of her old swains has probably prevailed upon her to stand up with him. She does occasionally still dance, and I own I like to see it. She is uncommonly graceful, and moves like a woman half her age."

They passed across into another room. From the doorway they had a view of all the players at whist, but neither her mother nor the colonel was present.

"Is there another room?" Katherine asked. "I don't believe the colonel is a gambling man, and I know Mama is not yet strong enough to dance."

But Tarrington did not answer her. He had stopped suddenly

and was squinting into a shadowy alcove. Abruptly he stepped across Katherine's line of vision, but not before she had seen a sight that made her gasp in shock.

Pressed against the wainscotted wall were Delia Amory and her gallant colonel wrapped in a very shameful, but obviously tender, embrace. Their lips had apparently just parted, and they were gazing at each other with eyes full of love.

Affection for her mother brought joy to Katherine's heart, but at the same time she felt the full weight of the blow she had been dreading all night.

"Katherine, I—"

"No, my lord." She did not realize how tightly her hand was now grasping his arm. "Take me back please. I—I want to sit down."

Silently he obeyed, but instead of leading her to where his mother sat fanning herself and exchanging laughing comments with an elderly gentleman, he drew her immediately out onto the floor. The musicians were just beginning a waltz, and Katherine, still numb, fell into it effortlessly.

After a moment, though, she began to struggle. "No! I do not wish . . . please, bring me back."

"Hush, my dear," Tarrington soothed her in a low voice, gripping her so tightly that she could only follow his lead and continue dancing. "It would cause more remark if you gave way now. It is better to pretend nothing is wrong until you have mastered yourself. Dance, now, just dance, and I promise I shall take you home if you wish it."

His voice calmed her, as if she were a frightened horse, and she tried to make her mind a blank, to ride on the waves of music, carried on the warmth of his closeness and his soft murmuring in her ear. She trembled with suppressed emotion, but resolutely refused to think. This was neither the time nor place to confront a complete re-examination of her life and her plans.

But thoughts forced themselves upon her. "Priscilla will be pleased," she said, as though thinking aloud. "She never thought very highly of becoming a governess, but she was too timid to object, and not clever enough to think of something else. Now she can live in the colonel's house and look after his children, and be called a dependent relation instead of a governess."

"Don't be bitter," Tarrington said gently. "It doesn't become you." He whirled her energetically, and before she could catch her breath to reply, he went on. "Try to see it from your mother's point of view. She is in poor health, has nothing but a small competence, no family to rely on, and a daughter and a niece to provide for. And I think, do you not, that she loves him."

"Yes, but . . . but I don't understand! Why didn't she tell me, and why was she so reluctant to come here?" Katherine looked up, pleading with him for answers, answers which she knew he could not give.

"Talk to her tomorrow," he advised. "Be happy for her." The waltz ended, and his hand slid from her waist like a caress. As they made their way back to the chairs where Mrs. Amory now waited with Lady Tarrington, the earl took Katherine's hand and squeezed it encouragingly, and she shook off her trepidation, especially when she saw the glow of happiness on her mother's face.

Still, she was glad that Colonel Dawson was not in sight, and she knew she could not stay. Above all, she wanted to be alone in her room to think over the changes in store and to prepare herself for an interview with her mother on the morrow. She was not ready yet to greet the man who would be her stepfather.

"Mama, his lordship has kindly offered to see me home. I'm afraid I have had a little bit of a headache the whole evening, but I didn't mention it because I did not want to spoil it for all of you. I'm afraid that it is becoming unbearable." She put her hand up to her temple in a convincing imitation of her mother during a bad spell.

Even Mrs. Amory's joy could not prevent her from wondering at this sudden headache striking her robustly healthy child, and her brow furrowed with worry. "Of course, my dear, go right home and get into bed. Have Minette make you a tisane like the one she made for me yesterday, and bathe your temples with lavender water, and—"

"Mama, it's all right. It is only a headache; all I need is a little rest," Katherine assured her, but her mother continued, ending with, "And sleep well, my dear, for I should like to talk to you early tomorrow before we go to the Pump Room. I have something very particular to tell you." Her joy lit up her eyes, and she looked quite young.

Katherine, though, felt very weary and old. "Yes, Mama," she said dutifully, but by then the earl had returned with her wispy evening shawl, and bidding the others goodbye, he led her away.

"Shall we walk, my dear, or would you like me to get you a chair? It is barely round the corner, but I know your fear of the night air." She saw his smile in the last light of the hall as the door shut behind them.

"Pray don't quiz me tonight, my lord," she said irritably, most embarrassed at the memory of the night she had avoided his company by that foolish ploy. Suddenly her fear of him and of her own feelings seemed incredibly silly. He had been so kind and brotherly that it was high time she accepted the friendship he had been offering her from the beginning, putting away her doubts and her hopes of anything more.

"You're right, Cousin. I'm sorry," he said, pressing her hand as they turned the corner.

If Lady Tarrington's Bath butler was surprised by their early return and by the absence of the others, he did not betray it by so much as the flicker of an eyelash.

"Is there a fire in the sitting room, Kent?" asked the earl, as he let them into the vestibule.

"No, my lord, but I shall have the footman make it up if you desire."

"Thank you, and please bring some brandy and two glasses."

231

Tarrington momentarily wished for his own well-run bachelor establishment, where such things as filled decanters and blazing fires on command at any season were commonplace.

"It is really not necessary, my lord," Katherine protested as he led her into the sitting room.

"Do you really have a headache?"

"Of course not. I'm never ill, only a little upset, but—"

"Then I think you had better sit down and have some brandy."

They were silenced by the arrival of the footman who worked incuriously over the grate, and at his departure the butler came with the brandy. Katherine hoped they were really as uninterested as they appeared. It was admittedly a little irregular for her to be alone with the earl so late in the evening. After all, he was a very *distant* relation. She watched with a little thrill of apprehension as Tarrington closed the door firmly behind the servants.

As he began to pour the brandy, Katherine stared into the licking flames of the fire, thoughts she had tried to suppress at the assembly rushing in on her all at once. She almost jumped when she felt Tarrington's light touch on her shoulder.

"Here." He handed her a glass of brandy. "Sip it slowly."

But it was too late. Such awkwardness had overcome her at finding him only a hairsbreadth away that she had taken the glass from him and had immediately swallowed the contents. When the fiery liquid reached her throat she choked, and sputtered and coughed, her eyes watering, while the thin trickle that worked its way down to her stomach did its warming work.

Tarrington shook his head and laughed. "Oh, Katherine, Katherine, my impatient, impossible girl." And taking the glass from her, he thumped her on the back. By then she was half-laughing, half-crying, the tears from the burning brandy mingling with tears of fear, frustration and anger.

Precisely when the back-pounding stopped and became a friendly pat, and when that patting turned into a warm caress, she could not have said, but no sooner had she regained her breath than it was driven from her again, by the unexpectedness of a crushing embrace.

Tarrington's warm, hard body was pressing against her own and his left arm held her close, while with his right hand he stroked her hair, her face, her neck. She was overcome with fear and excitement, and found herself staring helplessly into those changeable eyes, now deep green, now flickering brown in the rising and falling of the light from the fire.

"My sweet," he whispered, and though she heard it, she could not credit it. "So brave, so foolish, so utterly adorable."

The fuzzy thought crossed her beleaguered mind that there was no possible reply to this except to reprimand him for calling her foolish, but even that wisp of questionable reason was driven away by what happened next.

His face wore an expression of such intensity that she found it both a thrill and a torment to continue to look into his eyes, and soon he drew so close to her that it became a merciful blur. Katherine's eyes closed of their own accord, just before his lips met hers.

At first she felt soft, warm pressure, so new and surprising that it sent quivers down to the base of her spine, but then he let his passion have free rein, and suddenly, though she could not have said how, the tip of his tongue was in her mouth, tracing delicate lines inside her lips. She shivered with delight at the unexpected thrill of it, and clung to him, hoping he would never let her go.

By the time their mouths were completely open to one another, and she had, timidly relying on instinct, begun to return his intimate caresses, Tarrington was groaning with desire, and his hands had begun to move smoothly over her, up and down her back, around her waist, and upwards, breathlessly skimming the sides of her breasts so that she could not prevent a tiny sound from escaping her throat.

When finally he withdrew his mouth from hers, Katherine thought she would have swooned if the kiss had continued a

233

moment longer, but he was not yet done. Their bodies were so close that she became aware of something very disturbing and unfamiliar, as he pressed himself still closer against her, and she almost pulled away in alarm, but he had turned his attentions elsewhere, and she could not bear for him to stop.

After burying his fingers in her thick curls, he nibbled gently at her ear, and made his way down along her soft neck to the base of her throat, where he continued to press his kisses, lower and lower, past her collarbone, to the edge of her low-cut bodice.

Sanity, which had fled under the attack of this newly discovered passion, began to return the moment Tarrington's hands reached for the tiny sleeves of her gown and began to slide them over her shoulders. A part of Katherine desperately wanted to let him go further, sensing all kinds of forbidden delights in store, and the tingling and aching that had worked its way down her body begged for relief, of what kind she did not know.

But by now her eyes had been open long enough to recall herself to her surroundings, and her ears had detected the sound of the servants moving about in the hall, the rattle of a carriage on the street outside.

"Please," she whispered, "my lord, we must not . . ."

She moved, gently at first, to disentangle herself from his embrace, and finding that he was reluctant and only continued to caress her bare shoulders with his lips in a way that tried her resolve very painfully, she pulled away more forcefully.

Now he, too, came to his senses, releasing her so quickly that she staggered back against the sofa behind her. He gripped her shoulder to steady her, but when she flinched at the feel of those burning fingers on her flesh once more, terrified lest his touch reawaken that mindless need, he withdrew his hand quickly.

"My God, what have I done?" Tarrington's eyes were as wide as Katherine's own, his face as distraught. "My dear . . . Katherine, forgive me, I should never . . ."

He turned away and unthinkingly gripped the arm of the silk-covered sofa. Katherine, watching the hands that had so lately been on her own silky skin, shivered and averted her eyes.

When he turned back to her, his expression had changed, and he gave a short, mirthless laugh. "I have taken advantage of you, of your confusion, of your innocence. I, who only a few days ago stood in this room and styled myself your protector!"

Katherine still stood, clutching the sofa for support, her breath coming hard and fast, her thoughts in utter chaos. He was apologizing. Did that mean he hadn't wanted to kiss her? Was it only physical need that had driven him to it?

But no, he had known that she needed comfort, had been giving it, until then, in a quite unexceptionable way. She was sure of nothing, nothing except, for once, the strength of her own feelings, but a weight of gloom descended on her as she came to realize that for Tarrington the caresses they had exchanged had not amounted to a declaration.

He berates himself, she thought, for taking advantage of me, or else for putting himself in a dangerous position. Is this the way a lover would behave? He does not love me.

The thought was not accompanied by much bitterness, only the weary sadness of a doubt confirmed. His next words totally disabused her of any misconceptions she might still have.

"Katherine . . . Miss Amory"—he had stepped further away, and his voice lost more of its intimate inflection with each word—"I have betrayed your trust. I have been in a position of responsibility to you, and I have failed."

"But my lord—" She could not let him blame himself entirely for what had occurred, since she knew she could have stopped it at the very beginning. She simply had not wanted to.

"No, Katherine. I admit, I meant to do nothing tonight but help you accept the change in your situation, a change that seems difficult for you to face, with all your ideas of self-sufficiency. I have always tried to make you realize that you need not bind yourself to servitude to escape being a family

235

dependent. You will find, Cousin"—his voice was softer—
"that the most powerful of us are always dependent on someone for something."

"Even you?" she asked in a trembling voice.

"Even me," he said, summoning up a rueful smile.

Katherine wondered just what or who he was dependent on.
He was a man, a lord, with position and title and wealth, though
not as much as some men had. He lived his own life, answered
to no one, even his own family. He went off on his mysterious
rides, and disposed of family heirlooms as casually as if they
had been week-old newspapers; and no doubt he had ordered
every facet of his dead wife's existence, till she disobeyed him
and died. The thought made her shudder.

"Katherine, look at me," he begged. She did, and saw
determination in his features. "I know this may be difficult for
you, especially after what you learned tonight, but perhaps in
the long run it is best for both of us. I see my responsibility
clearly. I am not as wealthy as I once was, but I can offer you
the independence you crave. As the Countess of Tarrington
you would find plenty of scope for your active nature, and I
would expect no more of you than you feel ready to give.
Katherine"—he finally drew close to her again, and his face
very earnest, he gently took her hand—"will you do me the
honor of becoming my wife?"

Their gazes were locked, and Katherine felt raw shame flood
her that she could not hide her first surge of joy, then desperate
disappointment at his words. He spoke of honor, and of
excuses and responsibilities, but not of love.

It is what I would have wanted, she thought hazily, if
only . . . But he was not offering his heart, only his hand—
and his title. The money did not concern her; whatever he had
was more than she had ever expected to have. His past and the
sad story of his first wife touched her. However, the unsolved
mystery of his present activities, his odd acquaintances, and
his business with Mr. Oldbury, only partly explained by the
need to raise money, continued to nag at her.

All of this raced through her mind almost too quickly for it to really affect her decision. She felt his hand tighten on hers and she took a deep breath. "My lord . . . Vane." For the first time she whispered his name, and it was awkward on her tongue. "Are you sure . . . you are very kind, and I have not always been . . . that is, I have been horrid to you on occasion!" she blurted out. His answering smile warmed her a little, but she went on with trepidation, in one last attempt to wrest his secrets from him.

"Is there nothing else you would like to tell me before I answer?"

His eyes fell for a fraction of a second, and his lips tightened, so quickly that had she not been watching intently she could not have noticed it.

"Other than that I fear my overbearing nature hastened the death of the first countess, which is a sorrow I will carry with me always, there is nothing else you need to know. I promise I have learned my lesson, and shall leave you as free as you have always wanted to be."

His face and voice spoke less and less of the lover, and Katherine tried to ease her pain by considering her decision in total disregard of emotion. He is not a fool, she thought, and he must know I suspect all is not right, but he is an honorable man. Perhaps, one day he will confide in me. Or perhaps you will find it out by yourself, whispered a voice inside her.

Mentally she listed the benefits of the match. She would have a man she loved, but who did not love her; a measure of independence, but under a husband's watchful eye, despite his hasty words; a home of her own, children, perhaps. She felt an involuntary shudder of pleasure at the memory of his embrace, but turned her mind hastily to the facts. There was still a mystery to be solved, and whether the solution would bring joy or sorrow, there was no way of telling.

She squeezed her eyes tightly shut for a moment, swallowed the large obstruction in her throat, then said the only thing her heart would allow her to say. "My lord, I would be pleased and honored to become your wife."

When she looked at her betrothed, he was standing as before, but he had let go of her hand. He was wearing a grave smile that did not reach his eyes, and though there was relief in his face, there was no pleasure.

"Thank you, my dear Katherine," he said, then bent to place a chaste kiss on her cheek, managing to do so without touching any other part of her. It was as different from his first kiss as a waltz is to a country dance.

Suddenly he was a man of ice. Katherine was chilled to the bone, as if he, not the fire, had been warming the room.

"Rest assured that you will not have to suffer a repeat of tonight's scene at my hands during our betrothal, Katherine. I shall not embarrass you or myself that way again."

He led a dazed Katherine to the door and before she could form a reply, he was striding down the corridor.

She stood looking after him, weary and miserable to the core, feeling not at all like a young lady who has just accepted an offer from a very charming and handsome young earl. Her heart was full of conflicting emotions, and her tongue had been empty of the right words to express them. But then, she decided, there were no right words.

Chapter Eight

"*These* pantaloons, my lord?" Skempton looked contemptuously down the length of his nose at the garment in question. The worn-out pair of grey stockinette inexpressibles reflected poorly, in his opinion, on his master's taste and on his own reputation as a superior manservant.

The state of his lordship's wardrobe was a source of continual distress to a man of Skempton's sensibilities, even though it had been somewhat alleviated of late by the addition of new evening clothes, a new riding coat, and two waistcoats, on which purchases he had had the unutterable pleasure of advising his master. He was pained, however, that the earl had not seen fit to request his advice on the new pair of boots he had ordered on his last jaunt to London, but had been somewhat mollified when his lordship had assured him that Hoby, and only Hoby, would be entrusted with the making of them.

However, reflecting on it in no way abated his disapproval of the earl's choice on this fine morning. With a presumption perhaps unbecoming to a servant, he hesitated to assist his master into the garment. But the earl's will was not a thing to trifle with. The valet was rewarded with a scowl.

"As I said, Skempton, the grey ones. Look alive, man! I am in no mood to oblige you with an argument this morning."

"Very well, my lord." Skempton sniffed, and his lordship

stepped into the despised garment.

Tarrington stared grimly into his shaving mirror, carefully maneuvering a shining razor past his left ear. Skempton was a loyal servant and as skilled a valet as any gentleman could wish, but the earl insisted upon shaving himself, just as he always tied his own neckcloths.

There are some tasks, he thought, concentrating on his image in the mirror and ignoring the offended servant behind him, that one simply has to perform for oneself, if one is to be satisfied with the result. Had he not been engaged in the delicate operation of shaving, he would have smirked at himself in the mirror or given way to laughter at this thought. It would not have been joyful laughter, but a self-deprecatory snort.

Yes, he thought, I've done it well and truly, with no assistance from anyone. He had good reason now to regret having discarded too soon the habit of asking advice. The morning had brought with it some keen doubts and grinding anxiety about the wisdom of his actions the night before. He was not at all certain he had done the right thing in asking Katherine Amory to be his wife.

Though it had been many days since he had first realized how precious she was to him, experience told him that his affection was not yet returned, and there was no guarantee that it ever would be, or not in the way he would like. I have taken advantage of an inexperienced young woman in a moment of weakness, he berated himself. I only pray that she will not be too unhappy with her quick decision.

Though it was obvious to him, in the clear light of morning, that he ought to offer her an opportunity to withdraw, he resolutely put any such intention from his mind. He was certain that she would either take it as an insulting attempt on his part to cry off, or decide that she did not want to marry him after all; and this, despite his concern for her ultimate happiness, he did not want her to do.

Tarrington did congratulate himself on conquering her disinclination for marriage by what he considered an inspired description of the life she would lead as his countess. That, he thought, is what turned the trick. Although he imagined, not without pain, that there had been a hint of calculation in her eyes as she mulled it over right there before him.

The shaving finished, Skempton attended to the razor and then helped his master on with a fine, but carefully mended, shirt and a buff-colored waistcoat, watching in respectful silence as the neckcloth was tied and noting that his lordship appeared uncharacteristically careless about it today, then assisting with the black coat, taking care not to disarrange any of the previous preparations.

His lordship submitted impatiently to his hair being dressed, and grimaced as Skempton sprayed him with a mere mist of masculine eau de cologne, an affectation upon which he insisted before he would let his master leave the dressing room, Brummell's precept on the subject notwithstanding. Then the earl stalked down the hall to his mother's room. He must tell her and Sally what he had done, before they all met at breakfast.

Tarrington was in no doubt but that both of them, and Mrs. Amory as well, would be thrilled; and of course his friend Knolland would be excited unto incoherence, after his broad hints about remarrying. He had, besides, more than a small suspicion that Rodney felt that such a marriage might make his own romantic aspirations easier to realize.

And I, he thought, stopping abruptly with his hand raised before the door of his mother's boudoir, am I happy? After all, I love her. She is sweet, she is severe, she is quiet, she is lively . . . his pulses quickened at the mere memory of her yielding warmth in his arms. Katherine was altogether such a delightful contradiction.

She was intelligent, but unschooled; and he anticipated the joy of supplying her with all she lacked and of guiding her steps along the way to the maturity that awaited her. A tiny voice within him cried a warning at this—remember Cassandra!—but he shrugged it off.

Katherine is different, he told himself. She is not a heedless, spoiled child, merely a single-minded young woman unawakened to all of life's possibilities. And he was now a different man from that anxious, infatuated, intense young husband of a few years ago. This time, he vowed, I shall not make the same mistake. Then he lowered his hand to knock gently on the door.

At that very moment, in Mrs. Amory's bedchamber, there was a scene of celebration in progress. "My dearest . . . is it . . . can it possibly be true? Oh, my love!"

With one arm, Mrs. Amory clasped her child to her bosom, overcome with joy, while with the other she reached for her handkerchief. "You will be Countess of Tarrington! My daughter, my dear little Katherine . . ." She dissolved into sobs of happiness.

"Now Mama, pray be calm, do, else you will go off into a swoon and won't be able to see your future son-in-law at breakfast!" Katherine teased, returning her mother's embrace.

Outwardly she was smiling as delightedly as her mother and Priscilla, who stood by hopping with impatience till she could hug Katherine herself, but inwardly she was quivering with anxiety.

Had it been a dream? But no, the memory of Tarrington's kisses, the tautness in his voice when he offered for her and the peculiar rigidity of his expression when she had accepted, were engraved too deeply on her mind to be only the wispy remnants of dreams.

It had happened. She was going to marry the Earl of Tarrington. She need never worry again about securing her future. With that thought came an unexpected and inexplicable wave of melancholy. Luckily her mother and cousin attributed the wetness of her eyes to her happiness.

Though she no longer expected her love to be returned, it hurt her that, even at such a moment as the one last night,

Tarrington had been reluctant to make a clean breast of things, to answer her unspoken questions about the oddities in his life, actions that a prospective wife would have a right to know . . . or would she?

The intricacies of premarital relationships were still beyond her ken. She did not know enough about the subject to compare this sudden betrothal to others among those of Tarrington's class.

Though his advances could be considered compromising, no one had witnessed them, and surely he knew her well enough to feel certain that she would never raise an outcry against him. The earl could not have made the offer out of pity for her situation, either, for who besides herself, with her admittedly odd ideas, would feel pity for a girl who faced nothing less than a secure and comfortable future, under the roof of a doting mother and kind stepfather?

A girl of only respectable birth and with no fortune of her own could hardly do better. And the colonel would certainly have done his best to introduce her to some eligible men, so that she might have made a decent enough match one day.

Decent enough, yes, but how could she feel for any man what she had come to feel for Tarrington? Already it was difficult to drag her thoughts away from the memory that alternately horrified and thrilled her, those moments of enchantment and wonder in his arms, with his mouth over hers. . . . Too soon she was jolted back to the present.

"And when shall you be married, Kate?" Priscilla wanted to know. Katherine wondered if her cousin's joy was not unalloyed with sorrow in comparison to her own situation. It simply wasn't fair. Priscilla and Rodney were in love, and as vast a gulf separated them as if they lived on different continents, while she and Tarrington— But then she recalled, with a little smile, the first genuine smile of the day, Lord Knolland's plan. Perhaps some good would come out of this after all.

"I don't know, Pris, we didn't—"

"But of course Lady Tarrington and I will see to it that your wedding is perfectly lovely, my dear, whatever you and the earl decide," Mrs. Amory interjected. She clasped her hands together over her heart. "To think I was worried about you, though of course I would never have mentioned it, but I knew it would all come right in the end. And I haven't even told you *my* news yet!"

Katherine sent a silent prayer to Providence in thanks for that. On no account did she want her mother to know that it was her disappointment and uncertainty about the future once the marriage to Colonel Dawson took place that had driven her into Tarrington's arms, doubts and all.

Marriage without love, she knew, was a common enough phenomenon, especially where there were titles or fortune in question. But Tarrington's fortune was diminished, her own nonexistent. The earl's respected title alone, though, could have brought him the fortune of any wealthy tradesman's daughter.

Try as she might, Katherine could not see her betrothal as anything but highly irregular, and evidence of Tarrington's kindness and disregard for the conventions. She knew she should be satisfied, if not happy. But it was no use, and all that she could think of was the fire that had swept through her at his embrace, and of his face as he said the words, "I shall never so embarrass you again."

Inexperienced in love she might be, and the surge of response to his advances had frightened her for a moment, but she could not account for his behavior other than to think he had mistaken her surprise and docility in his arms for coolness to his advances or simply a need for comfort.

If he had, she thought with a sudden spark of anger, he had been extremely foolish. I'll show him how wrong he is, she promised herself, at the very next opportunity. He might not love me now, but I will *make* him love me one day.

"Katherine, dearest, I know your head is in the clouds, but surely you can pay attention for a moment. I want to tell you my wonderful news." Mrs. Amory jiggled her daughter's arm impatiently, but when Katherine sat down beside her and prepared to listen, she was suddenly shy and hesitant.

"Very well, Mama, go ahead." Katherine prepared herself to seem as happy as she ought to.

"I . . ."

"Yes, Mama?"

Mrs. Amory signalled for the cup of tea on her nightstand, and Priscilla brought it. She sipped and began again. "You may not have noticed, er, that is, my love, you might have wondered last night, when Joshua, I mean Colonel Dawson, of course, was so very . . ."

Katherine was touched at the shyness of her mother's manner. Why, she was like a young girl with her first beau. *In fact, she is more like one than I am, in love for the first time, in spite of everything that should have prevented it.* That awareness only made it more difficult, however, to keep pretending to be happy. She hurried the difficult scene to its conclusion, despite the trying meeting with her betrothed that awaited her downstairs.

"I think I know what you are trying to tell me, Mama," she said smiling with an effort. "Let me be the first to wish you both very happy." In spite of everything, she was grateful for the events of last night; only these had made it possible for her to accept the news in a manner appropriate for a loving daughter.

She hugged her mother, whose surprise at Katherine's perspicacity rendered her incapable of forming a complete sentence for some minutes. In the end, she only said, "So you knew! How very odd, yet I thought you might have suspected just a little, from the colonel's so very charming attentions to me all through dinner, and of course, though I had long forgotten it, from the letter."

"Whatever do you mean, Mama? Which letter?" Katherine looked at Priscilla for enlightenment, but her cousin only returned her question with a shrug and a look as blank

245

as her own.

"Why, the letter dear Joshua wrote in reply to ours, when you thought he was offering us positions in his household." A roguish smile crept over her face.

Katherine sat down, dazed. "Mama, you are not having one of your spells again . . . you do realize that you are not making any sense?"

Mrs. Amory blushed again and looked more sly than ever. "Well, at that time I was still so overcome by everything—your dear father's memory, as it always will be, of course, was still in my heart—and I was not utterly convinced that Joshua— That is, though our friendship was one of very long standing . . ." She looked away from her daughter's bemused face, and whispered, "It is rather shameful. You see, I knew the colonel before I ever knew your father, and at the time I was very—"

Katherine watched, amazed, as her mother flushed an even deeper pink, and Priscilla sat listening, equally fascinated.

"I was in love with him then, but he—he married Flora Parsons instead, and so when your father offered—not that I did not have the greatest respect for him—and of course, as time went on I came to love him dearly. But when your father lay dying and he begged his friend Joshua to take care of us, the colonel sent me this letter. Bring me that little box, please, dear."

Katherine brought the old leather box from where it sat on the chest of drawers, and watched while her mother rummaged through it and retrieved a much-folded missive from its depths. She clasped it to her bosom.

"Well, I thought it was only out of pity. I didn't believe he could love me as I had once loved him, as I still—" Tears choked her for a moment.

"Mama," Katherine said softly, "there is no need, I wouldn't distress you for the world!"

"No, child, you should know, and it doesn't matter now. We're so very happy—at last! Here, read the whole letter. When it first came, I only showed you the second page."

Katherine and Priscilla sat huddled together on the edge of Mrs. Amory's bed, their heads—one auburn, one chestnut—bowed over the well-creased page.

My dear Delia;

It was with surprise and pleasure that I received your recent letter, and I thank you for your kind condolences upon the loss of my poor Flora, may she rest in peace.

Young Katherine's inquiry could not have come at a better time, for, as you know, it is barely six months since the Lord took my faithful wife to his bosom. Even so, you must know that my feelings for you, though long unspoken, have not changed. Indeed, God forgive me, although you were already married to my best friend in the world, and I already pledged to Flora and unable to reveal my secret heart, they could not be denied, only concealed.

Since Walter's death I have begged to be allowed to assist you in some way, any way, but your pride would not allow you to give me the relief I sought in helping you. At that time it seemed that we would never belong to one another. And now, my dearest friend, we are both alone, and according to what your daughter writes, you will shortly have no home.

I pray that you will at least let me do for you what my heart, my conscience, my honor—nay, my soul—tells me is the right thing. I humbly beg that you will do me the honor of accepting my hand in marriage. I do not immediately post to Whitfield myself to ask it of you in person because I wish to give you time to think about it without being unduly influenced by my passion. I hope your heart will decide in my favor.

If you will not do so out of affection, which, though you may deny it, as for years you have very properly done considering our situation—I'll swear you have had for me from the first—then say yes out of pity for me and my poor dear motherless children.

We need you, aye, and Katherine and your niece as well. The girls, I am sure, are well taught enough to guide and teach the little ones. Walter often spoke with pride of Katherine's great talent for drawing; she shall teach my own daughters.

As for you, Delia, I could have no greater pleasure than to see you at the head of my household, directing and ordering everything in your efficient way. Well do I recall Walter saying we could not have done better than to engage you as quartermaster, so talented were you at managing.

The details can be arranged later; only come, come to Bath, where I wait for you to take charge of me and the children, and in return I shall see that you and the girls want for nothing. I await your decision.

Respectfully,
Colonel Joshua Dawson (Ret.)

The two girls finished the letter in silence interrupted only by the sound of Mrs. Amory's spoon clinking against the sides of her glass as she mixed a restorative that had been prescribed for her, and of which she was by now in great need. Then they looked up, glanced at one another, and began to laugh.

"Why, Mama, you sly thing, you have hidden it from us all along! How odd that I did not wonder at it when you showed me only the page beginning with "We need you." Though I would never have suspected you of concealing such a romantic past, I am happy for you." She kissed her again. "It has all turned out very well."

But when she was alone, Katherine reflected somberly that all her noble ambitions of independence had been no more than a phantasm, a hollow thing of bold words and intentions, with nothing to support it. There had never been a chance of any of it happening. Her mother had known very well what would follow upon their arrival in Bath, and had only been procrastinating until she'd known her own mind on the matter.

The colonel, Katherine knew now, would never have let them enter his employ as servants of any kind, even had her mother refused his offer.

And I am the biggest fool in the entire country, she thought, preparing with trepidation to go down to breakfast and face her betrothed for the first time before the others. Why cannot I be content, as any other women in my position, to have a roof over my head and a man to give me his name? Why must I long instead for even the lowliest level of independence possible in this uneven world?

But these questions were moot. She had cast her lot with Tarrington now, for better or worse.

Chapter Nine

The most miserable week in Katherine's life crept by with painful slowness, and so expert had she become at concealing her emotions that none of the residents or visitors at the house in Gay Street formed the slightest suspicion that Miss Amory was not reveling in her good fortune.

True, the house was constantly abustle, what with the arrival of the weary Lord Colesville, reunited at last with a suddenly demure but glowingly happy Sally, and the frequent visits of Colonel Dawson, who could hardly contain himself till the arrival of that day on which he would count himself among the happiest of men.

But Katherine wondered that no one seemed to notice how little time Lord Tarrington spent with *his* betrothed, and how stiffly he acknowledged the congratulations of their Bath acquaintances. Katherine could not help feeling the way he distanced himself from her, as if it were a nagging itch beneath a new wool gown, smooth on the surface but rough next to the skin.

While they stood close together accepting the good wishes of friends and family, he rarely looked at her. When they went out, her hand in his arm, she felt as though her warm flesh rested on the cold marble of a statue. They were rarely alone, it seemed to Katherine by design, and when they were, he had not once attempted to take her into his arms. In fact, he appeared to have forgotten the very circumstances that had led him to offer for her in the first place.

What was even worse, they had begun to quarrel. Katherine could not understand how the arguments came about at first. To be sure, she had from the first been at cross-purposes with Tarrington, but the friendship that had grown up between them seemed to have smoothed over much of their basis for disagreement.

The first inkling she had that he was displeased with her again was on the occasion of a small rout given by Lady Tarrington on the arrival of her son-in-law Colesville. His lordship was a calm, soft-spoken, somewhat pale man of medium height, with an expressive voice worthy of an orator and keen, intelligent grey eyes.

It gave Katherine a pang of mingled happiness and sorrow to see how much in love the Colesvilles were, though they strove to hide such an unfashionable affliction while in the public eye. Sally, at first filled with quiet joy, was even livelier than usual by the time twenty-four hours had passed since her husband's arrival in Bath, and was bustling about making ready to leave for their seat in the North, where they would spend the rest of the summer.

At first the Amory ladies had wondered at the contrast between Sally and her husband, but soon it became apparent that his dry, sly wit was more than a match for her ladyship's liveliness, and that they complemented one another to perfection. Very soon they found that they liked his lordship as much as they liked their cousin Sally, and looked forward to accepting their invitation to visit as soon as the various weddings had been accomplished.

In fact, it was while Katherine was dancing with Lord Colesville, and being vastly entertained by his intriguing tales of political figures and Parliamentary gossip, that she first chanced to incur Tarrington's displeasure.

Just as Colesville relinquished her hand at the conclusion of a set, and Katherine was still laughing delightedly at his last anecdote, she found Tarrington awaiting her, his arms crossed uncompromisingly over his chest, his face as stern as she had ever seen it. He greeted his sister's husband with a subdued smile.

"Here she is, Tarrington. Now let us make an exchange. I bring your fiancée to you—and you for heaven's sake please tell me where Sally has got to this time!" Lord Colesville pleaded.

"I believe she has just sat down for a chat with Mr. Fellowes," Tarrington replied, and Katherine followed his gaze to where his sister sat, one ear inclined towards a high-spirited Mr. Fellowes, while her eyes discreetly searched the room for an escape.

"Ah!" Lord Colesville rubbed his hands and started off, crying over his shoulder. "Nothing to make a man a hero in his wife's eyes like rescuing her from unwanted attentions, eh?"

Then they were alone, and Tarrington began immediately on the scold that Katherine had been expecting. He left her no time to wonder before he let her know precisely how she had angered him.

"Is it not enough, Katherine, that you expose yourself in that gown tonight? Must you shriek with laughter like a hoyden while on the dance floor before all these people?" His voice was soft, but its contemptuous tone was cutting, and for a moment she was too hurt to reply.

"That gown," she thought, is no more revealing than what any other lady present is wearing, and it was quite unjust of him to accuse me of exposing myself.

It was a garnet satin, cut low over her breasts, but discreetly so, and edged at neck, hem, and barely existent sleeves with puffs of the same fabric caught up with pearls. It skimmed her hips flatteringly, and made her look, Lord Colesville had gallantly informed her, as though she were already a countess.

And it was really too bad of Vane to say that her behavior on the dance floor had been inappropriate. The unfairness of it, combined with the fact that he had not once complimented her during the entire evening; or said anything that a gentleman should say to his betrothed, prodded her to express the outrage that had been slowly building at every instance of his neglect.

"I beg your pardon, sir, but when a gentleman takes the trouble to entertain a lady with an amusing story, it is only right that he should be rewarded with a laugh for his pains. And as for what you have to say about my gown"—she took a breath and met his eyes; they were cold and hard, and even the flickers of candlelight could not seem to ignite a spark in them tonight—"it is too absurd for me to even argue about it."

She turned away deliberately, and immediately there was a gentleman at her side, one of her former admirers, now freed to exert himself to the fullest to be gallant, as she was safely betrothed. She accepted the offer of a glass of champagne. "Oh, thank you, Lord Jamison, dancing makes me horribly thirsty. But no . . . do let me come with you . . . the *boulanger?* Certainly, sir. I am sure his lordship can spare me."

With one last glance at her betrothed, whose face was rigid with disapproval, she sailed away, her heart beating wildly at having dared such defiance.

But after all, she told herself, if I am to marry him, he must learn that I am not to be taken for granted. Again, she wondered why he had troubled to ask for her hand. Not for the first time, she considered if it would not be wiser to cry off. She had soon enough recovered from the shock of her mother's planned marriage, and a visit or two to Colonel Dawson's house had shown her that her life there would be no less pleasant, in most respects, than her current existence.

But there was a stubborn desire to capture this elusive thing that she had stumbled on all unaware. Love had come into her life, and she would not give it up without a struggle. What her life would be if Tarrington never grew to love her did not bear thinking of, but it could hardly, she thought, be much worse than this.

His lordship's attitude the next morning at breakfast told Katherine that her small attempt at rebellion had been useless. He was only colder and even more correct, if possible, than before.

A casual question from the Dowager Countess as to when he expected they would be married, brought the short answer, "In December, ma'am, at Whitfield." He did not even pretend to have consulted his betrothed on the matter, but grimly swallowed two cups of coffee in swift succession while Katherine struggled for words. How humiliating to have to admit that she and Tarrington had not even discussed it!

In the end, she lingered after the others had gone their separate ways, and when the earl would have risen, she detained him.

"My lord," she began, for when he was in this mood she could not bring herself to call him by his first name, and indeed, he had never invited her to do so. "I wish you would have asked for my opinion on the matter of our . . . wedding. If you had, I should hardly have chosen such a month as December, and certainly not Whitfield!"

He stopped, turned, and looked down at her. "Then it is fortunate that I did *not* ask for your opinion, my dear. At Whitfield, in early December. That will be best. Forgive me, but you have no other home to be married from, and four months should be more than sufficient time for the accumulation of wedding-clothes and such."

"But December . . . that is so soon. I had thought perhaps in the spring," she blurted out, in sudden terror at the thought of life with the stranger he had become. She bitterly regretted that she had not been able to master her surprise and disappointment on that night, so that he would never have seen a need to comfort her and those moments of madness need never have happened. She could still cry off. . . .

No, it was too difficult, even though he stood there staring at her with the oddest expression on his face. Perhaps this was all a ploy to enable her to do so with a good excuse. He knew very well that she hated to be told what to do.

But Tarrington's thoughts ran along very different lines. Too soon, he thought, she thinks December is too soon, and to me it is eternity. I was right, she is beginning to regret it, but I can't let her go now. After the marriage, after his delicate business had been completed, successfully, he hoped, they would be alone at Northfolde, and he would make her understand.

But it seemed that since their betrothal she had been going out of her way to irritate him. The effort of keeping his feelings pent up had put him so on edge, that the slightest things could set him off. How many times had he wanted to pull her into his arms and kiss that puzzled frown from her forehead, or to taste those sweet lips against his once again! But all he could do was armor himself against her beauty by insisting on correct and unemotional behavior.

And now she was looking up at him in mute appeal, begging him, he imagined, to release her from this engagement. Well, he would not, he decided. "In December, Katherine," he said, and left her staring after him.

Katherine brooded, alone in the breakfast parlor until Priscilla came for her, attired in a new cornflower blue muslin walking dress and leghorn bonnet with matching ribbons.

"What's this, Kate? Hurry, your mama is waiting to go to the Pump Room. She is eager to see the colonel, even though they saw one another yesterday. I vow"—she sighed—"I wish they were already married, the way they go on. Rodney says that the colonel is behaving like a moon-calf, and he does the drollest imitation . . . but come on, we shall be late. Rodney will meet us there later, after his ride with Tarrington."

She paused uncertainly, and dropped into a chair beside her cousin. "Oh, Kate, I think he is going to offer for me! I thought he would have asked me last night, but there were so many people about, and so he asked if I would be at the Pump Room today, and he said it with such a . . . a *meaningful* look on his face . . . do be a dear and leave me alone with him!"

256

Her cousin's anticipation was just the thing Katherine needed to distract her from her own thoughts. "Of course I will, you goose! Be sure to let me be the first to wish you happy, when it is all over." On the way there, Katherine consoled herself with the thought that her hasty engagement would at least bring happiness to her cousin and Lord Knolland.

But it appeared that she was to be denied even this consolation. They had been at the Pump Room for much of the morning, but Lord Knolland had not appeared. Priscilla and Katherine had to be content with hoping that he would arrive in time to escort them home. They sat by Mrs. Amory's side until the colonel arrived and bore off his bride-to-be to meet some friends newly arrived in Bath, and then Mr. Fellowes descended upon them, neglecting his usual ritual of greetings.

"My dear young ladies! Ah, how sorry I am that Bath will lose such perfection, just when we had been sure of gaining you for our own. Our future Countess of Tarrington"—he bowed to Katherine—"and if rumor is correct, our future Lady Knolland." He made a bow to blushing Priscilla.

"You are a bit premature, sir," Katherine admonished him, but with a smile. "Your sources of information must have a great deal of confidence, or perhaps a supernatural foresight, to divine Lord Knolland's intentions."

Mr. Fellowes smiled on them benignly and patted Priscilla's hand. "It needs no gift of divination to see that Lord Knolland is a man very much in love with a charming young lady. And where is our Romeo, by the by?" His keen little eyes traveled over the thin company.

"He is not arrived yet," Katherine said shortly. Sighting her mother across the room, she said to her cousin, "Pris, I have Mama's shawl here—I think she may need it. Would you be an angel and bring it to her?"

Priscilla rose eagerly, tired of sitting and watching the door for Lord Knolland. "Of course. And if . . . Oh, never mind." She took the shawl and scurried over to her aunt with it.

"Now, my dear Miss Amory, I hope that you may rely on my

humble knowledge to guide you, as you sometimes have in the past weeks. What advice do you seek?" Mr. Fellowes wanted to know.

"You misunderstood my little ruse, sir. I simply wanted to ask you not to speak of my cousin's betrothal as if it were a certain thing." Lord Knolland's failure to arrive that morning had worried her more than she wanted Priscilla to know.

"But, my dear, is it not?" Mr. Fellowes leaned forward anxiously, playing with the gold fob on the end of his watch chain. "After all, though your pretty little cousin has been quite popular here, his lordship was forever standing against the wall watching her, as though he dared not admire her as he wanted to. I confess I do not understand his hesitation unless . . ." He sighed. "Ah, but it is the fortune, of course, like so many others. Yet, since *your* betrothal, Miss Amory, there has been a marked change. Have you not noted it? Perhaps he thinks that where there is one wedding, there may as well be two. He is about to come to the point, my dear. Take it from a man of my experience." He nodded sagely.

Katherine could only agree. When Rodney had heard the news of the engagement, he had been beside himself with joy, hurrying to pump her hand, wishing her happy over and over, and clapping the earl on the back so many times that finally that gentleman had to beg him to desist. She had been sure that it would be only a matter of a day or so until everything was settled between him and her cousin.

But perhaps he had had some last-minute uncertainties about how Priscilla would accept his addresses, for instead of proposing immediately, he had begun to court her all over again, with compliments and bouquets. He had even lowered himself so far as to join the little groups that clustered around her at evening parties, though, to be sure, he was compensated by being permitted to bear her off triumphantly to dance the waltz. By now, Katherine thought, he must be sure that Priscilla returns his affection. They had spent almost the whole of every day together, and most of the evenings as well.

"Then why is he not here?"

Katherine did not realize that she had spoken aloud until Mr. Fellowes said, "Well, perhaps this is too public a place for him. Don't fret, my dear. I know that every young lady who is betrothed wants to see all her friends share her happiness. It will come about soon enough. It doesn't do to rush these things, you know."

It was in this same precept that the subject of their discussion was being instructed at that very moment, approaching Pultney Bridge. Knolland rode beside his friend Tarrington, struck silent by what he had just been told, but it was not long before even this understanding gentleman expressed his sense of injustice.

"Devil take it! I've waited so long, and now you tell me you're not *sure?* Why, I was about to ask her this very morning!"

"I'm sorry, my friend, but it would be wiser for you to wait a little longer, rather than raise false hopes in Miss Townsend. Besides, it was a hare-brained scheme in the first place! I could hardly credit it when you told me you'd actually mentioned it to Katherine."

It had been a painful moment for Tarrington when Knolland had revealed his conversation with Katherine. The inevitable reflection had arisen that the possibility of her cousin's marriage had been yet another advantage to accepting his offer.

What a fool I have been, and still am, he thought. I rate my own attractions far too low. What woman would have turned up her nose at an offer from the Earl of Tarrington? But now his doubts had driven him to caution Rodney against counting on the match to secure his future with Priscilla. He was not at all sure that Katherine would not cry off, after all. Her reluctance to agree to his proposed wedding date had cut him deeply.

"There's still no guarantee, even if Katherine and I do ever make a match of it," he told the disappointed Lord Knolland, "that your uncles will consent to your marrying her cousin.

259

They may like me, but I'm certainly not able to dower the girl, and you know that's what weighs with them."

As they crossed the bridge, Rodney sighed, and hardly seemed to notice the bright sun glimmering on the waters of the Avon, the busy shops lining it, and the pretty women strolling in their filmy muslins, shaded by gay parasols, darting interested glances at the two gentlemen riding by.

"I suppose you're right, as usual. I don't dare show myself at the Pump Room now, after what she must be expecting. In fact, I wish you will tell them I have gone to see to a tooth-ache, or anything you please. I can't face Miss Townsend today, after this. But I'll be damned if I'll lose her!"

He glowered at the earl. "You and Miss Amory had better make it up between you, whatever it may be. She'll make you just the wife you need, you know. Or at least, you should." He kicked his horse and trotted away ahead of Tarrington, who maintained only a sober trot, musing on his friend's words.

Amazingly, Rodney was right, though it was an unusual state of affairs. For a moment he thought of Cassandra, and for once, the memory did not bring with it that pang of regret and guilt. Her ghost had been put to rest, along with the shreds of his immature love. Now he must concentrate on Katherine, and on not making the same mistakes again.

I've already made a poor start there, he recalled. He had been unable to stop himself from commenting when he saw her, so vital and lovely, in that enticing gown, laughing and dancing in another man's arms, even if that man was his sister's husband, and rationally he knew nothing whatever improper was going on.

But it was all too easy to fall into the old patterns. And with the added pressure of a certain unfinished matter that he had been expecting each day to come to a head, he was in no way able to control himself around Katherine. The wisest thing to do for now, he thought, was to avoid her. It would be better than quarrelling.

It would not be for long. Mrs. Amory would marry as soon as

the colonel had observed a decent mourning, and he and Katherine would marry in December. There, at least, he would not give in.

But long before that, one of his main worries would be ended. The earl expected to meet later that day with an old acquaintance, the same curious-looking man with whom he had once met at the Black Horse, back in the village of Barton. If all went as he expected, his acquaintance would report that a certain interesting crime had been traced to a Mr. George Old-bury.

A partial solution to his problem blazed before Tarrington's eyes. I shall have to tell Katherine, he decided. She certainly suspects something, and it can only make things worse between us. It is perfectly safe now, so close to the end. Perhaps she will begin to understand me, he thought, and, with a sudden burst of speed, he overtook Knolland, smiling with real happiness for the first time in days.

When Mrs. Amory had drunk her two glasses and had been paraded proudly about by the colonel, she confessed to a desire to visit a shop in Milsom Street, and as the colonel, deplore it though he must, had another engagement to meet some cronies at a coffee-house, Katherine and Priscilla, who had finally given up hope of Lord Knolland's arrival, were elected to escort her.

Mrs. Amory's strength having returned to a great extent, she was able to walk, albeit slowly, all the way there, with the support of her daughter and niece. It was when they had just about reached the linen drapers' that was their destination, that Priscilla uttered a strangled sound.

"Oh, look, Kate," she whispered, her face pale with dismay, while Mrs. Amory was entering the shop. "It is Lord Knolland—and Tarrington is with him. Oh, I feel like such a fool. Why did I ever think that he was going to offer for me!" she wailed. The gentlemen were almost upon them.

"Come, let's go in," Katherine urged, reluctant to face them.

But it was too late. The two gentlemen had seen them, and in a moment they had walked their horses over to where the girls stood, and were dismounting.

Priscilla's face was fiery red with hurt and embarrassment, and Katherine looked away as Tarrington greeted her. Lord Knolland, to do him credit, looked quite as uncomfortable as anyone. He nervously ruffled his hair before replacing his hat.

"Lovely day," he commented, gesturing stiffly at the almost cloudless sky. "Tarrington insisted I join him for a ride— thought I was looking worn to a thread—I'm an outdoor man. Never feel so stout as when I'm out in the air, you know."

His imagination exhausted, he subsided into an embarrassed silence, while Priscilla treated his attempt at an explanation as if it had never been uttered.

"My aunt awaits me inside the shop. Katherine, are you coming?" She nodded coldly. "Good day, my lord." And without another glance at her tongue-tied and miserable admirer, she entered the shop.

Katherine was angry at Knolland's desertion when he had once more brought her cousin to the point of hope, but she felt that she could not question him again about his intentions in Tarrington's presence. Even if she had wanted to, Tarrington himself would certainly have prevented her. Nothing she did or said met with his approval.

"Go home, Rodney," the earl said to his friend. "I have something to discuss with Katherine."

To Katherine's annoyance, for the last thing she wanted was to be left alone with her betrothed, his lordship obeyed immediately. She attempted a desperate glance at Priscilla through the shop window, but her cousin only waved and did not come out to rescue her.

She turned and resolutely faced Tarrington. Surprisingly, he had lost the stern expression to which he had treated her ever since their betrothal, and he looked more like his former self than she had yet seen him.

"Katherine, I know that this is not the proper place or time, but . . ." He had taken her hand, and now he unconsciously squeezed it as he hesitated. His touch communicated a warmth that had been lacking ever since their betrothal. Suddenly the iciness that had descended upon him that night had melted away.

"There are some things I must tell you about—about myself, things that you, as my future wife, have a right to know."

By now Katherine was all but oblivious of the bustle of the street: people walking by them; carts, carriages, and sedan chairs passing; and vendors and chairmen crying out to attract business. It all faded into a blur of sound, and the thing she heard most clearly was the unspoken emotion in Tarrington's voice.

She saw nothing but his face, the earnest expression of his clear hazel eyes and the lines of worry etched deeper around his mouth. For a moment it was almost as it had been that day on the hilltop near Whitfield.

"I've already told you some things, Katherine, about selling some of my father's art collection, and I know that Knolland has told you about the death of my first wife."

At her silent nod, he went on. "I did not tell you the entire truth, my dear. After Cassandra—my wife—died in the accident two years ago, I found myself poised on the brink of ruin. I managed to save most of my fortune—but I did need to sell some things to keep afloat."

"I began with the things that reminded me too much of *her*. First to go was a pair of Chinese vases she had seen in a little shop and begged me to buy." A brief, pained smile flitted across his face at the memory. "I said no, but later I surprised her with them for her birthday." The smile was gone as if it had never been.

"They were ugly things, to me, but she was very proud of them, and they were much admired among our friends at the

263

time. So when I wanted to sell, I first asked a gentleman of our acquaintance who was an avid collector of such things."

Katherine was so involved in the story that she did not hear the post-chaise come rattling along the street and stop across the way before a lodging-house.

"He bought them for a very good price—more than *I* thought they were worth—and I heard no more from him until the day he came to see me at Northfolde, furiously angry. I had sold him a pair of forgeries, he said, and he threatened to reveal it to the world."

Katherine gasped. Her eyes fixed on his in mingled horror and sympathy, she did not notice the slightly stout, ruddy young man descend from the chaise across the street and direct his servant to see to his baggage.

"You must understand, my dear," Tarrington went on, his voice soft and intent, "that my social position was already shaky because of the scandal surrounding Cassandra's death and my own stupidity in living as a recluse for an entire year. I could not have stood any more scandal, especially when my fortune was not yet secure." He let out a long breath, and Katherine was impatient for him to continue.

"It was difficult, but I managed to convince him that I had not known the vases were fakes, and restored his money to him. Then I went to the shop where I had bought them, but of course it was long closed." He frowned. "I have learned since that such places commonly do business for only months at a time, then move on."

Katherine was more puzzled than ever by this explanation of his, which seemed to have nothing to do with all of the oddities she had observed in his behavior since she had known him. In what way, she wondered, does it concern our marriage? Distracted by this thought, she glanced away from him for a second and immediately a figure that had been intruding itself on the corner of her eye jumped into her line of vision.

The chaise across the street was pulling away, and its sole passenger stood, portmanteau at his side, giving orders to a servant who had emerged from the house. The new arrival in Bath, Katherine observed with disgust, was none other than Mr. George Oldbury.

"And so it was then that I determined—" Tarrington, following her gaze, had seen Oldbury, and immediately it was as if a curtain had been drawn between them. He did not trouble to finish his sentence, but shut his mouth, eyeing the man across the way as though he had seen a ghost.

Katherine thrust her surprise at Oldbury's arrival resolutely from her mind. All her attention was for Tarrington. "Yes, my lord? Please do go on. . . ."

But the silken cord between them had been slashed asunder by the appearance of Oldbury. The earl's features resolved themselves once more into lines of cool, distant courtesy.

"I find that it is of no consequence, after all, my dear." His voice chilled her. "I pray you will excuse me. Some pressing business has been suddenly brought to mind. We shall discuss all of this at another time."

In dismay, Katherine fixed her eyes on him and opened her mouth to protest, but he only snatched at her hand, pressed a hasty kiss on it, and took his leave.

She had only two things for which to be grateful. The first was that, if she hurried, she could duck into the shop and avoid Mr. Oldbury's catching sight of her. The second was that, before he remounted his horse, her betrothed pressed her hand once more and then bestowed upon her a last long glance. His mouth was as stern as before, but though she could not be certain, it seemed that his eyes still retained a hint of their former warmth. And with that she had to be content.

Chapter Ten

At an inn in one of the less salubrious parts of Bath, close to the river where the damp winds brought the threat of putrid fevers, a middle-aged man in a frieze coat descended to the taproom. He was grey-haired but unbent, obviously stout enough to fight off any illness the neighborhood might harbor. He shuffled behind the tapster who had summoned him from his tiny room, and was in turn followed by a ragged, mop-headed boy who tripped lightly down at his heels.

"What's this, guv'nor? Our gentry cove ain't never yet shown himself 'ere. What's ado?" The youngster took the last step in a jump, holding tightly to his oversized hat.

"Hush, now, young imp, and don't be giving us any of your jaw," said his companion, following the messenger into the taproom, his eyes, surprisingly keen and intelligent in his plain, low-browed face, searching the dim corners of that low-ceilinged chamber which was redolent of well-worn wood and spilled ale.

"I expect something has occurred as warrants my expertise, and the gentleman is callin' to get my advice on the matter, as I told him he ought," he said.

Just then the man he had been seeking caught his eye, and he gave his young companion a rough but not unkind shove in the direction of a corner table, where his visitor awaited him.

"Bilgrove." The gentleman, whom they had agreed would be addressed as Mr. Vane, gave a polite nod and gestured him to an empty chair. "And young Ted," he acknowledged the boy, who had lifted his floppy hat and now bobbed his chin. "I should have taken warning from your report last week, my boy. The lack of news ought to have made me suspicious." He lowered his voice and met the sharp eyes of the man called Bilgrove. "Our man is here in Bath. He's just arrived. What in God's name can it mean?"

Bilgrove's thick salt-and-pepper brows rose to meet the untidy fringe of hair that covered what there was of his forehead. "Begging your pardon, sir, but I hope it don't mean what I think it means," he said, scowling at the slatternly girl who approached them with tankards of ale, so that she nervously spilled some as she set them down. At the earl's reassuring nod, she scuttled away again quickly.

"And what, sir"—Tarrington was becoming impatient—"might that be?"

Bilgrove took a long swallow of ale, put down the tankard, wiped his lips, fastidiously though, on the sleeve of his coat, and met the earl's eyes. "It might be that you'll find yourself hoist with your own petard, sir, if you get my meaning. Unless, of course, we take action, and right quick."

"Explain yourself, man," said Tarrington irritably. The sight of Oldbury had forced him to flee and seek Bilgrove's advice, despite being in the midst of his revelations to Katherine. He could not have faced Oldbury at that moment. The fellow's arrival in Bath had been the last thing he had expected. He groaned, imagining what Katherine might be thinking.

"You see, sir"—Bilgrove spoke slowly and patiently, as if to a child, and little Ted, as well as the earl, listened intently—"you was expecting, and I don't say I wasn't expecting it myself, that our informants would carry word of the gentleman's activities in London once that painting changed hands. What we didn't count on was his passing right through London and heading on here." He frowned, and reached into a capacious pocket for his Occurrence Book, leafing the closely written pages.

"Let me see . . . the last we heard of the matter was after this Oldbury was trailed to London . . . they must have lost him there, clumsy fools . . . but then again, there's nothing easier. 'Tis a difficult place to keep a man in sight." He put the book away and looked up at Tarrington. "Could he suspect you? He's a cunning shaver, that Oldbury, more than we gave him credit for."

Tarrington shook his head. "He swallowed my story without a murmur, and paid well for the painting, too." He sipped meditatively at his ale. "And my inheriting that house could not have been more opportune. If he had lived in any other part of the country I would have been hard put to make an excuse to linger in his neighborhood. But as far as I know, he'd never heard of me before I arrived there. And he's never seen either of *you*, has he?"

Bilgrove looked offended, and clinked his empty tankard significantly. Tarrington signalled to the serving-girl, who hovered just out of hearing, and she quickly brought more ale to the Bow Street runner.

Young Ted piped up, "'E's never seen me, m'lud, I swears it! I kept my peepers open an' my mouth shut, an' the rest o' me out o' sight. But I'd lay my 'at"—he stroked the brim of the ridiculous headgear fondly—"that the cove was bit!"

The earl smiled grimly, then drained his tankard. "Let us hope, my young friend, that it is not *this* cove who has been bit instead."

After a few more minutes of huddled consultation, Tarrington paid the shot and, his face grim, bid farewell to his companions. The odd-looking pair departed from the inn some moments later, the boy melting onto a side street, blending with other children who dodged horses, chairs, and carriages, and the man meandering off towards the east.

Both of them appeared not much later in the vicinity of

269

certain lodgings in Milsom Street, which they kept under casual scrutiny, the boy prudently earning a few pennies by holding horses, the man blending into a knot of people before a print-shop window, and striking up conversations with old soldiers, all the while cocking an eye towards the house across the way.

Long before dusk descended to grey the gold-tinged whiteness of the city, their vigilance was rewarded by the sight of Mr. George Oldbury, who emerged from the house and imperiously hailed a chair. Without so much as one exchanged glance, the runner and his young assistant sprang into action.

Bilgrove, staggering as if from an excess of the very ale he had enjoyed that day, made his way into the street, and greeted one of the chairmen as though he were a long-lost friend, with drunken jocularity, weeping and laughing, clinging to him like a limpet, while the boy scampered away in the direction of Gay Street. By the time the irritated Oldbury and his chairmen had extricated themselves from the attentions of the slobbering inebriate, the boy was out of sight.

"How very odd!" Mrs. Amory said, searching Katherine's white face worriedly. "What could dear Tarrington have meant by it? I only hope that he was not suddenly taken with some, er, indisposition."

If Katherine had not been so shocked by it all she would have laughed at her mother's delicate phrasing. She had never seen anyone seem to take fright and run away, yes, run away, she told herself, there was no other way to express it, at the sight of someone as contemptible as George Oldbury.

The color was coming back to her cheeks. She had only escaped him narrowly herself. The moment Tarrington had gone, and before Oldbury could approach her, she had dashed into the shop like a mad thing, her heart fluttering dreadfully, her mind in total confusion, and blurted out the tale to her mother and cousin.

Priscilla was momentarily shaken out of her own distress. "Are you sure it was Mr. Oldbury, Kate? Whatever can he be doing here? Unless—" A smile, rare these days, brightened her face. "Do you think he can have heard, somehow, about your engagement, and has come to fight a duel for you with the earl?"

Even Katherine had to laugh at the absurdity of this, but she wondered if his arrival might not have *something* to do with her betrothal. It would be the likeliest thing in the world, she was sure, for Lady Tarrington to have written to some of her friends about it, and they might have told Oldbury.

"News of an engagement always travels fast," said her mother, echoing her thought. "But still, I don't think Mr. Oldbury, fond of you though he was, would come here with the intention of trying to dissuade you from marrying Lord Tarrington!"

The clerk presented her with a neatly wrapped parcel. "Come girls, if we are quick we may catch him before he goes in, though, to be sure, he will probably call on us before long."

Katherine breathed a sigh of relief that they had not been quick enough, for there was no sign of Oldbury. She could not believe that his purpose in coming to Bath was to renew his addresses to her, even if he did know she had become engaged. Their last conversation must have cured him of *that* intention forever. Nevertheless, she was very glad of her safety from such harassment. Tarrington, no matter what his true feelings for her, would not permit Oldbury to insult her ever again.

But whatever was her fiancé about, making such a public and hasty retreat? She had to do him the justice to admit that his expression, upon seeing Oldbury, had been more angry than frightened. And, of course, it was absurd to think that the earl would have any reason to fear such a buffoon. Then there were those fascinating revelations he had been in the midst of making—she had been cruelly disappointed by their interruption, just as she was on the verge of understanding him at last.

Despite her uncertainty, the black mood that had overtaken her since her betrothal had begun to lift. If only Tarrington would continue to confide in her. Today she had had a glimpse of the man she loved, the man who had been absent for so long, while a cold stranger had taken his place.

When next we are alone, she promised herself, I won't let him go until he finishes that story. And then . . . her skin burned at the picture that came into her mind, and she was glad that the forward poke of her bonnet hid her face from a casual glance.

But would he ever again show her that exciting side of him that only her distress had uncovered? The longing to make him respond to her made every moment of the trip home a torment, and she all but ignored the chatter of her mother and Priscilla, bursting with impatience to see Tarrington again.

Upon her return, she was crushed to find that he was not to be found, and casting all caution to the winds, she hurried to his room. But only Skempton answered her knock, and greeted her appearance with a shocked and disapproving sniff. She looked past him, but the earl was not in the room.

Katherine's mind was flooded with the memory of the day she had stumbled upon Tarrington in a state of undress, recalling her utter confusion, his warm bare skin so unnervingly close, teasing her and awakening the unvoiced desires he had evoked full force the night of their betrothal.

"I-I beg your pardon . . . I have mistaken the room . . ." she stammered, then blushed and escaped to her own bedchamber, unable to decide whether she would first scold Tarrington when she finally found him or fling herself into his arms so that he might complete what he had begun, the utter conquest of her heart.

She would contrive to be left alone with him the very first moment he appeared. But it seemed, to her frustration, as though this moment was to be put off indefinitely, for she did not see her betrothed again until shortly before dinner.

The family and several dinner guests were assembled in the

drawing room, when Tarrington at last came in. Katherine's heart sank, for at a glance she could tell that he was cool and distant once more. She tried to catch his eye across the room, but he steadfastly avoided her glance, and finally, feeling ridiculous but determined nevertheless, she went to him.

"Vane, I—"

"I'm sorry, Katherine, I can't— I haven't time to speak to you now. Please understand." His voice was tight, his face closed to her once more.

Pain stabbed through her, and anger at herself for being so foolish as to believe that he could ever love her. She struggled to compose herself, aware that others were observing them, and stepped back as Lady Tarrington and Sally approached.

He greeted them rather perfunctorily, and they, too, withdrew, puzzled.

"Don't worry, my dear," Lady Tarrington comforted Katherine. "You will find that men have their moods, and that quite probably it doesn't mean a thing."

But Katherine was certain there was a reason behind it all. She could not keep her eyes from following the earl as he attempted to disengage a glum Lord Knolland from the gossipy conversation of Mr. Fellowes. His expression seemed to signify that he had something urgent to impart, but poor Lord Knolland was trapped. Tarrington headed purposefully toward his friend, but before he could effect a rescue, a footman entered the room and sidled up to him, whispering frantically in his ear.

Tarrington immediately excused himself and slipped away. Katherine, luckily not detained in conversation with anyone, followed him unobtrusively, and hung over the balustrade as he descended to the hall, where a familiar figure waited to greet him. The young boy in the big boots and floppy hat was agitated, and some of his high-pitched words floated up to her.

". . . left 'is lodgin's not ten minutes ago . . . 'as a package under his arm . . . best make 'aste, or . . ."

But the event of which the boy had come to warn him was

too close on the heels of his arrival to do the earl much good, for at that moment there was a thundering knock at the door. The impatient visitor admitted by the footman was, to Katherine's bewilderment, George Oldbury. She crept a little farther down the stairs, still unseen and in shadow, but able to hear everything. Her former suitor wore an expression of the highest outrage.

"There he is! I knew I would track you, you villain!" Oldbury shook one fist at the earl while the other hand grasped a flat package under his arm. "You shall answer to me at once!"

Tarrington stood firm. "I shall give you the opportunity of explaining that remark, Oldbury, before I throw you out," he said.

"Very well, my lord." Oldbury had worked himself to a pitch of fury, and Katherine shuddered at the hate in his eyes.

"I called you a villain, and with good reason. You, sir, have perpetrated the grossest deception upon an honest man. This"—he shook the parcel he held at Tarrington—"is an outright forgery."

He set the parcel down on the hall table and began feverishly to unwrap it. Young Ted peered at him with a wisdom beyond his years, and said to Tarrington, "I shall fetch m'master. 'E'll know how to deal wi' this rum cove."

But the earl detained him. "No, boy. I want you here as a witness to this . . . gentleman's accusations."

Oldbury snorted as he slung the last of the paper away. "A fine witness, this urchin, criminal writ all over him. Your association with such as him would hang you without *this*." He stabbed a stubby finger at what was revealed by the undone wrappings. It was a small painting, but from the stairs Katherine could just barely make out its subject. The view was poor, but most certainly, it was the very painting she had watched Tarrington sell to Mr. Oldbury back at the Hall.

Words of defense leaped to her mouth, but she silenced herself in time, frightened of giving away her presence.

Young Ted protested vehemently. "Just because I talks flash

don't mean I'm one o' the crew. Why, my master—"

"Quiet, Ted." The earl interrupted. His eyes were fixed on the painting, in horror, it seemed to Katherine, until he tore them away. It was so quick that she wondered if she had imagined it. "Let the man say his piece."

"What I have to say, my lord," Oldbury continued, with a scowl at the boy, "I would prefer to say in private."

Tarrington paused, and stared at his visitor, almost as though he were looking through him; then he abruptly dismissed the wildly curious footman, before turning to Ted, and with a significant nod, telling him to go as well.

By now Katherine was trembling with apprehension. Though Tarrington had not told the whole of his story, she knew he must be on the right side of this dispute. Her fear was that he would not be able to prove himself innocent.

Oldbury, if he believed himself wronged, could certainly be vindictive enough to try to secure Tarrington's conviction. She was so intrigued by the scene below that she clung to the balustrade, unmoving, almost without breathing. But the two men were likewise intent on their business, so that Katherine underwent no danger of detection.

"And now, sir," the earl said in icy tones, "what is the meaning of all this nonsense."

Oldbury bristled, but not very convincingly, Katherine thought. It was plain that he had not really been prepared for the earl to withstand his first attack, and now that his audience was gone, he was uncomfortable alone with the man who had twice before intimidated him.

"I should not call it nonsense, my lord earl," he replied, but would not meet Tarrington's eyes. "It is a very serious charge I bring against you, and one, I have heard, that is no novelty where you are concerned." He gave a quick glance at Tarrington's face to see how this was received, but the earl appeared unaffected.

"Very well, sir, you force me to be unpleasantly blunt. You have been accused of this crime before—never mind how I

...ave discovered this."

Tarrington was mentally tracing his contacts during the past year to determine how Oldbury had found out something that his own mother did not know.

"The point is, my lord, that you will be revealed as the mastermind of a criminal enterprise, hiring men to forge works of art and then selling them as part of your 'collection.' This"—he stroked the painting lovingly—"will be my proof. It is unmistakably a forgery of a Van Meer, the original of which it is known that your esteemed father once purchased on the advice of the Regent. There is, however, one way to avoid such unpleasantness." His eyes gleamed with greed.

"I shall not trouble to ask you what that might be," said Tarrington contemptuously.

"Well, I shall inform you anyway. I think, my lord, when you have considered the alternative, that you will agree to my terms. And, of course, any attempt to implicate *me* in the matter will result in the most unpleasant scandal." Oldbury smirked knowingly. "I don't believe your reputation could sustain even another hint of *that*, my lord."

Tarrington eyed him coolly, and Katherine thought that she had never admired him so much as at this moment, as he stood up to the vile accusation and the blackmail of Oldbury. Even so, there was a lot that he had yet to explain, she thought, clutching the balustrade so hard that her knuckles went white.

The earl glanced casually at the painting. "If the original were found—"

"How could that be, my lord? If it were in your possession, it would only serve to prove your guilt in the matter." Oldbury smoothed his neckcloth, a satisfied smirk on his round face. "But I think that we understand one another, sir. I would hazard a guess that the original has been unfortunately"—his eyes slid over to the painting—"lost."

In two steps the earl was at Oldbury's side, and the man flinched in spite of his bold words. But the earl ignored him and only examined the painting more carefully.

It was an excellent copy, and it almost would have fooled him except that the artist, Oldbury's accomplice, had been just overzealous enough in coloring the sky, and had carefully painted ten cows where, as he very well knew, there were only eight.

But Tarrington, of course, had taken extraordinary pains to make himself minutely familiar with the painting before his attempt to sell it to Oldbury, and the sight of the forgery jarred him. It was so like . . . yet unlike the memory burned into his brain. His plan had fallen through, because he had made the fatal mistake of underestimating his opponent.

Experts would undoubtedly pronounce the painting a recently forged Van Meer. If only he could make a connection between Oldbury and the original . . . If Ted was as clever as he seemed, then perhaps he and Bilgrove would find a way to search Oldbury's lodgings before he returned.

But a moment's reflection told him that the original would not be found there; Oldbury was too clever to keep it near him. Yet his limited knowledge of Oldbury's character told him that no amount of greed or fear of exposure would make him destroy a work of art. Therefore it must still exist, and there was only one other place where it could be.

This should have been his moment of triumph, he thought bitterly. There would have been no doubt of the guilt of George Oldbury in this and other forgeries, especially with the evidence that he and the man from Bow Street had intended to produce. Of course as his involvement with the matter was well known to the authorities he was in no danger himself, but it tortured him that Oldbury might yet slip out of their hands.

There was only one way to prove without a doubt that Oldbury was the instigator of the forgery plot, and to salvage what he could of his original plan to catch him. And it required, unfortunately, that the man think Tarrington was caught neatly in this vile trap.

Almost sick at the necessity of pretending to cede the victory, the earl abruptly turned away, and to mask his expression of disgust, he raised a hand to his face.

Katherine watched him, horrified. Oldbury licked his lips like a dog who expected a treat, as Tarrington, in a voice of despair, asked him to name his terms.

"Five thousand pounds, my lord."

"You know I have no choice, you scoundrel," he said, turning to face his accuser. "I will pay what you ask, but you understand that it will take time. I will arrange tomorrow for a draft on my bankers, but it may involve disposing of some investments . . . I shall have to contact my solicitors."

Oldbury smiled greedily. "It is very sad that you were unable to enjoy the benefit of Sir Edwin Amory's fortune, as well as the responsibility of repairing his estate," he said. "However, when our arrangements are concluded, I shall be at leisure to see to it that the Amory fortune will not escape *me*."

"Are you insane, man?" Tarrington looked at him uncomprehendingly.

Oldbury laughed. "Ah, do you still imagine that you are too clever for me? Don't pretend, especially when the word is out that you have taken steps to secure that tidy fortune for yourself." His smile disappeared. "But pray don't forget that any interference on *that* score will dissolve our bargain. You'd best give up any idea of it right now, or . . . but I'm sure I needn't go into further detail."

He had always been contemptible, Katherine thought, dizzy and sickened by the outcome of this interview, but never before had Oldbury appeared to her to be so innately evil. And Tarrington, the man she loved, was obviously no better. Her world was being shattered around her, and were it not for the support of the balustrade she would have fallen down the stairs.

She was baffled, however, by the references to her uncle's fortune. Could Tarrington have been lying when he said that there was none? Before this moment, she would have refused to consider it, but now that the earl had all but admitted his guilt, she could well believe it.

Pain and disappointment made her chest constrict, and she forced herself to breathe, the tears frozen within her by the shock of these revelations. But still she could not force herself to go. If there were more, she should hear it. She would never allow herself to be so fooled again. It was a bitter reflection that she was truly as naïve as Tarrington thought her.

All the while she had rejoiced in the fact that he was confiding in her, he had very likely been preparing to deceive her. Or perhaps, to do him justice, only to describe how he had come to be involved in his criminal activity. She reflected with bitterness on the day he had rescued her from Oldbury's embrace, and on his casual exhibition of artistic knowledge. Obviously he had learned a great deal about the subject since his first experience.

"I am not, whatever else you may think, my lord, an unreasonable man," Oldbury was saying, going so far as to give a half-bow to his victim. "I shall give you twenty-four hours to produce the money."

His voice was suddenly hard again. "And don't try any tricks, sir. I am sure that the bankers in Bath can accommodate you, and you would not be so foolish as to attempt to leave the city. I am certain you would not wish the ladies"—he gave a nod upward, and Katherine shrank back into a shadow against the wall—"to know of your perfidy. Especially my dearest Miss Amory. I shall be trying my hand again at picking *that* plum as soon as our business is concluded, and, as I have indicated, if you are wise, you will not try to stop me."

"As to Miss Amory—" Tarrington began, but the simultaneous chiming of eight on the hall clock, and the sound of the company exiting the drawing room interrupted them.

Katherine jumped up, terrified of being seen on the stair, and made her way to her cousin Priscilla, who was just coming out, pale-faced and miserable, on Mr. Fellowes' arm.

"Why, Kate, where have you been? Your Mama has been asking for you, and Mr. Fellowes, too."

Hoping desperately that her distress was not too obvious in

her face or voice, Katherine took the gentleman's other arm and tried to smile, but she could produce only a weak grimace.

"I beg pardon, sir. I was detained by one of those annoying little feminine emergencies—a tear in my hem, and I clumsily caught my foot in it. But all is well now," she said lightly, wishing with all her heart that it were so.

Priscilla was satisfied with this explanation, preoccupied as she was with not looking wistfully at Lord Knolland, who was leading another lady in to dinner, but Mr. Fellowes looked at Katherine narrowly.

"Something is amiss, my dear. I know it in my old bones," he whispered. "And where is that fine young earl of yours?"

Katherine blinked back tears and this time succeeded in producing something closer to a smile. "I vow, you have the most suspicious nature, my dear Mr. Fellowes. Nothing is amiss. His lordship was called away on a matter of business. Vexing, when one is entertaining guests, but really most trifling." Her voice died away to a tight whisper, and Mr. Fellowes only patted her arm and troubled her no more.

She had begun the evening in anticipation of continuing the tête-à-tête with her betrothed, but she now dreaded his return, and wondered how she would manage to hide the fact that she had deliberately eavesdropped on his conversation with Oldbury.

With an extraordinary effort, she schooled her features to absolute unconcern, and vowed not to look at him the entire evening. Judging from the way he had treated her earlier, it would not be difficult to avoid him. Yet once their eyes met, all would be lost, and she was ill-prepared to face him and the frightening truths she had learned. But subsequent events made that dinner party even more of a test of her skill at dissembling than she could have imagined possible.

Tarrington had not yet made an appearance, and just before his absence began to be remarked on, a footman came to Lady Tarrington with the distressing news that her son had been called out of town on business once again, informing her that he made his most profuse apologies for deserting her, his fiancée, and his guests.

Lady Tarrington, with practiced ease and poise, made light of the matter, and the earl's chair and place were whisked away as if they had never been. Everyone ignored the suddenly uneven numbers, and the dowager countess put herself out to charm her guests, with assistance from Mr. Fellowes, but Katherine later met her eyes and saw the same pain and worry in them that gnawed at her own heart.

However, when the ladies retired again to the drawing room, Lady Tarrington gave her an encouraging nod and a little smile, and Katherine did her best to seem as unconcerned as possible. She wondered, for a moment, if she ought to confide in the earl's mother, but somehow she could not bear to jeopardise her ladyship's confidence in her son since her own had been destroyed by that scene in the hall. She doubted that his own mother would believe such a thing of him; Lady Tarrington would no doubt think her mad.

Somehow, she dragged through the evening, scarcely able to swallow a morsel, but it ended mercifully early, and only her mother commented on her wan looks and recommended a glass of port before bed. Before he left, Mr. Fellowes took her aside.

"My dear, you will not confide in me, and, of course, it is presumptuous of me to expect that you would. But if an experienced man of the world might give advice to a charming young lady whom he admires greatly . . ."

She managed a tiny smile. "Very well, sir. What is your advice?"

"That Tarrington may be a young fool, going off and leaving a lovely child like you alone for some nonsensical reason," he began, "but he's a fool who loves you. Anyone can see it," he insisted. "Don't be too hard on him."

He gave her hand a last squeeze, and stepped briskly out to his carriage, corsets creaking, entirely unaware of the terrible irony of his statement. She could not imagine why Mr. Fellowes would think such a thing, when all Tarrington had done since their betrothal was keep her at arm's length, and she dismissed it as the fancy of an eccentric. What would he have said, she wondered, if he knew what she had discovered today about her fiancé?

A note in the earl's hand, left on her mantelpiece, did nothing to encourage her to believe the best of him. His own face and his own words had proclaimed him guilty, though to her mind Oldbury, the blackmailer, was infinitely more contemptible. The note was merely an apology for his sudden absence, and begged that she would forgive him for leaving her unattended for the evening.

At the end, however, he said, "I am aware that our unfinished conversation will have awakened some questions. All will be answered to your satisfaction at the conclusion of this business." He sighed it simply "Tarrington."

It was hardly the note of a lover, but even less that of a guilty man. She did not know what to make of it, but the scene she had witnessed was unmistakable in its meaning. She held the note to her candle, taking satisfaction in the way the paper curled and blackened in the flame, and when it was only ash, the tears came.

She had seen her affianced husband accused of a crime, had heard him all but admit his guilt, and now he was running away. There was simply no other interpretation to be put on it. The story he had begun to tell her that day must have been the merest fabrication.

While her eyes were still wet, sleep came over her like a leaden blanket, a dreamless sleep that seemed to last only a moment and then left her awake on a radiant sunny morning, with the same thought still foremost in her mind. Her betrothed, the man she loved, was a criminal.

Chapter Eleven

Lord Knolland, suffused with good port and brandy, blinked up at the footman who had respectfully detained him on his way back to the drawing room after dinner.

"What's that? You say his lordship would like to speak with me?" He thought there was something very odd about this summons, and it took a moment, while the servant's face wavered before his eyes, for him to decide why, but at last it came to him.

"Can't be," he said with assurance. "S'gone. Her ladyship told us, told everyone, he was"—he fought to control an inconvenient belch before he could continue—"called away on business."

"I assure you, my lord, that Lord Tarrington is still here. He requests that you will come to him at once," the footman repeated, gently steering him toward the stairs. "In the front sitting room, sir," he said firmly.

To Lord Knolland's befuddled amazement, it certainly did appear to be his friend Tarrington who stood, clad in breeches and top-boots, in the shadows of the front sitting room. The wavering light of a single branch of candles flickered over his face eerily, and Lord Knolland hesitated on the threshold, mouth agape, as if unsure whether the earl were but a spectre.

"At my side in a trice, as ever, my loyal friend," the earl

greeted him dryly. His lordship decided that it was safe to enter the room, for no mere apparition could have attained just that familiar tone and slightly mocking but affectionate expression.

"Wh-what's amiss?" Knolland inquired, dropping his replete self onto a sofa. He fought to stay upright for a moment, but soon gave way to the forces of dinner and gravity, and addressed the earl with eyes half-closed, chin buried in his neckcloth.

"Told us you'd gone. Told us a good two hours ago. Thought that footman was bosky, for a moment." He frowned. "No good to let the servants make too free with liquor. Reminds me of a butler m'uncle James had. Fellow filched a case of port a month for years, no one the wiser, until one day—"

"Fascinating, Rodney, but I beg you will save your instructional tales for a less urgent time. Gather your wits about you, dear fellow. I require your assistance." Tarrington stood over the recumbent Knolland, his face calm, but the intensity of his manner eventually penetrated his friend's vinous haze.

His lordship ceased to sag against the leaf-green silk cushions, and almost, but not quite, sat up. "Of course," he said in more alert tones. "At your service."

Tarrington managed a little smile, and as if released from the tension that had held him immobile, began to pace back and forth before the sofa, crop in one hand, the other thoughtlessly ruffling his hair. This gesture alone, so unlike him, was enough to inform Lord Knolland that something very peculiar was afoot.

"There is a job that needs to be done Rodney, and I turn to you because there is no one else I can trust here to do it," Tarrington began. "I am leaving Bath tonight—never mind for where, it's best you don't know—but I hope to return by tomorrow evening, at about this time if all goes well. Now listen carefully. Do you recall that fellow back in Hampshire who had the impudence to mistake you for a highwayman?"

It required a moment of reflection. "Ol . . . Old something . . . Oldbury!" his lordship exclaimed in triumph. "How could I ever forget? Silly gudgeon!" He began to giggle, but at a sharp glance from the earl he desisted.

"Well, he's here in Bath and he's up to no good. What I want you to do, Rodney," continued Lord Tarrington, ignoring the way his companion paled at this news, "is see to it that he doesn't leave until I return. I'm not sure he will attempt it, but if he should find that I have left the city, he may lose his nerve and bolt, or even decide to come after me. Whatever you do, don't let that happen," he instructed the bewildered Lord Knolland.

"How can I? Don't know where you're going myself!"

Tarrington sighed and stopped pacing. "Never mind. Just keep him in sight for a couple of days. And be discreet." He studied his flushed, confused friend as if wondering if such behavior were possible. "Above all, don't let him know that you're following him."

"F-following him?" Inquired his lordship in alarm.

"Well . . . observing his movements, in any case. It shouldn't be too difficult. I doubt he knows anyone in Bath, and unless he turns up here, which I hope to God he doesn't, he'll probably stay near his lodgings. Here is the address."

He gave Lord Knolland a slip of paper, and smiled at the dismay on his friend's face. "Don't worry. I doubt he will give you trouble. And I am leaving you an assistant."

He stepped to the door, opened it a crack, and whispered to the footman who had stationed himself outside. In another moment young Ted, the runner's boy, popped in, hat, boots, and all. Knolland gazed at him in astonishment.

"Here now, what's this? Who is this urchin? Funny sort of assistant *he'll* make!" His lordship blinked, unable to believe his eyes.

"Don't worry, m'lud," said Ted confidently to his new master. "This cull won't escape us. If 'e tries it"—the boy took a bellicose stance—*"I'm* ripe for a mill!"

Tarrington flashed a grin at Lord Knolland. However, his lordship was still too stunned to appreciate the finer qualities of his newly appointed assistant.

"I'm sure my friend is very glad to hear it, Ted, but there's no need to sport your canvas just yet. I'd much prefer it if you went about it on the sly as usual. Especially now that our man knows you."

He dismissed the boy, telling him to make up a pallet in the kitchen and report to Lord Knolland in the morning.

"I can't explain just now what this is all about Rodney, but take my word for it that it is of the utmost importance that you keep Oldbury in Bath until my return. Ordinarily, I would have assigned that duty to Ted, but Oldbury would notice him in an instant, and his suspicions will be roused."

"But he's sure to notice me as well!" cried Knolland, recalling that dreadful time when he had been in Mr. Oldbury's power.

Tarrington picked up his hat from where it had rested on a satinwood table. "Certainly, but he has no call to think your presence here at all suspicious, if you are discreet and seem to be going about your own business." He smiled wickedly. "Besides, I sincerely doubt that, having once barely escaped with his life, he would again brave the wrath of Lord Bruiser!"

With the assurance that all would be explained upon his return, and an expression of the utmost confidence in his friend's abilities, he left poor Lord Knolland to ponder it all. However, it was much too fatiguing to a man full of beef, lobster, and wine, and ultimately he gave it up and rejoined the other guests, telling himself that he would worry about it in the morning.

But when he was shocked out of sleep the next day by what seemed a veritable blaze of sunshine, he had all but forgotten his solemn charge.

"The devil! Tol' you to leave the demmed curtains alone, you bracket-faced wench!" His lordship started up from his pillow, his hair a straw halo about his flushed face, until he recognized the instigator of this abrupt awakening.

"It's you, Finster! Sorry, thought it was that idiot of a

286

housemaid. Told her to leave the blasted curtains be," he explained groggily. "But what the deuce are you about, flinging them open that way? I imagine it's barely seven o'clock, and you know I don't get up much before ten, especially when I've a head like the one I have this morning." He threw himself back on the pillows again and groaned.

"Half-past, sir," corrected his valet. "And I venture to suggest that your lordship'll feel a mite better after imbibing a bit of this."

Finster, a kindly but iron-willed servant with a misleadingly cherubic countenance, held out a small glass whose muddy yellow contents were illuminated by a shaft of sunlight. "I'm under orders from his lordship th'earl himself that you was to be awakened early this morning, on account of there's something you will be wishing to do for him."

"I'll thank you to remember who gives the orders here. Think I'm a paper-skull? Does Lord Tarrington pay your wages then, too?" The effort was too much and he fell back on his pillows.

"No, my lord, your uncle does." Finster regarded him with complacency.

Knolland groaned again and turned his head away from the window, where not only the sunlight but the street noises had begun to interfere with the last remnants of drowsiness. A hazy memory of the interview with Tarrington crept upon his consciousness, but it only made him close his eyes again.

"Fellow couldn't find a truer friend than me"—he muttered into his pillow—"but I'll not be making a cake of myself . . . shouldn't wonder at it if that Oldbury wouldn't try to haul me away again. . . ." But despite his reluctance to perform the favor his friend had asked of him, he did eventually turn and raise his eyes to the light again, only to find Finster still there, holding out the glass as before, and regarding him with that stern glance that he knew presaged a lecture.

"Damn your impudence," he muttered, and snatching the

glass, drank down its slimy, spicy contents in a gulp. Then he allowed himself to be washed, shaved, and dressed in time to appear downstairs at what was to him an unreasonably early hour to breakfast.

He was startled and slightly embarrassed to see Katherine already at the table, apathetically consuming rolls and chocolate. No one else was down yet. He cleared his throat, and she jumped at the sound, but quietly returned his morning greeting.

Knolland was startled to see how wan she looked, but the oddity of his friend's sudden departure, he thought, was enough to account for that. Vane must be a greater fool than I am, he thought suddenly, if he thinks Miss Amory don't really wish to marry him. Dashed if I know what else she might be fretting about, but all this nonsense of his.

He wondered if he should venture to ascertain the truth of his suspicions while Tarrington was gone, but quickly decided that his life for the next few hours was going to be quite complicated enough without meddling in his friend's betrothal. It would just have to wait, though he was in dreadful fear that he was going to lose his chance with Priscilla if he did not do something about the situation soon.

To his strained remarks upon the fine weather Miss Amory replied absently, and she only showed some interest when she realized how uncharacteristically early he had arisen.

"What brings you down at this hour, my lord? Have you decided to come with us to the Pump Room today? I warn you it will be some time before *the others* are down."

She glanced at him accusingly, and he turned a little pink, knowing precisely who she meant. She could not know that there was nothing he would rather do than wait there for the arrival of a certain other, and that his promise to Tarrington was all that prevented him.

"Pump Room, no, no . . . thought I'd take an early stroll . . . have a look in at the circulating library . . . coffeehouse . . . maybe have my hair cut. . . ."

288

Katherine was looking at him now with undisguised curiosity. "How strange for you to have risen so early, then. There is nothing so urgent in that to have called you from your bed." She set down her half-finished cup of chocolate, and glared at him. "But perhaps you couldn't sleep. I know if I were you, my lord, and had caused so much pain to an innocent girl like my cousin Priscilla, I should not be able to sleep either."

And with this she got up and abruptly left the room. Lord Knolland stared after her in dismay. There was no way he could defend himself against this charge but he wondered if he ought to go after her and explain at least the reason for his early rising. However, the condition of his head decided him against it. He was in no condition to spar with Miss Amory. A servant entered with coffee and he applied himself to his cup, with a noticeable improvement.

The paper with Oldbury's address was in his waistcoat pocket, and he patted it nervously. Tarrington had said nothing about keeping his activities a secret, but he was not at all sure that in the current state of things, the earl would want Katherine to know of it.

Yet what was there in Oldbury's arrival to make him run off somewhere, leaving his friend to dog the fellow's footsteps? If the earl had a quarrel with the man, he ought to have challenged him then and there. However, this was quite enough cogitation for a man little used to it and in dire need of breakfast so Knolland soon desisted.

He had barely emptied his plate and was just going back to the sideboard for a second helping of eggs when he was interrupted by a commotion in the doorway.

"M'lady, I didn't mean no 'arm. Ow! I can't 'ardly breathe when yer does that. I promise I didn't take nothin'! 'Ere then, ask *'im!*" The speaker pointed a grimy finger at Lord Knolland. "M'master's gone away with the gentleman what lives 'ere an' today I works for his ludship there."

Young Ted, his collar in Miss Katherine Amory's firm grip, still struggled and protested, to no avail, as she hauled him into the breakfast parlor, deftly kicking the door shut behind her.

"Very well, but do be quiet," she told him. "I didn't accuse you of anything. I only wanted to talk to you."

Lord Knolland watched, open-mouthed, as she deposited the boy in a chair and calmly went to make up a plate of food. It had not escaped either of them that the boy's protests had been muffled from the moment he set eyes on the steaming trays and dishes set out on the sideboard.

"Here you are, young man," she said, "now hurry and eat this before the others come down, while I have a talk with his lordship." She fixed Knolland with a glance and he squirmed in his chair.

Ted's obedience to Lord Tarrington's instructions was no proof against the liberality of the breakfast spread, so much more enticing than bread and milk in the kitchen under the suspicious eye of the cook, and he fell to with a will, abandoning Lord Knolland to Katherine's searching eye.

Katherine, having for the moment gained a victory in apprehending the boy who, she reasoned, was surely a party to Tarrington's desertion, now herded Lord Knolland into a corner of the room and demanded to know what was the connection between the earl and that tattered specimen of youth.

"I observed him as I made my way to the stairs, my lord. He had just slipped out of the kitchen and was creeping past the stairs in a most suspicious way. When I accosted him, he insisted that he was under *your* orders," Katherine informed Rodney, searching his face for signs of complicity.

He evaded her eyes. "Nothing in it, Miss Amory. Just a boy's imagination. I swear, I've never seen the little fellow before!"

But under her uncompromising glance and in his own uncertainty about the mission the earl had assigned him, he could offer no serious resistance to Katherine's demands.

"Very well, then. He *was* supposed to work for me today," Lord Knolland admitted. "But if you want answers, you'd best ask Tarrington. It was *his* idea!"

"What was his idea?"

So far the morning's events had succeeded in bringing Katherine out of the grey misery in which the happenings of the past night had left her. The sight of that odd and familiar little fellow had acted like a spur to a weary horse, goading her into a determination to get to the bottom of the mystery.

Even if she could not salvage her happiness, she could at least find out what had contributed to the ruin of it. There was no doubt that the boy knew something of her fiancé's activities. But now, faced with the guileless countenance of Lord Knolland, she found it difficult to believe that the earl's friend had a part in it as well.

"It—it's to do with Oldbury," Lord Knolland finally blurted out.

Katherine felt the blood rush to her face. The memory of that shameful scene in the hall last evening, when the earl had stood accused by his own words, almost made her falter, but she pressed on.

"I know he has come to Bath, but what has he to do with you and this child?" She indicated Ted, who was greedily mopping up his plate with bread.

If he were to fulfill his duty to Tarrington he must be soon on his way, and he had no wish now for Priscilla to come down and find him being interrogated by her cousin while that absurd boy sat by swallowing slices of ham of sufficient size to choke a horse. Lord Knolland's only alternative was to surrender, and he quickly sketched for Katherine the content of his interview with the earl, urging her to let him and Ted go as soon as might be.

"Tarrington made me swear I'd not let Oldbury escape me," he embellished, "and I'd better get to Milsom Street before the fellow slips away somewhere."

Katherine frowned, uncertain of the import of this odd tale. The fact that Tarrington had actually confided in his friend before leaving did seem to mitigate his guilt somewhat, but, of course, it might have been a ruse, since he had not seen fit to tell Knolland of his destination or purpose. She came to a decision.

"I'm going with you," she said.

Lord Knolland stood up, alarmed. "Miss Amory! I don't think—"

"I haven't the slightest interest in what you think, my lord. Let us hurry, the others will be down at any moment. I will meet you in front of the circulating library in Milsom Street in no more than a quarter of an hour."

At the appointed time Katherine arrived in Milsom Street, having made her way there in great secrecy after giving the excuse of a headache to the other ladies. Though illness was unlike her, no one really thought it odd that she should wish to remain in bed for a few more hours today.

Each of them was preoccupied with her own affairs, Mrs. Amory with making her wedding plans, Priscilla with contemplating the ruin of hers, Lady Colesville with preparations for the journey home. Even the sharp-eyed Lady Tarrington suspected nothing, after her son's sudden defection the night before. She thought it no great wonder that Katherine looked so drawn and edgy, and to a great extent she shared her feelings, and vowed to have a serious talk with her son about his lack of consideration.

Lord Knolland was lurking self-consciously before the library, as if afraid to go inside. As Katherine approached, she had to stifle a laugh at the sight of him. Though it was early and the street not particularly busy, he was well occupied during his wait by politely touching his hat to every female that passed by, while Ted, the hearty breakfast notwithstanding, stood with his nose pressed against the window of a baker's a few doors away.

"Miss Amory, thank goodness you're here. Feel like a regular jobberknoll hanging about this way," his lordship greeted her, nervously peering about him. "People bound to

292

think I'm touched in the upper story, the ladies especially. I ain't much in the line of quizzing every female that walks by, you know. And what mutton-head would stay a quarter of an hour just lurking in a doorway except to do that very thing? Had to pretend I'm waiting for someone," he said, as he gave a nervous half-bow to a passing matron, who, with plain, stumbling daughters and a maid in train, regarded him with interest.

"But you *are* waiting for someone, my lord!" Katherine exasperatedly took his arm and steered him down the street, away from the curious ladies. "Have you seen anything of Mr. Oldbury?"

"Shhhh! Careful not to mention *his* name! Refer only to *O*, if you please. The instructions were to be discreet."

"But I'm sure that it's not necessary to—"

He forestalled her protest indignantly. "Think I don't know how to be a proper spy? Going to do a thing, then do it right, I always say." Katherine acquiesced but wondered if she could carry off so great a degree of discretion without going into whoops at the absurdity of it.

"Very well, my lord, *O* it is."

At the bake shop they bought a few buns for Ted, and before they could settle on any sort of plan for the safe surveillance of Mr. Oldbury's lodgings, that gentleman's familiar figure was seen in the doorway of the building across the way. They all three held their breath, shrinking back against the wall, to the great curiosity of the passers-by. Fortunately, Oldbury paused only a moment and did not glance their way, but headed off briskly in the opposite direction, on foot.

"Quickly, my lord, let us follow him!" cried Katherine.

"An' I'll follow *you*," suggested Ted, wiping his sticky fingers on his shirtfront. "So's he don't catch a peep o' me."

Knolland reluctantly allowed himself to be led across the street by Katherine, with Ted loitering a comfortable distance behind, out of sight should Oldbury suddenly turn.

He led them on a long and winding way, bypassing all the

better-known shops and fashionable lodgings. Oldbury seemed oblivious to their presence, but every so often when he paused at a shop or to allow a large party to pass him, Lord Knolland would clutch at Katherine's arm and pull her into the nearest doorway, ignoring all her protests and her fiery blushes as other morning strollers eyed them with amusement. In this absurd fashion they progressed for several minutes, until Katherine began to regret her determination to accompany Knolland on his peculiar mission.

Oldbury's first stop was at a second-rate inn, and despite having but recently broken their fast neither Lord Knolland nor Ted was averse to watching their prey tuck into a plate of chops, while they enjoyed a loaf of fresh bread and toasted cheese in an obscure corner.

Meanwhile, Katherine simmered with impatience in a milliner's down the street, trying on a dozen hats that she had no intention of buying, stretching out the time so much that at last the shopgirl began to look at her suspiciously. Still Lord Knolland and the boy did not come for her.

Finally she could not avoid making a purchase, and she stepped out of the shop with a very pretty chip straw bonnet trimmed with bright pink satin roses and ribbon. To her horror, Oldbury emerged from the inn, and began walking in her direction, so she ducked into the next shop, which proved unfortunately to be a tobacconists's.

The shopkeeper regarded her with wonder, as if he had never seen a lady before, but regained his aplomb in a moment and intoned, "May I be of assistance, miss?"

In a faint voice, she stammered that she was looking for a quantity of snuff for her grandmother, at which the man raised his eyebrows.

"Ah, I see," he said, though it was obvious that he did not see at all. "Well, then, which sort does the lady prefer?"

Between controlling her intense desire to laugh at her predicament, her impatience to catch a glimpse of Lord Knolland, and her desire to avoid Mr. Oldbury's catching sight of her through the shop window, Katherine suffered agonies, but at last she caught a glimpse of Oldbury's ruddy profile in between the gold-etched letters on the tobacconist's window. He turned neither to the left nor to the right, but proceeded haughtily down the street.

Now the tobacconist was recommending to her a particular blend of snuff said to be favored by the Duke of York, and Katherine saw Knolland waving frantically at her through the window, mouthing something undecipherable and waving in the direction Oldbury had taken.

With the hastily muttered excuse that she was afraid her grandmother did not at all approve of the Duke of York, she fled the shop and almost fell on Lord Knolland, stifling her laughter against her kid-gloved hand.

"None of this, now, Miss Amory. He's gone up ahead, and once he's over the hill we'll lose sight of him if we don't hurry!"

And so the chase continued, and though it was a tedious, wearying one, the little company of spies contrived to amuse themselves. Katherine, who of necessity found herself loitering in shops while his lordship and the boy pursued Oldbury into places unsuitable for a lady, spent freely of the money bestowed on her by Lord Knolland after she confessed her financial embarrassment due to the unexpected purchase of the bonnet. Lord Knolland and Ted, who his lordship was by now ready to praise as "fine young rascal," fortified themselves by eating and drinking at every opportunity.

And there were many of these, for among the stops on his morning jaunt, so far very innocent-seeming, Oldbury included a coffee-house, a pastry-cook's, and a confectioners' that happened in his way. Katherine had never realized that her former suitor was such a hearty trencherman and so addicted to sweets.

After purchasing the latest newspapers, he took them into the coffee-house, Lord Knolland and Ted close on his heels but observing him stealthily from a dark corner; and upon following him out, almost, but not quite surfeited, they informed Katherine that he had sat alone, drinking coffee and reading his papers, talking to no one but the waiter and seemingly oblivious of their pursuit.

She handed Ted the hatbox and the parcel containing a length of pale yellow India muslin she was sure would suit Priscilla, a packet of some tea that she knew would please her mother, and a card of fresh lace to retrim her one evening cloak.

After leading them circuitously past Bath Street, their quarry had stopped at a bookseller's, an apothecary, and a barber shop, passing perilously close to the Abbey and the Pump Room, where Katherine dreaded to be seen by her mother and cousin. Finally, weary and overheated, they found themselves watching from a safe distance as their prey entered the yard of the White Hart Inn and commenced a long harangue with the chief ostler.

Ted unceremoniously dumped the parcels and crept closer, blending easily into the bustling activity of the yard, while the others edged away and pretended to be observing the arrivals and departures. By now Katherine wanted nothing more than to sit and rest her feet, and Lord Knolland looked as though he agreed with her. His face was shiny and redder than she had ever seen it, and when Oldbury and Ted both seemed to have disappeared, he was so uncharitable as to wish his good friend Tarrington to the devil, completely forgetting the presence of a lady.

Katherine, too, began to hope that her betrothed was suffering some torment equal to that of traipsing about Bath on a warm day after such peripatetic quarry as Mr. Oldbury. As perspiration trickled down her face, she blotted it with her handkerchief, unconcerned with appearances.

In any case, no one around the busy inn seemed to be paying them the slightest attention. Just when she was about to demand that Lord Knolland bespeak them a private parlor and order a jug of lemonade, Ted popped up beside them, seemingly from nowhere.

"Trouble," he said darkly. "Mister *O* 'as ordered a carriage."

Lord Knolland revived. "Aha! Trying to slip out of our hands. Well, we won't let him, that's all!"

"I 'eard 'im talkin' to the ostler; got *that* close without 'em seein' me." He grinned and held up two fingers rather less than an inch apart.

"What did I tell you?" Lord Knolland beamed and patted the stained floppy hat gingerly. "Clever little rascal."

"But is he clever enough to have found out at what hour Mr. Oldbury—I beg your pardon"—she returned Knolland's warning glare—"I mean *O,* ordered the carriage to be ready?"

"Three o'clock," said Ted proudly. "Then 'e went into the taproom, an' looks ready to stay a good long time, if ye get's my drift." He crooked an elbow in illustration.

"Oh, dear," Katherine said, and shifted her weight wearily. "It is just rung twelve. I can't possibly wait here for another three hours, and I doubt if either one of you could consume another mouthful of food or drink without bursting quite open! Besides, if he has a carriage, how can we stop him from leaving? We can't follow him on foot! I don't dare ask Lady Tarrington for the use of her barouche, and—" She recalled with a sudden jolt that she was supposed to be at home in bed, and that the ladies would, on reaching home, certainly be worried at not finding her.

"I must go back, at least for now. I'm afraid, my lord, that you'll have to continue without me."

"Not to worry, Miss Amory. I'll just step in and have a word with 'em about hiring ny own carriage."

But this enquiry proved fruitless. There were no more vehicles to be had that day, and Lord Knolland was insisting that they try the livery stables to which the ostler had directed them when inspiration struck Katherine.

"I know one thing that might make him at least postpone his departure. Listen carefully, my lord."

At this point Lord Knolland had tired of the chase, and it took very little encouragement to bring him around to her plan. Finally, he agreed to do as she asked but insisted, "Tarrington won't like it."

Whereupon she shocked and saddened him by retorting, "I am sure that does not concern me in the least."

Knolland saw his last hope move completely out of reach. His friend was right; the wedding was by no means certain.

After summoning a chair and seeing Katherine safely off to Gay Street, Lord Knolland instructed Ted to return there as well, and await his orders. Then he smoothed his rumpled, damp neckcloth, wiped his face with his handkerchief, and entered the White Hart in search of Mr. George Oldbury.

Chapter Twelve

A watery grey dawn washed the sky, and the sun shed barely enough light to reveal two weary riders pressing their horses forward along a country lane. A laborer in his smock stopped and blinked as they rode by, then shouldered his hoe and plodded on.

The earl of Tarrington shifted his reins to one hand and raised the other to rub his burning eyes, hoping that his exhaustion had not led him to begin seeing things that were not there. But no, there was definitely the steeple of Barton village church, not a quarter-mile away. The long night's ride was almost over.

He spared a glance for the man riding at his side. Bilgrove, the Bow Street Runner, sat his horse clumsily, but he had maintained the grueling pace set by the earl with no complaint. He seemed as at home on a country lane as he was in the back alleys of London.

The man's tenacity and stamina had been a welcome surprise to Tarrington. He had once believed him to be just another lazy operative of an inadequate police system, motivated only by the lucrative prospects of thief-taking. But working with him over the past months had changed his lordship's opinion. Bilgrove had put as much thought and effort into the search as if he, and not Tarrington, had a personal wrong to avenge.

From the beginning of their journey, leaving Bath in the last of the dusk, they had spoken little, to preserve their energy for the task ahead. But now that the village was in sight a conference was necessary.

"I think we should stop at the Black Horse, m'lord. T'will do us no good to appear there covered with dust, hungry, and thirsty. Ye'll get no cooperation unless we appear to be just what we are: a representative of the law and an honest defrauded citizen."

Tarrington was reluctant. "Might we not make good use of the advantage of surprise? The servants will hardly be expecting anyone to arrive this early in the day, and if his accomplice is there, as I believe, then all the better if we go immediately, before he slips out of our hands."

But he was also hungry, parched, and tired of smelling his own sweat. It took little for Bilgrove to convince him that a stop at the inn for breakfast would do little harm to their mission. And they must, at any rate, hire a chaise to carry them back to Bath.

The only thing that made the prospect of performing such a journey twice in twenty-four hours bearable was the thought that this time they could travel post and bring with them, if they were lucky, the proof they needed to put an end to Oldbury's criminal career.

As Tarrington dismounted in the yard of the Black Horse, muscles trembling with fatigue, the thoughts that had tormented him through the night returned to plague him. Leaving that note for Katherine had been a gamble, a desperate wager that she might not condemn out of hand his hurried departure and his behavior on first sighting Oldbury in Bath.

He swore over and over to himself that the first thing he would do when it was all over and Oldbury was safely in Bilgrove's custody would be to pull her into a deserted room and take her into his arms. He had done it once, and though by all rights it should have only frightened her, it had won him the promise of her hand. Perhaps this time he could convince her of his deep and passionate love, and she would not, as she had every right to do, renege on that promise.

But at this moment he could spare no more thought than this for Katherine. The culmination of a year's work was upon him, and on its success or failure rested his self-respect and his future. The earl had little doubt that if he failed to bring positive proof against Oldbury, an uproar to make his last scandal look pale by comparison would ensue, and Katherine would turn from him in disgust.

Three-quarters of an hour later, after a hasty wash and a quick breakfast, the two men mounted fresh horses and set off for Bartonstead, the home of George Oldbury. Tarrington had a flash of panic, which he put down to fatigue, when he thought of how he had been forced to leave Knolland to see that Oldbury stayed in Bath and remained unaware of his absence. But it was too late to turn back. The moment was here.

The oaken door of the taproom was greasy under his hand, and Lord Knolland hesitated, unsure if he could perform his part as Miss Amory had instructed him. But he was forced to proceed because he was blocking the hall, where busy serving men and maids pushed past him with trays. Others struggled towards the stairs with baggage, and one plump wench gave him a sly wink as she trotted past, her ample charms scarcely hidden by her low-necked round dress and apron.

He tore his eyes away at last, cleared his throat, and finally pushed open the door, stumbling into the room, his nose assailed by a cloud of pipe smoke and the smell of customers in various levels of cleanliness. The room was not full, but a sizeable number of people were taking their ease and their ale on this warm day in Bath, and at first he could not find Oldbury. He advanced a little way in, eyes searching the far corners, noting that none of the inhabitants appeared likely to have any connection with the fashionable world. If Oldbury did his drinking here, he surmised, it was because he could not afford to hire a private room.

"The devil!" he muttered to himself. "What does Tarrington want with him, anyway?" Or was it, he thought a moment later, that Oldbury wanted something from Tarrington?

Mentally abusing himself for not having asked Ted in what part of the room Oldbury had seated himself, he approached the tapster and bought himself a pint. Then, nervously spilling some of the ale on his boots, with an inward shudder at the thought of the scold that awaited him from Finster, he started to search the room again, only to find that his quarry was practically under his nose.

At the end of a long table half-occupied by a group of old sailors and a sprinkling of yeomen, sat Oldbury, a pitcher of beer at his elbow, drinking solitarily, but not, it seemed unhappily. His flushed face bore a smile of satisfaction as he contemplated the table-top.

Lord Knolland took a breath and a swallow of ale, and the violent choking that followed served to attract the attention of almost every occupant of the table except the one whose ear he sought. Oldbury was too preoccupied to notice.

Knolland blinked his watering eyes and forced a greeting through the spasms in his throat.

"G-good day, sir! Mr., er, Oldbury, is it? Had the pleasure of makin' your acquaintance once before. How do you do?" His voice by now recovered, Knolland shifted his tankard of ale and extended his right hand, his face as congenial as he could make it, though his stomach was quaking.

Oldbury jerked his head up, and his smile vanished for a moment. But on recognizing the arrival, another spread over his face. It was a guarded, wary smile. "My lord ah . . ." A bead of sweat trickled down from his temple.

"Knolland," offered his lordship, seating himself without invitation on the empty bench opposite Oldbury.

"Indeed, indeed, sir . . . foolish of me to forget, after your generous forgiveness that unfortunate evening."

Knolland sipped at his ale and waved a careless hand. "Never think of it myself! Beg you'll forget it, too. It's just pleasant to see a familiar face here in Bath. Been preoccupied with sick relations here, you know," he extemporised. "Not much amusement to be had here this time of year."

Oldbury drained his own tankard and then said with elaborate casualness, "What? Not spending any time with your friend Lord Tarrington? I hear he is in town as well."

Knolland squelched a desire to smirk. Miss Amory had instructed him well, and Mr. Oldbury was falling neatly into the trap.

"Oh, of course I've paid my respects, been to dinner, that sort of thing. But Tarrington has little time for me today. He's occupied with some business or other. Thought I'd give the ladies a bit of diversion by taking them on a drive, but I've not my own carriage with me and there doesn't seem one to be had today." He busied himself with his ale, then looked at Oldbury through half-lowered lids.

He saw pleasure swiftly cross the man's face, and Oldbury did not trouble to keep it out of his voice when he replied, "Yes, I confess I've stolen a march on you, my lord, and with rather the same object in mind. I hired what I understood to be the last vehicle, with some idea of taking Miss Amory for a little drive this afternoon."

Knolland nearly sputtered into his drink at this interesting news, but relief followed swiftly on the heels of surprise. If Oldbury wasn't leaving Bath after all, then he would have nothing to worry about as far as Tarrington's orders went. Their plan to distract him into visiting Miss Amory was unnecessary, since Oldbury's own desires fell in with it completely.

Once Miss Amory had him in her charge, the whole silly chase would be over. Lord Knolland had the utmost confidence in that lady's abilities. Oldbury, he was sure, would not dare attempt to leave Bath while under her watchful eye.

If only Tarrington would return! It was quite tedious and exhausting, this spy business, and the sooner it was over, the better he would feel. But he had yet some more of his part to play.

"A capital idea! Miss Amory confessed to me that she feels a bit restless these days. Staying in Gay Street with Lady Tarrington, you know, and though it's livelier than she was used to, there ain't that much to amuse her. Only sorry I didn't think of it before, but . . . never mind."

He disengaged himself from the bench, praying that there would be no grease stain on the back of his buff pantaloons. Finster would have enough to tax him with as it was. "No use me loitering about here after a carriage that's already been hired. Sick relations very demanding, you know. Enjoy your drive, and good day, sir."

As the relatively cool air outside hit his heated cheek, Knolland breathed deeply and turned his weary steps back towards Gay Street. He had chased all over the hilly city by shank's mare after that dreadful fellow, and had no alternative but to get back the same way. He eyed a passing chair longingly, but resisted the temptation. A fine sight he would look, waving down a chair like an ailing dowager! He plodded on, imagining in fine detail the glorious release from his exquisite and expensive but suddenly very uncomfortable boots.

It certainly wasn't fair that, now it was Miss Amory's turn to keep Oldbury under scrutiny, *she* was to be permitted to do it sitting in a comfortable carriage! "Tarrington's taking this friendship thing a bit too far," he muttered.

Katherine turned and fidgeted, pulling at her crumpled sheets, tired but not at all sleepy, and irritable from lying in bed to no good purpose. The noise in the house indicated that the other ladies had returned from their morning visit to the Pump Room, yet no one had even sent to inquire how she was feeling.

304

It was tedious, but at least her ruse had succeeded.

She heard footsteps in the hall, and forced herself to remain in bed, but the steps passed and there was no knock on her door. Even if she really had been ill with the headache, she reasoned, no one would be suspicious if she appeared downstairs now.

She jumped up and pulled her morning dress on again over her shift, wondering how Lord Knolland was faring at the White Hart. If he succeeded in drawing Oldbury's attention back to her, then she would have the strenuous task of keeping him under her scrutiny for the remainder of the afternoon. She groaned at her tired image in the mirror as she arranged her hair. By tonight, she thought, if Tarrington had really meant to return, he would be back, and one way or another it would all be over.

At that thought, the cherry ribbons she was tying round her curls slipped from her fingers. She envisioned another frightful confrontation between the earl and Oldbury, yet steeled herself to go on, despite the almost certain outcome.

While the idea of Tarrington laboring to scrape up a huge sum to satisfy the demands of a greedy leech like Oldbury made her stomach squirm, it would be still more dreadful if Tarrington failed to pay and his crimes were revealed.

The betrothal, of course, must end. Though she could not pretend that her love for Tarrington had died, all respect had vanished in that moment when he had agreed to Oldbury's demand. She tied the ribbon firmly, ignoring the tear that seeped from the corner of her eye and slid slowly down past her cheekbone.

Her image in the mirror grew hazy, and it was as though she saw Vane instead, his changeable eyes laughing at her; his smooth, muscled, unclothed torso turned towards her, as it had been the day she had mistaken his room; and worst of all, the comfort and kindness in his eyes, which had turned to a passion whose demands she could not refuse.

Her heart had betrayed her into a hasty acceptance, and she

had been fool enough to hope that all would be well, but she could no longer deceive herself.

The girl in the mirror stared back at her once more, thick unruly hair barely contained by the ribbon, eyes cloudy and dark in a pale face. Katherine looked to herself as lifeless as a wax figure, and felt entirely drained of emotion. This chasing after Oldbury was surely nonsense, but she would play it out to the end. She owed Tarrington that much help at least.

Katherine flung down her comb, and turning away from the mirror, went to the door. She paused with her hand on the latch, suddenly wanting nothing more than to get back into bed and forget everything that had happened. But of course it was impossible. Nothing ever comes of running away, she scolded herself.

The others greeted her entirely without suspicion, and she joined them half-heartedly in a cold luncheon. Even the long morning of trudging about the city had not restored her appetite. Lady Tarrington inquired kindly about her health, and admitted her displeasure at the earl's sudden departure.

"I hope that you will be able to teach him better manners, my dear."

"Very shabby of Vane, I admit," said Lady Colesville, "but he has been behaving so oddly ever since the accident—" She stopped and eyed Katherine guiltily. "Well, I daresay you know all about it by now, though he made us promise not to mention Cassandra—but of course that's all over."

"Yes, Sally, I do know," Katherine said quietly. How she wished that she could discuss with either of them the horrible truth she had learned about their beloved Tarrington! He had betrayed them as well. But she could not destroy their trust in him.

Sally came and took her hand. "I know you will be very happy. You are so different, not at all the kind of girl that—" She flushed and bit her lip. "I mean that Vane will always be able to depend on you. It means a lot to us to see him happy again, and though it sounds absurd, I knew from the first time

306

you quarrelled with him that you were the one to make him so."

Katherine could only manage the brittlest of smiles and a tiny press of Sally's hand. She felt nothing but the sincerest relief when Lord Colesville descended upon them and carried his wife off for a drive to the Sydney Gardens.

Mrs. Amory was not at all perturbed by her future son-in-law's absence, being too happily preoccupied to notice anything amiss. "I daresay dear Tarrington will be with us again very soon . . . Priscilla, my love, when next you go into Milsom Street I wish you would look out a bit of lavender ribbon for me. I do so want my old grey silk to look a little smarter when the colonel presents me to his brother next week."

Katherine glanced at her cousin, who replied listlessly, "Yes, Aunt Delia." Priscilla seemed to have lost all the sparkle she had gained in the last week, and she did not even pretend to flirt when two of her most fervent admirers, albeit middle-aged and confirmed bachelors, were announced after luncheon.

The other ladies strained to entertain them, but they soon left, disappointed that Miss Townsend was not disposed to reward them with so much as a smile to fight over. The arrival of Mr. Fellowes added a bit of levity to the distracted group in the drawing room. As usual, he complimented all of the ladies extravagantly, and even managed to draw a giggle from Priscilla, by comparing her beauty to some cool, refreshing ices he had enjoyed the day before. Then he begged leave to escort her and Miss Amory to the shop to sample them.

"Shall we, Kate?" she asked her cousin, with the first sign of genuine animation she'd displayed since Lord Knolland's defection. Katherine would have loved to accept the invitation, for she was sorely in need of Mr. Fellowes' innocent and entertaining distraction, but if Lord Knolland had done as she'd instructed, she would soon be receiving a visit.

"You go along, dear. I can't . . . I'm expecting a caller."

The others looked up, mildly curious.

"Who is it dear?" asked her mother. "Is it Miss Martin, or Lord Jamison—he seemed to admire you excessively the other evening—or that handsome Mr. Tripham we always meet in the library, buying prints? Have a care, my love, else you will be making dear Tarrington jealous," she said playfully.

Katherine swallowed and stared down at her hands, which were pretending to be busy embroidering the initial T on a damask napkin. "It is . . . Mr. Oldbury, Mama. You do remember that he is in Bath."

Mrs. Amory nodded and went back to her own embroidery. "Of course. Nothing could be more natural than that he'd wish to pay his respects to us, especially, my love, to you. I do hope he is aware that you are engaged, Katherine, or else I fear he will suffer an unpleasant surprise. The poor boy is rather sensitive, and you have not been kind to him."

Katherine grimly assured her that she would break the news gently, privately reflecting that the afternoon was going to be strenuous enough to bring on a genuine headache. She could not afford to be severe with Oldbury this time, even if he should take up his old ways and begin to insult her with his advances. Tarrington's honor, or what was left of it, was at stake, and that she could not cease to care about, no matter what he had done.

"Oh, that is too bad, Kate," said Priscilla. "Why must you stay home to wait for that horrid Mr. Oldbury? Just because he wanted to marry you once doesn't mean that you have to miss this treat! Besides, he'd much rather talk to Aunt Delia; she likes him and you don't," she pointed out.

Mr. Fellowes regarded her with interest. "What's this, Miss Amory? Have you a rejected suitor in your past? How sly of you to keep it from me! But I insist that you remain to tell him, tenderly, of course, that there is no more hope for him. How fortunate for him that his lordship the earl is temporarily absent." He chuckled. "It is always so amusing when young people get themselves into such predicaments. Now come, Miss Townsend, and let us go cool ourselves with an ice," he said, ignoring Katherine's glare.

Priscilla sent the housemaid for her sunshade, bonnet, and gloves; and in a few minutes was ready to set off with Mr. Fellowes, but before she could escape from the drawing room, she suffered a serious setback at the entrance of Lord Knolland, fresh from a severe scold by Finster and newly dressed, with unwilted neckcloth and pale yellow pantaloons.

They met on the threshold, he turning pink, she pale, and Mr. Fellowes looked on in sympathetic amusement. His lordship uttered a strangled, "Good day," but Priscilla only lifted her chin and swept out of the room without a reply.

Despite the camaraderie of their morning's adventure, Katherine had not yet forgiven Lord Knolland for toying with her vulnerable cousin's heart, and offered him no succor. Mrs. Amory seemed to be of the same mind, though she nodded kindly enough in response to his greeting. Lady Tarrington, finding she could get no information from him regarding her son's whereabouts, gave up the attempt and turned back to perusing a periodical.

After wandering restlessly about the room, his lordship perched uneasily on a settee a few feet from Katherine and endeavored to attract her attention. A slight hand gesture went unnoticed by her, but Mrs. Amory lifted her head from her work in time to see it so his lordship pretended to fan himself vigorously.

"Warm, very warm," he announced.

"Indeed," said she, eyeing him with concern.

His lordship, undaunted by Katherine's lack of response, pressed on.

"*O,*" he muttered.

There was no response.

He tried again. "*O . . . O,*" he insisted.

Lady Tarrington turned a page and looked up. "Is something wrong, my lord?"

"Nothing!" He started guiltily. "No, no, nothing at all," he assured her, assuming a vacuous expression. His eyes slid towards Katherine. After a moment of silence, he murmured something that sounded vaguely like "sweet heart."

Mrs. Amory glanced at him sharply. He reddened and cleared his throat. When the ladies seemed absorbed in their activities once more, he tried again.

"Splendid work, Miss Amory, those tiny stitches and all— never could understand how you females do that sort of thing without going blind altogether."

Katherine glanced at him in surprise.

"Would you like to see how it is done? Come sit next to me, then, my lord, and I will show you."

For a moment he stared at her in perplexity. "Why would I want to see— Oh! yes, certainly, much obliged."

He dragged a chair close to hers and bent over the needlework, while Mrs. Amory stared suspiciously at them, and Katherine's chest ached from holding in a laugh. She bent closer, but heard nothing from Knolland. Exasperated, she looked at him and found that he was mouthing something at her, now and then darting frightened glances at her mother.

"What's that, my lord? Did you say you preferred the *old* stitch?" she asked deliberately. He looked at her blankly. After a very long moment, comprehension dawned on his face.

"I've done it," he whispered just loudly enough for her to hear. "The *White Hart, O*—he'll be here soon!"

Katherine had entertained some doubt of his succeeding, but it came to her now that Oldbury would be unable to resist the temptation of gloating in her presence at his triumph over Tarrington. Even so, it was a relief to hear that he had taken the bait.

"Where is Ted?" she said in an undertone.

"I sent him back to the inn, to make sure *O* don't slip away," he whispered back, poking an awkward finger at the design on the damask between her hands.

"Very good. Now you'd best go. You shouldn't be here when he comes."

"Where should I go?"

310

Katherine stifled a sigh of exasperation. "Why don't you go for a walk, my lord?"

He regarded her with as much dislike as his essential good nature would allow him to muster, and promptly took his leave.

"Mama," Katherine said when he had gone, for that lady had kept her eyes fastened on them throughout and she could tell that Knolland was rapidly falling from favor, "Lord Knolland says that he has met Mr. Oldbury in the street."

"Why, how interesting, to be sure, my love, but why should he feel it necessary to whisper such a thing to you, and in such a peculiar way." She frowned. "He has not been . . . that is, he *is* the earl's best friend, but . . ."

"Mama!"

Mrs. Amory sighed and went back to her embroidery. "No, you are right, I'm merely being foolish. And of course, Lord Knolland is in love with Priscilla . . . or he was. The poor child! I am afraid he would make her a most unsuitable husband, in any case."

Lady Tarrington agreed. "Rodney is a perfect gentleman, of course, but I fear he has not the strength or constancy of mind one could wish for."

Katherine thought it fortunate that Priscilla was not present, for she would, despite her hurt at his failure to come to the point, have defended Lord Knolland with her last breath. When it is all over, she vowed, his lordship is going to be made to explain himself, to me at least.

But before that there was still the ordeal with Oldbury to endure, and mercifully, she had not long to wait before it began.

He was shown in by the butler, whom he addressed as "my good man" and from whom he received a frigid glance for his pains. Looking as self-satisfied and sounding as pompous as ever, he bowed and smiled and said everything proper.

The two older ladies received him kindly, but Katherine shivered as he took her hand, feeling tainted by his touch.

Why, she wondered, had she not felt that way about Tarrington? He was a self-admitted criminal. But there was something so vile about a blackmailer that Tarrington's crime seemed trivial by comparison. She could hardly find it in her to believe that Oldbury and the man who was her betrothed were of the same species.

"My dear Miss Amory," he began, when he had satisfied all Mrs. Amory's inquiries about everyone back in Barton, "I come to offer you a bit of diversion in the form of a drive out of the city. I do hope that you will grant me the honor of your company for an hour?" His recent triumph, Katherine observed, had at least made him polite.

Quickly, before her mother could mention her betrothal to Tarrington, Katherine accepted. If she were to keep Oldbury at her side it would be better if he knew nothing of that. Not, she thought, that it would discourage him very much, but she hoped to avoid discussing the earl, lest she give something away or learn something else to his discredit.

She had already had her fill of revelations, and wanted nothing more but to perform this one last service for the man she loved before she let him leave her life forever.

If Oldbury was surprised by her ready acquiescence, he hid it well. Mrs. Amory, however, despite her fondness for the gentleman, was so far from thinking it proper that she was moved to protest. "Don't you think, my love, that with Lord Tarrington away, it would not be—"

"Nonsense, Mama. I am sure his lordship would be the first to say I should take some air after being inside all day."

If Oldbury noticed the quick reference to the earl, he made no comment, and there was no sign on his face that he understood it. Katherine relaxed and sent for her bonnet and gloves.

It was only a few minutes later that she found herself beside Oldbury in his hired curricle, a somewhat dilapidated vehicle which had probably once seen better days in the stables of a wealthy man.

Fortunately, he seemed little interested in the subject of

Tarrington and chatted on for some minutes about his latest acquisitions. Katherine feigned an interest but winced inwardly, recalling that painting whose purchase had proved so tragic for Tarrington.

She managed to summon up enough pretended fascination to keep him talking until they were past a tangle of carriages, chairs, and people at Queen Square. A sudden commotion behind them made her glance around, and to her mingled relief and horror she saw young Ted, hatless, his tangled curls bouncing as he dodged carts and carriages and people, following them gamely. He caught her eye and gave an encouraging grin. She shook her head warningly, and motioned him off, but he kept up with them easily, so slowly were they travelling along the crowded street.

She turned back quickly before Oldbury could notice her preoccupation, but luckily he was busy negotiating the narrow street. When he had leisure to speak again, his conversation, as she had known it would, turned to their last encounter.

"You may be surprised, Katherine, to see me in Bath again after what occurred upon our last, er, meeting," he began, darting a glance at her, and moistening his upper lip. "And I, in turn, am surprised to be so kindly received by you. You were not so happily disposed towards me back at Whitfield."

This was no time, Katherine reflected, for the truth. Suddenly she regretted sending Knolland away. Glancing up at Oldbury's sly and expectant face, she realized that her task was going to be much more difficult than she had assumed.

"Why, sir, you know that it is not in my nature to hold a grudge for long. I believe we understand each other now, and it is unnecessary for me to continue being angry with you," she said, with what she hoped was a forgiving and innocent air. She hazarded a glance behind them. Ted's tousled head was still in sight, though farther away than before.

"Hmmm! Very nicely said, my dear. Of course, if you are of the same mind, I shall no longer importune you upon the subject that caused you such distress. But, allow me, as an old

313

friend, to assure myself that you are happy in the path you have chosen."

"Very happy, sir," she said firmly. "Our future in Bath is quite secure. But I own I am surprised to see you in this city." She moved swiftly to a change of subject. "I hope it is not for health reasons?" she ventured.

"Oh, indeed, not . . . a matter of business . . . a trifling thing or two to do with my collection . . . along with a desire for a bit of amusement, and of course . . ."—he half bowed, almost losing his grip on the reins, to which one of the hired pair objected by tossing his black-maned head—"the desire to assure myself that my friends and former neighbors were faring well."

They had finally progressed through a muddle of traffic and were approaching Milsom Street, and Katherine was sanguine in her hopes for an uneventful, if somewhat tedious, drive when she heard herself addressed in those high, slightly shrill tones that belonged unmistakably to her cousin Priscilla.

"Hallo! Kate! Oh, *do* turn round. ., . It is she, Mr. Fellowes, is it not? I cannot . . . oh, she sees us. . . ."

Katherine turned and found her cousin and Mr. Fellowes, presumably well refreshed and full of ices, approaching them, Priscilla waving in a fashion Katherine would have characterized as excessively vulgar if it had not been accompanied by a vague stare and a surreptitious squint, the gentleman displaying a determined smile that she knew boded ill for her chances at escape.

She twisted nervously in her seat. This meeting could only lead to uncomfortable questions. Her sole consolation was that for a few minutes she would be relieved from the necessity of having to entertain Oldbury alone. Out of the corner of her eye she saw Ted dart into a side street, out of sight.

By now Oldbury had seen Priscilla and had pulled up before her and Mr. Fellowes. He, too, seemed irked at the coincidence, his thin lower lip almost disappearing in what she recognized as a sign of annoyance. Perhaps, she fretted, despite his dis-

314

claimer, he had intended to renew his attentions to her after all. The knowledge that Ted was following them was ridiculously comforting, though she feared the consequences if her companion recognized him.

Introductions accomplished, Katherine became aware that her cousin and Mr. Fellowes were regarding her with pity, a result, she was sure, of Priscilla's having regaled him with the story of Oldbury's persistence and general unpleasantness. Priscilla's eyes held that hazy inte' ' that was as close as she ever came to being determined, an .o Katherine's dismay she lost no time in coming to the rescue.

"Oh, Kate, I only wish you would have gone with us! The ices were of all things most delightful," she said, ignoring Oldbury. "But I'm so glad that we met you, because I saw the most charming bonnet in a shop just down the street, and I need your advice. Do step down and see it, and then you can walk home with us."

"But Pris, Mr. Oldbury—"

"Oh, I am sure he will not mind." She bestowed an icy smile upon their erstwhile neighbor.

Katherine glanced at him, but he appeared only mildly discomfited at this bit of rudeness.

He laughed hollowly. "Ah, Miss Townsend, I am not quite prepared to relinquish your cousin to you yet. We have only just begun our drive."

"Oh, but you can drive with her another time."

Katherine intervened. "Another time might not suit Mr. Oldbury so well, Priscilla."

"Yes, I know very well what you mean, Kate. Why, Lord Tarrington will very likely return by tomorrow, will he not?" Her pointed face glowed with triumph as she saw the means by which she could separate her cousin from her persecutor.

The look Katherine gave her, however, was anything but grateful. "What has that to—"

"Is his lordship not in the city then?" Katherine felt Oldbury tense beside her. "I had hoped to have the

315

opportunity of furthering my acquaintance with him." There was a change in his voice that made Katherine's skin crawl.

"Oh, no," Priscilla said before she could think of an evasion. "He left quite unexpectedly—"

"—to attend to something for Lady Tarrington and we expect him back in time for dinner this evening," said Katherine, control slipping away from her by the moment, "and his presence or absence has not a jot to do with my driving with Mr. Oldbury."

Priscilla looked shocked. "Why, don't you think he might object, considering—"

"How silly you are, Pris!" Katherine forced a little laugh. "Why should he or anyone object?" She shot a desperate look at Mr. Fellowes in the hopes that he might understand that she meant their rescue attempt to be abandoned.

To her chagrin, he promptly misinterpreted it. "Indeed, and it is getting on for four, and I meant to have this young lady back early," he patted Priscilla's hand. "Why not step down and walk with us, Miss Amory? You young people ride too much. All the physicians here agree that walking is of great benefit to the constitution." He held out a hand to help her down from the carriage, and winked conspiratorially.

Katherine nearly screamed with frustration. "Thank you, *no*, I prefer to ride." She turned to Oldbury, who was watching her closely. "Drive on, sir. I fear any more delay will make us waste this lovely sunshine." Indeed, there was little of it to be seen between the gathering clouds. The heat of the day was dissipating, and a breeze was moving damp air across the river.

Without any more encouragement, he whipped up the horses, and they soon left Priscilla and Mr. Fellowes behind, staring and wondering at Katherine's inexplicable behavior.

Very soon, though, Katherine ceased to rejoice at her close escape, and she began to wish she could abandon the entire idea of keeping watch over Oldbury, because his appetite had been whetted for news of Tarrington.

It took all of her ingenuity to convince him that she knew

nothing of the business that had taken him from home, that he had not talked of an extended trip, and that he had assured them he would be home to dinner that evening. Still he persisted.

"And did I detect, my dear Miss Amory,"—his manner was a shade less conciliating than it had been—"some concern on the part of your family as to what his lordship might think of my calling on you?"

"There is nothing at all in that, sir," she assured him. "It is only that Lord Tarrington feels a responsibility for all of us as relations, you know, and has a tendency to interfere in aspects of our lives which otherwise would be none of his affair." How horrid I once thought it of him, she thought, and how kind it really was. Some part of her was refusing to believe, even now, that he could have committed a crime.

Whether this glib explanation would have satisfied Oldbury or not, she was not to have the opportunity of knowing; for as they were nearing Pultney Bridge, a carriage containing Lord and Lady Colesville approached them from the opposite direction. Katherine held her breath, but to no avail, for Sally's sharp eyes were quick to see her seated in the curricle next to Oldbury.

She nudged her husband, they both waved, and nothing could be done but to pull up to them and make the proper introductions.

Lord Colesville expressed pleasure in meeting Mr. Oldbury. His wife did not. She greeted him briefly and immediately plunged into conversation with Katherine.

"How fortunate that we left the Gardens when we did, or we might not have encountered you. And to think I wanted to linger, but Colesville would insist that it was coming on to rain, and we had much better go." Her lower lip was extended in a playful pout, and her hazel eyes were dancing. "But what are you doing driving out at this hour, Katherine? Did you forget that we expect the Brockton's to tea?"

Katherine knew very well that there was no such

engagement, and even Lord Colesville looked surprised, but his wife went on before he could protest. "Come, now. Get down this instant and let us take you up and bring you home. Your mama will be most displeased if you are not there to greet our guests."

Lord Colesville's brows drew together. "My dear, I do not think that—"

"Oh, hush, my lord, I know very well what I am about," she whispered, a bit too loudly.

Katherine reddened and wondered why she should be blessed with so many good friends who seemed bent on making things difficult for her. "Thank you for reminding me of it, Sally, but I am sure that Mr. Oldbury will bring me back in good time."

A flash of ginger caught her eye, and she noticed Ted darting past them. Whatever was the boy up to? If he did not have a care he was going to attract Oldbury's attention, and then all would be lost.

Sally was adamant, however, in insisting that Katherine return with them, and Katherine just as persistent in refusing. Lord Colesville, sensing some female mystery, had given up reasoning with his wife and stood by, listening in idle amusement.

Lady Colesville attempted one last ploy. "If my brother were here, I'm sure he would be most displeased with you, Katherine, though I am sure it is entirely his fault for running off in that infuriating way!"

Oldbury's reaction was not at all what Katherine expected.

Instead of being angered by the persistence of various people in attempting to remove Katherine from his company, his smile had grown bigger with each of her refusals to leave. Katherine thought it odd, but she was too preoccupied in resisting yet another rescue attempt to wonder what this might portend.

As a result, when Lady Colesville had reluctantly surrendered the field, and the curricle was moving across the bridge unhindered, Katherine was totally unprepared for Oldbury's next words.

"My dear Katherine, let me relieve you of your apprehension. There is no need for you to dissemble. I see it very clearly, my dear, that you wish nothing more than a return of my addresses. This reluctance to quit my company, despite the earnest entreaties of your friends, convinces me as nothing else, that you have reconsidered your hasty dismissal of my proposal."

He shifted the reins to one hand in order to place the other one on hers, and it was all she could do not to fling it off. Here was a dilemma, indeed! She swallowed, her mouth suddenly dry, and looked around for Ted. He was nowhere to be seen. The carriage was moving at a brisk pace at last, she realized, and it would have been impossible for him to keep up.

"I—that is . . ." If only she could swiftly disabuse him of this ridiculous assumption, as every nerve in her being longed to do!

"Say nothing, my dear. I know the remorse which must have forced you to keep silence for so long. Yet though I was pained, very pained, by the manner in which you last refused me, think not that I am too proud to ask again. It seems, from the manner in which his opinions are considered among you, that his lordship the earl of Tarrington would be the person to whom I should address my proposal. If you will just tell me, my dear"—his hand tightened on hers almost painfully—"where he can be found, I will hurry to him and we can be officially betrothed this very evening. Now what road did he take out of the city?"

There was a gleam of greed in his eyes, and with a chill she realized just how vulnerable her position was. Would Tarrington give her to Oldbury if he threatened blackmail again? She could not bear to believe it of him.

"Come now, my dear, you must know where he has gone."

"N-not far, sir. He will return this evening," she repeated, but he was not satisfied, and then everything happened at once.

The skies, which had become more threatening by the

319

·moment, opened and raindrops splashed on Katherine's lap. There was a cry behind her and the carriage was jolted as Ted leaped from the little groom's seat, where he had been curled up in hiding behind them, and dashed back onto the bridge.

"What was that? Why, the ruffian was riding behind us!" Oldbury, distracted, caught a glimpse of the ragged figure and Katherine cringed at the recognition that crossed his face. "I know that boy!"

With an effort he pulled the curricle over and turned it around, and by the time they were in a position to pursue Ted, he was far ahead, but they were gaining.

Katherine plucked at Oldbury's arm. "Really, sir, it is not worth your trouble to chase after an urchin in the rain. I would much prefer it if you would take me home now. After all, he has done no harm."

To make matters worse, Katherine really was uncomfortable. Her gown was quite damp, and she gathered from Oldbury's sly sidelong glances that it was clinging to her in a most immodest way.

"I have reason to believe that the boy is involved in some activities of a nature I would rather not discuss with a young lady. It is my duty to find him and question him," he replied.

Katherine was unable to think of a reply. She was sure Ted could contrive to slip out of Oldbury's hands, and that he would deny knowing Tarrington if caught, but that would not keep Oldbury in Bath. His suspicions aroused, sooner or later he would attempt to go after the earl, and she would have failed.

Through the curtain of drizzle, she could see a rider coming towards them. Her heart leaped for a moment in fear and joy, but as they approached she saw that it was only Lord Knolland, and not the man whose return she dreaded and desired. She sank back into her damp seat with disappointment and relief. At least, if she could prevail upon Oldbury to take her home, she could give Lord Knolland the task of delaying him after that.

But the next thing to happen left her breathless with surprise. Ted was dodging and darting ahead of them with an amazing speed and agility. Lord Knolland had stopped before a shop and was dismounting to seek shelter within when the boy nipped past him and with lightning swiftness possessed himself of his lordship's watch.

"Here, what'd you go and do that for, you little—" And Lord Knolland had joined the chase. Either the boy was winded at last, or as Katherine suspected, he slowed down deliberately, but Lord Knolland soon had him by the collar and Katherine could swear that they were whispering to each other.

By the time Oldbury's curricle pulled up to them, however, all that could be heard were his lordship's threats and the boy's sullen replies.

". . . didn't take nothin'."

". . . my gold watch, you miserable young shaver. I demand you give it back."

Mr. Oldbury slowly began to descend from the carriage, examining the captive boy carefully. "Why don't you turn him upside down and shake him, my lord? His crime is sure to reveal itself. In fact, I would like to have a word with him regarding—"

Lord Knolland held up a hand, and grinned insolently. "No, this boy is my prisoner, and I'm taking him straight to the magistrate. My duty, you see, to rid our streets of such ruffians."

"But my lord!" Oldbury nearly fell into the street, he was suddenly in such a great hurry, and Katherine huddled in her chill damp corner of the carriage and looked on in astonishment as Lord Knolland remounted, Ted leaped up behind him, and they rode away.

"This is most irregular! Shocking!"

Oldbury would have gone on, but Katherine begged him most earnestly to take her home. As she was beginning to shiver in earnest, he complied, though not without grumbling.

In the end, to avoid the questions he resumed asking about

the earl, and to assure that he would remain in the city, she was forced to invite him to dinner that evening. If Tarrington did not return that night, then Knolland would have to watch over Oldbury without her assistance.

In her room again at last, and getting out of her wet clothes, after suffering a fervent press of the hand and a humiliating inspection by Oldbury, Katherine found it impossible to resist succumbing to her bone-deep weariness. She flung herself upon her bed and closed her eyes. Never had she lived through such a day as this one, and she hoped earnestly never to experience another like it.

Chapter Thirteen

"But the master is not at home, I tell you!" A sleepy footman in greasy, nondescript livery peered out of the cracked-open door. "I don't see—"

"You'll see right enough, my lad, if you doesn't make this house available to us right now, and as for yer master—"

Bilgrove, catching the slightly built servant off-guard, forced his stocky shoulder against the door and was inside Bartonstead in a flash, the Earl of Tarrington close on his heels. Ignoring the protests of the rumpled footman, they began to move through the house. "Your master may think he's a downy one, but we've got him all right and tight this time," said Bilgrove over his shoulder.

A frightened housemaid with a duster scampered out of Tarrington's way as he strode determinedly up the stairs, and a slatternly cook in a stained apron bustled out of the kitchen corridor, dusting flour from her hands and shouting at Bilgrove as he inspected each picture, vase, and bibelot in the front sitting room.

"Ye have no right, no right at all! Forcin' yer way into a gentleman's 'ouse!"

"Bilgrove of Bow Street has ev'ry right, woman. I'm h'empowered to search and arrest on suspicion. And I've a perticuler suspicion that your master ain't no gentleman."

The cook shut her mouth in mid-shout and scurried away.

Tarrington, meanwhile, was searching the upstairs rooms meticulously, but did not find what he sought. He did find, however, that word had gotten around quickly that the master was in deep trouble. He saw a housemaid in the dining room desperately scooping a collection of gold tea-spoons out of a drawer in the sideboard and into her apron, and the footman who had vainly tried to prevent their entrance was methodically appropriating every gold or silver candlestick he could find.

"Here now, this will not do at all, my friends," he said, fixing them with a deceptively placid gaze.

"That it will," replied the footman, continuing his depredations, "if the master goes to jail, what happens to the likes of us? Best collect our back wages"—he winked at the sack of riches he had accumulated—"and take ourselves off."

"I strongly advise against it, my friend, unless you wish to follow your master into jail."

The two servants, seeing a man who obviously meant what he said, dropped their booty, but before Tarrington let them go he managed to extract from them the information that there *was* a guest in the house, "a queer silent fellow with paint on his hands" as the footman put it, who could usually be found in a room under the eaves.

He took the stairs two at a time and opened the first door at the top, to be rewarded by the sight of nothing more suspicious than a sparsely furnished servants' bedroom. The next door opened on a tiny room stacked with picture frames and half-finished canvas. The third room found him face to face with Oldbury's accomplice, the forger.

"Who the de—"

"Allow me to introduce myself as one of your former dupes, sir." Tarrington drew the small pistol he had worn concealed beneath his coat. "And to repay you and Mr. Oldbury for all you have done, I am going to take you on a little journey to Bath, where you and he will be reunited. There is a gentleman from Bow Street who has some very particular questions to ask you, and if I'm not mistaken—ah, Bilgrove."

The runner was puffing a little from the climb, but when he stepped into the room his face was all satisfaction. For behind the tall and gangly man who sat on a stool before a table, obviously copying the design of an exquisite vase onto a plain-fired piece of pottery of similar shape, there hung Tarrington's Van Meer landscape.

The thin, balding man in the stained smock blanched when he saw Bilgrove, and a slow smile spread over the runner's face. "Martin Trubbs, is it? Tell me why I ain't so surprised it's turned out to be you."

"J-just don't shoot me! I never meant—"

"The way you never meant it the last time when I all but caught you passing stolen goods? Lucky you were, then. But your luck's gone, lad, and mine's just begun. A rare price you'll bring, with your record. A regular thief-taker's prize."

Bilgrove rubbed his hands together, and shook his shaggy head. "Talented man, this Trubbs," he said to Tarrington, who had put away his pistol and was taking down the Van Meer. "But never yet used his gifts for any honest purpose."

Tarrington was turning the painting over in his hands, and examining carefully the underside of the canvas. "I think you'll find this is all the evidence we need to confront our other suspect," he said, and showed it to Bilgrove. Faintly inked were the Tarrington crest and the date the Fourth Earl had purchased the painting.

The runner began to rummage through a stack of canvas, making noises of appreciation or interest. "Now here's one I know for certain hangs this very moment in a viscount's town-house," he observed, examining a biblical scene. "Ain't it curious that Mr. Oldbury has got one exactly like it hanging downstairs. Your work, Trubbs? Or just a coincidence?"

The forger made no answer.

Bilgrove gave a long whistle. "Well, what've we here? Mighty popular theme, them windmills." And he produced yet another copy of the Van Meer. "Good hunting today, my lord." He nodded at the earl.

"Take them all, Bilgrove," said Tarrington with a smile. "I know a fellow in Bath who will be quite surprised to see them."

Trubbs glared at them, his eyes hot with fear and anger. He made a swift move towards the door but Tarrington was there before him, the pistol once more in his hand.

The forger's eyes were darting about the room, searching vainly for an escape. Below they could all hear the sound of the servants hurried footsteps, no doubt resuming their scavenging before deserting the house.

"Stop them! Are you going to let them ransack the place?" cried Trubbs.

"Don't concern yourself with it, my friend," replied Tarrington. "We've already sent word to the magistrate. No one will leave this house with anything of value. It's all to be held for evidence and restitution. Let us instead turn our attention to you. We haven't much time."

He handed the painting to Bilgrove and drew up a chair before the forger. Crossing his long, booted legs before him, he eyed the man with casual good humor.

"Now, would you prefer to be hanged, or would it rather suit you to be transported and to practice your arts—legitimately— in the Antipodean regions? I'm told that once a convict works out his sentence he can do very well for himself in Australia. But hanging, on the other hand . . ."

"I'll talk." The forger hung his head sullenly.

Bilgrove got out a stub of a pencil and his Occurrence Book, and he and the earl exchanged a smile.

"It was all Oldbury's idea . . . ," began Trubbs.

"We rather thought it might be," said Tarrington.

"Why Kate, what has come over you? Why would you invite Mr. Oldbury, of all people, to dinner?" Priscilla pulled off her bonnet a little too roughly, and her carefully arranged auburn curls came undone. She pushed them out of her eyes impatiently and turned to her cousin, awaiting an explanation.

"Come now, Pris, we must not be uncharitable. After all, Oldbury cannot trouble us any more. And Mama feels sorry for him, so I thought she wouldn't mind."

Katherine desperately tried to sound casual, and yawned, sitting up against the pillows. Priscilla had bid Mr. Fellowes goodbye and immediately burst into Katherine's chamber, waking her from the first truly restful moments she had had all day. Now her cousin sat on the edge of her bed, fidgeting with the bonnet.

"Well, I think you are all about in your head!"

"Wherever did you learn that expression?"

Priscilla looked away and busied herself untying the knot she had made in the periwinkle satin ribbon. "I heard Rodney—Lord Knolland—say it once." She bit her lip, which had begun to tremble.

"Oh, Kate, what could have gone wrong? I thought that he—I could have sworn that he was going to offer for me, in spite of what you said about my not having any fortune . . . really and truly I did!"

"I'm as baffled as you are, my dear," Katherine confessed, glad to be telling the absolute truth for once.

"You are so lucky. It's plain that Lord Tarrington would never deceive a lady about his intentions. How happy you will be!"

"Oh, Pris," said Katherine, and impulsively hugged her cousin. If only she could share the dreadful burden of the truth, but her gentle cousin was certainly not the one to turn to.

Priscilla pulled away after a moment and looked up at her. "But Kate, oh, *why* wouldn't you let us spare you from that drive with that horrid Mr. Oldbury? One would almost think that you *wanted* to be with him!"

"As I said, it never hurts to be kind to someone. It costs me nothing but a little time, and in my position"—she forced what she hoped was a joyous smile—"I can afford to be charitable to the poor man."

Priscilla shrugged and gathered up her bonnet and gloves. "You certainly have changed, Kate. But I suppose there is no harm in it, as long as you make him your own dinner partner, and do not inflict him on anyone else."

Katherine promised solemnly that she would.

When Mrs. Amory was informed that her daughter had invited their former neighbor George Oldbury to dinner, she was not nearly as pleased as Katherine had expected. They were all assembled in the drawing room, Colonel Dawson, the last guest, having just arrived.

Lady Tarrington merely raised an eyebrow, and Lady Colesville made a sour face at Katherine, but her mother took her aside and whispered, "Are you sure that was wise, dear? Lord Tarrington is expected back tonight, and we would not want to cause a disagreeable scene."

"Oh, I doubt Vane will make an appearance in time to dine with us," said Sally, "He ought to have been here by now. How very disobliging! You must scold him for it, Katherine."

"Well, then," said Mrs. Amory, relieved, "I suppose I am worrying for naught." She looked thoughtfully at her daughter. "You did tell Mr. Oldbury that you are betrothed to the earl, did you not?"

Katherine smoothed the skirt of her poppy silk dinner dress and accepted a glass of sherry from Lord Colesville before answering. "Our drive was cut short by the rain, Mama, so you see I—"

Just then the object of their discussion was shown into the room, and made a beeline for Katherine. He bowed and kissed her hand moistly, before greeting Mrs. Amory. She received him with kindness, as usual, but looked worriedly at her daughter. It was only luck that the colonel came to bear her away before she could say another word.

"Have you given your mother the happy news, my dear?" Oldbury retained a painful grip on Katherine's hand, and she attempted vainly to withdraw it. It was only when he noticed

328

Lord Knolland, who was wandering the room restlessly, that he dropped her hand, intent on another matter entirely.

"Come, Katherine, let us go and speak to his lordship. I should very much like to discuss with him that curious incident that occurred this afternoon," said Oldbury, moving towards him with a determined step.

Knolland glanced at Katherine helplessly, and she tried to wave him away as inconspicuously as possible, but he stood rooted to the spot, his eyes darting wildly about in search of an escape.

To Katherine's intense relief, dinner was announced and Lord Knolland hurried to Priscilla's side, as if to a safe refuge, begging leave to escort her to the dining room.

Katherine watched her cousin blush with pain and pleasure, and then it was her turn to be embarrassed as Oldbury ostentatiously offered her his arm. "We will speak together privately after dinner, won't we, my dear?" he said pleasantly, but in a voice that brought a chill to her spine. "And I really think I will have a word with Lord Knolland over the port."

Dinner brought some slight distraction from her current troubles, as both she and Oldbury had also to converse with the persons seated on either side of them, but time and again her stomach would knot with fear lest someone let slip a word about her betrothal, or remark on Tarrington's not returning. She managed to force down a few spoons of soup, but not much more than a few bites of the fish, fowl, and meat courses.

Just before the ladies withdrew, Oldbury placed a hand on Katherine's and whispered, "I hope you do not think me too impatient, my dearest Katherine, but I am dreadfully disappointed in Lord Tarrington's continued absence. I think we will simply have to do without his blessing. Shall we announce our betrothal?"

He knows, oh, he must know, Katherine thought, desperate. Why else would he be taking such exquisite pleasure in tormenting her about the earl? Suddenly she realized that she was in danger of being used as a pawn in a hazardous game of greed.

If Oldbury knew that she was engaged to Tarrington, then would he think that her silence about the betrothal meant that she was aware of his involvement with the earl? Would he expect Tarrington to have confided in her? She must keep him unsure of her until Tarrington arrived. Strangely, she had not yet given up hope that he eventually would.

"Oh, but . . . but his lordship has been so kind to my family, it would be most ungrateful of me to . . . to enter an engagement without his approval," she said, feeling the turbot, goose, and rare beef she had only just tasted congealing into a painful lump in her stomach. She bared her teeth in an awful travesty of a smile. "I am sure he will arrive very soon, and then we can speak to him—*together*."

Mr. Oldbury squeezed her hand, and she clenched the other one in order to keep it from trembling with disgust and fear.

"Very well, my dear, it shall be as you wish. But of course, should his lordship have any objections to our union"—he smiled mirthlessly and his eyes were like flints—"he and I will have to discuss the matter. I am sure it will take very little persuasion to induce him to reconsider."

Katherine reclaimed her hand and got up clumsily. Oh, *where* was Tarrington? At this rate she would never be rid of Oldbury. She had no idea what she would say to her betrothed, or how he would react when he realized that she knew of his perfidy. But there was no time to think of that now.

She shot an encouraging glance at Lord Knolland, wishing she had had time to consult with him before Oldbury's arrival. His quick thinking in keeping Ted out of Oldbury's hands that afternoon had surprised her, but now there was much more at stake, and she doubted that he was up to it after the lengthy meal.

Both men had been drinking, and yet to come were the bottles of port to be consumed by the gentleman after dinner. She had not much confidence in Knolland's ability to maintain the pretense of ignorance under Oldbury's questioning, not without further coaching from her.

But it was too late. Oldbury had already left his seat and taken the empty chair next to Lord Knolland. Katherine followed her mother out of the dining room, but excused herself.

"I shall be down in a few minutes, Mama. I have a little farewell present for Lady Colesville in my room, and I wanted to give it to her tonight. I am sure she will be too rushed tomorrow morning to appreciate it."

But when she had retrieved the gift, a sketch she had made in the garden at Whitfield, she did not return immediately to the drawing room. She was feeling far too restless to sit and gossip or embroider, or worse, to evade further questions from her mother.

She paced her room, looking out of her window onto the street, but nothing rewarded her glance except for a passing gig and a few pedestrians. Finally, she descended the stairs once again, but before she could reach the drawing room, Oldbury emerged from the shadows of the narrow hall and blocked her way.

"Ah, Katherine, I have been looking for you. Your dear mother assured me you would return at any moment, so I thought I would wait for you here. I have had a most edifying talk with Lord Knolland, and am looking forward to our little chat with great pleasure."

Katherine swallowed on a dry mouth, and began to wish she had drunk more of the wine at dinner. Then anger restored her to her usual confidence. The sketch was being crumpled in her fist.

Why was she allowing herself to be tortured this way? It was obvious that Tarrington had deceived her as he had deceived everyone else. It was painful, but it had to be faced. She had spent the day hardening her heart against him, but it was still the most difficult thing she had ever done.

No matter. She would no longer allow Oldbury to frighten her merely for the sake of shielding a criminal, even if that criminal happened to be the man she loved. If Tarrington had

331

done wrong, he must pay for his crimes like anyone else.

But not like this, not as the victim of a blackmailer. Nevertheless, he had not returned as he had promised, and she was, after all, under no obligation to protect him. No obligation, that is, but that she had loved him from the first and knew she always would, no matter what he might have done. Still confused, not quite knowing what she would do, she allowed Oldbury to take her arm, numbly, as if the limb belonged to someone else entirely. The paper fell from her hand.

"Very well, Mr. Oldbury," she said, leading the way to the empty, rear sitting room. "I have something very particular to discuss with you as well."

The post-chaise rattled into Bath from the direction of the London road, and as they approached the Paragon, two of the three silent, weary passengers were suddenly jolted into attention. A diminutive and very distinctive figure in a very damp, floppy hat stood forlornly at the side of the wet road, squinting to make out the identity of the passengers of each passing vehicle. In the long dusk of the July evening, Lord Tarrington could recognize the features of Bilgrove's boy Ted.

Obeying instructions from within, the yellow-jacketed postboys brought the vehicle to a stop, and after a quick conference, Ted was taken up and the chaise continued on its way. The earl's face was grim in the half-light, and heedless of the city traffic, he shouted to the postboys to spring the horses.

Katherine stood with her back to the mantel of the small sitting room fireplace. She was reminded of that other interview with Oldbury, back in the shrouded sitting room at Whitfield; but this time there would be no fortuitous entrance of Tarrington to spare her Oldbury's demands.

Oldbury had followed her closely; now, despite the fact that she had taken a chair and invited him to sit also, he stood over her, his thin moist lips in a loose smile, his eyes gleaming with greed. Katherine had been unable to keep from shooting an anxious glance towards the door, as he had shut it carefully behind him.

"And now that we are in privacy, Katherine, perhaps you would like to decide on our wedding-day. Of course I beg leave to hope that it will be soon, very soon," he gave a dry laugh and rubbed his fingertips together. "Bartonstead is waiting to welcome its new mistress, and I trust you will find it comfortable. My collection"—he put an almost tender emphasis on the words—"adorns nearly every wall and table, and though that should be beauty enough for anyone, I will not trouble to deny that the benefits of your fortune will give Bartonstead the elegance it deserves. Oh, what treasures we will collect together, my sweet!"

He had moved behind her as he spoke, and Katherine shivered as she felt his soft damp hands close on her shoulders. But even her revulsion could not overcome the utter confusion at his casual mention of a fortune.

"My . . . my fortune?" Her voice sounded faint to her own ears, her throat too tight from the war of fear, anger, and curiosity within her.

"Pray don't toy with me, Katherine." Oldbury's hands tightened on either side of her neck. "Your Uncle Edwin himself told me of it. To be sure, I was afraid that you would foolishly squander it on trips to town and female fripperies; of course, you are too young and untrained to properly deal with such sums, but I trusted that once we were married, I would safely have the handling of it, as your uncle intended."

He had to stop talking, because beneath his hands Katherine's shoulders were shaking. "How"—she choked on a hysterical sob of merriment and horror—"how absurd! Oh, to think that Uncle Edwin . . ." She could not put an end to the half-laughing, half-crying fit his assumption had provoked. Oldbury shook her brutally, and when her teeth began to crash against one another, her sobs subsided.

"Are you mad? What is the meaning of this, Katherine? I demand to know—"

Katherine at last drew a long, ragged breath. "I . . . I will tell you, Mr. Oldbury, but I'm quite sure you won't like what I have to say."

Taking advantage of the fact that he was no longer pressing her into the chair, she rose and faced him. Just then a slight movement caught the attention of her eye. Oldbury, red and incensed, did not appear to notice it. The door handle was turning, slowly, slowly. . . .

Oldbury was approaching her again. She stepped back. The look on his face frightened her; there was something not quite sane about it.

"It was all a hoax, a bubble, a Banbury tale," she said. "Sir Edwin used to tell us the same thing, that he had a marvelous fortune, that he had hardly spent a penny of it, that it would all go to Lord Tarrington."

From her new position she could see that the door was open a crack, and that the crack was widening. Who would enter the room in such a way, and for what purpose?

"What you are saying is impossible!" roared Oldbury. "Sir Edwin left his fortune to *you!* He swore it to me! He assured me that if I married you—"

Katherine laughed again, with real mirth this time. "And I was such a simpleton! I could not imagine to *what* I owed the compliment of your persistent courtship!"

"This is no laughing matter, you stupid little bitch," growled Oldbury. "Do you think I would tie myself to a woman, *any* woman, except for the sake of a fortune such as the one your uncle told me he was leaving to you? And Tarrington—"

"He was the one who told me it wasn't true. He said there was nothing left but the house and a bit of land."

The door was almost half-way open now, and she had managed to move so that Oldbury always kept his back to it. Over his shoulder she could see Lord Knolland peering in, and when he caught her glance, he began to make grotesque faces, rolling his eyes, and jerking his chin towards the stairs. When she only looked blank, he pointed towards the window.

It was a great struggle, but she managed not to convey by her expression that she saw anything unusual at all. Oldbury still stared at her in disbelief, his eyes bulging in his puffed-up face, his hands clenched.

"One of you is lying! There *is* a fortune, I know it, the Amory fortune, Sir Edwin told me." He was totally out of control, and saliva appeared at the corner of his mouth. "It's Tarrington then, he's got it, hasn't he? And he wants you, too, eh? Well then, he shall have you and be damned but not the fortune, by God."

Grimly she thought that might even be true. But she neither knew nor cared at this moment that Tarrington might have lied about there being no fortune. He could keep it and be welcome to it, if only he arrived in time to confront Oldbury himself and spare her any more of these maniacal ravings.

"It should have been mine! I was promised . . ." Oldbury wailed like a child denied his treat, but never taking his eyes from Katherine. Her maneuvers had finally positioned her with her back against a wall, with only a few feet separating her from Oldbury.

Katherine spared a glance at the door. Lord Knolland was still gesticulating, but this told her nothing more than before. Uncertain of whether he could help her or not, she wavered on the brink of beckoning him in, but when next she gave her full attention to Oldbury, her mind had been made up for her.

His right hand was emerging from his coat and in it he carried a small but rather effective-looking pistol.

With an immense effort she managed not to scream, but spoke to him quietly. "Mr. Oldbury, I realize that it is a severe shock, but you know that I had nothing to do with it . . . I have been fooled just as you were . . . you knew my uncle. Wasn't it just like him to mount such a deception, simply for his own amusement?" She tried to keep her voice even and unafraid, but he was obviously beyond reason. The hand holding the pistol trembled.

"You're lying," he said softly. "Sticking to your story, going to try all your cozening tricks on the great Earl of Tarrington, because he's got the fortune after all." His voice rose to a horrible mad falsetto. "Take me to him. Take me to him at once, or . . ." He gestured menacingly with the pistol, his eyes completely without mercy and without sanity.

The door was almost fully open now, and Knolland stood uncertainly on the threshold. When he noticed the gun in Oldbury's hand, Katherine saw her only chance and took it.

At that same moment the door crashed fully open and Knolland crossed the room in long strides, Katherine, seeing Oldbury distracted by Rodney's entrance, wrenched the arm holding the pistol away from her and pointed it towards the wall, struggling to make him drop the weapon.

"Here now . . . careful with that, old fellow."

"No! . . . No, my fortune . . . my fortune."

None of the three heard the light footsteps at the door.

"Rodney! When I saw you had not returned to the drawing room, I knew that I must find you, because I cannot keep silent another . . ."

A shot pierced the wainscotting, leaving the echo of an explosion in the room and a burn mark in the wall. At almost the same moment a scream pierced the air.

"No, you mustn't . . . oh, I shall die if he is shot . . . please, oh, please, Lord, don't let him be dead. . . ."

"Pris, whatever are you doing here? It's all right . . . don't cry . . . just get out of our way . . . Mr. Oldbury is still—"

"There now, I'm all in one piece, Miss Townsend. The ball's gone into the wainscotting there. I'm not a bit . . . M-Miss Townsend! Is it really true? Do you . . . I mean would you . . . Odd sort of time to ask but— Oh, the devil with what Tarrington said!"

"Oh, yes, *yes*, Rodney! I've loved you from the first moment I saw you ride to my rescue . . . so very brave, my love."

"This is all very well, and I wish you both very happy, but you *must* help me with Mr. Oldbury, my lord, he's . . . Oh!"

A crash resounded throughout the room, and when the echoes died away George Oldbury lay sprawled on the Turkey carpet, a rather large bruise on the back of his head. Lord Knolland stood over him with a fire iron in his hand, while Priscilla clung to his other arm.

It was only now that they heard cries of surprise and shock from the drawing room, feet hurrying along the corridor, and the unmistakable sound of at least one pair of boots belonging to a large man pounding up the stairs two at a time.

The owner of the boots reached the sitting room before any of the group from the drawing room could do so.

"Kind of you to spare me the trouble. But did it really take all three of you to incapacitate him?"

The Earl of Tarrington stood on the threshold, barring the doorway with his arms, the others crowding behind him. His face was etched with lines of exhaustion, but his smile was triumphant, and his eyes sought Katherine's immediately.

He stepped aside, and let his mother and Mrs. Amory, with the colonel and the rest of the party, stream into the room. There were cries for water and sal volatile, questions and demands, shouts and replies, and over it all, ignoring the persistent tug of her mother's hand on her sleeve, the happy sobs of Priscilla and the proud tones of Lord Knolland, Katherine simply looked into the eyes of her betrothed, hardly knowing what she sought to find.

She looked at him until her eyes began to tear, yet he took not a single step towards her. Now behind him appeared a familiar figure, a stout man wearing a very shabby and travel-stained frieze coat, and in back of him the floppy hat of Ted popped into sight.

Katherine picked up the skirts of her gown and flew past them all, evading Tarrington's arm as he reached for her. She pounded up the stairs to her room, and did not look back.

Chapter Fourteen

"I quite understand why you don't want to come down, my dear, but I think that in all fairness to yourself and Vane, you should do so."

Lady Tarrington's voice was quiet. The only other sound in the room was that of the bed creaking as Katherine turned to face her.

"How can you—" Her voice died of its own accord. Her ladyship seemed not at all disturbed, but then she did not know enough, as Katherine did, to begin doubting whatever her son may have told her.

The Dowager Countess took her hand. "Vane would like to speak with you. Whatever passes between you is, of course, your own affair, but if you should decide . . . if you would prefer not to marry him . . ."

Katherine winced and evaded Lady Tarrington's eyes. It was what she had intended ever since she had unwittingly become aware of his secret, but now that the moment had arrived, thinking of it brought nothing but pain.

"It is your choice, of course, my dear," Lady Tarrington continued, "but . . ." She hesitated. Her clear green eyes looked directly into Katherine's, as if searching out her soul. "Please don't hurt my son. He has been hurt enough. I don't know what the quarrel is between you, and I don't wish to know. I only ask you to deal fairly with him. If he has somehow offended you, then at least give him a chance to apologize and explain."

She rose from the corner of the bed, where she had been sitting since Katherine had finally answered her soft but persistent knock.

"There now, that's enough meddling from a foolish old woman." She dropped a light kiss on Katherine's cheek and softly left the room.

Her own mother, Priscilla, and Sally had all attempted to rouse her, but for almost an hour she had lain on her bed, torn by indecision, and unable to overcome her leaden reluctance to ever face her betrothed again. Lady Tarrington was the only one she could bear to see, the only one, she thought, who could possibly love the earl enough to understand what she was feeling, if only she knew what Katherine knew.

Tarrington's arrival had done nothing to relieve her distrust of him. But in all fairness she had to admit that she had been too overwhelmed by the events of the evening. She had not even thought to give him a chance to say a word in his own defense. Lady Tarrington is right, she thought, and swung her feet to the floor, keeping that reckless surge of hope firmly contained, nevertheless.

She made her way down the steps slowly, hesitating on each one. There was a quiet murmur of voices from the drawing room. She could make out those of her mother and cousin, Lord and Lady Colesville, and Lord Knolland. She paused for a moment at the bottom of the stairs, but no hint of Tarrington's deep, full-throated tones reached her ear.

Then the door to the sitting room opened. The erratic glow of the candlelight in the room beyond framed his head and shoulders. He was a silhouette, tall and featureless, with a reddish halo about his sandy head. Then he stepped out into the pool of light from the sconces in the hall. His eyes were wearier than she had ever seen them.

"Katherine."

She shrank back for a moment, but she was lent courage by the grave humility in his voice, the question in his eyes. He stepped aside, and held the door of the sitting room open. She took a very deep breath and walked towards the light of the open door as though she were walking into the flames of hell itself.

He stood aside, just enough for her to brush past him, and even that slight contact enflamed her senses, as the heat of his body and the slightly brandied scent of his breath seemed to reach out for her, caressing the bare skin of her bosom and shoulders.

Katherine felt sure that she was in imminent danger of being caught up in his arms, and after that she knew that she would ask no questions. It was all to difficult as it was to think of him as evil when the very sound of her name on his lips tugged at her heart. If he touched her she was surely lost. She moved quickly out of reach, and he followed her at a distance. She thought she heard a tiny sigh as he closed the door.

Unknowingly, she sank into the same chair she had occupied when Oldbury had hung over her earlier, in the very same room. But Tarrington stood a yard away, his back to the grate, his profile to her. She hazarded a glance, and observed for a moment the proud line of the forehead, the strong thrust of his nose, the generous curve of lip and firm chin held high over a pure white neckcloth.

Still without facing her, he folded his arms behind him and began to speak. "It was only two days ago, was it not, when I began to tell you a story. At the time you seemed sympathetic; I could tell that you were interested in hearing what I had to say. Tonight, it appears that you have experienced a change of heart. It may even be"—he glanced at her momentarily and looked away again—"that you intend to put an end to our betrothal."

Katherine was aware that she had made a sound, and that her hands were white-fingered on the carved maple arms of her chair, but he did not look at her again.

341

"If this is so, then I will free you, now and forever, from any promises we have made to one another, and I will not ask you for a reason. But neither will you require me to explain anything further. A marriage without mutual trust would be a sordid thing, Katherine."

She wanted to speak, but her throat closed around her words. Her pulse was pounding at her temples, and her eyes began to sting, her vision to blur, because she was so intent on her internal struggle that she simply forgot to blink.

"No!" She all but choked on the word, and he swung to face her immediately. "No, my lord, I . . . I apologize for running away when I should have known that . . . please say what you wished to say. I have not made any decision."

"Katherine!" He was at her side, crouching beside her chair, one hand on the back of it, the other on her chin. She could not meet his eyes, yet. He sighed, released her, and stood slowly.

"I had begun to tell you of my experience as the victim of an art forger," he said, pacing the room. "And of course you thought it very odd that I should run off that way at the mere sight of George Oldbury. But it is all connected, you see."

A wave of mingled sickness and guilt washed over her at the sound of Oldbury's name. She was already dizzy with anxiety, and Tarrington's nervous movements were not making it any easier. "I beg of you, my lord, sit down. I—I can't bear to watch you stalking about the room this way!"

He flashed a brief, tired smile and drew a straight chair up across from her. He bent forward as if to reach for her hands, but desisted at the last moment. In the end he clenched his hands on his knees, and continued staring straight at her, though she still could not bear to face him. She studied the tiny space of carpet between them.

"After I had come so close to being plunged into scandal, I heard of others who had undergone a similar experience, and I determined to seek out the villain who was creating these forgeries and placing them on the market. I managed to interest Bow Street in my cause, and with help of Mr. Bilgrove"—he smiled—"a gentleman you no doubt saw me entertain for the first time at the village inn in Barton, and others, we traced the sale, distribution, and manufacture of certain cleverly created but undoubtedly bogus works of art to a certain part of Hampshire."

"But how—"

"It was difficult. It took the better part of a year. Some of the places where the works were sold were legitimate shops, but most reputable dealers were too experienced to have such goods foisted on them, or to wish to foist them upon their customers. Our investigations did, however, eventually lead us to a chain of buyers and sellers. There was, for example, a man who worked in a Staffordshire pottery. He had access to discarded pieces, glazed and fired but unpainted, and these were passed along, for a consideration, to certain persons who would arrange for original designs to be copied onto them or cleverly disguise them as antique specimens, with chips and cracks. Such were the pair of vases that drew me into this affair. I took heed of these clues and continued to search for the man who owned the originals of that design."

Katherine felt the burden of misery begin to lift from her heart, and she raised hopeful eyes to him. Then the memory of the blackmail scene she had witnessed intruded, and she studied her own hands instead. But she hung eagerly on every subsequent word.

"There were others who set up shop in London for a period of months. Mingled with their genuine wares were a goodly supply of forged paintings and *objets d'art*. These shopkeepers—I will not allow them the dignity of being called art dealers—proved elusive and difficult to trace, but as I said, the trails eventually led to one of the major suppliers of such goods."

Katherine dared not ask a question. She fixed her eyes on his face, but now he stared ahead unseeing, as if watching the memories of his long quest parade before him.

"We knew it had to be someone who had access to a large

collection of original art; all of the forgeries we had come upon were definitely copies of *something*, not just tawdry imitations of a style to be pawned off on the ignorant. No, it was the mystique of owning something rare and valuable that caught most of the victims, some even more highly placed than I. My last contact but one gave me the name of the person we sought. It was, of course, George Oldbury."

Katherine was hardly surprised at hearing the name, but more confused than before. "How could it be?" she asked. "He is known in these parts as a devoted collector, but forgery—why, I happen to know he cannot even create a decent sketch such as any eleven-year-old girl could produce!"

Tarrington smiled, and this time he did lean forward and take her hands in his. "Such skills can be had for a price, my dear, and our Oldbury did well enough to be able to afford the skills of a very practiced and expert forger indeed. He was in the ideal situation, because, though he had a large and varied collection, to which he continually added, ignoring all other demands on his resources, he lived out of the mainstream of the art world. He had never been abroad, he was mostly unknown to that close community of *aficionados* and collectors, and he took care to travel to London only when he must, and to maintain a certain anonymity in his purchases, especially with those who were in league with him to distribute his false masterpieces. This is how he managed to remain undiscovered for so long."

Katherine's mind was whirling with suppositions and undigested facts. All of her previous beliefs built up from the day she had met him were slowly toppling, but the fact remained that she had seen Tarrington agree to pay Oldbury five thousand pounds to keep silent. Her hands felt warm and safe in his, but she slowly withdrew them.

Avoiding his eyes, she said, "I know—indeed, you will probably be angry with me, and you would be within your rights—but last night I . . . I followed you out of the drawing room, and hid on the stair. I—" She swallowed very hard, and finally looked at him. His eyes were cool, his mouth hovered on a smile.

"I heard and saw *everything*," she confessed. "I saw Mr. Oldbury show you a painting. I assumed it was the one that you sold him, after what you had told me about wanting to meet with him, and he said it was a forgery. You told him you would—"

She stopped, astonished, for Tarrington was chuckling and he looked relieved.

He stood and pulled her to her feet, and she felt his heart beating as he pulled her against him. She did not resist, but came to him with a sense of finding her true home. It does not matter, she thought hazily, basking in the warmth of him, what he says now.

"Oh, my sharp little cousin, my dear suspicious love! It was a trap. I sold him one of my paintings, to see if we could trace its forgery and the sale of the fake. But I was unaware that he was suspicious of me. I underestimated his instinct for survival."

Katherine let herself melt against him, and his fingers entwined themselves in her curls, totally disarranging the careful style in which they had long ago begun the evening. She shyly slipped her arms about his waist, and felt him sigh, while he stroked her back with his other hand, his long fingers delicately teasing the flesh at the nape of her neck.

"I was in despair of finally proving Oldbury's guilt," he said into her hair. "I pretended to be caught by his blackmail attempt, knowing I could use the time to hasten to Bartonstead and search for the evidence."

Katherine raised her head reluctantly from his shoulder. "You—you went all the way to Barton and back in one day?" Impossible as it seemed, despite the laughter in his eyes, the lines in his haggard face told her it was true.

"We rode all night, Bilgrove and I, and in the morning had the luck to find my original painting and other evidence, as well as the hired forger himself. We traveled post-haste all the way back, and met Ted, Bilgrove's young assistant, who told us Oldbury was with you, so we—"

He stopped, his forehead lined with bewilderment. "How the devil *did* Oldbury come to be here tonight? I know that I told Rodney to keep an eye on his activities, to make sure that he stayed in the city, but—"

Now it was Katherine's turn for mirth. She trembled with giggles in his arms. "Oh, if you only could have seen it!" She went on to describe to the bemused and delighted earl their stratagem to keep Oldbury in Bath and unaware of his absence, until they were both laughing in each other's arms.

Finally the earl disengaged an arm to pull out his handkerchief and wipe his streaming eyes. Katherine watched him, feeling as though her whole body glowed with pure happiness. She felt light enough to float now, and could hardly wait for him to finish so that she could be close to him again. What a wanton she had become!

But she was to wait a bit longer before being held in his embrace once more. He drew back and searched her face, his eyes burning into hers until she blushed with confusion.

"I can well see how you might have doubted me after overhearing that scene with Oldbury, but the fact that you went to the trouble of helping Rodney carry out my request at the same time that you believed me a criminal . . ."

The handkerchief was gone. His arms slid up to her shoulders, gently kneading her bare flesh. "Katherine, this *does* mean what I think—"

But she was not yet ready. "One more question, my lord," she whispered, her voice husky. "Tell me about the . . . the Amory fortune."

His fingers stroked the sensitive skin of her soft white neck unmercifully, until she shivered.

"Little vixen," he said gently. He bent his head, but she avoided his searching lips.

"Tell me," she said, keeping just out of his reach.

His expression changed, and his teasing fingers stilled. "Do you still doubt me, Katherine? Look at me."

She struggled against the compulsion, but gave in to herself and him, and locked her gaze with his. The green flecks had begun to appear in his eyes again, but his mouth was no longer laughing.

"Oldbury said . . . he said Uncle Edwin had told him the fortune was mine. *That* is why he was so persistent, but of course I realized . . ." She tried to look away but could not, and her hands found their way up to his shoulders, where they remained.

"It is only that I was afraid . . . you are *not* ruined, are you? For a moment I feared—not that I should care if you were a pauper, except that . . ." Her voice grew very small under his demanding gaze.

"What did you fear, Katherine?"

"I don't think you can *afford* to marry a girl with no fortune, my lord!"

His eyes blazed with passion and delight once more as he drew her close against him, and she clung to him as if afraid that it would be the last time.

"Foolish darling . . . I'm *not* a pauper. Look." He disentangled one arm to show her his shirt cuff. "New. And you shall have as many new gowns as you can wear, despite the fact that there is no Amory fortune, and hasn't been one for longer than you have been alive. Now, my love, there is something I have been burning to tell you, and to hear from your lips as well."

"Oh! Well, that's all right, then. Heard you laughing; knew all must be well. Stands to reason, wouldn't laugh so loud if you were quarrelling, would you?" Lord Knolland, a starry-eyed Priscilla on his arm, had appeared in the doorway, and Katherine hastily jumped out of the earl's embrace.

"Oh, Kate, I'm so very, very *exquisitely* happy!" Priscilla flung herself at her cousin and almost danced her about the room, while Lord Knolland advanced on his friend and shook him heartily by the hand.

"Told you my idea would work!" He planted a chaste congratulatory kiss on Katherine's cheek, then shot a hasty glance at the earl. "It's all right, ain't it? We'll be related and all."

Tarrington assured him, eyes twinkling, that he had no objection to a future relation by marriage, kissing his intended.

"Exactly what I thought!" Lord Knolland's hand captured Priscilla's once more, and he frowned.

"Oughtn't to bring it up now everything's settled," he said to his friend, "but it was too bad of you to warn me off that way. Why, I could have been an engaged man a fortnight ago! And you call *me* a cod's head! Why, anyone with eyes can see that she loves you!" He chuckled, while Katherine blushed fiery red.

"Should have asked my advice, but you never do. I could've told you! Anyone who couldn't see it must be a regular mutton-head."

"That will do, Rodney." The earl's tones brooked no disagreement. "I will grant that you are quite astute and that I shall remain forever in your debt. And I apologize to Miss Townsend for unwittingly causing her pain by my interference in your affairs. *There,* will that satisfy you?"

He had an arm around Lord Knolland's shoulder and was leading him to the door. "Goodbye for now, my dear fellow."

Ignoring Knolland's protests, he gave him a last friendly shove out of the door and immediately swept Katherine into his arms. His swift move left her breathless, and she closed her eyes, her lips hungry for his kiss.

When she opened her eyes, a veritable mob greeted her sight, and she gasped with dismay. Not only did Priscilla and her betrothed linger just outside of the door, but her mother and the colonel nodded and beamed, Lady Tarrington smiled knowingly, and behind them she saw Bilgrove smacking his lips over the good brandy he had just sipped from the glass in his hand, while Ted, oversized hat in one hand, was wriggling through the assemblage to the door, where he caught sight of the earl and his beloved in close embrace. For a moment his mouth hung open in surprise, but he quickly regained his precocious confidence.

"'Ere now," he said, motioning the others away and taking hold of the door. "Ain't this a gentry cove, ken? If a cove can't 'ave a bit o' privacy in 'is own 'ouse, where's the good?" And he shut the door firmly.

"I'm afraid that I don't understand more than half of what that child says," Katherine confessed laughingly.

Tarrington took her hand and drew her to a sofa. "A lady shouldn't; but if you insist, some time or other I shall enlighten you. But right now my love . . ."

He drew her down onto his lap, and buried his face in her neck.

"Right now there are some other matters on which you would prefer to enlighten me, is that correct, my lord?"

His mouth worked its way up to hers, pausing frequently to leave kisses at each area of interest, until Katherine felt so positively boneless that she slid off his lap and found herself half-reclining.

He shifted and gathered her into his arms. "I believe I had begun to do so once before . . ." he murmured, admiring the way her hair sprang from her brow and spread over the silk cushions. "Now stop me if I cover some previously discovered territory."

"Oh!" Katherine gasped and imprisoned his head between her hands. "No, my darling, I shall not stop you . . . nothing will ever stop us again. . . ."

Not a single word was spoken for a very long time, and the ginger-haired youngster who stood guard outside the door finally winked at his master, tugged on his floppy hat once more, and happily abandoned his post.

THE BEST IN HISTORICAL ROMANCES

TIME-KEPT PROMISES (2422, $3.95)
by Constance O'Day Flannery

Sean O'Mara froze when he saw his wife Christina standing before him. She had vanished and the news had been written about in all of the papers—he had even been charged with her murder! But now he had living proof of his innocence, and Sean was not about to let her get away. No matter that the woman was claiming to be someone named Kristine; she still caused his blood to boil.

PASSION'S PRISONER (2573, $3.95)
by Casey Stewart

When Cassandra Lansing put on men's clothing and entered the Rawlings saloon she didn't expect to lose anything—in fact she was sure that she would win back her prized horse Rapscallion that her grandfather lost in a card game. She almost got a smug satisfaction at the thought of fooling the gamblers into believing that she was a man. But once she caught a glimpse of the virile Josh Rawlings, Cassandra wanted to be the woman in his embrace!

ANGEL HEART (2426, $3.95)
by Victoria Thompson

Ever since Angelica's father died, Harlan Snyder had been angling to get his hands on her ranch, the Diamond R. And now, just when she had an important government contract to fulfill, she couldn't find a single cowhand to hire—all because of Snyder's threats. It was only a matter of time before the legendary gunfighter Kid Collins turned up on her doorstep, badly wounded. Angelica assessed his firmly muscled physique and stared into his startling blue eyes. Beneath all that blood and dirt he was the handsomest man she had ever seen, and the one person who could help beat Snyder at his own game.

Available wherever paperbacks are sold, or order direct from the Publisher. Send cover price plus 50¢ per copy for mailing and handling to Zebra Books, Dept. 3325, 475 Park Avenue South, New York, N.Y. 10016. Residents of New York, New Jersey and Pennsylvania must include sales tax. DO NOT SEND CASH.

ZEBRA ROMANCES FOR ALL SEASONS
From Bobbi Smith

ARIZONA TEMPTRESS (1785, $3.95)

Rick Peralta found the freedom he craved only in his disguise as El Cazador. Then he saw the exquisitely alluring Jennie among his compadres and the hotblooded male swore she'd belong just to him.

CAPTIVE PRIDE (2160, $3.95)

Committed to the Colonial cause, the gorgeous and independent Cecelia Demorest swore she'd divert Captain Noah Kincade's weapons to help out the American rebels. But the moment that the womanizing British privateer first touched her, her scheming thoughts gave way to burning need.

DESERT HEART (2010, $3.95)

Rancher Rand McAllister was furious when he became the guardian of a scrawny girl from Arizona's mining country. But when he finds that the pig-tailed brat is really a voluptuous beauty, his resentment turns to intense interest; Laura Lee knew it would be the biggest mistake in her life to succumb to the cowboy—but she can't fight against giving him her wild DESERT HEART.